THE BEAUTIFUL IS FREE

The Beautiful Is Free

Fourteen And Over

ASHLEA RAYWOOD

CONTENTS

~ thirteen ~
The Sum Of It

~ fourteen ~
Those Birthday Blessings

Sneak Peek

What's The Story, Morning Glory?

~For you, reader~
May these journeys enlighten you on yours, and may they give you all that you need from their company.

ONE

The Kidnapping

~ One ~

LIFE AS THEY KNEW IT

~ 1 ~

Wyatt Fineman sat with his two best and only friends at the park by the town's infamous waterfront. He's seen as the ideal son to the outside world and the epitome of perfect in his mother's eyes. He began to feel the familiar chill of late afternoon air, his personal notification home time looms. It's August and the weather had lately been decent enough to spend time outdoors, although these three boys would try to go out rain or shine.

"Down the track tomorrow?" His best friend Ricky asked.

The third boy, named Ryan; replied with a low tone of internal irritation that his friends are used to, so much so they knew what's coming. Unlike Wyatt, Ryan isn't regarded with the same pride at home. "Ethan has a football game, so I can't hang out tomorrow." He said gathering up his few Pokémon cards as he announced his departure from the park.

Ricky turned to Wyatt. "See Wy? I told you it'd just be us again."

Wyatt looked to Ryan with a smile. "Don't worry, we won't go down the track without you. Though there's not much else

2

Gerryville has to offer."

It satisfied Ryan to hear this. They hadn't been down there much over the years, and it's the perfect place to explore.

"Yeah, I mean it's not much fun with just Ol Wylie Coyote here anyway-hey hey!" Ricky said with a lonely chuckle.

"Okay, please *don't* start calling me that." Wyatt said irritated.

Ricky seemed delighted with himself.

"Thanks guys." Ryan said. "How about the next day, Sunday after Wyatt's church thing?"

Both Ricky and Wyatt agreed. With that sorted, Ryan set off for home.

"It's called mass and you know it!" Wyatt called after him. He'd leave to follow shortly as his house is only a few streets on from his, he just had some card swapping to sort with Ricky first.

Ryan walked along the path with his own Pokémon cards in one hand, the other raking fingers through his floppy but neatly cut, bright blonde hair. His unmatched blue eyes looked over the grassy greens creeping over onto the pathways. He's never aware of how the light of the darkening sky gives them a chance to challenge its rich colour, and his face a handsomely grownup appearance. In some ways, he *is* more grownup than his other classmates. Not that he's boring in the slightest, he just seemed a little more mature, he's a very deep person compared to his peers.

His long-time friend Ricky knows him better than anyone, understanding he's like he is because of what things are like at home, especially since the aunt moved in nine months ago. Ricky had never let on however, that he knows these things to a deep extent and thinks him to be a rather brilliant person, admiring him unconditionally.

Ryan thought of that bitter thing. He doesn't like his aunt Thelma Kersh, the adopted sister of his mother, the very thought of her makes him want to throw up his insides and stab himself in the neck with his own Sharpie highlighter.

She was friendly towards him but definitely not when they're alone. The accusations he had against her were of course nonsense to the ears of his parents. They weren't completely terrible parents, but they tended to be stupidly blind and favour his seventeen-year-old brother Ethan.

Looking at the sky always made him have a nice feeling though, helping promote a view of something hopeful rather than dead-end sorrow. He began to walk with a faster pace as his thoughts turned to dinner.

~ 2 ~

Richard 'Ricky' Benson ate his spaghetti dinner with gusto. He wanted to go muck around in his bedroom before the good shows come on. He ate the last wriggly pasta from his bowl, heading straight to his room without even putting his dishes in the sink. For his last birthday he'd gotten a practical jokes guide from his parents, they're always amused at his silliness and encouraged it in friendly ways. He planned to put some of these pranks to good use on Wyatt one day, he's always so composed and sensible so he seemed like a perfect target.

Where they'd hang out tomorrow he doesn't know, probably just meet up and wander around or stay at Wyatt's house to do something there. Wyatt's place is okay but in Ricky's opinion the most exciting thing there is Wyatt's sixteen-year-old sister Candice.

Stretched out on his bed looking through the book, he became aware of the light rain tapping on the window, reminding him to shut his curtains. The idea of somebody lurking outside the house, outside his window in the dark disturbed him, especially when he'd go to get changed or something. He closed the curtains and walked over to the messy volcano he calls his 'wardrobe.' Now in his pyjamas, he headed to the bathroom for a good old teeth brushin' time.

In the mirror he stared at the familiar reflection, his striking green eyes sitting safely behind his nerdy glasses. His hair, as always, an organised mess. With the bright hue of the bathroom light, its brownness took on that reddish tinge the sun also gifts it.

One day I'll use contacts, hopefully one day I'm rich enough to buy them... and a vintage sports car...
He went out to the lounge, happy to see he had the TV to himself. His mum and dad were getting ready elsewhere for one of their adult night outs. He sat on the bean bag with the remote in his hand, pointed it towards the TV and pressed the power button with a big, satisfied sigh.

"Oh Christ." He mumbled realising the channels wouldn't come up again, it flickered back and forth from solid blue and black screens. It'd been playing up for the last few weeks now, but it always came through in the end so no plans for a new one yet. After a couple of frustrated minutes, he sat back down to enjoy the evening alone.

The television occupied him for a good hour and a half before he decided he's tired enough for bed. The parents had gone by now, probably talking and dancing the night away with their friends or something he supposed. He went and slipped into bed, thinking about an advertisement for the army he saw on telly.

That's probably something bloody Wyatt would do.... Nah who am I kidding?...
Ricky isn't entirely sure what he wants to be, the ideals always change. He figured he'd be whatever he will be, as long as he has fun. Of course, his mother wants a more structured future career plan than a freelance funny guy. His father feels the same

but understands his boy, having no doubt Ricky will be a great man someday.

At the thought of Wyatt he remembered there's a chance of going to his house tomorrow. With that his thoughts turned to Candice Fineman. If ever there were a perfect star to play the role of girl next door in any schoolboy's fictionally sexed up daydream, it would be her. The way she has the reputation of church going goody two shoes while simultaneously keeping the idealistic popular-girl-in-high-school persona is understandably intriguing. She has it all, and Ricky wants her and has done so for years.

For the past few months however, he'd been giving her the cold shoulder. Back in April when he was due to turn fifteen, he came across her once again. Over the years he's had many teasing run-ins with her, but this one time really got to him for some reason.

He was returning to Wyatt's bedroom from the bathroom when she came walking up the stairs with her very popular and obnoxious best friend. Ricky politely said hello to her like he always did, when this time the friend brutally insulted him for no good reason. The worst part is that Candice didn't defend him at all and seemed to agree with her. That threw gasoline and a lit match onto the already burned Ricky. He confidently shrugged it off just as he normally did in any such situation that didn't agree with him.

Later that night he cried himself to sleep.

Now, even though he still feels the same way about her, he tries to ignore her and act as if she doesn't exist when she's around. He dozed comfortably off to sleep with the few good memories of her lighting his hazy mind.

~ 3 ~

Wyatt sat at his family's upper-class dining room table eating his Saturday breakfast, plain old cornflakes today. He wondered what he and Ricky would get up to as the day would unfold. He loves both his friends but hanging out with Ricky one on one is quite enjoyable, even if it does mean you get twice the teasing and jokes.

He's never sure about bringing him around to his house now, he tends to be a real moron when it comes to his big sister. Over time it became common knowledge that he's infatuated with her. Wyatt couldn't understand why because really all it did was cause grief for him after Ricky's gone. Although he has noticed it hasn't been as bad lately.

Besides, he swears Candice is repulsed by Ricky.

He finished his breakfast, drank the rest of his orange juice, cleaned his dishes and went upstairs to get ready to go meet him at the milk bar. As he walked along the hall to his bedroom, Candice came out of her room clad in her night gown, hair a mess, mobile phone in hand with a girl's voice emitting from it like an angry parrot chattering worse than Ryan's pet bird. This parrot's name is Bethany and it seems she's furious about some guy named Trip or Trap or... Who really knows?

Candice seemed to be only half listening to the death threat sounds coming from her phone, she looked like she'd just woken up which wouldn't be surprising.

"Hey what's wrong with Beth?" He asked out of pure curiosity.

She covered the phone with her hand so that Bethany couldn't hear them speak. "Meh, just the douche she met last week. You wouldn't understand lil' bro." She gave him a half smile.

Wyatt replied defiantly. "I'm only two years younger than you."

She raised an eyebrow in judgement. "Dude how could I forget, but right now you're still thirteen, because you're a little baby. Now if you'll excuse me, I need to pee." She walked past him to the bathroom, still with the parrot raving on.

Wyatt frowned at her remark. "I might have a friend over today so please try not to have her yelling or whatever when he's here."

She turned to look at him with her normally long dirty blonde hair, looking somewhat like a hardcore-sleep induced afro. "Which one? The little weirdo with his morbid drawings or the little douche that thinks he's charming?"

"That's Ryan, and Ricky. I know you know their names." He said with an annoyed tone.

She rolled her eyes. "Does it look like I care?!"

"It's just Ricky today. Why do you care anyway?" He replied defensively.

"I just like to know what I'm up against." She said this with a funny, almost devilish smirk turning for the bathroom, taking Bethany off speaker and talking to her with the phone to her ear.

Wyatt finally got to his room dismissing the brief encounter with his sister. Not without first thinking maybe later telling Ricky what she looked like this morning just to gossip about her behind her back. Call it a little friendly sibling rivalry.

He finished dressing for the day by putting on one of his many polo shirts, today seemed like a good day to wear the grey one with the blue trim. He combed his brown hair over to the right in a fashion similar to the old college contour of the fifties not much seen these days amongst fourteen-year-old boys, maybe on the old men that went shopping on Thursdays or hobbled along to Sunday mass.

Over the last few months, he'd slowly grown out from his

familiar chubbiness into a more slender, slightly taller version of himself. While he doesn't pay much attention to these details, others do. His subtly well-developed physique now gave him the occasional unwanted attention from girls and left him open for the senseless attacks by intimidated male bullies at school, but he's still considered to be owner of the blandest personality in his class. Not far behind Ryan, but that's only because he keeps to himself so much, or rather everyone is intimidated by him. It's the eyes Wyatt had concluded, they're quite intriguing and intimidating in their own right. Lovely but, different.

About his own, some say grey eyes are great, but secretly he wished he could have something more exciting, green or blue like his friends. Even Candice's are more exciting than his.

Looking snappy in his mirror he left his room hoping he took long enough for Candice to have finished with the bathroom. He really needed to tinkle. He came out to see her walking towards her bedroom, no longer talking with squawking Bethany. Unlike him his sister is an adept 'cool kid' and immensely popular at school.

She gave him one look and spoke harshly. "You're such a dork. Sometimes I wonder if we're even related." She came over to him to run a finger through his hair as he pulled back with an irritated grunt. "One of these days I'm going to *make* you let me give you a haircut." She walked off inside her bedroom and shut the door.

It's his go to haircut; she's just being mean he always figured. He went to tinkle before he left for the front door. He didn't need to take anything with him today but his pocket money for the milk bar. Yet, he felt like he was forgetting something...

His hair!

He had to fix what she'd interrupted on his head. After clearing that up he went back downstairs to find his mother. If he left the house without giving her a kiss goodbye, he'd never ever hear the end of it. He didn't mind, he loves her just as any son may love their mum. Her protection of him is boldly motherly but there's certain lines a parent can cross without feeling they're crossing one. In some respects, Patricia Fineman's 'love' for her son is far beyond that line, it's so far in fact that anyone not as specially moulded as Wyatt would realise sooner rather than later that she's obsessive and downright cruel in some ways.

Not a single time had he forgotten to kiss his mum goodbye, she made sure of that.

He started at a relaxed pace along the sidewalk with the destination fixed casually in his mind, where he'd soon see Ricky, and that's always the perfect way to start any day's events.

~ 4 ~

Whilst her little brother was on his way to meet one of his pesky friends in the Main Street, Candice Fineman undressed in the bathroom. She felt the need to clean herself after the morning she'd just woken up to. At first, she was hearing all about Bethany's recent experience about this guy. Over time Candice turned all her friend's boyfriends into one guy, it just made it easier to deal with. Being Bethany's 'best bitch' meant that she's subject to many girly talks of fashion and her escapades as a connoisseur of the promiscuous kind. Today after complaining about the current dude, she began once more to try and urge Candice to accept the advances of Rob Brannon, one of the hottest and most popular boys in their grade at school.

Almost every day she would hear "But Candice you'd have to be completely insane not to go out with him! He's just so... Happening."

Cue eye roll.

But what really garnished the shit over the day was that she'd

just had a little argument with her mother. Well, it seemed like
a little argument but they both know it was bigger than that. All
Candice had done was suggest she doesn't go to mass tomorrow
and her mother responded with great hurt and aggression, as if
she'd just found out the church priest was a secret Satan wor-
shipping child killer. That's what Candice felt the reaction was
like anyway. There was almost no point in asking and she knew
it. Tomorrow she would once again attend Sunday mass with
the rest of the 'bible zombies.'

As she stepped into the shower and turned on the water, she
felt as annoyed as a caged tomcat. Her hazel eyes began to tear
up a little as the water created a waterfall of flowing dark gold
over her head. She's sixteen and not permitted to miss a single
day of church to hang out with her friends on the weekend.

It's like torture or something...
She began to hum the sweetly cagey tune to Pete Murray's 'Bail
Me Out', figuring she'd give that song a spin later when her
mum's gone. Her dad was already out with his mates.

Living life how he wants to... Unlike me...
With the thought of loud music ceasing the recent anger surge
her church loving mother had created, she soaped her body's
skin as she wondered why Bethany even bothers to talk to her
about her boyfriends. This time it was Tray she was pissed off
at, some dude she met last week that works in the Launceston
Kmart.

Candice hadn't actually been into the dating thing, despite
popular belief, so really the only advice she could give Bethany
were things she'd picked up off the television and in magazines,
not to mention learning from her friend's past endeavours.
Also, unlike Bethany she's very much a virgin and didn't really
mind this fact, although there's pressure from her friends who
basically urge her to change this little fact about herself. It

seems everyone is obsessed with sex. She just isn't. Suppose it has something to do with her upbringing, in this household anything sexually related is completely and absolutely frowned upon. There were times she thought she should just give in and say yes to Rob, but if she were to become his girlfriend he'd surely try to get in her pants at some point.

Nope not happening, just no... Gross on steroids...

She did however; enjoy driving her little brother's nerdy friend crazy.

Without having seen the little twerp for a while she felt it was time for some good mocking of him. Thinking it over every now and then she decided she may have been too mean a few months ago. Only because she noticed he'd been ignoring her in a way she found maybe more irritating than him actually irritating her with his petty glances of admiration in her direction and attempts to engage her in a play of words. It was really Bethany that sent Ricky into a surge of Candice related silence that's lasted these months. Suppose it may have been a little weak of her not to say something when Bethany looked Ricky in the face and told him to 'take his lame style and over-ripe sense of self confidence and beat off into a sock somewhere very far away.'

Finishing up by washing the pollution of conditioner out of her golden waterfall, she now stood in front of the bathroom sink looking at her reflection in the mirror, wondering why she isn't like everyone else, why couldn't she relate to her friends, why couldn't her mother see she's upset and....

Is that a pimple coming through?...

She sighed deeply and left the room.

In her bedroom she'd wrapped herself up in her bath towel with the bundle of another towel drying her hair. She figured she'd just chill out in her room today, and when her brother comes back with his nerd she'd 'accidentally' stumble across them- *maybe literally...* She thought with a tiny chuckle.

As she freed her hair from the towel-turban, her mother called out from the bottom of the stairs. *"Candice I'm leaving now. If you see your brother, please make sure he's not up to anything silly with that friend of his!"* There was a pause. *"And please don't think you're being punished. One day you'll thank me for making you open yourself to God. I'll be back later with your father!"*

Candice had no intention to answer but did so out of the underlying respect and unspoken knowledge that if she didn't answer it'd make it worse. "Yes mum, I will. Have a nice time and I love you!" She called out reluctantly.
She's just happy that now she could blast her music without interruption.

~ 5 ~

As Wyatt found Ricky in the Main Street and Candice rocked on in her bedroom by herself, Ryan was miserably sitting in the audience bleachers at the local football oval.

His brother Ethan had a game on and their parents were sitting beside the aunt who had Ryan seated beside her. Whenever an intense situation unfolded on the field making the audience very involved and occupied, Aunt Thelma gave Ryan a stern nudge with her elbow, looking down at him with her critical eyes. Her maroon dyed perm sitting under an enormous ugly hat. shading those dark eyes soaked with bad intentions. Her wrinkly mouth made her look like a saggy old witch and the fact she had makeup caked on in a horrid way made her look even older than she actually is.

"Go and get me a drink will you boy, I'm thirsty." She passed him a five dollar note; at least she gave him money this time. Usually, he was left to use his own money or ask for it from his parents. "And if you keep any change, I'll make sure you get a whuppin' for stealing."

He got up from his seat for the canteen where a small line of people waited. A young couple, behind them a teenage girl, Ryan figured she was probably one of the player's girlfriends by the way she's done up all pretty and such. Behind her a middle-aged man stood with a young boy who's really hungry by the sounds of his whiny nagging. Then here he stood behind them.

He didn't really know why he obeyed that horrible woman; sort of just did it now like he's just used to it. Ricky once said he wants to pull a really good practical joke on her and teach the old hag a good lesson on why not to mess with young boys.

Ethan hasn't been the same lately, but Ryan hasn't seen any-thing strange happen. But with that said, has anyone else when it comes to how she treats him? Apparently not. Ethan's usually a standoffish tough type that's nearly a bully to his brother, but lately he hardly sees him and when he does he's either overly moody and mean or even stranger still -he's really nice towards him.

After the man got his son an ice cream and a bag of chips, Ryan walked up to the counter and asked for a bottle of water. The lady took the fiver off him and turned around. Her face appeared again as she passed him a bottle of natural spring water with the change. "Thank you ma'am." He said with a sweet smile, rarely seen nowadays, though a natural form on his face.

"No worries, have a nice day." She replied happily.

Yeah right... He thought as he walked back towards the seats. The idea to make a run for it to his friends crossed his mind, even though he had no idea where they even were.

He got back to his seat handing her the drink and money, stop-ping mid action to imagine earthly vines of deep green slowly creep out from behind her and begin to wrap around her stout neck. He stood by as she sat looking at the field with no reaction while these vines gripped her tightly- maybe her neck could break at the grip, before they retreated, disappearing into nothing behind her again. He squeezed his eyes shut in an attempt to get a grip on himself.

"Well it's about time boy, I was starting to think you'd left us for good and taken my money." She said looking at him as though he's street trash looking for freebies.
Ryan thought that was such a ridiculous thing to say, who runs away with five dollars? "Here's your water and here's the change." He said with as much politeness as he could muster. She snatched it all off him and put the money in her purse.

She unscrewed the cap, wrapped her disturbing lips around the top of the bottle and took a long slurping gulp of water, resembling a hungry bottle-fed calf sucking the milk out of the latex teat. Although honestly a calf has a lot more class than her.

This sight made Ryan so uneasy that he had to look away, looking out onto the field to try and spot his brother. He had no idea what was going on, he isn't much of a football fan, or of any sport really. He's more of an art guy; his favourite subject at school is art. His drawings are random and often overlooked by most, but the art teacher Mrs Monroe liked them. The drawings are mainly people, people he saw down the street, people he saw on television and people he saw in books, even dreams. Ricky suggested that he draw naked girls which he quickly declined to do, he wouldn't even know what exactly to draw. Wyatt liked them too but thought some of them were a little creepy.

His aunt turned towards him, blatantly 'dropping' the water all over the front of his body. His mum and dad didn't see of course, no way would they have seen because they're concentrating on Ethan and wouldn't have been able to see past her round body anyway. She yelled in a sorry tone so fake it was near plain obvious. "Oh, my goodness! I'm so sorry dear boy!"

He stood up in a huff of fury to ask his mum if he could be excused because he's covered in water. "I'll just go to one of my friend's houses and get home before dinner?"

His mother looked at him in minor shock, deciding it's okay. "Very well, you're not supporting your brother very well anyway. Don't do anything else stupid." She was looking back at the field before he could answer.

He gave his aunt a blank look of disgust and could swear there's faint dirt stains on her throat. He looked away and quickly left the area, rubbing his neck at the uncomfortable thought of it snapping. Her stupid bullying worked in his favour this time and he's now free to have the rest of the day to himself. He didn't even care that all the people he would pass could see his clothes stuck to his thin body, even his dark pants appearing to be peed in. He set off for Wyatt's house finally relieved.

~ 6 ~

"Why don't you go and talk to her Wylie Coyote?" Ricky said through a cheeky grin.

"Okay firstly, no. Secondly stop calling me that and thirdly, you're saying it wrong anyway. It's Wile 'E' Coyote." Wyatt replied in his classic, polite bossiness.

The 'her' Ricky referred to was a girl with long dark hair that'd been staring at them while they were in the milk bar. Beside her stood a magnificent looking dog, medium sized but big enough to leave Wyatt with discomfort. From where he was standing he could see its eyes looking on with great honour, like a royal guard.

"Come on Ricky let's get out of here."

They left the milk bar with their precious snacks, Ricky hardly caring about the girl as he opened his Wicked Fizz with all the casualness of such an innocent action. "Yeah I reckon she was staring at me anyway, seems more likely." He said as they walked along the sidewalk.

"I'm totally sure about that. Maybe your huge ego was poking her in the eye."

"Oh come on that's a little harsh Ol Wylie! It's not an ego if it's the truth."

"One of these days you're going to piss off the wrong person, I just know it."

"Well come at me I say." He now yelled with his arms outstretched. "Hear me haters?! Come at me I say, I SAY!"

Wyatt shook his head wondering if Ricky ever realised how much plain coolness he just naturally emits, especially this year. He secretly wished he could be as authentically awesome as him with his streetwise dress sense and bouncy hair. Reserved and sensible is Wyatt's normal essence but sometimes the coolness is an attractive fantasy.

Before eating more of his vanilla ice cream he turned to instinctively look over his shoulder- no girl there. They walked on towards Wyatt's end of town, much to Ricky's silent excitement.

~ 7 ~

After a long but peaceful walk Ryan finally reached Wyatt's house. His clothes had dried significantly but were still a little damp.

Is that Kylie Minogue?... He thought to himself as he got closer to the front door.

It must be his sister, there's no way she'll hear me knocking...

He tried anyway just so no one could say he didn't. No answer. He opened the door and went inside. "Mrs Fineman? Anyone here?" No answer, just the music coming from upstairs. He went up for Wyatt's room, opening the door before realising he should ask the sister if she knows when he'll be back.

He turned around and started back towards her bedroom. As he stood outside the door, he tried to get himself ready for an irritated girl having a go at him. He hardly ever spoke to the sister. "Candice? You there?" He knocked a few times; the knocks seemed to go with the beat of the song. "Candice?"

He slowly opened the door and saw a scene not exactly frightening, but it made his stomach drop with a feeling like fear. He wanted to look away, but it was far too fascinating. Yeah that's it, fascinating.

Oh god, I shouldn't be here... He thought with panic and excitement, closing the door to walk rather quickly back to Wyatt's room where he planned to sit quietly until his friends got there. Sitting on the floor in front of the bed, he began looking at all the scientific stuff in the room, his eyes fell to the tiny crucifix on the wall.

He laughed a little as he realised that it definitely was Kylie Minogue she was listening to.

~ 8 ~

Candice was having an absolute ball. The feeling of being free by the simple task of dancing alone in your bedroom is amazing to her. This feeling of freeness was also due to the fact she never got dressed, she simply threw the towels to the hamper and danced to her mix CDs. She moved to the sound with her modesty nowhere to be seen, her body moving in tune while her semi dried hair waved and bounced in such a fashion it could be considered an artform. She found herself dancing to some Minogue song when she thought she heard something from outside her door.

Shit maybe the twerps are back, or worse, mum...
She looked out the window careful not to show any of her naked self to the neighbours and saw no cars, telling her that her

mother isn't back. She quickly got some clothes on and flopped herself down on the bed with a big sigh of pure satisfaction.

~ 9 ~

About twenty five minutes after Ryan's encounter, his two friends walked through the front door. By this time the music had been turned down but still loud enough to be heard from downstairs. As they walked up, a song came on, stealing Ricky's attention.

"Oh what?!" He said with quirky surprise. "She's playing Runaway!"

"Yeah she plays it all the time now." Wyatt said with little care.

Ricky ran up the rest of the stairs to her door. For a minute Wyatt panicked at the thought of him doing this. He didn't want any interaction between these two right now, especially negative interaction.

"I'm going to knock or something." Ricky said totally enthralled.

"Nah don't, she'll just get annoyed. Let's go to my room." Wyatt groaned.

"No I gotta say something." Ricky persisted.

"It's just Bon Jovi." Wyatt said in a matter-of-fact tone.

"I don't care about the political bullshit, their music is-" Someone emerged from Wyatt's room and into view.

"Ryan?! What are you doing in there?" Wyatt asked with surprised interest.

"I got water spilled all over me and they let me go early. Why are you guys standing outside that door?"

Ricky replied to this with what sounded like upmost confidence and sincerity. "Oh, I'm just about to ask Wylie's sister for her hand in marriage."

"I've seen more of my sister's arse than you ever will." Wyatt scoffed.

Ryan giggled nervously.

Ricky reacted with a high-pitched voice. "Oh my, cover my ears and soap out his mouth! Does your mother know you talk such filth?!"

Wyatt sighed unimpressed and walked to his room. "You guys coming?"

Ryan followed and Ricky went reluctantly after, mouthing the lyrics as they played through the hall.

Wyatt sat on his desk chair as the other two sat on the bed while Ryan told them the story of how it's the aunt's fault he got to leave the football game early. He did contemplate whether to tell them that he believed he may have forcibly hallucinated seeing vines wrap around her stupid neck, deciding he wasn't ready to say something like that just yet, if ever.

"She's such an old hag." Ricky stated. "At least you aren't blood related to the thing."

Ryan nodded with indifference. "I'm just so sick of her."

"That time she told you your parents wanted to abort you was such a horrible thing to do." Wyatt recounted, concerned.

"I don't hate that she said that. The part I hate is that it's true." He answered sullenly.

"Well if it makes you feel any better Wyatt has a girlfriend now." Ricky informed happily.

Wyatt replied with a confused tone. "Ah... No, I don't?"

Ryan's greatly intrigued at hearing this.

"Yeah you do. That girl having a good look at us in the takeaway shop."

"That doesn't mean she's my girlfriend."

"Did you talk to her?" Ryan asked.

"He didn't, I think he was too shy." Ricky answered amused.

Wyatt answered disregarding Ricky. "She was freaky. Besides, you know I don't talk to strangers."

"No, you just can't talk to *girls* boyo." Ricky teased. "And she wasn't freaky looking from what I could see."

Ryan started to get confused. "Okay so why was she weird and what do you mean by 'from what you could see'?" He asked.

Ricky began to say "We were at the counter and his girl-friend was-"

"Not my girlfriend! She was outside, across the road with a big dog." Wyatt finished with an uneasy gaze.

~ 10 ~

Feeling especially thirsty and peckish, Candice decided it was time for a kitchen run.

Must've been all that dancing...

She was at the pantry with a glass of apple juice, looking at the selection of food when she heard a cough from behind her. She jumped a little from the sudden noise causing some juice to spill onto her fingers, making her hand sticky.

It was that Ricky in the doorway to the kitchen, leaned up against the doorframe. "Hiya Candice, how ya doin'?" He asked with a dorky grin.

"Well I was going pretty well before *you* appeared." She placed her glass on the bench and went to the sink to wash her hands.

"Oh don't be like that, thought you'd be happy to be graced with my presence."

He observed her clothes, a casual shirt that's slightly too big for her and a pair of denim shorts that never leave much to the imagination. The hair freely hanging down her back. He loves the casual look on girls, especially when they reaped the 1980s kind of casual.

"Yeah totally. You just keep believing that little Richard." She snarked with a smirk while she cleaned her hands. "I just love how when you're around my hands are instantly sticky."

He had no idea what meant, only thinking of the Rolling Stone's album 'Sticky Fingers'. "Ah, so you're calling me *Little Richard* now? I *am* younger but I'm not *little*."

She turned to look at him with one eyebrow raised. He winked at her.

Bethany once said he was kind of cute, like a puppy always following her. She also believed him to be a twerpy creep. "Play any jump rope or hopscotch today *Big* Richard?" She asked with an innocent face, walking over to the bench drying her hands with a tea towel.

He laughed while he walked around to the other side of the bench so they're facing each other, to mention he heard her play Bon Jovi earlier.

"You know that band?" She replied with happy interest.

"Yeah you bet your trousers I do! I even have some albums on vinyl. You like Bed of Roses? It's the only vinyl single of theirs that I've got. And it's not an easy one to get a hold of mind you."

"Don't get too excited Skippy." She said trying to repel his attempt to have an actual conversation with her.

"I'm into all sorts really, a jack of all genres if you will." His hand proud against his chest as he spoke of his taste in sound. "I love rock from all around the world, but I do tend to have a soft spot for older Aussie bands and shit; you know like INXS, Icehouse... I'd say Crowded House but say they're Aussie to the wrong person and you're askin' for an argument." He finished with a laugh.

"I don't really know what's from where." She answered trying to sound uninterested.

"Come on, I know there's a little rock rebel in there somewhere." He said in such an almost affectionate way it reminded her of when adults are talking like delinquents to a baby and the infant just looks at them like they're an insane threat.

"Okay I know a few of their songs but I'm not totally into that sort of thing alright. I like new stuff." She answered confidently.

He crossed his arms and gave her a look of sly disbelief. "Name it then."

Taken aback by the name game, she tried to keep the confidence going. "Dancey, like dub step... pop."

Ricky simply shook his head uncrossing his arms. "I mean a band or singer."

"I know, duh." She didn't. "I was just messing with you dork face." She began to struggle finding the words, trying to carry herself confidently. "I just love, you know stuff like Nicki Minaj and Iggy Az- whatever the name is. Can't go wrong with Ariana Grande-"

"Stop, stop, stop. You're going to kill my ear drums just by mentioning their names." He said amused but obviously unimpressed.

"Hey you asked, don't diss my music." She said with faux pride.

"That's bull."

"Excuse me?" She said now getting defensive.

"No it's not your music, it's your *friend's* music." He said flatly. Before she had a chance to react to the sudden wisdom, Wyatt came in and exclaimed that Ricky should come back upstairs.

"You're so rude sometimes mister. Can't you see I'm having an adult conversation here?" Ricky said in obvious non-seriousness.

"Well just don't be too long. We have to get the game going before mum gets home." He left to go back upstairs, frowning from the sight of the two.

They both now had their elbows leaning on the bench.

"So what game are you little kiddies playing today? Duck, duck, goose?" She asked him seriously.

"Ha-ha very funny. We only play that on Wednesdays, not Saturdays."
Candice shrugged her shoulders in mock understanding and took a sip of her sweet apple drink.

Ricky continued by saying "It's actually a PS3 game about a guy with wings and long ears trying to stop an insane serial killer dressed as a clown in a business suit."

"So it's Batman?"

"Very good ma lady, it is indeed." He said with a posh British accent.
Candice rolled her eyes, like she usually does when he's around.

"So do you always have loud Bon Jovi concerts alone in your bedroom?" He asked her, his playful eyes casual.

"Meh." She thought for a moment, deciding to tell him the truth of her musical outburst. "My mother is keeping me caged in her religion and I use music as my outlet."

It stunned him that she spoke in such a serious way. "Well, is there a better way? I mean music is brilliant, is it not?"

"Yeah, guess you're right dud head." She said smiling.

"Just next time you should totally invite me over to join." He leaned closer. "You'll be happy once you give me a whirl." He picked up her glass to take a big sip, looking her right in the face. She stared back in surprise, his verdant eyes piercing her hazel wonderland from behind the confines of his glasses.

"COME ON RICKY!" Wyatt yelled out from upstairs.

He put down the glass and turned to leave. "Well bye bye. I'm being summoned to Gotham City."

She spoke unexpectedly, making him turn around in the doorway. "Touch my drink again and I will end you, Benson."

"Well you didn't offer me one." He smiled as he turned to walk away.

She stood there for a moment and called out just before he left around the corner. "Hey, I do like that song by the way, love it."

"That's because you're not full of shit." He said in an almost serious tone.

"You know you're pretty cool, for a friend of my little brother." She said feeling like she's taking a shot in the dark.

"Thanks Candice." He said in a thoroughly wholesome way before leaving.

She decided to just get a vegemite sandwich. She made it up and went to take it to her room when she realised that her drink would now have that dude's spit swirling around in it.

It's just a waste if I poor it out, it's not like he's diseased or something...

She grabbed her glass and took it with her.

~ 11 ~

After a super long Arkham Asylum session in Wyatt's room, Ryan looked at the time on the alarm clock, realising it was nearly time for dinner. God forbid he be late. "I'm gonna have to go now guys, don't do any more without me okay." He mentioned it reluctantly.

"We've been playing for far too long anyway, it's bad for your eyes to look at a screen for too long." Wyatt informed sensibly.

"Yes, we know. You tell us *all the time* Coyote." Ricky exclaimed, rolling his eyes. "Hey, I'll just go too so you have company on the way home." He said to Ryan.

"Okay awesome, see you tomorrow, Wyatt." Said Ryan as he got up to leave.

"See ya round man." Ricky waved as he followed.

"Bye guys, and stay safe out there."

They looked at him in confusion.

"I guess that girl earlier kind of gave me the creeps."

"We will." They replied in unison and left his room.

"Hang on a sec Ryan." Ricky stood outside Candice's door and knocked lightly.

Ryan felt a little uncomfortable, so he turned the other way to look at the wall adorned with sensible family portraits hung up like a photography exhibition.

Candice yelled out "Come in if there's a good reason!"

Ricky opened the door and stuck his head inside. Ryan couldn't hear what he was saying, it was too light and muffled. She was laying on her bed holding a magazine, looking up at him in the doorway with a face full of caution.

"Just thought I'd recommend an album." He said trying to hide his timid demeanour.

"Oh? What is it, The Wiggles?" She said trying to verbally burn him.

He rolled his eyes. "It's 'Soul's Core' by Shawn Mullins. I reckon you'll like it."

"*Shawn Mullins?*" She said with suspicion of his efforts.

"You'll love it, trust me."

"Okay. I'll look into it, if I remember." She nodded awkwardly.

"Okay. Bye."

"Cya."

He then shut the door and turned to Ryan, who stood by prepared to leave.

"Okay you ready?" Ricky asked trying to keep his marbles in line after that.

"Yeah let's get outta here already." He replied, relieved to go.

On the other side of the door, Candice was dealing with this weird feeling after they left. The Ricky dude seemed more grownup than usual, and she didn't even really taunt them as much as she'd planned.

Since when did he have the balls to knock on my door?... Mullins...
She looked the musician up on her phone, discovering she knew one of the songs that came up. It reminded her of back in the sunny days with Bethany before the obsession of adulthood found their friendship. It's such a good song with its comforting lyrics alongside the nostalgic music of bouncy rhythm.
Now she thought she might give it a whirl and look into the dork's recommendation.

Give it a whirl?...

"How long have I been using that phrase?" She said to her empty bedroom.

~ 12 ~

"I just recommended some music Ryan, not ask to *do it* right there in the hallway."

"Yeah I know, it's just that I think Wyatt is like, annoyed or something."
They walked along the road as the sky aged into a dark purple.

"Well maybe he should take a chill pill and realise I'm not his property. I'm always open for inspection."

"What the hell? Anyway, I don't mean he's jealous, he's like, man I don't even know."

"He's jealous that he's losing his friend to his sister. Man, what a noob, seriously."

"Yeah, I guess. Just don't make it worse."

"Nah what Candice and I have is purely physical Ryan, nothing for little jealous Wyatt to worry about."

"Yeah *so purely physical* that you're recommending music to her."
They laughed together as Ricky gave him a friendly nudge in the arm with his elbow.

Ryan had one of those moments where he wished he could just go home with Ricky instead of back to the oblivious parents, the perfect brother and the witch that he's supposed to call his Aunty. They reached his house much to his dismay, with the lounge light on, the curtains shut.

"No doubt that grouchy old hag is watching Neighbours, ordering ya mum to hurry up with the dinner." Ricky said with his voice deepened in hatred.

"Yeah well, I better get in there before I get a 'whuppin' from her for being late."

"Okay. You know the emergency drill, see ya buddy."

"Yeah, I remember, thanks Ricky. Bye."

He watched him go up the street and out of sight into the dusk-soaked town. He once told Ryan that if anything ever happens, he can go straight to his house, no matter the time. Ricky's parents wouldn't mind because they love Ryan. He loves them, and Ricky, but he doesn't love his own home. And he certainly doesn't love Kersh.

He walked through the front door to the smell of veggies roasting in the oven with a chicken. His stomach rumbled with excitement. "Hi mum." He greeted when he entered the kitchen. "Dinner smells nice."

"Thanks. Did you have fun with your friends?" She continued to turn pages in her magazine atop the bench, not looking to him.

"Yeah, I did. We played some Batman and stuff."

She replied with an almost uninterested 'Hm'.

"Dinner almost done?" Ethan asked from behind him.

"Hello sweetie, give it maybe ten minutes." Her grin greeted Ethan, still not looking to Ryan. This wasn't on purpose, he knew that. It's just how things are.

"Kay cool." He said before whispering to Ryan. "*You're not gonna be happy.*"

"*What do you mean?!*" He whispered back with complete concern.

Ethan just walked off down the hall, using one of his strong hands to rake his sandy hair back over his head.

"Come here boy!" Thelma called from the lounge. "I know you hear me!"

Ryan walked on into the lounge where he saw Neighbours on the television and Thelma sitting in one of the recliners with her feet up. A glass of red wine residing on the side table, and she was painting her toe nails a dark red. It looked like she was painting them with somebody's blood.

"We had no chicken, so I suggested using that squawker of yours for dinner tonight." She states in a low, horrid voice.

Ryan knew that they wouldn't have done such an uncivilised act, but he also knew she could be saying such a thing to introduce something bad. He ran straight out of the lounge, down the hall, through the back entryway and out to the undercover area of the backyard. The birdcage he kept his parrot in is now empty. Bird toys and feeding bowls, even bird shit's there, but no bird.

His bird. His bird is gone.

He looked around for a moment then ran back inside to the kitchen. "Mum where's Perry? He was there this morning I saw him, and I just checked he's gone!"

"Sorry I forgot to tell you honey." She said when she turned to him, her plain face prepared to say something undignified. "We had to move him on to someone else because he was too loud and smelly."

"But he was MY bird. Why didn't anybody say anything?! That's *so* not fair!" He yelled furiously.

"Don't take that tone with me. It's not fair that a bird should be able annoy the people of this house."

"It was *her*, wasn't it?! It was Thelma!" He exclaimed with such a deep frown he could be mistaken for a Star Trek character.

"Stop yelling or you can go to your room." She remarked lowly, clearly worried about the embarrassment.

"Don't worry I'm going anyway. I hate you; I hate you all!" He left the kitchen and ran upstairs to his room.

"Well don't expect any dinner tonight!" She yelled after him. His door shut with an anger generated slam.

He lay on his bed crying in the dark of his room for what felt like hours. He always hated himself when he cried. His dad had always said it's a sign of weakness that could get you killed at the right moments of the wrong time. Ryan didn't even know what that meant. Even still he understood that it's emotion his body's feeling. To make it worse, his stomach kept gurgling in distress, asking for food like a caged bear unable to hunt. He wiped his eyes once more, letting his mind wander to anywhere but here, settling in the moment he opened Candice's bedroom door. He remembered her as the tears slowly dried and the sobs eased up on his tired body.

He thought of her closed eyes, the hips swaying slowly side to side, the sunlight through the window catching her hair making it seem more golden than he ever noticed it was, her breasts bouncing like there was no gravity, the hands free from care as they dangled at the ends of her delicate arms while she danced. All this stirred in his head, having him feel that familiar sudden urge.

He got up, flicked the lamp on, got his art supplies out, sat at his desk and began to draw.

~ Two ~

THE TRACK LEAVES TWO AND AN UNEXPECTED NIGHT IN

~ 1 ~

Sunday afternoon and mass is over. The family of four Finemans were leaving the church for the family car when the youngest of them thought he saw a girl in the cover of the long willow branches lining the church grounds. No, not *a* girl. *The* girl.

The long, wispy branches of the old tree swayed in the light wind, it appeared she swayed *with* them.

He turned to tell Candice but when he looked back, she was gone, nothing but the willow vines. Typically, he thought: *Must have been imagining it. But if I see that again I'm going to really freak out...*

~ 2 ~

Ryan spent the whole Sunday morning at Ricky's house while they waited for Wyatt to be free.

He told him all about how they'll never see Perry again because that horrid woman didn't like him. Ricky cheered him up the only way he knows how- by being himself.

31

They're the most peculiar fourteen and fifteen year olds when they're at their most comfortable. They held hands forming somewhat of a circle, jumping around so enthusiastically in the loungeroom that you'd think it's a scene from one of those early morning paid presentations selling a product that's practical but overly expensive.

Ricky's taste in music varied but he seemed to be a soul living in the vintage and retro times. This, coupled with his uplifting presence helped you forget the problems grasping at your enthusiasm for life.

Ryan's happiness shone through the bright, laughing grin on his face.

Ricky bounced around the room making them both jive about like moths around a fire. He sang out 'Have You Ever Seen The Rain?' with absolute carelessness. He stopped to walk over to the stereo, now fiddling around with it for a minute. Then turned back to Ryan with a waiting look about him.

The music started with a short and quirky keyboard opening, then the gutsier instruments pitched in with Ricky playing a great air guitar. He was jumping and singing 'Holy Grail 'at the top of his lungs. Ryan couldn't help but to join in with him, it was far too inviting.

As the song played on they sang in perfect timing together. They smashed out on their wicked air guitars with some dorky moves, yet it actually made them look like they knew what they were doing. Taking on a lower tone of voice as they sang out together, they danced, letting go of all things that could be possibly pulling them down.

Ryan realised that he completely understood why he saw what Candice was doing in her room, it was like this but she was naked. And he doubted it would be a good idea to get naked and dance with his mate.

Ricky sang solo once more to the song's last hopeful lyric. When it ended, he turned the stereo's volume dial down and flopped himself on the couch with a soft thud. "So what's the new art you've brought to show me?" He asked Ryan who was now sitting comfortably in one of the armchairs. Ricky's house isn't as glamorous as his and Wyatt's and it isn't a two storey either but it has a nice, warm, homey feel to it.

"What makes you think I have new art?"

"Dude, I've known you for freakin' years. Usually when you have a new drawing, is when you bring your art bag."

Ryan looked over to where his bag was sitting. "Oh, yeah. Well, it's definitely new alright."

Ricky sat up intrigued.

Ryan got the drawing out of his bag while the songs from Pink Floyd's 'The Wall' haunted softly. The both of them like that album, the movie too. Ryan was introduced to it by Ricky and was always so fascinated by the animated scenes throughout it. It gave him a lot of artistic inspiration.

"You're not allowed to laugh or anything okay, you gotta promise." He now stood in front of Ricky who gave him one look and said "Of course I won't."

He offered the paper over with upmost trust, holding his breath.

Ricky stared for a moment. It's only in black and white. He'd used only a grey lead to draw a girl; nah it's not a girl, it's a *woman*.

Boobs. There's boobs.

She looked like she was dancing, a soft sketchy darkness loomed around her, making her the brightest point to look at. It's beautiful really.

"Wow." He said.

"What does that mean?"

"It means wow man, I was not expecting to see that."

"Why are you being so serious, you're freaking me out." He asked with uncertainty.

Ricky *was* being serious, but he had to start his comedic trade again, the moment was too weird. "You're all grown up. My boy is all grown up!" He exclaimed with fake tears.

"Come off it." Ryan said with a chuckle.

"You know what this means Ryan? I don't need to pay for porno mags now you're doing this shit!" He said excitedly.

Ryan grimaced. "Dude, that's nasty."

All Ricky did in return was open his arms wide, nodding proudly as if to say 'that's what I'm here for'.

Ryan put his dancing girl away, suggesting they get ready to meet Wyatt.

~ 3 ~

Wyatt was already standing at the road where the Track started when the other two reached it. It's rare for him to be late for anything. "Guys it's about time!" He exclaimed as they approached him. "For a second, I thought you weren't coming. It took me ages to convince her to let me go out. She insisted she drop me off."

"Well I know you're a mummy's boy, but she doesn't usually say no to you so much." Ricky replied unapologetically.

"She's still worried over that little girl that went missing months ago. Every time she hears something bad on the news she fears for my life. I mean I get it, but still sometimes it really annoys me." He said with a serious face.

"Ah yeah, mum's craft friend's kid." Ricky stated in remembrance of his mum's own sadness and fear of the missing girl.

"All well, you're here." Ryan said positively. "We're all here, unlike Perry. Thelma got rid of him just to upset me."

"What? No way!" Wyatt gasped.

"Yep, Merry Perry is gone thanks to the old Ronald McDonald look alike." Ricky said without a smile.

Wyatt looked rather sad to hear it. Perry had amused them on many occasions, even getting him used to birds. "Ricky don't say clown! You know I hate them." He said with a small laugh trying to lighten the mood.

"Ah mate, I'm sure I can safely say one of the things the three of us morons have in common, is the dislike of those colourful kiddy fiddlers." He states with a humorous authoritative voice. "But still I'd rather one of those to be in your house than her, and that's the truth." He assured Ryan.

They all laughed at this as they started along the track, Ryan in the middle with Ricky to his left and Wyatt to his right.

As they crossed the small bridge, Ricky pulled out his phone to put his music on shuffle, Guns n Roses began to sing about Yesterday.

"My mum would have a fit if I played that in the house." Wyatt thought out loud.

Ricky giggled. "This is like, one of their most innocent songs."

"I mean that music in general. I like Guns and Roses, but you know what she's like."

"Frank Sinatra and church hymns." Ryan said amused.

"Hey I like that shit." Ricky said sounding serious, causing them both to look at him. "It makes the stuff us normal people listen to sound even better."

"Oh ha ha you comedian." Wyatt teased.

"By the way Wylie Coyote, it's Guns N Roses, not Guns AND Roses." Ricky exclaimed.

Wyatt responded with a distasteful face he pulled in his direction.

"How come your sister can play good stuff but you can't?" Ricky asked genuinely curious to know the answer.

"Candice is just careful, whereas I don't bother really. You know how it is." Wyatt answered honestly.

A few steers in the paddock to their right watched the boys pass with big, shining eyes of curiosity as they chewed their earthly snacks. Their dark coats shone quite nicely in the sun. Ryan thought they look like big black gems sitting in a sea of waving brown and green, the look of the scene made him think of it in the way of water colour pencils. If he could pull it off that would make a great piece. Ricky spoke his name, causing him to pull out of his artistic imagination.

"Wy, you gotta see Ryan's new drawing." He winked at Ryan. He tended to wink a lot, one of his many talents he once boasted.

"Oh no, don't think you'd like it." Ryan said trying to avoid the situation.

"No it's okay, I want to see." Wyatt persisted with intense innocence.

Ryan reluctantly pulled out his drawing.

I mean really, it's not like he'll actually recognise it as his sister... It's not even really her anyway...

He handed it to Wyatt, who let a cringe rest on his face as he looked down at the piece of paper.

"How cool is that aye?!" Ricky asked with enthusiasm.

Wyatt just stared at it before looking to the others. "What... Like, why? She's naked Ryan."

"I'm pretty damn sure he's noticed that Wyatt, you know sometimes I really worry about you boyo." He said with a bad Irish accent.

Ryan spoke up by defending it. "Look, I said I didn't think you'd like it. It's just something I thought I might do."

That was followed by a good old fashioned, hearty laugh from Ricky.

Wyatt realised he'd been offended. "No I think it's really good, well done. Just that I wasn't expecting nudity. There's something familiar about her to be honest."

At this point Ryan got a little too nervous and took the drawing back from him to put it away and out of sight.

"What do you mean? You've been seeing naked girls without telling us?" Ricky said with clear interest.

"Oh wow Ricky. No, I haven't been looking at naked people. I mean the person itself." Wyatt said as he shook his head and began to walk on.

He'd only seen his sister naked. With her acting like a loon in her room when the parents were out it was bound to happen. But that definitely didn't count; Wyatt thought nothing of seeing his family members free of their clothes.

'The body is God's creation, but modesty is courtesy to respecting yourself and others. You should only ever be naked in front of your wife.' His mother had always said to him. She never even lets him sit in sex ed at school, thankfully the other boys always let him know what he misses. Though their grades merge for it, so he doesn't get to see first hand how the teachers are passively amused by Ricky with his silly yet relevant questions and answers.

Up ahead on the track, Ricky spotted a small figure planted in the middle of the way, but before he had a chance to say 'Hey what's that?' it flew off to the side with silence. Really, he couldn't tell if it flew, ran or slid away. "I think I just saw a fox or something." He said, pointing to the spot where he'd seen it.

The other two boys looked curiously.

"I don't see anything." Ryan said trying to catch sight of something. "I wonder if we'll see it again if we're quiet enough."

"Or Ricky is making it up." Wyatt suggested.

Ricky defended himself by assuring them he wasn't making it up.

Ryan's interest in seeing a fox was shown even more when he suggested Ricky turn his music off to make less noise, which he did.

"I really don't think there was a fox, I mean really the chances aren't that great." Wyatt said with scepticism.

"Well maybe it's a Tassie Tiger!" Ryan exclaimed with excitement.

"Ryan, the chances of that happening are way worse than a fox. The Thylacine is totally extinct, foxes aren't." Wyatt replied informatively. "Besides, there especially wouldn't be one just hanging out in this town of all places. The chances are really too preposterous."

They stood there a moment as Ryan took a deflated sigh.

"I just love it when you use big words like that Wyatt, honestly." Ricky giggled.

Wyatt looked away shyly towards where the mystery animal had been.

They walked on cautiously in case they caught a glimpse of it in the bushes. Wyatt unhappily told them about how he'd seen a girl at the church that looked a lot like the one from the milk bar. They weren't sure what he was actually trying to confide as he was always the 'logical' one.

Ryan finally asked "So you think you're being stalked or something?"

"No I don't know. I thought I was going senile, but Ricky saw her that day. She really gives me the creeps."

Ricky piped in with reassurance. "Well hey, don't worry about it." He went over to him and put a comforting arm around him. "Nothing will happen to you with us as friends, isn't that right Ryan?"

"Oh yeah of course." Ryan confirmed.

Wyatt spoke up from underneath Ricky's arm. "Ryan! We

could go to the cops and I can tell them that I'm worried about being stalked and you can tell them about your aunt!" Both of the other boys looked sullen at hearing his suggestion.

"Well it was a good idea I thought."

"Yeah but my family..." Ryan began, looking to the ground. "I just can't be bothered with them."

"But it'd-"

"Just NO Wyatt, I'm fine with going for you but I'm not saying shit about my aunt, I'll just get fricking hell rained down on me. There's no point."

"Okay, never mind." Wyatt's eyes looked anywhere but his way.

Ricky stayed unusually quiet, now walking in the middle of the trio as they went. They remained in silence until he pointed out that they'd reached the cemetery. "I never knew you could get there from here." The other two just stood looking around without a word to answer the lonely sentence. It's obvious they're still unsettled by Ryan's anger before. "Guys come on it doesn't matter, I mean who cares right now? We're here and that's it. Let's just enjoy being out okay, jeez."

"I'm not going inside that cemetery, okay." Wyatt said flatly.

"We don't have to, I was just saying." Ricky wanted nothing to do with the cemetery anyway. Horror movies have really successfully given them a bad name.

"I might just go home. Have fun guys, I'll see you later." Wyatt said turning to leave, causing Ricky to role his eyes.

"Oh come on Wy, it was just a little lover's spat. You don't care do you Ryan?"

Ryan looked around with a scowl. "Nah Ricky if he wants to be a little sissy 'cause of something so stupid he can, not my problem."

Wyatt took a step towards Ryan. "I was trying to help you!

That's what good friends are for! It's not my fault you want nothing done and prefer to sit around all day wondering why your life sucks! You wanna know why it sucks Ryan? Because you do nothing to fix it!"

Ricky stood by shocked as Ryan stepped closer to Wyatt, making their faces close enough to be sharing a short piece of spaghetti together.

"You know what Wyatt? Why *don't* you just go back to your precious home and curl up in mummy's arms, telling her all about the devil boy who hurt your feelings and disgusted your sensitive little eyes by showing you a naked person?!"

Wyatt screwed his face up with small tears forming in his eyes. "Don't talk bad about my mum!"

"I wasn't. I was talking bad about *you*." Ryan answered in classic smart arse style.

Next thing they knew Wyatt had pushed him to the ground. He landed with the hard thump of sore betrayal.

That's when Ricky tried to step in with a worried posture and a slightly panicky voice. Wyatt and Ryan went at each other with every bad intention they could muster from their argument. Ryan now had Wyatt on the ground with him, rolling around kicking up dust from the track, Ricky standing by the commotion yelling at them to stop.

"Guys stop! Stop it please! Stop! Fucking STOP!"

They both stopped to look up at him. His panting had the look of sad disgust on his face. This caused Ryan to stand up first, brushing his clothes off with both hands and Wyatt soon followed.

"You know what?" Ricky said slightly looking down on them as he's a little taller than them both. "I don't need to witness my best mates having at it like a couple of hobos after the same piece of cardboard or some shit. Either make up or I'm flipping out of here."

Wyatt's head turned from Ricky to Ryan, who had no trace of apologising about him, and back again. "Nope, don't worry about it, because I'm out of here and I'm not hanging out until he says sorry."

"Oh 'cause it was totally just me and all." Ryan replied angrily. Wyatt turned away with red cheeks and walked off back down the way they had only just come from.

"Yeah well, we don't need you anyway! Run off home and pray to Jesus!" Ryan called after him.

"What the hell is wrong with you?! That was so messed up! I don't even know what the hell I just witnessed." Ricky stated giving him a hard nudge with a closed fist on his arm just below the shoulder.

"Well I'm sick of his bullshit."
Ricky looked at the back of Wyatt walking down the road on his own, not knowing but expecting tears running down his dirty face as he sobbed.

~ 4 ~

It wasn't long before Ricky turned up at Wyatt's house to see how he was. Now a few hours after the fight, he wanted nothing more than to make sure he's okay and home safe. To his relief, Mr Fineman answered the door. There's been many a time his wife answered instead, promptly accusing the Benson boy of being dirty and un-showered right to his face. She doesn't like Ricky as much as she likes Ryan, she thought her son's too close to him and doesn't like the fact that he's from the 'bad end' of town. Her husband didn't seem to completely share these views with her. Although he never shows a great liking towards him it's perhaps even better that he shows he almost couldn't care less.

Candice came out from behind her father and explained that

the riff raff is there to see her, to help on ideas for Wyatt's birthday present. His birthday's still a month away, but she knew he'd fall for it.

"Okay missy but, as your mum would say; don't let him touch you or steal anything." Mr Fineman said quietly to her ear, although Ricky heard it anyway and cringed in irritation.

He went inside and followed her upstairs, promptly headed to go to Wyatt's room when she stopped him by exclaiming something peculiar, in total casualness. "Hey, where you goin?" She looked genuinely serious.

"To... Wyatt's room." He replied slowly.

"He's not even home."

"Oh, okay. So where is he then?"

"I don't have a clue, thought he was still out with you guys doing whatever you do."
Ricky thought that maybe he was somewhere cooling off or at Ryan's house making up or even possibly out with his mother because it's clear she isn't home.

"So you coming in here or not?" She said gesturing to her bedroom door.

Ricky quickly decided to do so and as he walked over, he couldn't help but think of how she lied to her dad just to have him in her room. He grinned to himself excitedly as he walked through the door frame and into the fresh, fruit scented room he always thought about.

~ 5 ~

As his friends went about their quiet business, Wyatt had gone out of view. He thought about how this would be a perfect time to have a mobile phone so that he could contact his mum to come and pick him up. She had always knocked back his request to get one no matter how much he pointed out the pros over cons. Only when he turns sixteen she will let him get one, even though Candice was younger than he is now when she got her first mobile.

What had happened just now? The trio of friends never fight. Not seriously anyway, especially physically like that.

"*Oh just stop sooking.*" He whispered, trying to reassure himself before hitting the main roads. Taking a deep breath, he veered to the right side of the track to simply pluck a small leaf from the dense bushes lining an old wood post paddock fence. As he did so, his entire self felt engulfed by somebody from behind, now struggling into the bushes due to a totally frightening force. Ruthless arms had wrapped around his upper body and head, holding a dirty, chemically doused cloth forced over his face making him almost gag to death. He struggled as much as he could with his sad tears turning into tears of fright for what felt like an eternity before his conscious mind gave in to the nasty fumes he breathed in.

You see he was right, he *was* being stalked. But it wasn't just by the girl he thought he was seeing. There were men following him, and they're possibly the worse kind of man there is; the kind desperate for money no matter how much they had to their names, the kind that had next to no care of how they got it. They'd been stalking him because in this town word of mouth is strong; it was just known who was wealthy and who wasn't, so naturally these men had snatched him in their greedy hopes.

The man pulled Wyatt's body through the brush and under the wire of the fence into the paddock obscured by the bushes and trees. He was pulled over to a car, not a van, just a normal everyday sedan. Another man waited, leaning against one of its doors. He opened the boot of the car when he saw his partner in crime coming with the bundle of human money.

"Help me get him in Al." Said the man that had dragged

Wyatt.

They lifted him into the boot of the car, trying not to damage him anymore than they already had. He was laid down in there with a blanket underneath him and one thrown over the top of him before being shut in the darkness of the trunk.

The men got into the car with Al in the driver's seat. "We good to go Daz?"

Daz put the nasty cloth into a black backpack, carelessly throwing it onto the backseat. "Yeah. We're good to go." An evil smirk appeared as he thought of the profit they were going to make.

They drove carefully through the paddock and out the gate, reached the street and drove casually down the road amongst to the rest of the busy townsfolk.

~ 6 ~

Ryan wasn't in the mood for anything at home so it was to his great relief that the only person there was his brother, the rest were out at a celebration at the RSL for some sort of work party from where his dad works. It was specially held on the Sunday because of the long weekend.

After Wyatt had left them, all they did was sit there and talk, drawing things in the dirt with sticks, not really talking about anything in particular, avoiding the subject of Ryan's sudden outburst at Wyatt. After a while they had departed and went their separate ways as Ricky continued on to the Fineman house.

He walked into the living room where Ethan sat watching the television, eating cereal with a bag of chips beside him. Something they had in common other than DNA is that they're both always at their most comfortable when nobody else is home.

Ryan sat on the armchair beside him and just looked at the telly showing a rerun of some old sci-fi show about the ocean, it had a dolphin swimming around friendly with some young, blonde haired diver boy.

"Want some?" Ethan offered, handing him the chips without even looking.

"Yeah sure." He took a handful of chicken flavour crinkle cut.

Ethan looked over at him and asked what the hell happened. He's all scruffy and covered in a thin layer of dirt.

"I got into a fight with a friend."

"That can't be good."

"No. It's not."

They sat there together watching the TV, barely saying another word. Simply brother beside brother with no antagonising outside world to harm them.

~ 7 ~

"Okay Candice I'll be back later tonight, your mother is meeting me at the museum function. Remember that it's the long weekend so you can stay up until ten tonight."

He looked at Ricky and then back to Candice while he was standing in the doorway of her bedroom. "And if anything, you know, *happens*, do not hesitate to call us and the police. Call the police first. And make sure your brother doesn't get up to no good, wherever he is. Probably with Ryan. Let him know I'm not happy with him not telling."

"Yes daddy I know. Enjoy the night out." She said in a funny, submissive tone that made Ricky giggle a little on the inside. They said their goodbyes with him telling her not to have her door shut while she had a visitor.

She waited to hear the car pull out of the driveway before she got up and shut her door. It made Ricky nervous. "What he doesn't know won't hurt him, agree?" She says cheekily, walking to her bed.

"Oh yeah, totally." He answered trying to come off cool.

"So I listened to that album."

"You did, already?" He asked excited. "Did you like it?"

She thought for a moment. "Well I'm not gonna lie. At first, I was kinda like 'hmm...' But then it warmed on me, and I've been listening to it literally all day."

"Aw man that's awesome. Told you you'd like it. I know my shit you see."

"Yeah, I just wanted to thank you for telling me about it."

"Ah-huh. You couldn't have just thanked me at the door?" He asked without thinking it through.

She was quiet for a moment before answering. "Well I just thought we could sort of, hang out."

He simply looked at her, smiling helplessly. "Yeah sure, no worries ma'm."

She returned the smiles.

In the years that had gone by with Ricky coming in and out of the house to hang out with Wyatt, these two had never been so friendly to each other.

"So what was your favourite song?" He was dying to know.

"Hmm, well I don't really have one, but I already liked Lullaby and that one towards the end about shimmering is really nice."

"Yeah, I'm not surprised you say that. Gulf Of Mexico is great too but I love them all I guess, because the album is just *so* brilliant."

"Yeah, so it is." She looked around awkwardly for a moment after observing his obvious passion on the subject. "Did you want a drink or something? It's getting kinda cold so I want a hot one."

He went to answer but she cut him off by continuing with "Or I could just get you like juice or something, or water. There's the tap but we have bottled too."

He couldn't help it, he laughed at her innocent drink offering.

"What's so funny?" She asked feeling embarrassed, unsure as to why.

"I'll just have whatever you're having, okay." He confirmed in a giggling voice.

"Alrighty then, let's go downstairs."

They left the room and headed for the kitchen. He followed her out and couldn't help but think suspiciously to himself.

What the hell is going on?...

He offered to make the drinks, insisting she sit on one of the stools at the bench and not look. She warily obeyed the weird demands.

He boiled the water as he tried to convince her that he was about to make the nicest cup of Milo she's ever had.

"So much so that you'll hire me to make them in the future, I guarantee it."

She answered with a playful "Mmhmm, I'm *so* sure of that, barista Benson."

"Yeeees." He replied sounding like a clown. He started by putting two and a half teaspoons of Milo in each mug. He then looked through the cupboards and draws for the special ingredient.

They have to have it, they're rich and buy everything...

He realised the obviousness of the large pantry sitting in the corner of the kitchen basically screaming 'Just look in here you dumbass!'

He walked over and had a look inside to see the small walk in pantry with several shelves of organised food behind the door, searching around the packets of God knows what fancy food and tins of stuff. Many containers of homemade goods no doubt made by Mrs Fineman. He spotted the bag of powdered milk, happily picked it up and went back to the kettle that had finished boiling. He poured a generous unmeasured amount of the powdered milk into each mug followed by a portion of the fresh milk he'd gotten from the fridge.

Next is the hot water he slowly poured in over the contents. Then he carefully stirred them both as they frothed up on the surface looking rather appetising. Lastly, putting all the ingredients away trying to respect being in someone else's house. "Voila! Ze drinks are fin-eshed and are reedy to be drunk Madame." He exclaimed, trying to sound as French as he could for no actual reason.

"Okay, let's have a taste then shall we." She didn't actually believe it would be as great as he was saying but she took a sip and fell in love with the creamy warmness that is this Milo. She contemplated whether or not to let him think she thought it was shit or just say it was amazing. She opted for both.

"So, how is it?"

"Look I'm sorry but um, it's not that great I might just tip it out and make another one."

He looked at her suspiciously.

"Yeah, I'm joking it's amazing! What did you put in it?"

"That's for me to know and you to find out. One day. Maybe." With that they wandered on back upstairs where she sat on her bed, and he sat comfortably on the desk chair. Together talking, having conversation after conversation, laughing wholeheartedly simultaneously. Candice hadn't enjoyed herself in this way for such a long time. She talked with Bethany all the time, but it was never this interesting. All they spoke about was boys, fashion and general gossip.

With this guy it's music, movies, games, their teen problems and he's funny, boy is he funny. It's no wonder her brother always hangs out with him.

The day slowly greyed into night outside.

She showed him her CD collection upon request, the homework she had for school which she complained about and she told him all about the troubles Bethany got her involved in.

"Bloody hell, I think that girl gotta slow the heck down! I mean soon she's gonna have no guys left in the state to prey on!" He teased of her.

"Yeah I know!" She said totally humoured. "And most of the time when she's crapping on, I have no idea what she's talking about."

"Whatcha mean?" He asked while swiveling on the chair back and forth.

She didn't actually know what to say now, at risk of being personal with him. "Well, I guess like, I haven't been around as much as her, if you know what I mean."

He burst out laughing for a solid thirty seconds before realising she was serious. "You're joking right? I mean, that's not what everyone else thinks."

"Yeah well maybe everybody should shut their mouths." She said with sudden feistiness, crossing her arms.

They were quiet for a minute before he spoke agian. "Me neither, sister."

The awkwardness was still present when she said "Well that's not surprising because you're only fourteen."

"Oh you're playing *that* card are you?" He bantered in a high tone. "Besides, I'm fifteen."

"I mean because you're younger, you know what I mean!" She felt stupid now.

"That means nothing nowadays Candie my friend." He stated confidently, nodding.

Calling me Candie, that's funny... "Oh so you've had some girl-friends have you?"

"Um, well no."

"Never even kissed a girl?"

"Never."

"Ha, okay."

"I know, it's surprising isn't it?" He meant it to be a self-deprecating humour.

"Well it's just that you sort of don't act like it." Her shyness crept upfront with that.

"Oh I don't do I? How so?"

She felt uneasy as he asked her this, with that familiar devilish grin on his face whilst he lit a match to relight the tea light candle for the scented wax melt in the oil burner she has on her desk.

"Ah well, I dunno." She spoke absentmindedly, looking at the outline of his posture with the light of the world outside her window behind him. The puffy jacket he wears looking rather comfortable as he sat there on the chair making himself at home, his grey jeans and slightly browned white socks ever noticeable now.

His hair a somewhat muddled mess on his head, his black framed glasses showing themselves out from under his scruffy fringe. At this point she realised she'd never had a male in her room before, other than family and there was that one time, surprise surprise, one of Bethany's male friends was in here for a few minutes once.

But now there's a boy hanging out in here with her, in *her* space, and she found that she liked the turn of events. It occurred to her that she's possibly perving on her little brother's friend that's younger than what she is. That's some pretty nice hairdo though, she wouldn't blame herself.

A year younger to be exact, not that bad...

Besides, it didn't really feel like she was perving on him, it was different. She was *admiring* this boy.

"Pfft how do you not know? You're so weird, you know that?" He stated in humoured judgment of her, as he put the used match in the bin under the desk.

"I have an idea." She sat up straight to build her confidence.

"Of how weird you are? That's weird." He said smiling.

"No, of something we could do." She replied sheepishly, trying not to be.

"Oh? Lay it on me. An idea for a prank on Wyatt? 'Cause I'd love that. I mean he wouldn't, but I would." He said with a goofy gaze looking off into the space of thinking.

"Well no. I was just thinking that because neither of us have ever kissed anyone..." She paused, astounded at herself. "...we could use each other?" She began to talk faster. "But you know if you don't want to, we don't have to it was just an idea."

He stared at her in plain amazement and shock, mulling it over in his brain before he simply said "Meh, why not hey?"

"Okay let's do it." She said in disbelief of herself.
They both stood up and stood awkwardly before each other. She suggested they sit on the floor. They sat down at the same time, both crossing their legs like kindergarteners ready for a story.

"You ready?" She asked slightly shaky, trying to sound composed.

What the hell am I doing?!...

He gently nodded his head as he moved in towards her face. Her heart beat so fast she thought she might die sitting here looking at the emerald jungle of his eyes, safely behind the glass of his geeky glasses. She could see the skin of his neck bouncing to the rhythm of his heartbeat. She felt she had to close her eyes just to be able to get through it. A most strange feeling.
A warm hand slowly glided up the side of her face with the fingers gently entering the softness of her hair, where only the

hands of her parents and best friend had ever entered, her ear now sitting comfortably between his thumb and pointer finger. The anticipation proving intense while she waited for something to happen.

Rather than a touch on her lips, she hears him whisper gently into her ear. *"Sorry love, but I'd prefer it if my first kiss didn't have anything to do with being used, or just for the sake of it."*

She opened her eyes with his face still beside hers, finding she'd like to do more than just innocently kiss him but let's not go there.

He got up with a proud smirk on his face and went to leave the room; she looked up at him with surprised amazement.

"Where you going?"

"Well, now that it's gotten awkward as shit in here, I figured I better go home and act like a good lil' boy." He explained, now sounding like that dominating whisper couldn't have been this silly, shy guy right here.

"No it's okay, you can chill here. I don't mind." She remained casual. "We can just pretend that never happened. Or never nearly happened... Whatever."

He thought for a moment. "Right, let's get some tunes on the go. You got board games?" His hands clap together, as he's ready to ignore what 'never nearly happened.'
She grinned as she went to get the board games and playing cards from downstairs.

When she got back to her room, he was sitting on the floor with his back resting against her bed waiting. He'd put on some sort of playlist, Bluetoothed to her speakers. They now sat on the carpet hearing The Smashing Pumpkins playing 1979 as the two of them started going through the games deciding what to play, surprisingly more comfortable with each other than ever.

~ 8 ~

Wyatt woke up sore, confused and totally terrified. Now in a room, on a mattress with clean bedding and a towel folded on the end of it. He looked around to see it looked just like a normal room in a house with pink walls, except it's very small with no windows, just a single, naked light bulb in the middle of the ceiling. A blue bucket in the corner with a fold up table in another. He slowly got up off the mattress to have a look at the table to see crayons and blank paper sitting on it. The sight reminded him of those set ups they have in retail stores in the city to occupy little kids while the parents are busy talking or shopping.

He staggered over to the door and reluctantly tried the handle. Just as he expected, locked. Trapped in a strange place away from home, away from his mummy and daddy, away from Candice and away from his friends. He began to sob at the thought of being tortured and killed by people who are dirty and have the devil in them.

There's no way to even tell if it's daytime or night-time, or what day it even is.
He tried to remember what happened and felt more terror at the memory of being pulled into the bushes and restrained. He wanted to get out right *now*.

He closed his eyes and prayed, he prayed to get home safe to where nothing could hurt him and where he could be hugged by everyone. His whimpering whispers were the only sure sounds around.

"Please Lord, I'm sorry for my sins. I realise my wrongs. I promise I'll make it right if you get me home safe. Amen." He opened his wet eyes, sobbing a little harder thinking of his home.

His polo shirt's covered in dirt from the scruff with Ryan but the whole right side and back of his body is caked with dirtiness from when he was dragged along the ground.

He listened for something, but all he could hear were muffled voices and sounds. It was very, very faint but he was sure there was a television on out there somewhere and he's here, terrified and in fear of his life. Something odd, maybe a door, followed by heavy footsteps came closer towards him from out of nowhere. They must be coming down a long hallway.

Wyatt sat huddled in the corner under the table, his breathing rapid. He had never been so scared in all of his 'almost fourteen' years.

The clomping steps approached the outside of the door, then the sound of a key entering the lock and turning, followed by the cautious opening of the door to his captive tomb. He didn't even notice the urine running down his leg with the anticipation of the certain death he's about to endure.

~ 9 ~

Ryan had gone and had a shower to get dressed into clean, warm pyjamas. He made his way back to the lounge where Ethan was still sitting, just as he'd left him. He sat back in the recliner beside his brother when Neighbours came on.

"Man I freakin' hate that show." Ethan said out of nowhere, changing the channel to something random. Now a man in a huge, green crop field spoke about season harvesting.

"Yeah me too. It's so boring."

"I never found it interesting or whatever but now it just reminds me of Aunt Thelma."

Ryan looked over at him. "Me too." He replied. "Is she *mean* to you Ethan?"

"Oh man, I just wish she wasn't here. Fricken hag."

Ryan looked back at the farmer talking about crops and decided to tell him how she makes him feel; dreadful.

"I know she's a bitch to you man. There's nothing I can do about it." He stated flatly.

"But mum and dad like you more so you could say something."

"Like what exactly?" He sounded annoyed.

"You could say that her being here is affecting your schoolwork or your sport and stuff. She's so mean Ethan, she got rid of Perry. *Perry*."

"Yeah, I dunno. You know that friend she has over all the time, mainly while mum and dad are at work?"

"Yeah, I hate her too. 'Mutton dressed as lamb' my friend calls her."

"Yeah well she, ahm, Hm." He shifted in his chair and didn't finish his sentence.

"What's going on?" Ryan asked concerned.

"Nah don't worry about it."

Ryan felt kind of worried now, he's being especially weird. "Okay sure."

"Let's just watch some TV and enjoy the peace." Ethan said flicking through the channels.

"I'll put the heater on." Ryan said. He used the remote to turn on and control the air conditioning. He wondered what they were up to at the RSL. His dad worked at the power station in the offices. They wore business suits, but Ryan had no actual idea what they did. There's numbers and stuff involved, and whenever he hears anything of that nature he shuts off and zones out. His mother works as one of those bank ladies behind the desk.

Ricky's dad's a mechanic at the petrol station and his mum's working in the local Woolworths.

Wyatt's mum is the owner of the florist in the Main Street, not surprisingly named 'Flowers of Heaven'. Wyatt always says he'd rather it be called something more creative. Anyway, that's why inside the Fineman house they always have so many vases of fancy flowers. His dad works as the curator for the old art and history museum in the city and is the owner of the Gerryville Heritage House and Museum.

They're probably talking and laughing about the things actual adults laugh about, eating big plates of nice food, possibly dancing to songs he's never heard of.

He wondered if Ricky had spoken to Wyatt like he said he was going to.

Eventually both brothers fell asleep, the television still glared at them into the lounge room.

~ 10 ~

The night was getting on, Ricky and Candice had played a few games of Guess Who with Ricky winning most of them, next was Snap and Go Fish with the playing cards.

For a while now they'd been playing UNO. Candice's yawns were getting more frequent, and he noticed. He tried to think of something to do to prevent her from saying it was late and time for him to go, he was having too much fun.

"I'm done with these cards, how 'bout a game of Twister?" He raised his cheeky brows.

She was going to automatically say why not? But then thought of being close to him, no doubt having parts of their bodies touching and so on. "Nah I'm not really in the mood." She decided she was being wise and responsible, acting her age.

He slouched and rested his elbow on his knee with his chin in hand. "Oh my God, I know what we can do!" He spoke excitedly, springing up with great enthusiasm.

She watched as he tinkered around with his phone. She blinked slowly due to her growing tiredness, another sign of how unusually comfortable she is.

"Oh my God." She heard herself say as he came towards her, jiving to the opening of 'Teenage Dirtbag'.

He held out his hands, she allowed hers to be held by his and pull her to her feet. She laughed as he sung out in a hilarious voice along with the chorus, still dancing.

"Come on, sing with me!" He exclaimed as a verse played. He went over and turned it up a bit more.

She was felt self conscious now, unsure of the situation. She usually did this sort of thing on her own.

"Don't worry, it's not a talent competition!" He said loudly. He mimicked the voice of the female's part, gesturing encouragement with his arms for her to join in.

Finally, they mimicked in girly high pitch tone together.

Ricky looked so happy and excited it rubbed off on her, causing her to jump straight into the last chorus without hesitation.

They both giggled like girls by the time the music faded out.

The next song came on, she startled him by grabbing his waist and hand the way a gentleman does with the lady he's waltzing with. The entire thing's near perfect, like when it's December and you're waiting for Christmas all month and you're so excited it's almost uncomfortable, then the final week of waiting is left and slowly the days go by until you get up on the morning of the 25th and can finally run out to the lounge to rip open your presents, and the feeling is just so right it's near euphoria. That's how Ricky felt at this moment.

He followed her lead as she did a strange tango/waltz around the room before bouncing and singing in their best Morrissey voices. She didn't even know the words very well.

"That's the way Fineman!" He encouraged loudly.

They danced, sang, yelled and jumped with song after song, it's like this visit was happily never ending. Some of the songs

Candice had never heard before but that didn't matter, she's free, and to make it even better there's somebody here to be free with her.
To think they're the same people that spoke with each other in the kitchen that very morning is quite remarkable.

They kept going until near exhaustion, never hearing the phone ringing several times downstairs.

"Man I gotta stop!" Ricky said, puffed. She nodded her head in agreement with a panting smile.

He turned down the music and collapsed onto the floor in the middle of the room. She stepped over him, walked over to the light switch and flicked it, she then jumped onto the bed and lay down too, from there she turned the bedside lamp on, lighting the room once more.

"I'm gonna to have to go home." He said from the floor.

"Here use this. You can stay here."

He looked over and saw her offering a blanket. "Thanks, man this thing feels like it's warm enough to keep me alive in Antarctica." He said as he rolled himself up in it like a caterpillar in a cocoon. "Wyatt's kind of frightening when he's angry." Ricky stated randomly.

"Yeah, like a male, chubbier version of our mother. Guess that's where he gets it."

"I've never really seen your mum *too* angry, she's scary when she's normal."

"Dude you don't wanna see her in a rage, trust me."

"Sheesh, I don't intend to." He said closing his eyes with sleepy temptation.

Wonder what would make her that angry...
He's definitely cosy. It wasn't long before she heard him breathing heavily, turning to light snoring.

Giggling to herself at his complete randomly, she turned the lamp off and climbed under her doona, listening to the foreign snoring in the air.

It seemed Candice Fineman had unexpectedly found a friend.

The moonlight soaked her room in a comfortable hue, a light she isn't much used to in her space. Usually she shut the curtains before it got too dark.

She lay looking at the shadow on the floor that's indeed her new friend, watching the rise and fall of the blanket from his breathing, just happy that it's there.

Is it still 'admiring and not perving' if I wonder what he looks like without clothes?...

She felt sleep come over, her eyes closing and finally staying that way.

~ Three ~

THE DEVIL'S CONTACT

~ 1 ~

Mr and Mrs Fineman were in the car heading home to their beloved children, completely unaware that only their daughter was there in her room with that riff raff boy, their only son being held captive by strangers in an unknown place and scared for dear life.

"I simply can't understand how Linda can trust that gardener after the incident at the other property." Patty Fineman said to her husband.

"I don't know dear, sometimes I can't understand a single thing anyone does in this town. Respectfully, of course."

Gossip helped keep the circulation of that 'small town virus' flowing. Gerryville is known for its seaside attractions and old time feel. It's a favourite for tourists that visited the state wanting to see original buildings and landscapes. A wonderful place to visit but a different story to some of its residents. Underneath its maritime beauty were streets full of violence, sex and drugs. Bogans ruled most of the areas where the upper class people didn't live. The Main Street almost always had a scene unfolding on the sidewalk. Yelling and swearing was a common occurrence that barely lifted the heads of residents passing by, only looking to make sure it had nothing to do with them directly. Even the local police were so used to it they pretty much only responded to intense situations such as robberies, near fatal bashings, murders, and things involving children. Most of the teenagers in and surrounding the town were lost causes. The select well looked after teens and adolescents kept their noses clean and steered clear of the groups of tatty people their own age that rode bikes too small for their bodies, had badly cut mullets and rattails, baggy pants and singlets. It was a disturbing sight for the adults who had been raised properly, or anyone that had been raised properly. Most bogan children went to Pier Ripple school because it was the cheapest of the two schools in the town.

Due to its small residency, it's amazing if something happened to you and the rest of the town didn't know within the next week, even mere days to hours. It was never discussed how a tiny detail of your life was suddenly known by everyone in town, it was just one of those things you get used to over time and don't think about.

"Yes, well if our son keeps fooling around with the thug boy who knows what will happen to him."

"Oh Patty, I've spoken about it several times with him. I'm more worried about Bethany."

"I've heard some things about her too, but Candice has been friends with her since kinder."

"Wyatt loves the boy, and to be honest he's never really done anything too bad by me. In fact, I left him with Candice before I left."

Patty turned her head so fast it appeared she snapped her neck. "What? Alone at the house? Donald did you really?"

Donald shifted in the driver's seat not looking from the road. "Well... Yes. I told her to call us if anything happened."

She started to speak louder sounding genuinely panicked. "How could you? She's probably been left half dead and pregnant, with all our valuables stolen!!"

"Oh my world, Patty the boy is fifteen. They were just meeting to discuss Wyatt's birthday presents."

She scowled at her husband in disbelief. "You *believed* that? I can't fathom this right now." She looked at the timer in the car; it read 11:52pm.

"Patty it will be fine, you'll see."

"Donald, you'd better hope so."

They pulled into the driveway of their home, it was a rather large house in the 'swish' end of town where all the houses were pampered, hardly ever a blade of grass out of place. From the driveway you could see Candice's bedroom window high on the house where Mrs Fineman saw the curtains were still open.

"Donald quick, her curtains are open, she's always hated that."

They walked up to the front door, unlocked it hurriedly and both headed for upstairs, passing Ricky's shoes without noticing.

~ 2 ~

Whilst her parents were in the front yard, Candice quickly went to try and wake up Ricky. At first it was not successful but after a lot of hurried whispering and shoving he finally woke up.

"Holy god what's happening?" He said sleepily.

"My parents are back, I don't know what to do. If they see you're here we're both dead, for real."

Ricky felt for his glasses on the floor beside him and put them on. He thought for a moment in the dim light. "Can't you just say I slept over? You know, the *truth*?"

She made a panicked groan. "Rick I'm serious we gotta do something."

He realised the actual terror she was feeling and suggested he try to hide.

"Under the bed!" She suggested. "Hurry up I hear them!"

He scampered towards the bed, perfecting an epic slide manoeuvre across the floor straight into the darkness under her bed, hitting a wall of stuff underneath. "What the?" He said rubbing his hip. "You could have warned me! I can't fit there's heaps of shit there I can't see."

She could hear them inside getting closer and closer. "Okay well just come here." She moved onto her bed, pulling his clothes at the shoulder. She got under her blankets and pulled him viciously over the top of her with his body crashing uncoordinated beside her and the wall.

"Since when are you a sumo wrestler?" He asked in humoured astonishment.

She pulled the covers over his head with an assertive 'Shhh' and left it covering her shoulders so that her head was out.

Her door opened somewhat slowly, she saw both parents peaking in at her as she pretended to be just woken up. "Mum? Dad? What are you doing it's late?"

"Just checking you're okay honey, go back to sleep dear. Rest well." Her mother said and made a blowing kiss gesture at her. Both left leaving the door shut.
She heard her dad say something outside, but it was too muffled to work out as they went to Wyatt's room to check on him.

Ricky pulled the blankets back down to reveal his head. *It smells like fruit 'n laundered freshness under there, wish my bloody bed was that decent...* His thoughts were thankfully private.

"Phew, can't believe that worked. Although they might have noticed if they turned the light on." She said quietly, never sounding more relieved.

"At least now I can tell everyone in my class I've been in bed with an older girl." He said with nervous humour.

"Oh shut up!" She said giggling.

He was nervous alright, although he was usually pretty great at pretending he was calm and in control, on the inside he was a blubbering mess. Now he was in the fruity scented bed owned by the girl he's had a crush on for years, with her in it, next to him, and they were so close they were touching.

Is this even real?...

He didn't like the situation he was in, well actually he felt he liked it too much which made him resent himself in a way, causing him to not like being in the situation.

He could feel how warm she is, could feel some part of her body, what it was he didn't even know. She was being so innocent in the dark while he was here thinking about, or trying not to think about, her body laying here next to his with her beautiful face right there by his head. He believed in heaven and so contemplated whether or not he'd been killed by something during the day.

Her whispering about something made him smile even though he had no idea what she was saying, he just lay there listening to the sound, hoping the parents don't come back. She shifted and rolled around a little closer to him, he felt something graze his belly and instantly felt he had to get out, before he embarrassed himself by his body showing its natural gratitude for her.

"Well I better work out how to get home then. I'll climb out the window or sneak out through one of the doors." He quickly but quietly stumbled out of the bed and stood in the dark of the room with his back to her.

"I was just giving you suggestions, weren't you listening?" She said perplexed.

"Yeah, I gotta go. See you when I see you okay?" He spoke urgently, wanting to leave.

"Okay... Tomorrow?" He could hear her smiling with hope when she said it, having to turn and look at her.

"Sure, of course."

"Yay!" She said excited but quiet.

"Oh no actually, I'm doing shit with my parents tomorrow. You got a mobile?"

"Yes, of course I do."

"I was just asking because I do, but Ryan and Wyatt don't so... Dunno, I knew you had one, I'm just dumb. Give me your number?"

They exchanged numbers and he turned to go out the door. "Bye Candie."

"Cya Benson!" She said with a little wave he saw only faintly lit by the moon.

Then he was gone from her space. She lay there now alone, maybe wishing she wasn't.

Ricky sneaked almost professionally through the house downstairs and out the front door, he even knew the code to the security system. He was always so laid back in situations like this almost never caring if he got caught, probably the reason why everyone thought he was 'riff raff'.

He carelessly shoved his shoes on and was finally out in the street breathing in the chilly night air. It was really on the road with not even a cat skulking in sight.

He got around the corner when he stopped for a moment and breathed in somewhat triumphantly and irritated at the same time. He looked down at his crotch.

"I seriously *hate* you right now." He said through gritted teeth in a low tone.

He straitened his glasses and walked on, shaking his head in spite of himself as he headed for his own home.

Hey I never saw Wyatt... he must have gotten back at some point...

~ 3 ~

As you know he certainly was not at home.

He was now sitting on the mattress his captors had provided for his 'comfort.'

A man claiming himself as 'Al' had come to give him some food to eat. He didn't want to eat, even if it did look safe enough. The man had left behind a burger and chips accompanied by two bottles of water.

When Al had seen Wyatt's wet trousers, he said it was lucky he was here to give him some new clothes. As he sat reluctantly eating the food, he reminded himself it's good that at least Al didn't hurt him at all, if anything he was really nice despite the circumstances. He told him that he wanted to go home, Al replied by saying that he would soon, just not yet.

He'd gotten changed into the clean clothes about ten minutes after the thug had left the room.

He now wore a plain white t-shirt and grey track pants, his dirty clothes folded next to the bucket in the corner of the room. His tears had dried but his feelings were still raw. Once he'd changed clothing, he concluded that he must still be around Gerryville if the takeaway food is like this; it was proper and home-style. If they were somewhere near the city surely they would just get McDonald's or Hungry Jacks, they're cheaper and it's doubtful they would purposely spend more money on him than they had to.

Why did they take me? It must be money...

He took big gulps of water nearly emptying the first bottle in one go.

Somebody must be looking for me by now, surely...

He lay down on the mattress and closed his eyes to sob as he thought of his mum, her hair done up in a church style bun, her pearl necklace with a dull glisten, the smell of sandalwood and flowers. He wanted to hug his mum and never let go.

Al had warned him that it wouldn't be wise to yell and shout. He wanted to do so right now and that's for sure.

As the time passed, he lay there wondering what exactly it was he'd done to deserve this. All he could think of was the unexpected fight with Ryan.

Ryan, and Ricky...

What if they were here too? They were at that track thing with him, maybe they got snatched too....

Or they'd been killed...

He sobbed harder with the tears running onto the pillow making round wet marks in the fabric. He stayed as quiet as he could. Not only had he been warned about yelling, he didn't want any thugs hearing him cry like a baby literally because he wants his mum.

He still had no clue how long he'd been here or what day it was. Rolling over onto his other side to face the wall and wait for something to happen, it occurred to him that last time he'd woken up in his own bed in his comfortable house he had no clue he'd be here now.

If nobody saved him now, he might die.

I might really die...

~ **4** ~

Monday morning was so far as casual as every other day, except its public holiday status.

Patty Fineman sat in the study sewing. She had recently decided to give clothes making a go for an extra hobby and was elbow deep in soft brown and teal fabrics, creating her first self made dress.

Donald Fineman sat at the dining table reading the paper. Nothing really interesting in today's copy, except maybe the article on local vegetation planting. They were planting native brush in parts of the area and there were now penalties for vandalism.

He turned a few pages and saw the silly little comic strips. He took note to save them for Wyatt. That's when he realised it was 10:00am and he hadn't heard or seen him today, he usually got up early.

Maybe he's having a bit of a sleep in, taking advantage of the holiday...

The house phone rang out for all and was quickly answered by Patty, who had gone from the study to the hallway to pick up the phone.

"Fineman residence, Patricia speaking." She stated friendly into the telephone.

A most disturbing computerised voice began to speak, Patty thought it to be the devil with what it was saying. *"We have your son. He's safe but he won't be if you don't give us something. We'll exchange him for all that money you have tucked away."* It hung up leaving that familiar beeping in Patty's ear.

Her heart sank as she dropped the phone handle, leaving it to hang itself by the wall. She couldn't help but scream.

"DONALD! They have our boy, someone has taken my son!" She sounded as though she was dying a horrific death.

Candice jerked awake at hearing her mother's blood curdling cries, her heart immediately beating hard. She jumped straight out of bed and ran for downstairs.

She found her parents in the hallway near the phone, her mum kneeling on the floor blubbering and her dad holding her, trying to understand what she was talking about.

"Daddy, what's wrong?" She asked scared, feeling thoroughly disjointed at the sight.

Her mother tried to speak, her face red and wet from tears. "They.... Wyatt is...he's been taken... They're going to hurt him if we don't.... If we don't pay them... Thousand... My baby..."

"Candice, go to your brother's room and see if he's there, right now!" Her father demanded in the panic.

She turned and ran straight back upstairs as fast as she could, she didn't have time to think of safety resulting in tripping at the top of the stairs. She bounced back up straight away and ran to Wyatt's door, her flowing hair flying out behind her in fearful motion. She bashed on that door, yelling his name, not hearing his familiar voice talk back to her.

She turned the knob and barged in, she only saw his belongings, there was no Wyatt.

The only thing to do now is go all the way back to her parents and tell them the news.

Why wasn't he there? She thought to herself. *How long for and where is he now?...* "Didn't you check on him last night?" She asked them confused.

"We thought he was in there. I'm calling the police." Her father declared. She'd never seen him like this before, it scared her. She turned and went back to her room away from the sounds of her mother crying in despair.

She sat on her bed in a zombie trance, breathing low. Her little brother was gone, Wyatt was gone. She looked over at the mobile phone on her bedside table, her hand reached out for it and slowly brought it back to rest against her chest. Tears began to run down her face as she clutched her phone between her breasts.

She looked down to interact with the screen of the phone while it lit up her sad face.

Going through her contacts, hovering her thumb over the dial button beside the name 'Little Richard'.

She didn't ring it, she only sat there in silence, failing to truly fathom the situation.

~ Four ~

ROSES ARE RED, BUT THEY'RE ALSO BLUE

~ 1 ~

Wyatt sat in his captive room wondering whether he should try the door to see if it was still locked.

You know it's locked, you heard it... If they hear the door being tampered with, they'll probably kill you...

He crawled from the mattress to the door and lay on his stomach, his head tilted onto its side on the floor trying to peek under. It was very dimly lit out there which gave him chills. He thought of sitting in a room in the middle of the abyss, all by himself with a man-thug named Al, bringing him cheap food to keep him alive until they felt like killing him. He didn't cry this time, he seemed to have no tears left.

What if they're like the paedophiles Ricky sometimes jokes about?

Colourful kiddy fiddlers and white collared rock spiders...

A weak, subtle smile crept over his face at the thought of Ricky's ridiculous names for some things.

He stood up, automatically brushing his clothes off to sit sideways on the chair by the table, facing the room where he looked at his situation once more.

A bed, a towel, a bucket, and a table with crayons... Maybe they want to keep me as their kid?

At that moment he heard a soft sound from outside the door, the kind of sulking a little girl in tears would make. It startled his nerves causing him to jump out of his skin. He listened to it, too scared to get close to the door.

What if it's a kidnapped little kid?... What if she's hurt?...

He felt he had to make some sort of contact in the spirit of a true Superman fan.

"H-hello?" He said cautiously.

The sobbing stopped as soon as the 'oh' in his greeting hit the still, cold air of this place.

Listening with his ear now against the door, he timidly asked if there was anybody out there.

"Uh, hi." A girl's voice said from the other side.

Wyatt jumped backwards in frightful surprise, he hadn't heard any footsteps or anything indicating the approach of a person anywhere in front of him out there.

With a hand to his chest, he breathed deeply to try and regain what was left of his composure. "Were you just crying? I hope you're okay."

"No, I only just got here." She said sounding confused. *"I hope you're okay though."*

"Oh, well I'm not really okay." He replied not knowing how to handle all this.

"What's your name?" Her voice was steady and deep in that feminine kind of way. Comforting in its own way of strangeness to his situation.

What would a girl be doing here? She must be a prisoner too...

He walked back over to the looming door. "My name is Wyatt. Who are you?" He could hear scuffling on the ground out there before she spoke again.

"I'm Rose." She replied calmly.

He sat back a little in preparation of what was unfolding here. "What are you doing here, were you stolen too? Can you get me out?"

"Hold the questions for a sec, I can come in." She replied as she clearly played with the lock.

"Sure you can come in." Wyatt said realising that he'd spoken before thinking, it's not like he had a choice in what goes on here.

The handle began to move. He stepped backwards towards the mattress as he watched a girl with shoulder length, light brunette hair come in with great caution. She wore a wavy dress patterned with colourful flowers, black leggings covered her legs, a baggy purple cardigan keeping her torso warm. Her shoes were the kind of ankle high canvas sneakers- obviously Kmart knockoffs, the cool girls wear to the bogan school. Her eyes looked tired but definitely not as if she were just crying.

She looked at Wyatt and smiled awkwardly.

～ 2 ～

Rose Brandis was alone in her backyard as she usually is. She can be happy, imaginative and is one of the few people born with the ability to carry appreciation of wonder into the older years of her life. The kind of person who can pick up one of thousands of tree leaves and look at it as an individual, as a piece of amazing emerald treasure.

She was also immensely sad and disturbed underlying the great feelings of her childhood and adolescents. Not in a total bad way, more of a troubled way.

Rose isn't much of a social girl. She has a few acquaintances but there was only really one friend. Hannah's quite the funny girl at times, could always light up a moment just as easily as breathing. Rose was always happy at the thought of seeing her even if most of the time it meant going to school. The only other friend is her best; her brother.

Except recently she's made friends with a girl she hasn't seen at school. She met her when she was mucking around at the beach across the road from where she lives. This girl is younger than her and kind of weird looking but really nice.

When Rose tried to explain her elusive new friend, Hannah thought she sounded freaky. Rose sometimes found herself questioning whether to continue as this girl's friend, but she couldn't deny the fact that she seemed to turn up at times when she was feeling low, which is unfortunately often. She would offer light-hearted conversation and outlooks in her own weird way.

The backyard was getting darker by the minute, but she decided she'd stay out until her mother would call her in, which might or might not happen. That would depend on whether her mother could be bothered giving a damn about where she was this evening.

All she'd been doing was sitting in the huge tree that stood in the wide backyard. Its branches were thick at the base and got smaller as they got closer to the top, slowly turning into tree-top twigs. This made it easy to climb high and sit relatively comfortably to scope the land beyond the backyard. Even if it's just a few other spaced out houses, sheds and paddocks, seeing the world beyond always gave her an adventurous feeling of hope, the same feeling as when she'd look at the sky above her in all its wondrous glory.

Before too long, her mother's unpleasant screech beckoned her to come eat the dinner she'd microwaved. Honestly, her and her brother preferred the usual days when the woman didn't bother to try and feel like a housewife and mother.

She carefully climbed back down to the ground to walk solemnly along to the back door of the house. The solidly round head of the house bull terrier lifted to watch her approach from where he sat, tied to the house by thin chain link near the large gate to the front yard.

"Hey Bully-Dog." She greeted from where she stood at the door. He doesn't bother to greet happily anymore, rather he lay his body down and place his head over his front paws. Even the spirit of an innocent dog was killed thanks to this household.

They were having distasteful micro-waved beef tonight, much to her twin brother's disgust. Jack wanted to be a vegetarian, but their mum's boyfriend thought it to be lunacy and far too queer. 'Meat is man's food' he'd been told numerous times.
And of course like every other topic of life, their mum agreed with her boyfriend.

Rose understood Jack, they are twins after all. Not identical but similar all the same.
Jack has a clear feminine handsomeness about him, with his dark spiked up hair and shiny, light copper eyes deeply soaked in marijuana, the odd pimple here and there on his lightly freckled, milky complexion. It isn't surprising he has a lot of girl's attention at school.

Rose sat next to him at the dinner table after he patted the chair beside his. He leaned over and whispered to her. "They actually have a kid, I swear."

Rose looked back with a grave expression. "You serious? This is bullshit. I hate it."

"Me too." He said looking at his plate full of dead animal.

"I'm going to talk to him, or her." Rose said confidently.
Jack turned his head fast and tried to explain why she shouldn't and just stay out of it.

"Well I am. I told you that if it actually happened, I'd do

something about it, and if you want to make sure I don't mess up, come with me."

"Ohh Rosey why?" Jack quietly whined. "I don't want to get into trouble with *him*."

"Jack seriously, there's a scared kid down there. What if it was me that'd been taken, and some dude just ignored it because he was scared of his mother's boyfriend."

He frowned at hearing this. He didn't like the example at all and now felt like a complete, selfish prick. "Okay, I'll keep watch while you do whatever. What exactly *are* you gonna do?"

She didn't answer right away, but when she did, she was playing with her food using the fork. "I'm going to make them comfortable and feel safe, then I'm going to help them escape."

Jack squirmed at the certain trouble and severe punishment they were going to get themselves in. He nodded to acknowledge that he'd heard her when he became painfully aware that Daz had entered the room, he'd promptly walked over to the fridge to routinely get a beer out. The twins stayed dreadfully quiet as if to try and wait out a terrible ordeal. With good reason too because on his way back past he lingered around Jack, probably seeing if he'd eaten the meat yet.

"Eat your damn dinner." He demanded in a deep, guttural voice.

"Yeah, I will, pretty much just sat down." He answered cautiously.

For that he felt a hard thwack to the back of his head, quietly cringing at the pain.

"Hurry up and eat what your mother gave you. Ungrateful piece of..." He looked at Rose now. "You too, ya little brat." He swaggered off into the lounge room without hanging around for an answer or reaction.

Rose stabbed the piece of meat on Jack's plate with her fork and placed it onto her own. She couldn't endure seeing Daz violently terrorising her brother but knew that taking the burden of meat eating away she was helping him personally and that was worth acting on.

Jack looked at her with a grateful face. He knew his sister was destined for great things, doubting himself at the same time.

He didn't care what happened to himself, he just wanted to leave this life knowing he'd gotten his sister to a point in her life where she could be as great in the world as she is on the inside. A chance to live normally and comfortably blissful with as much peace as possible.

They just somehow needed to get far, far away from here.

Their mother laughed away in the lounge at something on the blaring TV while she ate her well cooked takeaway dinner, a large box of cheap goon sat beside her on the table.

Chewing on the tasteless meat, Rose collected her nerves as she thought of actually making her way down to where the kid currently resides. From her place at the dining table, she could clearly see the doorframe to the darkened laundry. It seemed to plead at her to hurry and fix this.

"Fuck it, I'm in." Jack suddenly stated in a quiet tone.

She looked to him and saw he was also staring at the darkened doorway. He looked at her to share a silent look of a mission's pact.

Together they would save somebody from their own home.

~ 3 ~

Jack now stood outside the door to the victim's 'cell'. When he heard Rose speaking to the captive, he thought the kid had a nice voice. It was innocent and fluently polite, not like the ferals he was used to hearing such as the bulky, brain dead bullies at school. It also sounded a lot older than what he was expecting.

He stood there uptight as his sister talked to the poor guy behind the door in that stupid room, listening out for Al or Daz. He didn't have a clue what to say if one of them came along, suppose he'd just try to say they were bored. He waited anxiously for her to come back out.

Inside the room Wyatt had no idea that there was another person out there, nor would he really care if he did know.

"What, w-what are you doing here?... Did you help put me here?" He asked timidly looking to her, shaking in anticipation of what was happening here.

Rose sat on the ground in front of him and began to talk. "You have to stay quiet and do everything they tell you to okay, or our efforts to get you out safely without your parents paying them a cent will be ruined. And most likely we'll all end up *dead*, I wouldn't put it past him."

Wyatt soaked in what Rose was telling him, joining her on the ground. "Who's *he*? And *they*? And how do I know I can trust you?"

Rose shook her head. "You have to trust me, what else can you do? And *they* are Al and Daz. Daz is my mother's boyfriend, unfortunately, and Al is his buddy. They're total crooks and have recently decided to take up kidnapping. I think they mess up or freak out before really doing a ransom. I want to help and stop all this."

"I just really want to go home." He said in a pitiful voice.

She just looked at him as he was facing his head down. "How old are you?" She asked calmly.

"I'm fourteen." He simply answered, not looking up.

"I'm fifteen." No reaction from him. She felt around in the pocket of her dress and pulled out a homemade bracelet. It was made from colourful plastic strings. It's pretty, intertwined colours looked like a rainbow. "Here, have this so when we're not here you know you have people here to help you. I just thought I'd give you something. I didn't want you lonely down here."

He took the unexpected gift with confused gratitude and looked at it, he smiled ever so slightly. "Thanks Rose." He put his hand through the loop, leaving it wrapped snug around his wrist.

"Okay well we better get outta here before we get caught." She stood up and headed for the door. "Don't worry kid, we'll getcha out. We'll be back later." She said with a sad little smile leaving the room, looking back at Wyatt until she was gone behind the door. It shut with a soft click and then there was the noise of the lock being played with.

He sat there alone once more as he heard his new hero walk away as quietly and hurried as she could. He looked down at his bracelet gift, his lip began to tremble as he sat in the resumed quiet.

Hang on... She kept using plural words... But she was alone... Wasn't she?...

~ 4 ~

The twins were sitting on their bedroom floor eating lollies while Jack grilled Rose for information on what happened with the boy.

"He was so sad I almost cried Jack. It was terrible. He is literally just sitting in there with next to nothing."

"Well let's just call the cops anonna-moose... annamously." He took a moment to regain his bearings of speech. "Anonymously." He suggested with little faith.

"Nah. Something tells me that'd go down bad." She said biting on a coloured snake.

They sat quietly for a moment before Jack began to ask what the captive boy looked like.

"Umm, he has like, sorta dark brown hair, sort of greyish eyes and stuff. I don't know."

"Sounded like he had a really nice voice." Jack said almost like asking a question.

"Yeah, I suppose he was really nice considering. Being held hostage here probably means he won't want anything to do with us when he gets out."

"He also sounded older than what I was expecting."

"Yeah, he was more like our age. He said he's fourteen." Jack looked up at the open window of their bedroom thinking about how the boy only has a light bulb for light.

"And Jack." She said with one eyebrow raised looking at her brother. "He's most likely straight."

"Yes, yes, I know. I don't mean, you know. Don't be stupid." He said shaking his head looking at the floor.

She laughed a little before remembering they're dealing with a kidnapped person.

Jack noticed her silence and the serious expression she had. "Don't worry sis, we'll get him out." He reached his hand out and sat it on her shoulder. She looked up at him and smiled with tiny tears forming beneath her eyeballs.

"I know. I'm just scared." She replied.

"I am too but not as much as he must be. Down there probably scared shitless."

She sniffed in a successful attempt to stop mucus running out her nostrils. "I want to go back and get to know him better." She stated boldy.

"Wyatt is such a weird name." Jack said taking a bite out of a lolly snake.

"I guess. You going to come in with me?"

"But then who'll keep watch?" Jack replied.

"Oh yeah, true. Well, we can always take turns in talking

to him."

"I will go in, but just not yet." He said scratching the back of his head. "We gotta actually start trying to figure out what exactly the plan is."

They talked about it for a good half-hour before giving up on the subject. Jack finally just suggested a simple set of events.

"Look why don't we just plan a time to go down there and get him, bring him up and just go for a super run for it back to wherever he lives or even the police station."

"But what if we get seen by Al or Daz, or mum?"

His voice took on a higher pitch as he replied. "Well we'll just take the out of view routes!"

"Yeah maybe a quick and reckless approach will actually work with this. Man, I hope we can do this..."

"Okay what day you reckon?"

She thought about it. "How about... Tomorrow night when mum's shopping and they're at Al's drinking?"

"Yeah. That could work." He looked over at the alarm clock beside her bed. "Okay we've still got a while to have the place to ourselves. If you want to go back down there to talk, we'd better do it. Maybe we should just do it now?"

"Nah, I'm not ready. I'd prefer to be prepared for possible hell."

Without answering, Jack crawled across the room to his bed and promptly reached inside his pillowcase to pull out a zip-lock bag of greenery before crawling back to his previous spot, leaning his back at the foot of Rose's bed. He indulged in a deep sigh as he rolled his joint of relaxation. "Why'd it have to be us, huh?" He asked meaning it to be rhetorical.

Rose looked from her stoning brother to the wall where a small photo of their dad sat on the inconspicuous spot beside the end of her bed. "Could be worse I guess." She answered lowly.

"Ha, *yeah right.*" Jack scoffed, retrieving the lighter from his pants pocket.

She too sighed deeply, shrugging her shoulders in thought.

~ 5 ~

Wyatt lay on the mattress once again. There wasn't much else he could do.

He wondered why God would punish him so brutally just because of an argument with his friend.

He looked at his wrist decorated with the bracelet Rose gave him.

At least now I have some sort of real hope... Candice was right, God is overrated...

He tugged the bracelet softly and thought how nice it was that she actually sat there and made this for him before she'd even met him. At that he started to wonder if it was all planned or something, but couldn't help but feel he could trust her. His gut told him it was okay, or was that delirium clinging to hope, or maybe it was God... Maybe Rose is actually an angel of sorts, God's soldier here to help him.

He began to slowly drift away into sleep, the first time since he'd woken up in this hell hole. His drifting was soon interrupted by Rose coming back in. Wyatt was so on edge that even in his light slumber he jolted awake and upright before she'd even come in.

"Oh, I'm so relieved it's just you. I thought it might be the men."

"No only me." She smiled.

As he sat back more comfortably, he asked her how she was.

"Um, I'm good. You don't need to pretend. I know this isn't normal." She forcibly giggled as she raised her shoulders. He looked down at his crossed legs.

She sat on the floor near the bed. "Do you like the bracelet

Wyatt? Silly question I suppose because..."

He looked at her and said "No, I mean yes, I do. I really do. Thank you again." He smiled the weary smile that maybe a man living roughly on the train tracks riding across the countryside would display.

It pained Rose to see it.

He continued "It's very random for you to think of it. I mean it's a really beautiful thought and all."

"Oh, well I had the initial thought, but I didn't know what to make. My brother suggested a friendship bracelet type thing. He made it."

He became alert to the fact she'd said she has a sibling. "You have a brother?"

"Yeah, my twin. His name is Jack. Has good ideas and stuff but there's not a week that goes by he hasn't got a joint, I swear to God!" She exclaimed with light laughter.

"Oh, okay." He replied with fake laughter.

"He's keeping watch out there." She pointed her thumb to the door.

It made him feel a little safe knowing she had a sibling standing outside the door, like one of God's bodyguards here to save his life. He imagined what the Angel looked like out there keeping watch of the door to death, just waiting for the moment the Devil's henchmen appear. He could be the tallest angel known to heaven wearing a modest robe, his hair flowing in strands of elegant brown as the shoulders of his strong wings of white towered over head.

Wyatt didn't answer her, so she began to speak again.

"Okay so here's what we're planning." She told him all about it, even the route they'd take to stay out of the road view. He sat nodding his head getting more excited to leave and more eager for home, if it were even possible to feel any more eager.

After they agreed on the plans, she offered to invite Jack in so he could meet him quickly before they left for the night.

He replied with a simple "Yeah okay" of indifference.

She got to her feet. "I'll see you tomorrow sometime, rest well okay."

He waved his hand at her, he didn't really want her to go. "Yeah, I will, you too."

She went out and almost immediately there he heard mumbled, rushed whispering.

So that's what it really sounds like when angels whisper...

It stopped, the door began to open again but this time it certainly wasn't Rose, it was a boy of maybe the same age as her and maybe even a little prettier. He looked like the friendliest teen male Wyatt had ever seen, other than Ricky and Ryan. Especially Ricky with his almost constant laughing and happy mood.

The Jack boy stood in the exact spot his sister had been sitting not even two minutes ago. He wore tracksuit pants similar to what Wyatt had on now and a red hooded jumper with a stylish sports reference on the front. His sneakers weren't well kept but his black, boyish hair done up rather well like one of those classic cool kids made up for that.

"Hey there, I'm Jack." He held out his hand with a certain wistful coolness about him. His voice seemed a little hoarse, like an unnatural taint to his otherwise lovely sound.

Wyatt reached up and shook his hand without much hesitation. "Hello. I'm Wyatt."

Jack smiled and revealed a set of even teeth in only the very slightest pale yellow to complete his near perfect appearance. Their hands fell away from each other. Nobody spoke for a small amount of time, although the silence made it feel like forever.

Jack felt he needed to apologise for what had happened here. He decided that sitting down at his level would be better, so he did.

"Ahm... I'm super sorry for what's happened. Me and Rose hate it but we're getting you out. Somehow."

Wyatt looked over at one of the walls trapping him in and felt anger seeping into his feelings. "Your sister has told me that a few times. I just want to get out of here. Can't you just call the police?"

Jack leaned back uncomfortably, thinking about how that's what he had suggested. "Yeah, like I totally get that but we're just dumbass kids remember, and I'm scared shitless myself."

Wyatt felt a smile come over his face followed by laughter. Whether or not it was fear, nervous giggles or if it was because he thought it was funny, he didn't know.

"Hey." Jack said perplexed. "What you laughing at dude?"

Wyatt looked to him, speaking as his giggles slowly ceased. "I don't really know, just that... the fact you said 'scared shitless'. I think I'm over tired, I've hardly slept."

Jack nodded his head in understanding. "Do you want to be left alone to rest before we go tomorrow? Or attempt to go I should say." He asked courteously.

"No, I don't really like being alone in here. Can you stay for long?" He replied eagerly.

"A little while, we really don't wanna be caught being somewhere we shouldn't. Um, Daz, the one with more hair, is a real piece of work and I don't really think it would end well for me and Rose, if we did get caught trying to help you and stuff."

"Oh okay... So, they do just want me for my parent's money?"

"Well that's all I've figured." He shrugged.

Wyatt looked down at the putrid looking hardness of the cold ground and the paisley mat covering most of the room.

Jack was aware of Wyatt's gloomy change. "So, tell me a little about yourself. What's your last name? Do you have pets?

What's your best friend's name?"

Wyatt bounced his head up in comforted surprise. "My last name is Fineman, I have no pets and my best friend's name is..." He paused, causing Jack to look at him expectantly.

"... I have *two* best friends, Ricky and Ryan. I was with them just before I was, you know."

"What're they like? They both must be awesome to have the name of best friend." Jack replied happily.

"Ryan is great. He can draw really well and stuff like that. He's usually really nice even though his parents obviously like his brother more, but for a while now he's been uptight because of his stupid Aunty being mean to him."

Jack grimaced at hearing this. "That must suck. At least he has friends to get through it." He gestured his hand positively toward him.

"I guess you're right." Wyatt reciprocated, smiling.

"What about Ricky, what's he like?"

"Oh Ricky is totally great. He's *so* funny *and* a great listener, and nearly *always* has the perfect thing to say."

Jack looked through squinted eyes accompanied by his smirk at Wyatt describing Ricky. "You guys have girlfriends or anything?" He asked him casually.

"No, I've never had one. I've never gone anywhere near a girl like that. Ryan was dared to kiss one once. Ricky on the other hand seems to be comfortable with girls and all that stuff but as one of his closest friends, I know he's never been near one. Just like me." He spoke proudly.

Rose popped her head in and smiled at the sight. Her brother and the sad prisoner were sitting with each other looking somewhat happy. "Guys I think we'll have to give it another five minutes before we go."

Wyatt nodded as Jack replied. "Kay sis." She left them to their conversation to resume her watch duty.

"Well I can't wait to meet them." Jack said grinning. "What's your favourite song?"

Wyatt thought for a moment before answering. Usually if asked this question he'd say something like 'Let It Be' by the Beatles or 'Superman' by Five For Fighting, or anything created by Simon and Garfunkel. But being here and gone from all that he's ever known, he felt it was right to say "Send Me On My Way by Rusted Root."

"Oh, cool." Jack said of the answer. "I don't think I know what that is." He shook his head in the slightest way.

"I haven't actually heard it properly for years, not since I was really little with my family. My dad used to make my sister and I laugh by singing along to it and dancing with us. That was so long ago now."

"Sounds awesome." He replied knowing how dear sweet memories of youth are.

"Yeah it was. What about your favourite song?" Wyatt asked the nice boy.

"I guess right now it'd have to be a tossup between..." Jack began as he tilted his fine head in thought. "Okay maybe, I'd have to say, 'Shadow of the Day' by Linkin Park, 'It's Too Late' by Evermore, and 'I Just Wanna Live' by Good Charlotte."

"I don't think I know what they are either." Wyatt laughed, to which Jack shrugged his shoulders, returning the laugh.

"Dude when we get outta here I am *so* showing you Linkin Park. Stuff me man, it's amazing." The strange boy informed as though he was describing the full taste of a good wine.

"I'll try to be open to whatever it is." Wyatt replied willingly but cautious.

It was then that he realised how ludicrous this was. How can he be having a conversation like this when he's in such a perilous situation?

His thoughts forcibly turned to the goings on of outside that door. "So is your mum bad like those kidnappers?"

Jack squinted with thought for a moment before trying to explain the strange circumstances of the answer to that simple question. Maybe mysterious simplicity was the right answer. "Umm, she's just there." He replied.

"Sorry about my prying, that was rude to ask." Wyatt shook his head with a look of disdain before he bowed his eyes to the bare floor between them.

"Nah, ask anything you want. I mean look what they did to you." He answered obviously trying to let him know he wasn't offended. One of his hands reached over to touch his left forearm.

Wyatt's emotional catalogue couldn't recognise what he was feeling, it was a stand-still fullness of nothing as he watched Jack shift closer to inspect the grazes on the skin of his arm. Almost like built up sound in the climax of a loud chorus, he urged himself to suddenly pull his arm away and tuck it behind the other one against his stomach.

"Sorry man." Jack said looking up at his face, seeming to be slow to the situation.

Wyatt was feeling extremely odd now and so asked what school he and Rose go to without first reassuring Jack about the apology.

"We go to Pier Ripple. You?" He answered with conversational ease.

"I go to Our Lady Sacred. So do my friends. They both used to go to Ripple, but their parents coincidently moved them to my school at the same time. I think something dodgy happened and freaked their parents out. They were already good mates at the other school before they met me."

"Oh okay, wonder if I knew 'em. Did you say you had a sister?"

"Yeah I have an older sister called Candice."

"Just a sister like me!" He exclaimed excitedly. "They can be a real handful can't they, just between you and me." Wyatt nodded and smiled.

"Well I'd better get a move on so that you can rest before the big escape." Jack said as he got to his feet and headed for the door.

"Okay, stay safe out there." Wyatt answered, not wanting him to leave him alone again.

Jack turned to look at him again, thinking. He put a hand in his pocket to pull out a bag of mixed lollies. "Here, have these. Just make sure you hide the packet or something." He gently threw them at him, catching the bag swiftly.

"Thanks!" He said surprised.

"That's okay." Jack smirked. "You look good with that bracelet on by the way."

"Yeah it was really nice of... Oh yeah you made it! Thank you."

Jack simply replied with a "Catchya later Wyatt" and a wink of the eye, just like Ricky.

"Hey Jack?" He said quicly before he was gone. "What day is it?"

He thought for a moment as his inner self sifted through the remaining plant smoke in his mind. "It's Monday the... 20th of August. And we're in Tasmania in case you didn't know." He said with a quiet chuckle, that turned into a minor cough.

"Oh okay... Thank you."

Jack went out the door still smiling and once more it was locked behind him.

As he lay back on the mattress sucking on some sort of raspberry flavoured lolly given to him by Jack, he felt more tired than he'd ever been in his life. Under normal circumstances he wouldn't indulge in lollies of any kind really. But what has he got to lose at this time, it's not like eating them would change his life at all. Unlike the meals the captor brought him to eat, he trusted in the angel's sugary gift. He finally swallowed the sweet tasting food and rolled over to fall into the dreams that were waiting to be had. It occurred to him that although the twins were out and free to roam, they were just as much as captives as he is at the moment.

He knew that Jack was just making conversation with him to get his mind off being kidnapped, it didn't really help but it was really nice to talk about normal things with him.

He began to think of getting out and seeing his family and friends again. His eyes closed, leaving his other senses to pick up the slack a bit. The smell of an over bleached room currently in use by a scared teenager inhabited his nostrils. The sound of... nothing in his ears. He could hear his own heartbeat though, it promptly helped him fall into a deep slumber. The packet of mixed lollies fell onto the floor beside the mattress while his deep breathing continued without interruption.

~ Five ~

WHEN DOVES CRY

~ 1 ~

At Monday's midday, Ryan ran from his house into the street and went straight for Wyatt's place. Living only a few blocks away made such actions easy to carry out. He'd gotten a phone call from Ricky telling him that he was told by Candice that the police were at the Fineman's place because Wyatt was missing. Ricky didn't know exactly what was going on, just that he was missing, and everyone's upset. It was enough news to make Ryan panic.

He ran so fast through the streets it could have looked like he was flying. He had so many things running through his head, even contemplating whether or not it could be a prank.

He turned a corner now running on unpaved grass. He heard somebody call his name out from behind him. Slowing, he turned to see Ricky coming towards him down the road on his bike, the wind blowing back his plaid shirt.

Ryan stopped running, trying to catch his breath as Ricky slowed to a stop beside him on the road.

"You okay man?" Ricky said looking at Ryan's red and panting face.

"I... just wanted... to get to Wyatt's... fast as I can." He said breathless. Ricky kept looking at him as if he knew he had more to say. Ryan picked up on that. "What if he left... because of that stupid fight?"

Ricky felt sympathy and dismounted his second-hand Schwinn to hug his friend. Ryan clung to him as he sniffled and stifled back tears. "C'mon Ryan, maybe he's just being an arse and not going home. Or maybe it has absolutely nothing to do with anything. No need for tears just yet buddy."

They broke apart, standing on the grass while Ryan wiped his face with his sleeve. "You're right, he's probably fine."

"Here, take my bike and I'll walk the rest of the way."

Ryan looked to him with great gratitude and affection. "You're the best friend ever, you know that, Ricky?"

He laughed, nodding at the compliment. "So I've been told. Now let's go before we turn forty."

Ryan swiftly mounted the bike, gave Ricky a quick nod and started to pedal up the road. If it looked before like he was flying when running, it now looked like he was hovering in super speed while he was riding. The red body of the bike flew past the light traffic of the road, the drivers in their cars just saw a boy riding his bike as fast as he could for fun, but in Ryan's brain fun was nowhere to be found.

He reached the street the Fineman house was on, the bike nimbly turning the corner with his guidance. He zoomed up the road and into the driveway, careful not to hit the police car parked beside the nature strip or the family's car sitting outside the doors of the house's side garage. The bike came to a dramatic skidding stop leaving blemishes on the concrete. Mrs Fineman would complain about the marks on her driveway at a later date.

He leaned Ricky's bike up against the wall of the shed beside the house before he ran up to the front door and knocked rap-idly. He waited for a moment before the door opened to reveal Candice's worried and expecting face. Ryan wondered who she was expecting to see... Wyatt finally coming home or Ricky's 'doofus' head?

"Hey Candice. I came around as soon as I heard, Ricky told me."

She looked at him with a distant, slightly perplexed face. "Thanks kid, where's ya friend?" She asked looking past him down the street.

"He's on his way. He shouldn't be long."

"Come on in. Just don't get all funny 'cause of the cops in the dining room."

Ryan walked in behind her, she left him to close the door. He turned inside the hall and noticed faces peering through the curtains of houses across the street. He closed the door, shutting out their curiousness.

Following Candice to the living room, he could only just see Mr and Mrs Fineman and two police officers sitting at the table in the dining room. Mrs Fineman sat there, staring into nothing, her eyes were red and puffy. Mr Fineman sat beside her with his hands on his knees listening to one of the officers.

The talking cop had a burly appearance about him although he wasn't a large build. Clean shaven with a faint but noticeable scar on his cheek, his hands waved around a little as he spoke with a stern voice.

The other cop, obviously younger, sat on a kitchen chair with his skinny arms crossed, his navy blue cap with the police shield on it sat tightly on his head. It appeared that it was all new to him.

The tougher cop looked at Ryan as he entered the house, his eyes not leaving his until he was out of sight.

He now sat on a lounge chair near Candice. Not a word was

said, an awkward scene where nobody had anything to say, or knew what to say. Ryan and Candice nearly never had anything to do with each other, so this moment was especially strange given the circumstances. Every now and then she broke the room's silence with a small sniffle.

Finally she sprung up and left for the door, Ryan's perplexed expression faded as he noticed through the lounge window that Ricky was walking up to the front door.

A few minutes later they entered together, she sat back in the same chair crossing her legs like a lady, Ricky sitting on one of the fancy foot stools.

"Man those cops are kinda not what you'd expect hey?" Ricky stated.

Ryan shook his head slowly in agreement. While sitting here, he couldn't help but notice the glances of glistening eyes the other two keot throwing each other. "When was the last time anyone saw him?" He asked them.

"Honestly the last time I saw him was when he walked off on us." Ricky said sounding glum, even though he was trying not to. He always naturally felt like it was his job to be the happy one that kept the mood light in times of sadness, but this time was very sad, very real and very scary.

"The last time I saw him..." Candice began "...was yesterday when he left to meet you guys after church."

"So he's been out all night? It's not like him at all..." Ryan said to the floor.

They sat in silence once more while Ricky nervously rocked the stool back and forth. The polished wooden clock on the mantelpiece ticked softly away as it always had, leaving a disturbance in the psyche of all three teenagers. It's ticking suddenly sounding like their only connection to their lost brother and friend.

An unfamiliar voice made them all jump, giving their attention to the young cop that was now in the room. He had simply said hello.

"Well kids, I guess you all know why we're here today." They each looked at him, nodded their heads in unison.

"I'm officer Rogan, but you guys can call me Jeff." He said as he sat on one of the other foot stools. Ricky giggled at learning his name is Jeff, careful not to let him see.

"I ah, I know this must be difficult and everything. I apologise for the loss."

"He's missing, we haven't *lost* him." Candice snapped, not hiding any anger she was feeling at hearing that sentence.

"Yes, you're exactly right. I'm, yeah sorry." Jeff looked down at his little note pad. "So we've spoken to you miss, but you guys, what are your names?"

The boys looked at each other, Ricky nodded at Ryan to say it's fine for him to go first.

"My name is Ryan Jonson. I'm a friend of Wyatt's."

"Mm-hmm. Cool." Jeff said as he wrote down what he heard, then he looked over at Ricky.

"I'm Richard Benson and I'm also a friend of Wyatt, and his sister." He said looking quickly at Candice and back to Jeff. She lifted the side of her mouth to form a small smirk.
Jeff wrote down those details and asked another question, one that they were silently expecting. "Okay guys, when was the last time you saw..." He looked at his notes "...Wyatt?"

They explained that they had both last seen him the day before down that track off Augustus Street.

"Okay, was he acting strange or did anything out of the ordinary happen when you were together and stuff?" He was asking his questions sounding like he was trying too hard, it was obvious he was new to the job and clearly very green.

Ryan stayed quiet, a little reluctant to admit that the last time they saw him there had been a big argument that turned physical. Ricky answered Jeff by telling him about the weird girl Wyatt kept thinking he was seeing in random spots.

"Ah... what did this girl look like?" Jeff asked.

"I only saw her once at the milk bar." Ricky explained. "She was young, I dunno maybe like twelve, thirteen? She had really long dark hair, and I didn't see her close up so I can't tell you much. She had a big dog with her, one of those collie looking things."

As Jeff concentrated on the notepad he scribbled details in, Ricky encouraged Ryan with hand gestures to speak up about it, about the argument. Candice looked on in curiosity.

Ryan knew it was the right thing to do but still felt like shit at the thought of telling the police about it. Did it even really matter anyway? "Um, officer Rogan?" He said quietly.

"Yeah man? I mean kid."

"Yesterday when we last saw him, he was walking off because I had a fight with him. It was the biggest fight he'd ever had with either of us."

Jeff nodded at Ryan's confession. "Well, you didn't kidnap him and then call his parents for money, did you?" He asked smiling.

The two boys looked to each other, both wearing the expression of 'what the hell is this?'

Ryan looked back to Jeff to reply confidently. "No, I didn't."

The smile left Jeff's face, he looked shamefully down at his trusty notepad. "So uh, did he ever talk to the girl?" He asked still looking down.

"Nah, she creeped him out. He said he saw her at the church yesterday." Replied Ricky.

Candice sat up in surprise. "What? He never said anything to me! I didn't see any weird girl! I mean *it is church* so everyone's weird, but still."

"It's Wyatt, he doesn't like talking about things that make no sense." Ricky said trying to console her.

"Okay everybody I'm going to go back into the um, ah... Other room in there. If you think of anything that could be helpful or whatever just go in and pipe up okay." He got up and left them, the mantelpiece clock seemed to chime louder without him in the room.

"Man, that guy needs a few more years of training or some shit." Ricky stated unamused.

Ryan and Candice nodded in agreement.

"I can't handle hearing them in there anymore." She said unexpectedly as she got off her chair. "I'm going to go to my room." She hesitated for a moment. "You guys can come too if you want. I mean you did come all the way here, I don't expect you to sit here alone not knowing what to do, like I was."

"Yeah that clock is giving me hives." Said Ricky when he stood up with casual ease while Ryan became instantly reminded of the last time he saw the inside that room, when Candice was in there literally butt naked.

The other two left to go upstairs. He thought of his friend out there all alone and scared. He figured Wyatt would think him to be a moron, not being with loved ones at a time like this because of silly things like that. He sprung up from the chair and caught up to them as they ascended the stairs.

~ 2 ~

Ryan sat on Candice's bedroom floor realising he needed to relieve his bladder fairly soon or wet the carpet where he sat. "I'll be back." He said to the others as he left the room for the toilet.

Candice sat on her bed quietly while Ricky sat on the desk

chair once more.

He watched Ryan leave before looking at the things sitting on the desk. There was a bunch of girly things like perfume bottles with fluffy lids, sticks of lip-gloss scattered here and there, sticky notes with random shit scribbled over them, a little teddy bear ornament holding a pink present with a straw hat on its head leaving the ears poking through. It made him smile until he heard light crying coming from over at the bed. He turned to look and saw Candice with her face in her hands. Without giving it a thought he rushed over to her with nothing in his male mind, just the intent to comfort his friend. He sat down beside her causing the mattress to give way, making her body naturally lean closer as he asked her what was wrong.

Oh good one you bloody idiot he thought of himself.

She tried to stop the flow of tears. "It's just that, I can't get the sound of... Of my mother screaming out of my head. It was the worst thing I've ever heard." She gave in and let the tears flow once again.

He honestly didn't know what to say, so he let his instincts take over instead. He put his arms gently but firmly around her, making her feel the most secure she'd felt for a long time. She cried a little harder at the feel of his pure care and warmth. She turned to be facing him with her head now pressed against the breast of his chest, her tears wetting his t-shirt. Her hands clung onto the front of the red plaid, as she did so his embrace tightened around her tender frame.

"Everything's gonna be fine." He reassured in a low comforting voice, he didn't know what else to say.

It didn't seem to him like he was helping much, she just kept crying.

Moving his face from her shoulder to sit over her head to do a most peculiar thing, he opened his nervous mouth and began to sing softly.

"Please look at your life, see how it's all for you and me..."
The sobs eased a little...

"Don't let small minds fool you, there's so much more to see..."
They started to cease now, he figured it must be working.

"I won't go around if you're not there, 'cause this I just couldn't bear...
Don't look away, someday you'll want me to stay..."
He stopped when he felt her giggling, followed by the girly sound of the act. Relieved that at least the strangeness of him singing had her laughing and not crying about her missing brother and hysterical mother.

"Hey why'd you stop superstar?" She asked cheekily from the safety of his grip.

"Well you see it's kinda hard for a superstar to continue when he's being laughed at by his audience." He said with obvious hilarity.

"I'm sorry." She said sincerely. "It's just that I've never been sang to like that."

"Ha, it was weird for me too, trust me."
They separated and looked at each other, awkwardness expectedly present.

"I don't even know what possessed me to sing, I mean really what the hell?" He said starting to feel embarrassed now they could see each other's faces.

She looked at him as the colour in his cheeks slowly turned scarlet, she couldn't resist her thoughts asking her if he could look any cuter. "It was awesome, don't worry." She said wiping the wetness off her face with a tissue, followed by a dainty blow of the nose. "And I don't even know the song."

~ 3 ~

Ryan had finished up in the bathroom, now on his way back

to Candice's room. He observed those family portraits that had hung around the walls of the hallways since he first ever visited here. There were a lot of people he didn't even know in some of them. He was about to enter the bedroom again when he felt the urge to go into Wyatt's room. Feeling a loss inside him, he wanted to be close to him somehow, so he guessed going into his bedroom where he'd spent several hours with him and Ricky when times were simpler would be a good start. Worried that Mr or Mrs Fineman or even the cops would tell him off for going in there, he tried to keep quiet while he did it.

Opening the door to see the room was indeed empty, it felt so off. Maybe he was hoping to see Wyatt sitting in there on the floor happy and content, he'd say this whole thing was a big mistake.

He walked further in, looking around scoping the room. It felt weird being in here, not having a single clue where the owner was or how he is, not knowing if he's dead and rotting in the gutter somewhere...

While he took in the surroundings neatly cluttered with Wyatt's belongings, Ryan vowed to himself that when, not if, but when he saw him again he's going to apologise for that stupid fight so much he'll promise to be his slave for the next ten years.

Walking over to the big plastic tub that Wyatt kept his comic book collection in, he picked up a random Superman comic. The cover had a colourful print of the Man of Steel and his leading lady Lois Lane. They were in some sort of alien peril, but this illustration gave you the idea the day will be saved again. It humoured him, the thought that Wyatt enjoyed reading this sort of thing when he was so scientific and quick to not believe in the unordinary. He took the book over to the bed and there he sat reading it, like his lost friend would have done so many times before him.

~ 4 ~

There wasn't much sun shining through the windows today, it made the premature mourning of Wyatt all the more present. Glum weather almost always has that effect.

Candice and Ricky sat side by side, she made him incredibly uncomfortable by asking him to put his modesty aside and sing again.

"Candice honestly, I don't think I can do it again. On the spot anyway."

She sighed and let her body have that deflated and tired look. "Fine." She said with unfulfilled softness. "What was up with that girl my brother was scared of? And why did him and Ryan fight?"

Ricky rolled out the details as he knew them until she began to sob again. He put his hand on her and began to slide it back and forth across her shoulder blades in another attempt to comfort.

She made a whiny noise as she cried harder.

"You're going to cry a river and drown me." Ricky said trying to lighten her up. "He'll be fine alright, you'll see." He closed his eyes in reluctant preparation before he began to sing again. *"It's a dreaded old rain again, but even the drops are new. What's on your mind when it washes away your clue?"* Now he got a little louder and smiled as he recited the lyrics, trying to lighten the mood. She looked up at him and giggled at the sight of his swinging arms as he continued.

"You hold back loving what you know is good for you. I can wait for sense to see you through..." He grabbed her gently by the wrists to sway her arms from side to side with him. Her sadness lifting for the moment. *"Please look at this now, flowers torn with age. They'll*

always have beauty, just look at them on their stage..."

She laughed as Ricky stood up and took her with him, enabling their swinging to go free.

"Your ties are burdened with a rule and I for one see it as cruel. Don't look away because I know you'll want me to stay..." He sang lifting an arm to the air like a Shakespearian poet.

Still with tears drying on her face, Candice let him guide her around the room a little so they were dancing like drunk colleagues at a Christmas party. *"It's a dreaded old rain again, but even the drops are new. What's on your mind when it washes away your clue...?"*

He stopped the singing to encourage her. "Okay you gotta do it with me now!"

"What? I don't even know the words or anything!" She said in protest.

"Oh come on Candie, remember it's not a talent competition." He teased with a wink, still guiding her around in carefree swing. She smiled in an accepting way.

"Hold back loving what you know is good for you..." Ricky sang, nodding his head in encouragement. To his honest surprise, she sang the rest of the line.

"But I can wait for sense to see you through..."
After admiring her little solo, he sang a new line.

"All I can do is pray that someday you'll ask me to stay..." He gestured for her involvement again. "Same line again." He said quickly as if there's actually music to keep in time with.
Together they sang.

"All I can do is pray that someday you'll ask me to stay!"
Their harmonising excited him through his entire being, she could tell by the enormous grin he had on his face. It almost didn't even feel like there was no music around them. Perhaps it all anticipated her next move, so unlike her that it made it even

more exciting.

Without warning to him or even herself, she grabbed him by the front of the plaid, her glossy lips met his in an almost catastrophic collision. He pulled back in shock for a small moment before lifting his hands to hold her head, as if the taste of her salty tears gave him an indescribable hunger. It felt as if her whole body would melt at the feel of his hands on either side of her face, like she's been unknowingly waiting through the hours for it since he'd touched her the night before.

With their eyes closed, touch was their guide through this passion. Her hands freely slid from his chest to hold the sides of his body under the flannel of his top shirt, moving him closer to her as she pushed him backwards towards the bed on which they now sat, still not opening their eyes.

She didn't even know *how* she was kissing him, she just was, like one of the most natural things on this planet, maybe beautiful instinct.

She moved her face to the side when he moved his hands down to her neck, his fingers gently holding the hair at the back of her head, the dark gold flowing through them like water through smooth rocks. She moved in even closer, holding him tighter as she began to kiss the warm skin of his neck, temptation was far too strong after being close enough to smell the scent of his young masculinity.

A small moan, she couldn't tell which one of them it was, nor did she even care. His breathing was heavy and rapid, driving her senses into a fury of want and need.

In the midst of the recent saddening events, she knew within herself that she wanted this and she *needed* him.

Her hands found themselves trying to sneak down to his lower belly, making him shy away gently before she reached the belt hidden under the t-shirt, they felt the denim it was on, feeling for the buckle, sliding the fabric out from the steel, she paid no attention to the rest of the world, just concentrating on pulling the belt back to free it, on the way it felt to have him holding her...

She pulled it free of its silvery attachment and unbuttoned that single button. What her intentions were she didn't think about, it was just happening.

She reached for the final barricade, that last step, her finger tips touched the zipper... before he pulled himself away and ceased all her efforts.

He held his hands up as if she was a dog in training, growing impatient and misbehaving because it wanted the treat before it deserved it. "Erm.... that escalated fast." He said in high pitched awkwardness, though clearly excitedly amazed.

"Sorry." She simply said, looking away as she moved herself back.

"Pfft." He sounded amused as he straightened his glasses. "Don't be sorry, I'll probably be calling myself a dickhead later for stopping you."

She started laughing, at least her eyes were free of tears and she's grinning instead of crying again, she looked absolutely gorgeous when she laughed, just as anyone does.

"Man you're vicious when you wanna be, bloody hell." He said shaking his head.

She crossed her arms and nodded her head from side to side. Ricky began to do his belt back up as Candice watched on in a kind of disappointment at her failed efforts.

You idiot! Your parents and the police are downstairs talking about your missing brother...

As if the world had read her mind and decided to punish her misguided actions, her mother opened the door and stepped into the room, drowsy and innocent.

Ricky stood up in reaction with his hands still on the half buckled belt. Mrs Fineman's face turned to shock of horror, her hand clasped over her mouth with a hollow smack, her eyes wide and reddened.

"Mum nothing happened I swear!" Candice said quickly, each word nearly stumbling over the next.
Ricky stood frozen not knowing what the hell to do with himself, he was shit scared to say the least.

"Get... Out... You dirty child." Mrs Fineman ordered of him through gritted teeth.
Candice now stood beside Ricky, looking like he was about to be bombarded by a hail of pitch forks and she was there to help fend them off.

"You... Your brother is missing and you're up here slutting around with this boy!" She said angrily pointing to her daughter.

"Mum I swear to God noth-"
"Don't you bring God into this, but you can bet your britches later on you'll be praying for forgiveness Candice." She turned to Ricky who was still. "I said get out right now. NOW, GET OUT!" She began to yell.

"Well I would Mrs Fineman but you're kind of... In the door-way." He explained, not intending to be rude or funny.
Candice let out a forbidden giggle that didn't go unnoticed by her mother.

"You think this is *funny*?!" Mrs Fineman grunted growing loud again. "It's too bad they didn't take YOU instead of your brother! I'm sure you would have entertained them well!"
Candice grimaced with hurt. Ricky saw her face and couldn't help but to try and defend her.

"Now look Mrs Fineman I'm not a parent myself but-"
She scoffed at hearing this like she didn't fully believe that statement, but he continued. "...that was really out of line. You

ought to believe her when she says nothing happened. We're devastated about Wyatt."

"I SAID LEAVE! LEAVE RIGHT NOW, OUT OF MY HOUSE!" She screamed at the top of her lungs.

Ricky turned to Candice with a sorry expression, then left for the doorway, squeezing past the monster that's an exhausted and depressed Patricia Fineman.

He saw Ryan in the hall and quickly gestured for him to follow, which he did.

They passed the officers and Mr Fineman on the way down the stairs. They all looked concerned and confused as the boys rushed past.

The older cop grabbed a firm hold on Ryan's arm causing him to look around angry, the touch reminded him of that Thelma arsehole.

"Tell me, what's the matter here?" The cop asked sternly.

"I have no idea and that's the truth." He replied with confidence, freeing himself of the man's hand. He joined Ricky who waited for him at the bottom of the stairs. They walked quickly out the front door together, put their shoes on and went straight for the bike which Ricky wheeled off the property with Ryan behind him.

They were halfway up the next street when Ryan finally enquired about what happened back there. Ricky stopped and turned to face him, still holding onto the bike.

"Um, Ricky, what's up with that?" He asked pointing to Ricky's belt and laughing.

Ricky looked back at him unimpressed "That, my dear fellow, is why we'll never be allowed under that roof again."

"No, WAY!" Ryan began to howl with laughter, the peering heads in neighbouring houses looked on in astonishment.

"That's right, laugh it up." Said Ricky as he finally did his buckle up. "You won't be laughing when it's *you* in this situation one day you douche!" He began to laugh with him.

"*You* made out with *Candice Fineman?!*"

Ricky scratched his head with a smirk of proud realisation. "That's right, I went where no guy has been before."

"What about that Rob Brannon weirdo?"

"Nope, she's never gone near him."

"Holy shit man." Ryan said in plain amazement.

"But seriously we just kissed a little. None of the other stuff."

"Well what was it like?" He asked with fascination.

"Kinda gross, if I'm honest." He answered with an honest cringe.

Ryan looked at him with an understandable eyebrow raised.

"But epic for a first kiss I reckon." Ricky said reassuring him he was happy with it happening.

"Aww my little Ricky is growing up!" Ryan said imitating him.

"Shut your face!" He answered laughing with him.

They felt guilty because of Wyatt but it was laughter that was overdue, if you don't laugh you cry.

"C'mon let's go before I get a grenade thrown at me." Ricky urged, walking on.

"Well, it's about time if you ask me." Ryan said encouragingly. "You and Candice I mean."

Ricky grinned at him as he guided the big bike along beside them.

He called it 'The Ferrari', pretty much to boost the *bike's* confidence. Every other kid around had brand new ultramodern sports monsters whereas The Ferrari was from the mid-nineties. It may have be older and a little rusty here and there, but Ricky loved it. It worked like a bike and did its job, that's all he needed, he didn't need a new one with all the bells and whistles. When he first got it (a birthday gift from his mum and dad, they had picked it up at a garage sale for $50) him and Ryan spray painted it red, leaving the glistening silver areas to shine like it had for decades. Ryan put masking tape on either side of the large bars in the frame to stop it from being painted there. To this day it reads THE FERRARI in the original chrome green paint it has under the red. That's all the writing on it now, not even the Schwinn name to be seen except for the brand badges. It was totally his and one of a kind.

The three of them headed for Ryan's house to pick up the generic bike he owned. Then they would ride over to Ricky's house to discuss their next move in this mess that's now their lives. They hated having a member of their threesome out there somewhere and being together felt better to them. If there was any chance they could find him, they'll take it.

~ 5 ~

Candice was trying to defend herself against her parents now that she was alone with them. The cops had gone back down to the dining room after learning the commotion was just teenage bullshit gone wrong. Jeff of course had internal amusement at what had unfolded.

"Daddy please believe me." She pleaded.

"Candice I wouldn't expect anything like this from you, but your mother wouldn't make that up. You're grounded, you are not to go anywhere except school, you have the day off tomorrow but after that you're going there and nowhere else. I don't want to hear of anymore shenanigans, we have to put all our energy into getting your brother back."

If there weren't the perils of Wyatt's absence on his mind, he would have remembered to confiscate her mobile phone.

He left with his wife beside him, who slammed the door behind them.

She sat back down on her bed sad and alone. She didn't believe she could feel any worse than she did right now. Her insides felt shredded and raw, the emotions were feeling like actual physical pain.

Laying on the bed, closing her eyes, they opened slowly at the sound of her phone dinging with a message for her. She had no enthusiasm for Bethany's input right now, she picked it up anyway to see.

It wasn't Bethany, instead the letters were 'Little Richard' sitting there bright and ready to be tapped on. When she did open it, small tears came rolling down her face as she smiled at the simple five word message:

'Don't you cry pretty girl :)'

Her hand held over her mouth as the tears flowed harder at the pure appreciation she felt for him in that despairing time.

~ Six ~

BAIL ME OUT

~ 1 ~

With his long snout pointed at the water, fascinated dark brown eyes watched the aquatic bugs skipping happily around the surface. Although he was a good boy it didn't matter. He's here for this now. Not the loyalties he once held for his smelly upright.

Soon he would help one of *them*, the new uprights. This one was fearful under the grip of the bad. The bad didn't know best and this good boy didn't like the bad, he knew it was taking over and that was just as bad as the bad itself.

He heard something in the wind, his head now up and alert as he sat regally with the tips of his ears pointing towards to the sky.

The invisible master was speaking, her voice ran through him, telling of the things that were to come. He understood that it was even sooner to the moment he was to contact the other one of *them*. He could do this, it's what he's here for. He would do as he is asked and obey, he isn't just a good boy. He he's a *loyal* good boy.

He now lay down beside the creek with his bugs.

~ 2 ~

Al's on his way to the hostage with some more junk food and water, he carried it in a plastic shopping bag as he walked into his mate's girlfriend's laundry.

He crouched over in the corner of the room and lifted a floor mat, similar to the one Wyatt was constantly looking at. The lifted carpet revealed a door it was hiding underneath, like the trap doors in castle basements they mentioned in fairy tales or witch's dens in scary stories.

He put his finger through the rope handle and with a swift move he lifted it up. He'd done it many times.

His body descended stairs with steady footsteps, he was sure to close the door behind him and it wasn't long before he was at the bottom of them now on flat ground. Before him, a long hall-way badly lit with LED lights placed uncoordinated on the walls all the way up to a door. He walked on towards it with his bag of food supplements for the poor little tike. He didn't much like this job, but he did like the money it could possibly pay. Besides, if he said he wanted out of the business he'd look like a pansy and pansies don't have a good time with the crowd he's around.

He placed a bandanna over most of his face before turning the knob of the lock. He walked in to see the boy passed out on the mattress.

Oh shit, he better not be dead!...

"Kid, hey kid." He said through the bandanna to see if he'd react or just stay there. He sat up fast and moved himself to rest his back against the wall, still sitting on the mattress, staring at Al with wide begging eyes.

Al noticed the lollies sitting on the floor near the bed. "Where'd they come from?" He asked with in a flat tone.

Wyatt hesitated with the unknowing of what to say, he was

careful to not let the bracelet show on his wrist. "They ahm... I had them the whole time."

"No you didn't." Al said flatly.

"I... I did. You just didn't see them in my clothes." Wyatt tried to sound confident while he was dreading what was promising to unfold.

It seemed the man believed him after a moment of thinking it over. He placed the bag on the floor and left the room without another word.

Wyatt sighed a breath of relief and began to eat the junk. He couldn't hold out any longer and just had to eat the food.

As he ate he hoped it was now Tuesday, the day his Angels would help him escape.

With a chunk of salad roll being chewed in his reluctant mouth, he picked up the small bag of lollies and put them in the pocket of his pants.

~ 3 ~

Rose walked through the carpeted hallway of her school with her backpack over her shoulder. She had just gone to the loo and left Jack waiting for her near the classrooms. It was now recess, they were going to go outside and have a much needed snack, she didn't have breakfast this morning. You'd think they'd be used to living with Daz by now but if they could, they attempted to avoid him at all costs.

So, this morning whilst Daz was about in the house they had once more skipped their breakfast and left for school. They walked two and a half kilometres every day they went, rain or shine. They understood they're privileges of having a roof over their heads and the opportunity to even go to school un-like many other kids, but they felt the only good thing about their life was that they had each other. They'd always be in it together.

She thought about later tonight when her and Jack would help Wyatt escape the room. It amazed her that all these other students were going about their lives with all the cares and worries they each personally had, not realising the true extent of what real worry is.

She casually walked through the hall as she had a million times before, now seeing a group of four bullies picking on someone who was curled up on the ground shielding his face with his arms. As she approached, she realised it was her brother.

Not again she thought as she saw red, *nobody touches my brother...*

She walked faster as her bag swung side to side with her fury. "Hey Harley!" She yelled at the main antagonist. "Why don't you go castrate yourself with your buddy's teeth?"

Harley turned his round face around to look at her. "What the hell did you just say?" He said angrily, amused at the same time. Jack looked up at his sister with relief and regret.

"You heard me. piss off and leave him alon,e you toad." She said firmly.

"He's a faggot." One of the other bullies stated in laughter.

"Where'd you hear that?" She asked angrily.

"Everyone's sayin' it." Harley growled.

"Oh, so hearing rumours gives you the right to single him out then, does it? Seriously, piss off and don't touch him again." She said when she kneeled down to help him up.

"Hey it's a free country, if I don't want to be slapped on the arse by a fag, I have the right to get rid of it." Harley said proud of his political statement.

"Freak." Rose said as her and Jack began to walk off.

"Yeah go home and do it with your sister you shitty fag!" Harley called out after them.

This time Jack turned around. "Okay so if I'm a fag, why would I be 'doing it' with my sister?"

Harley's face screwed up. "You're not so scared with your bodyguard to protect you. Hopefully you'll get fuckin' AIDS and die you stupid cocksucker."

Rose turned, leaving Jack's side. Her freckled face turning as red as her name when she grunted "You inbred piece of *SHIT!*" She walked right up to Harley with a closed fist, striking him hard right in the pudgy nose on his stupid face. He bent down in pain and his buddies simply stood by in shock.

The grade 7 teacher Mrs McNeil came along at that moment to see what all the commotion was. There was no way he'd admit he just got punched in the nose by a girl, especially the girl that has a faggot for a brother.

"Everything okay?" Ms McNeil asked concerned.

Harley looked up at Rose. "Nah I walked into a door that was opening. Stupid door."

"Be more careful next time and watch your language please." The teacher walked off, telling the other students to move on before recess was finished.

The twins finally got out into the yards and sat side by side on the benches seated near one of the schools brick walls.

"I don't even know what I did to make them think that." Jack whined, eating a Monte Carlo biscuit they'd nicked from the teachers office.

"You know how it is." Rose replied referring to the fact everyone knows everyone's juicy business in this town.

"But I don't even act like it or anything." He said saddened.

So far as the twins knew, Jack had tendencies that indicated he had the potential to be as gay as the day. Daz hated queers, thought they were scum. Their mother agreed just as she did with anything Daz said, which made Jack try to deny himself.

Rose often thought that the arsehole must not look in the mirror much if he thinks gay people are scum.

She looked at him sympathetically. "Jack you are who you are. You can't help it, and you're the best. Just be glad you're not like *them*, don't worry." She continued to munch on her own biscuit.

He tried to soak in her encouraging words, he tried all the time. It was still too hard to try and just be comfortable when 24/7 you were questioning your very existence just because you were more inclined to like boys as well as girls. It was stupid and unfair, what was so bad about it anyway? He didn't necessarily hate himself, he resented everyone else for thinking *him* to be the freak when *they're* the ones who have brains too small to comprehend that a human is a human, just like them. Gay or not gay, fat or thin, male or female, short or tall, rock star or janitor, horse or cow we're all the same. He understood this so why couldn't so many other people? In the years going by he was beginning to believe more and more that the human society was crumbling slowly. People were getting too political and too comfortable with being evil, especially to each other and the planet.

People who were true and pure were becoming rarer than the Tasmanian Tiger, which is saying something.

Rose felt this way too. Together they hoped they weren't the only youth who thought along these lines, if they weren't then maybe there was still some sort of hope for the world.

"I even had a girlfriend." He said sullenly.

"That's it Jack, it was probably her!"

"Why would Chelsea say shit to anyone? I never said anything to her about it."

"Yeah but she's a total arse who probably only liked you because of the fact she could get Mary Jane out of you whenever she pleased."

Jack pulled the hood of his jumper over his head in a move to signify he was done talking and wanted to stew in his own thoughts. He absolutely wouldn't put it past Chelsea to spread rumours, but he didn't want to think about it. Instead, under the isolation of the hood he began to think about the song he'd looked up last night when he was unsettled in bed. It was the one that poor, kidnapped and undeniably cute Wyatt guy had said was his favourite. After investigating the plucky randomness that is that song, Jack was now fond of it himself.

The perkiness of Hannah suddenly sat beside Rose, completely happy and unknowing of what had just happened in the hall.

"Hey Jack." She greeted in a light flirty tone the twins always noticed but chose to ignore.

"Hi Hannah." Jack smiled back after pulling the hood off his head, stroking his hair back with his fingers. He's aware Hannah has fancied him for a while now. He liked her of course but really wasn't interested in her as more than a friend. "Did you hear about Rose's punching match with Harley?"

Hannah looked surprised as she swiped a lock of blonde hair behind her ear. "Oh what? No! Do tell guys." She replied interested.

Rose shook her head as Jack dramatically recited what had happened.

~ 4 ~

By 12:43pm on this Tuesday, Candice sat waiting in her room. Waiting for her brother to be home safe, waiting for her parents to be normal again, waiting to hear Ricky's voice fill the emptiness she now realised she felt when he wasn't around.

There was another waiting she was feeling, she couldn't put her finger on it though. Maybe it was just restlessness dancing on her mind. Feeling especially guilty because of her joyous time with Ricky whilst her little brother was being snatched by evil sons of bitches, she got up and walked over to her window for no particular reason, just to look out. You could see the tops of so many houses from here.

Wyatt where the heck are you?...

Movement on the ground below made her look down.

There on the lawn of the house was a dog, not a big dog but still a decent size. It was looking up here, looking at her window. She noticed that it was looking at her, yes it was, it was looking *right at her* and nowhere else.

She thought for a moment before deciding she had nothing to lose by going to see if it had a tag on its collar. At least if it was lost, she could return it to the worried owners. Yes, she thought of Wyatt when deciding this.

She put a jumper on and went downstairs. Her dad was now sitting asleep in an armchair by the phone. Candice felt sorry for her own dad at the sight. Her mother had been taken into hospital care because of her hysterical behaviour. After the incident with Candice and Ricky there was no settling her down, she even began having a go at the cops.

Those dudes had gone off to do something, she didn't know what to be honest. She'd seen kidnappings on TV shows and stuff but this was different, weren't they supposed to have some guy with technical equipment hooked up to the phone waiting for the kidnappers to call again?

She went to the front door and walked out without bothering to put shoes on.

The dog looked bigger up close but she wasn't scared in the slightest, it's so cute.

It ran over to her excited, she scratched it behind the ears and checked for a collar.

No collar, great...
It didn't have a typical doggy smell either. It smelt more like dirt or something. It actually reminded her of the trip to the mossy, rainforest-lush wonderland of the Gorge her class went on last year.

"You've been running around in the bush?" She asked the friendly animal in a high pitch voice. "You haven't seen a young dude with a bad haircut walking around, have you?"

The dog just simply went on wagging its tail viciously and panting happily.

"You're a good boy." She said after noticing his male appendage.

Suddenly, he turned and ran up to the corner of the street, there he stood to bark at her in encouragement.

Candice stood up to stare at the good boy with furrowed brows. She began to follow him. When she got closer, he went further at a faster pace. Now she was walking faster to keep up and not lose sight of him.

It went further and further away from her, she sped up now, running awkwardly with the bare underneath of her feet colliding with the black ground. She made the smart choice to move onto the strips of grass, it felt so soft and inviting compared to the rough surface of the road.

She was now ran with the grey-blue sky throwing wind through her hair. The clear beachside air tasted like a forbidden freedom.

Chasing this random dog through town felt right for some reason, she wanted to see where he was going. After all, he was acting as though he wanted her to come with him.

She followed her new canine friend through the streets for a while, passing people who watched with startled faces, past house after house, down streets she never gave a second thought to. She felt puffed out but didn't dare to give up now.

The scruffy good boy turned into another street and out of her sight.

Damn it! Don't go missing now!...

Slowing down at the corner of the street, she looked around expecting to see the dog gone -which he was. She began to walk down the sidewalk noticing that most of the houses were run down or messy looking with things scattered in the yards, like machine parts and kids toys. Alot of the lawns weren't cut short either, it was sort of long and brown with coarse weeds.

She kept walking with her panting easing up until she saw the dog sitting by the open gate on a driveway. Walking over to him with a smile, he wagged his tail once more at the sight of her still there and happy to see him.

She got closer, reaching her hand out to greet him when he casually turned and went into the yard past the gate. Further down the driveway he trotted and sat comfortably by a flowered bush at the corner of the house, past it the stairs to a concrete verandah. Above the bush there's a big closed window with an opening between the two curtains. Surrounding the window were brick walls that enveloped the home of a loving family, it wasn't the prettiest house but boy was it a charming little place. It seemed familiar to her, but she's slow to the realisation.

She raked through the memories of her mind trying to figure out why it was familiar. It was only a minor familiarity but it was definitely there.

She was younger and sitting in the front seat of the car with her dad driving, Wyatt was in the backseat, they'd just argued about who was going to sit in the front but obviously Candice won because she was older. She was looking at the small screen of her first ever mobile phone, it had taken weeks of nagging and good behaviour to get it.

They pulled up on the side of the road to let Wyatt out for his first ever time playing at a friend's house, he'd been bragging about it for days-

"Oh my god, no way!!" She said aloud with a grin.

She looked up from her phone to see Wyatt walking up the drive-way to the house, two other boys came running out excitedly to greet him. One was slightly shorter than the other and wore those denim overalls, the taller one had big glasses and looked as happy as anything shouting something she didn't understand. They both had toy weapons of some sort.

'What nerds, no wonder Wyatt is here.'

Then she looked back at her new device that was blinking with notifi-cations, she didn't think twice when the car drove away.

She went further in hoping nobody was home just in case her expectancy was invalid, there was no car but still, somebody could be there.

The tatty covered carport beside the house showcased a big gate at the end of the way. The light shining through the roof of the carport had been turned dimly green by the time it reached Candice who was now under it. She carefully walked right up to the gate trying not to stand on anything lying on the ground that could harm her feet. She got a grip and held onto the crusty surface of the gate with her body supported by her feet on her tippy toes.

Her eyes peered over the top, looking around to catch a glimpse of some sort of sign to show that someone she knew lived there. She was about to give up when a red figure caught her eye.

"Yes!! I knew it!"

She was indeed looking at The Ferrari, sitting in its home place under the shelter of the house, able to only just see it from where she was but knew exactly that it was Ricky's bike. She had seen it outside her house many times over the years.

Turning around to see the dog sitting loyally behind her looking up in expectation, she kneeled in front of him praising his effort to bring her here and of course, telling him he's a good boy.

Together they walked back around to the front of the house. Carefully she squeezed the right side of her body up against the bush that was sitting forever under that window. Peering inside the house with her face on the glass, her hands cupping the sides to ensure the light wasn't shining, it was darkened but she could still make out most of the room. She saw a cluttered lounge room with a big stereo in the corner, an average sized digital television, a worn couch accompanied by two armchairs and a few bean bags taking up some space in another corner. There were photo frames on the walls, but they weren't all family shots, some were memorabilia of all kinds. The mantelpiece over the old fireplace was covered in random quirky ornaments.

Removing herself from the wondrous sight of the lounge room window she turned around with curiosity satisfied. It was slowly getting cooler as the afternoon approached. Covering her hands with her jumper sleeves, Candice sat on the front steps of the Benson house with the dog that had led her there. Instinct told her to wait around rather than knock on the door.
They sat like that and waited for whatever would happen when someone came home to see them.

~ 5 ~

Sally Benson stood at the front door of the Jonson house having a long, friendly conversation with Evelyn, the mother of Ryan and Ethan.
Ryan sat in the car with Ricky, waiting for them to finish up their chat so that she could take them back to their house.
"Man, I wish she would stop gas bagging and bloody hurry up." Ricky said looking over at his beloved mum.
Ryan looked over there too now, wishing the same thing.

The never-ending school day was over. It was pretty average other than the shadowy cloud that was Wyatt's loud absence. They didn't tell anyone what they knew, they just tried to act normal to get through the day. Thankfully there was barely a whisper about the kidnapping from anyone.

Finally, she was saying her goodbye to her somewhat wealthy acquaintance and walking to the car, getting in the driver's seat. "Okay boys, Ryan I'm allowed to have you for a couple of nights. I didn't think she'd agree because it's the start of a school week."

"Thank you so much, I think they're all sick of me at the moment."

She turned in her seat to face him "Ohh don't be silly! Take it from me who has to raise this big, bumbling, bundle of baby Benson."

"God, could you have found another 'B' word to use?" Ricky said cringing, shaking his head.

"That can't be possible." She continued dismissing her son. "Maybe the stress of Wyatt being gone has gotten to them too."

Ryan shrugged his shoulders at her kind but faithless suspicions. Ryan never told them about Wyatt.

She started up the car and left the driveway turning the headlights on, making sure to look as posh as she could while she did it.

"Oh mum, they'll never suspect your high position as checkout lady." Ricky said playfully.

She shook her head smiling. "You be quiet you cheeky little turd."

Ryan giggled at them teasing each other, they always amused him, especially when Ricky's dad was around. Many years ago, when Ryan was still a small boy, he had a habit of calling Mr Benson 'Uncle Noah' which he still did to this day.

"So what happened at the door to hell today, Mumsie?" Ricky

asked seriously.

"If you're referring to Ryan's front door, next time you ought to choose better wording Richard." She advised, turning the wheel.

"Mum you know what they're like, just ask the expert in the back there." He pointed his thumb back at Ryan, who sat quietly.

"Richard behave yourself or I won't let you go back to Wyatt's house."

Ryan couldn't help it, he tried he really did, but the laughing hysterics flowed out blissfully at the memory of what had happened the previous day.

"Ryan shut up. That's okay 'cause I don't wanna go around there anyway. It's not like I can help find Wyatt." He was trying to speak through Ryan's laughing. "Although from what I've seen I'd do a better job than the cops anyway."

She turned the car into their street. "Okay guys... what am I missing here? And don't say bad things about the police, they'll get him back."

The headlights were bright in the dulling light of the day, neighbour cats scattered at the approach of the car.

"Don't say anything Ryan, shut your face!" Ricky said amused but a little panicked.

"No no, do tell Ryan." She said slyly.

"Okay so we were there yesterday when Ricky and-"

"Candice?!" Ricky exclaimed confused.

Ryan looked out the windscreen to find out what had made him say her name like that. They'd pulled into the driveway to see a strange dog and yep, there was Candice. Here and in the flesh.

"Isn't that Wyatt's sister?" Sally asked smiling although confused as to why the girl was there.

"Yep... It sure is." Ricky said in a near whisper.

The three of them watched her get to her feet and wave nervously. She looked like she was shivering a little from the cold. The dog stood beside her quiet and sensible.

~ 6 ~

The Brandis twins were in the security of their bedroom, both changing into their darkest and most ninja style clothes. This actually meant that Jack was wearing dark grey track pants and a black hoodie. Rose was sporting black leggings and a long sleeve shirt that Jack believed to be too thin.

"Nope. I won't allow it. It's too freakin' thin, you'll freeze to death outside." He nagged before turning to go through the pile of clothes on the end of his bed.

"Oh my gawd." She said in an exhausted tone. "It's fine! I don't have anything warmer that's a dark colour. We'll probably be running and stuff anyway, so I'll get hot."

He handed her one of the black jumpers he'd pulled from his belongings. "Just wear this would you?!" He sat down beside his pile.

She slid it over her head and left it to sit loosely on her body. "Happy now, mum?"

"Don't be stupid, if I was your mum, you wouldn't be in this fucking mess in the first place." He sat down on his bed with his face in his hands. Rose began to feel the true seriousness of what they were trying to accomplish.

What if they really did get caught?

"Rosie, I'm not gonna lie. I'm *shitting* myself." He said nervously tapping his heel on the floor. "For real, gonna slide down my legs."

She only relaxed her shoulders looking at him, before walking over to offer a hug of support.

Out in the kitchen their mother was preparing to leave for

the shopping centre, looking in the fridge and cupboards to see what they needed more of. She had to do the shopping on her own because her only children decided to be lazy and not help her tonight.

Her boyfriend was out having a drink, it annoyed her how he never invited her. He did once but she messed it up by getting too drunk and acting the fool in front of all his mates. Daz wasn't the best person in the world but at least he was with her still after all these years, unlike the father of her kids whose surname they have. He died in a car crash on one of the dark highways between Gerryville and its neighbouring towns.

The stupid man (as she called him) was a sucker for the fluffy wallabies and other animals that roamed the state's thick under-brush and misty paddocks. She has no doubt that he managed to get himself killed by trying desperately not to hit one that night, leaving her alone with two toddlers.

Daz came along when they were about seven. Ever since then she's been following him and doing everything he asks because according to him, if it wasn't for him they'd be destitute. Now she had to drink her way through what operates out of the very home her children lived in. She did love them but so many nights she wished them away. Wished *herself* away.

She ignored the fact that every now and then there was a group of men gathered around her kitchen table sorting drugs or if there was a child being carried through and left beneath the house. It didn't matter if she paid no attention.

"Alright you two I'm outta here! If I forget something you need it'll be tough tiddies!" She called out through the house.

"Okay, have fun!" Rose yelled back from the bedroom.

The twins sat and listened to their mother leave the house, get in the car and leave.

They looked at each other with grave faces, knowing what they had to do.

"Alrighty, we've gone to the shitter so we don't need to pee when we're panicking, got the dark clothes-"

"Jack let's just go already." Rose said to her anxious sibling.

"Yeah, let's just get the little birdy out of his cage already." He answered with a nod of readiness.

She smiled and left the bedroom for the room where Wyatt has been staying, he followed close behind her.

They made it to the door, Rose unlocked the knob. "Wyatt?" She whispered before opening the door.

"Rose? That you?" She heard from the other side.

She opened the door and walked in with Jack staying in the doorway.

"I've been waiting for you, I can't wait to leave, I really can't." Wyatt said to her. He stood ready to go with his little bracelet still cosy around his wrist.

She nodded. "C'mon, let's get the hell out of here."

They walked out the door with Rose in front and Jack last. Wyatt had finally stepped outside the room for the first time since Sunday. His angels were really saving him, he knew they would. Superman may be spectacular to read about with all his brilliant saves but these two were real life heroes and he would never forget what they had done for him.

He felt secure between them. Their large white wings would have been folded against their bodies in this small hall.

He turned around to see Jack, who looked back at him and smiled. His angelic, saving eyes warmed Wyatt through to the core.

~ 7 ~

The three Bensons, Candice and Ryan were in the quaint lounge room Candice was spying in on just hours before. Mr

Benson had gotten home from his workplace not ten minutes after his family got home.

Whilst his parents sat in the armchairs, Ricky sat on the couch next to Candice who had Ryan on the other side of her.

"So why exactly are you here again?" Ricky asked her still astonished at what she'd said.

"Oh, Ricky! Don't be rude." His mum said trying to make Candice feel comfortable.

"No, it's okay Mrs Benson, I know it sounds crazy but I really did follow that dog here."
The dog was outside on the lawn not giving any sort of care to the night.

"But... *Whaaaat?*" Ricky said quietly, still perplexed.

Candice giggled, she just *had* to tease him. "I guess he was just coming back to the only place he'd know he'd surely find flea repellent."

"Yeah, Rick's untidy bunker filled with dirty shorts and dishes he likes to call a bedroom." Noah Benson finished with a cheeky grin looking at Ricky, who now hid his face with his hand, sighing at the sound of them working together to tease him.

Ryan laughed a little, it was a nice moment to be a part of, even if it still felt wrong to be happy.

"Right on Mr Benson!" Candice said back impressed with the goings on.

"Call me Noah sweet-art." He replied with a friendly at-home feel.

"I wouldn't mind seeing this bunker, if you don't mind?" She said to Ricky beside her.

He was contemplating things in his head, well really, he was trying to think back to whether or not his room was presentable enough to be seen by the most precious thing in town. He decided it was good enough.

Who am I kidding? She won't care anyway, yesterday she was trying to rip my clothes off...

"Yeah okay." He stood up and left the lounge. She quickly did the same, hurriedly trying to catch up before she didn't know where to go.

"Door open guys!" Noah called in a mockery of sternness, causing Ryan and Sally to giggle.

"Would you guys just drop it already?!" Ricky called out just as humoured as his dad. *"So immature!"*

Ryan stayed seated on the couch with Noah and Sally's conversational skills keeping him occupied. They were mainly saying funny things about their little Ricky liking a girl.

Ricky led Candice into his bedroom. He'd spent so much time here on his own thinking about her and what it would be like to have her in this very space.

Her first impression was that it was nothing like what his dad made her think, or even of what she thought it would be like. The wardrobe's the untidiest thing in here with its doors open and clothes entwined with each other nearly spilling out like expanding foam.

The tidy bed has a shelf on the wall going over the head of it. Full of stuff like the mantelpiece in the lounge except he had them placed neatly. No desk, an untidy stack of varied books near the bed, a record player in the corner to the left of the doorway and the vinyls horizontally stacked to either side of the stand it sits on. A big window loomed across from the doorway with its curtains wide open.

"Who are they?" She asked pointing at the two large posters on the wall by the shelf above his bed.

"Okay, so that's Morrissey back when he was in The Smiths. And that's Michael Hutchence with INXS." He answered fondly informing her.

"They look pretty cool." She answered honestly.

"Dude, trust me they are and were." He replied nodding his head. "Sorry for calling you dude." He continued awkwardly.

She shrugged her shoulders with little care of his name calling.

"I gotta shut the curtains, don't want the neighbour girls getting all jealous because you're in here." He spoke with one of those winks of his.

She laughed and had a good look at the rows of vinyl albums.

"I have some singles too but they're in that box." He pointed to a cardboard box near his volcanic wardrobe.

"I'm really sorry about my mum yelling at you." She said apologetically.

"Nah it's fine. Guess I won't be allowed to go there anymore." He answered laughing at himself. "Would you even be allowed to go back to church after handling riff-raff?" He continued seeming to not even care about being disliked so much.

Candice shook her head at him, pretending she was unimpressed with his wit. "That message you sent really did cheer me up." Butterflies took flight in her stomach.

"Oh? You're welcome, I guess." He flashed a modest hand. "It wasn't the greatest message of all time. Next time I'll be sure to type out a poem." He said thinking he was funny.

"It was perfect how it was, honestly."

"I guess I could say the same about my first kiss." He said with a grin of pureness.

"You're pretty cute sometimes. Of course, in a totally annoying and nerdy way."

"You never answered me though." He replied a little shyly.

"I know. I'm sorry." She looked back to the vinyls. Their faint, dusty smell was somehow comforting.

"They're all original you know, the records." Ricky said proud and informative. "I actually searched for an original working player for months before I found it with some old guy. It'd been sitting in his shed for ages. I then mowed lawns for weeks and even worked at the counter of the petrol station where my dad works just so I could get up enough money to buy it."

"Wow, I'll never look at it the same way again." Candice said now knowing the little history between the record player and its current owner.

"It's basically my baby." He said humbly.

"That's cool. You're like an old soul or something." She said somewhat melancholy.

Ricky smirked. "That's what my parents say. I kinda live vicariously through them because I never lived through the good decades. If you know what I mean."

She turned to face him now. "Your parents don't even seem that old. And what's wrong with the decades you *have* lived?" She asked, almost offended for her generation.

"I mean as in everything was just so much better back then. The music, the clothes, the general feel." He looked to the ground and continued "I don't know, they just... the older the better, you know?"

"So that's why you drool whenever *I'm* around." She teased.

"Wait you noticed? I mean, I so don't drool." He replied with faux shifty eye movement.

"Yeah I'm pretty sure I once suggested to Wyatt that he should start carrying around little hankies to wipe it off your chin." She tried to keep a serious face.

"No way." He said laughing. "You're totally lying!"

"Wyatt always got so defensive when I'd say something mean about you." She said looking away into sullen thoughts of loss.

"Hey Candice he'll come home, don't worry." He said sounding nearly as hopeless.

She reached her hand out to him and after a small hesitation he took it with the gentlest steadiness. He placed his other hand over the top hers so that it now sat warmly between. She stepped forward before he let go of her hand and embraced her in the privacy of his room.

This wonderfully comfortable embrace was the only place she wanted to be all day. Though it was a completely foreign contact, he seemed to be so comforting due to the familiarity of his essence. She buried her face in his shoulder when she felt more tears on the way, once they came there was no stopping them. She didn't want to cry but this was so near perfect and her little brother was still out there, maybe not even alive.

There was sudden, loud howling dog barks from outside. They were both startled, without discussing, they ran straight out to the front yard, Ryan joined them when he saw they were going out to investigate the insane noise.

"What the heck is wrong boy?!" Candice asked the mystery dog.

He stopped his crazy barking when he saw his friends come to his calls. He stood on the grass wagging his tail. Unbeknownst to them, once warm and clear on the air his breath now only remained stagnate in the cold.

"Uh oh." Candice expressed. "I know what this means."

"What do you mean?" Ricky asked concerned.

"I mean he wants us to follow him."

"We can't just go following a weird dog into the night." Ryan stated in worry.

"Well he took me here, didn't he? Obviously, I needed to be here. Otherwise, that's one hell of a coincidence." She defended of the dog's logic.

They were quiet before Ricky spoke. "Yeah, she's right. It's nuts but let's just go."

Ryan sighed, he knew they were going to go whether he went or not. "Okay I'll come."

"Mum we're just going for a walk... To find this dog's owner!" Ricky called out to his parents.

"I don't like it Ricky, but I'll let you go! Be back in half an hour, an hour tops!" She called back from the lounge.

"Whoa, can't believe she said yes." He mumbled, surprised.

"I need shoes." Candice rushed to say.

Ricky looked around the doorstep. "Just use my mum's, she won't care."

After Candice quickly put on the borrowed shoes, the three of them left the porch after closing the front door and followed the good dog into the night.

Ryan smirked when he saw the other two holding hands as they all walked on, leaving their faith and trust with this four legged guide trotting happily along the sidewalk, occasionally turning his head to look at his trusty group.

~ 8 ~

The escape from Wyatt's place of holding was going smoothly until they'd been interrupted by what they were never expecting.

Wyatt wore only the white t-shirt but didn't care about the goose bumps on his arms, the cold promising to try and freeze him, he concentrated solely on walking away from that horrible place once and for all.

They had reached the back door to the small, messy house when Rose spoke up. "Your shirt is white, you'll stand out. Jack, give him your jumper."

"But I don't have a shirt underneath, I'm not gonna walk around with no clothes. That kinda defeats the purpose, doesn't it?"

"Wait..." She crossed her arms. "So you complain my shirt is too thin to wear and then you wear nothing but a jumper? Far out Jack." She debated.

Wyatt stood by worried as they argued about clothes. "Guys, I don't want to be nagging but if we don't go, we'll surely be caught."

"He's right." Rose agreed. She took Jack's extra jumper off herself and handed it hastily to Wyatt. "Here just take this one, quick."

He quickly wriggled it on. It was a near perfect fit, just a little bigger than what he would prefer.

"There, you look perfect." Jack said fixing the hood around Wyatt's neck, who felt funny in the stomach, like the feeling you get on the first day of school at the beginning of the year.

I must be nervous to get out... he figured to himself.

They walked out of the house and into the back yard where Rose had sat alone for so many years. She felt she may never spend another minute there again. It saddened her but couldn't deny gladness at the thought of taking Wyatt away, possibly saving her and Jack from possibly a worse fate than what had happened to him.

They'd gone through the steely gate of the driveway, the pebbles beneath their shoes crunched uncomfortably loud as they walked.

Rose tried to be as quiet as possible when she put the chain back through that held the gate to its post. She didn't know why she was trying to be so damn quiet with everything she did, it's like she's worried that Daz or somebody would hear it from where they are. The homes that neighboured where the twins live are spaced out, giving each resident some space to do what they will.

Wyatt realised he could hear the ocean, it was a sound he

wasn't expecting but he was so glad to hear it, feeling gratitude at the crashing waves.

They walked to the side of the road and jogged across. There were no houses on the other side. He could feel they were now on long grass. It wasn't especially long but it was untamed and uneven. The sound of walking through it sounded twenty thousand times louder than the pebbles of the driveway.

"Just be careful because there might be rabbit holes and stuff around." Rose said to Wyatt behind her. He nodded in response, not thinking about whether or not she saw him do it.

Jack sounded utterly surprised when his tired voice exclaimed suddenly. "Violet?!"

The other two turned around in the dark lit dimly by the pale moon. There beside Jack was a girl dressed in white. Wyatt looked on in complete fearful surprise. He'd never seen her this close, but he was instantly sure that this was the girl that had been stalking him. *The creepy girl.*

"What are you doing here?" Rose asked concerned.

Wyatt shivered with worry, if she could sneak up on them in this grass, what else could?

"I came to help." Violet said softly with little hesitation.

"What?" Rose replied with confusion.

Jack moved closer beside Wyatt. He whispered "*Creepy mother-fucker*" as he nudged his shoulder. Wyatt didn't really react, he was freaking out at Violet's sudden and unusual appearance at this terrifying time. The hair of her extremely long and jet black, her white dress flattering yet clearly not usual and immensely out of ordinary in a setting such as this.

"Just come with me, come on and follow." Violet said in her kind but still unnerving voice.

They followed her with weary caution, they did feel as though they could trust her. Even Wyatt, who was still unsure of her general presence.

She led them through the darkened area off the grass and onto a small dirt path that wound itself through bushes of tea tree and tall trees of pine.

The sound of waves still there, only muffled by the wall of foliage now surrounding them. They couldn't see much now that the trees caged them in, although Violet skilfully walked along with ease as though she'd done it a million times before now. Wyatt squinted at the dark to try and look at the dangling wake of Violet's dress. To his further astonishment, it looked as though she was doing all this barefoot.

The smell on the air fresh and clean, even to Wyatt, glad to have Jack walking beside him. Rose and Violet were in front and if Jack wasn't there he certainly wouldn't have felt as safe as he currently did.

"What's this path? I was just going to go on the big one closer to the beach." Rose said to the strange friend she had in Violet.

"This one is better." She replied pointing ahead of herself.

Wyatt tried to refuse his urge for urination. He'd only gone once, twice if you include the time he wet himself. It's as though his bodily functions just shut down while he was in there and now that he was free and hearing the distant roar of the ocean it became evident, he needed to go now. He tugged at Jack's sleeve to get his attention.

Jack squinted to look at him. "You okay dude?"

He replied in a low tone, trying not to let the girls hear him. "I need to go."

"Yeah, I know, that's what we're doin'. We'll be safe soon."

Wyatt moved closer in irritation and spoke even lower. "No, I need to *go*. I need to *tinkle*."

Jack started to giggle profusely, sounding the gayest he's sounded since he entered the story.

"Tinkle, that's so cute." He said through his giggles.

"It's not funny, I'm serious." Wyatt answered annoyed. Rose turned to see what was so funny.

"He needs to pee." Jack explained, stopping the giggling as if he'd get into trouble if he continued.

"Oh, well just go over there. We'll stay here." She said to Wyatt.

He only saw where she was pointing because of her white hand floating in the dark. He looked into the blackness of bush. "What if something grabs me in there?" He asked in fear.

"I'll come with you, bro." Jack pushed him along with guidance into the blackness.

"Hurry up guys, we gotta leave." Rose said after them. She was left standing on the dirt with Violet, who was now looking off into the direction of Wyatt's nature toilet.

~ 9 ~

While the others were waiting for Wyatt to relieve his bladder, Ricky, Ryan, Candice and the dog were still walking. They'd walked through the streets and had now reached the outskirts of town.

"It's starting to feel more and more like a waste of time following this guy. I mean what the hell are we doing out here?" Ricky said puffing in his breaths.

"I don't know. I do know I'm exhausted though." Candice reciprocated.

Ryan strode along with a lot of curiosity raging within him. At first, he thought it was a bad idea but now that they had followed the dog this far it was feeling like it was on an incredibly strategic mission. A mission to take them somewhere important. Stray dogs didn't act like this.

They walked along on the roadside gravel. There were no cars tonight, only one had passed them a little way back. They had no idea it was the mother of Wyatt's presumed angels on her way to get groceries, taking an extremely long detour through various streets to prolong her time alone with herself.

"I've never been out here on foot." Candice continued.

"We have. Ryan and I rode our bikes out here a few times." Ricky said fondly.

"Did Wyatt ever come out here with you guys?" She asked saddened.

"Not a lot. Cause yeah, he doesn't have a bike." He replied nearly apologetically.

The canine guide suddenly turned and trotted over the road, they automatically followed him and stopped in sync on the other side of the tar when he glided into the darkness of pine trees.

"Whoa, I'm not walking in there." Ricky said cautiously. "Dog or no dog."

A light breeze, a whistle of precious wind, then the furred head of the dog appeared again and whined, as if talking to them.

"He wants us to go. We can't just stop after all that." Candice said trying to convince her new companions.

"Yeah, I agree with her." Ryan said to Ricky.

"Hey you were the one trying to convince us not to go!" He argued right back at him.

"Yeah but I'm okay with it now, there's something about that dog."

Ricky looked back at the darkened, expecting face of the leading dog. "Fine. Alright let's go, but I'm thinking we stay close to each other." He said reluctantly.

They entered the darkness behind the happy tail of the good boy. It wasn't long before they realised they were on an actual path, it's little, but one they were glad was there. It would have been hell trying to walk through the bush blindly. There'd be tripping and scratching, all sorts.

"My mum's going to murder me." Ricky said with a small laugh.

"My dad doesn't even know where I am." Candice said sounding disappointed in herself.

"My parents probably wouldn't care if they *did* know." Ryan joined, followed by silence.

They walked on through, for a while all they could hear were the little scurrying noises out to the sides of the path, the occasional rustling of possums in the odd eucalyptus tree and the guide sometimes snorting as he trotted. Now they could hear the muffled sound of waves.

"Huh, the beach." Candice said amazed that they'd actually come this far, even though the whole town is beachside. She had her left arm wrapped tightly around Ricky's right one, the dark scared her a little even at the best of times.

The dog picked up his pace making the teens go faster behind him. If they lost the reason they're in this situation they'd probably freak out and run back. The way the dog was starting to pant and snort worried them a bit. He was acting like someone was there, someone he knew.

"This beats all the games of Murder in the Dark I've ever played." Ricky stated in a careful voice.
They heard small footsteps up ahead, only faintly against the sound of waves rolling on the beach.

"Shit shit shit!" Ricky exclaimed panicked to leave, freaking the heck out of Candice.

Ryan stood, squinting ahead. The dog ran up to something and reared his body up to greet it.

"Guys wait, I think it's okay."

Ricky and Candice stood behind Ryan, watching as four people came towards them behind the dog happily jumping along in front.

He's a good boy, he'd done his job.

As the hoard drew closer to them they could make out two girls, they were young, the shape of one was slightly familiar to Ricky. Behind them were two boys cautiously following the girls' steps. They'd gotten a few metres closer when Candice started to cry and leave Ricky's side.

"*Wyatt*! Oh my god!" She yelled as she ran between the two girls, attaching herself to her little brother. He held her back tightly and began to cry with her.

"Candice, I can't believe it's you!" He said shaking all over.

"What the, where have you been?!" She asked not really caring what the answer was, just relieved he was here and alive.

"I got taken." He replied sobbing.

"The boys are here too, guys come on!" She said to the dark.

Ryan and Ricky walked over to the siblings and were greeted with firm hugs from Wyatt, who was still sobbing from happiness at their presence around him.

The twins stood by watching and listening, astonished at the turn of events.

Violet and the good boy stood side by side sensibly, both happy at what they'd accomplished so far.

"Oh man Wylie. I've never been so happy to see your little self!" Ricky expressed affectionately.

Wyatt replied with another big hug, he clung to him with great relief. Ryan couldn't help himself, he embraced his friends with all the love and care he had within himself.

They broke apart as Wyatt briefly explained who the twins are. Candice walked over thanking them both with hugs of gratitude.

Jack and Rose stayed rather quiet; to be honest they were a little shy at being joined by them.

When the initial shock was over, Jack turned to see that Violet and that random dog weren't there. "Ohhh-kay... That's not creepy at all."
They all turned their attention to him, realising what he was talking about.

"Let's just leave, please?" Wyatt pleaded.

"Yeah let's go." Ryan agreed.

The six of them walked back along where the dog had just led, eventually coming out from the confines of foliage, back out to the road. Rose began to feel strong concern at being out here, they could get seen.

Wyatt was gleeful at having his sister and dear friends with him, but thought it was incredibly unhinged that Violet and her dog were still out of sight.

"Okay we gotta move it." Rose declared. "Where do you guys suggest we go?"

"Let's go back to my place, it's the closest. Then we'll tell my parents and they'll involve the police." Ricky said authoritatively.

"I like the sound of that." Jack said in a friendly tone. "Just lead the way sir." He held his arm out to escort him ahead.

Ricky smirked through a deep, suggestive voice as he walked to the front of the group. "I will do."
Wyatt smiled at their silly interaction with Candice's arm around his shoulders.

They all walked hurriedly along the roadside, much to Rose's mistrust.
As if to punish her for not speaking up to warn everyone about being near the road and not out of sight, a familiar drone began to chime up the road in front of them.

"Oh god, we gotta run!" She yelled startling everyone except Jack, who knew what she was talking about. An old van appeared on the tar, almost skidding off the road past them when its driver pumped the brakes abruptly.

Of course they have the van, mum has the car... Rose thought panicked.

They began to run behind her when someone called out. It was a horrid voice, full of evil and greed.

"Get, the fuck, back here!" It called from behind them.
Rose froze, obediently turning around. Daz had Jack's head in a tight grip, one of his hands over his mouth so that he couldn't talk, and in the other hand a hunting knife.

"Get in the van or I'll cut the little idiot." He looked directly at her.

Jack tried to signal for them not to, but his wriggling was stopped by a hard nudge to the hip from Daz's knee.

"What do we do?!" Wyatt asked the terrified group.

"You get in the fucking van is what you do." Daz grunted foully.

Rose began to walk back to the van. As she walked through the other four, she spoke in a tear stained whisper: *"I'm so sorry."*

They all followed her to the van when Daz yelled. "Al open the back!"

His accomplice jumped out of the driver's seat, ran around the back of the van and opened the doors.

Rose got in first, followed by Wyatt and Candice, then Ricky and Ryan, then Jack who'd gotten shoved in there by Daz. The doors were shut mercilessly behind them.

There was nothing in the back but the smell of old rust and things that shouldn't have been. In the dark of the steely walls, Rose held her brother and knew it wasn't just business now, it was staying out of prison.

Daz and Al had been seen. Their faces were now in the minds of all six teenagers.

~ Seven ~

TO CATCH A THIEF

~ 1 ~

Ethan Jonson wondered what to reply to the message he'd gotten on his phone. An invitation by one of his mates to join a party in the city. He wanted to go, but had to regretfully decline. Tonight, Aunt Thelma had her stupid friend over, the one he didn't like at all. She's a creeping, disturbing, slime of a woman who thought she looked like Elle McPherson but really just looked like a raisin trying to dress up pretty for a thirty year school reunion.

'Ur loss m8 th girls r hot.' He rolled his eyes, chicks are getting boring anyway.

He had to stay to have dinner, his parents expected it of him. Sometimes he wished they *would* treat him like they do Ryan. Ethan's old enough to have realised they're only like it because Ryan's the product of an unplanned conception, and is bold enough to act as himself, most of the time doing what he pleased. Whereas Ethan is the shining promise of the Jonson name really making a mark on the world. Or that's what it felt like his parents were expecting from him, and at an early age became their toy soldier.

Downstairs, they were all seated at the well-dressed dining table. He sat across from his aunt, beside her resides the raisin, at either end of the table his parents had perched themselves. They couldn't be further apart.

"Nice of you to finally join us." His father said to him with typical authority.

"Hello Ethan." Raisin said in a far too friendly tone, making him gag internally.

"Hello Georgina." He answered with a false smile.

"You're bigger every time I see you, I swear." She stated from across the table.

"Am I?" He gave her no eye contact as he used his fork to stir the veggies around his plate.

"Yes you are. As I always say you'll be a great man one day." She said taking a sip of wine, stroking his shin with the toe of her high heel under the table, making him quickly tuck his feet beneath his chair.

"Can't say the same for the other one, causes trouble here and there. He's a bad egg and always will be." Thelma Kersh declarded to the diners.

Ethan looked up to see his parents' reaction, to see there wasn't one. "He's not even that bad though." He defended by himself.

"You say that but really you have no idea. I saw a picture he made, of a naked woman." She announced to everyone in a slow and raspy tone as if she were telling a horror story.

Mrs Jonson looked up surprised. "What? You've got to be joking!"

"Is that so?" Georgina the raisin asked impressed.

"I just need to visit the loo." Ethan said casually.

"You only just sat down. Why didn't you go beforehand?" His dad asked sternly.

"I was worried about being late to come down."

"Fine, off you go."

Leaving the table to go upstairs as they spoke about this star-tling discovery of Ryan's nude drawing capabilities, he went straight for his brother's bedroom. After turning the desk lamp on, he looked around the room, finally catching sight of the art portfolio Ryan put his finished drawings in. He looked through all the drawings he'd slaved over.   Portrait after portrait, a few landscapes flashed by but no naked ladies. He placed it back down, rushing to find the drawing in the rest of the room. At last, in a plastic pocket under several pieces of paper and other bits and bobs inside the bottom desk draw, he found the nude lady.

This confirmed to him that Ryan either showed their Aunt this picture which was extremely unlikely, or she snooped around the room and found it in that hiding spot.

He wondered for a moment where the guy could have gotten that inspiration, figuring he must have looked it up on Google or something. He put it back where Ryan wanted it to be and went back downstairs.

If she's going through his stuff then she's probably going through everyone's. Why?...

"Darling your dinner is going cold." His mum said to him, she was obviously over the shock of hearing about Ryan's naked art. Silly really, she has two teenage boys and expects to not hear anything about naked girls. She was a prude but certainly not as bad a prude as poor old Patty Fineman.

"Where is that little tike anyway?" Raisin asked.

"Oh he's out at one of his friend's houses tonight." Answered Evelyn after swallowing a bite of her roasted meat.

"Shame about that friend of his being taken." Kersh stated without sincerity.

Ethan and his parents looked up concerned.

"What do you mean?" Mr Jonson asked seriously.

"You mean *kidnapped*?" His wife asked her sister in concern.
Thelma stopped eating, noticing that everyone was staring at
her. "I ah.... I heard it through the grape vine. Not to mention
the news. Evelyn, don't you watch TV?"

"Well, I never heard about this!" Said the worried mother.

"It's probably just a hoax, I wouldn't worry." Said his father
continuing to eat his meal.

Ethan was not convinced. By pure untrusting instinct he
decided right then and there that something wasn't right. After
dinner he will snatch his aunt's mobile phone and snoop the
hell out of it.

~ 2 ~

Nobody had spoken the whole short drive back, not even
when they were being taken back down into the little room
where Rose and Jack had just freed Wyatt from.
They'd been locked in and left there, hearing the men arguing
all the way back up the little hall, then there was nothing.

Under the light of the single bulb that Wyatt had stared at
for days, they could now all see each other properly for the
first time.

Jack was in fact the first one of them to speak since they'd
been caught. "Well, that failed. We're now trapped under our
own house."

"What?! You *live* here?!" Candice asked surprised, her arms
crossed in fearful uncertainty now looking to her brother. "You
failed to mention that in your into, Wy."

"Long story, but trust me we're nothing like them." Jack added,
trying to calm her down.

The group sat in a circle on the paisley rug for another five minutes more of silence.

Wyatt sat between Ricky and Candice, Ryan was beside Candice and Rose was between him and Jack who was next to Ricky, completing the circle.

"I don't think they'll be back for a while." Rose suggested, hoping it's true.

"Hey guys." Jack started. "I'm really sorry about not being able to fight him off and knock the jerk to the ground." They all looked to him with emmpathetic eyes.

He continued "I mean I probably could have, but me and violence don't mix well."

"Nah man, it's all good." Ricky said to him, tapping a friendly hand on his shoulder.

Jack looked over at Wyatt then back to Ricky. "I mean it, I work out. I could totally get him next time we see him. Here feel." He flexed his arm like he was impersonating a burly strongman at the circus.

Rose slapped her forehead in spite of her flirty brother, even at a time like this.

"He's not joking." Ricky said slightly amused to the others as he innocently stroked Jack's arm.

Wyatt didn't think much of the interaction, not surprising considering the fact he's back in the room, except now people he cared about were in danger with him. It was getting a lot more personal; he began to feel rage rather than fright.

Candice saw the whole situation for what it was. "Maybe you should stop feeling everyone up and come here." She now looked directly at Jack with a stern face, he sat back with his limbs to himself, he understood exactly what she said.

"I'm quite fine where I am, *Candie*." Ricky said back to her playfully.

"*What?!*" Wyatt questioned with high pitched confusion, he

looked past Candice at Ryan, who nodded with confirmation. "How long was I *gone* for?" He asked, shaking his head in disbelief.

"Too long!" Candice said putting her arm over his shoulders again.

"We have to work out how to leave." Ryan stated eagerly, wanting start their venture out of the unbelievable situation. "Does anyone have one of those bobby pins or something?"

"No, sorry." Candice replied disappointed.

Ryan looked expectantly at Rose, who found herself stunned at the close sight of his swirling blue eyes looking at her. He seemed really familiar to her somehow. "No I don't either, sorry." She looked away, rejecting the innocent yet intriguing gaze.

They all looked at Jack, who wasn't impressed with the way they all assumed he'd just happen to have a bobby pin. He doesn't even use them. "Sorry to disappoint everyone, but no." He said sternly.

"Then what are we going to do?" Ryan asked exhausted.

"Well there is one thing we can do." Ricky began in a serious voice, they all looked to him trustingly, waiting to hear something that could help them get out and survive the night. "We could... Sing Kumbaya."
Ryan and Candice sighed, rolling their heads back at the same time.
Wyatt laughed a little in his exhaustion, he'd missed Ricky's stupidity.

"Does anyone have a mobile?" Rose asked. "Sucks they took ours."
Everyone shook their heads before Ricky asked Candice where hers is.

"I left it at home, yours?"

"Yeah it's in my room." He replied deflated as he thought of it sitting on his bed.

"I can't believe nobody has a mobile right now in this day and age." Candice said disappointed.

"No doubt they would have been taken off you anyway." Wyatt said wisely.

"So what was up with that girl? The dog took us straight to you guys." Candice enquired curiously.

"That's Violet." Said Rose, then began to tell the tale of her weird friend.

Candice replied by explaining to everyone what had happened from the moment she looked out her bedroom window to see the pooch sitting on the lawn.

"Ricky, remember the creepy girl outside the milk bar that day?" Wyatt asked.

Ricky's face lit up with recognition while he realised that he'd seen the dog before. "How did I not notice? So dumb." He said to himself aloud.

"What do you mean?" Rose asked them suspiciously.

"We've seen your friend before I came here, that dog too. She's given me the creeps a few times now and I find it weird that she turned up here." Wyatt explained.

Jack shook his head in confusion. "Wait, so why didn't you say something?"

Wyatt shrugged his shoulders. "You guys might have thought I was crazy or making it up."

"No, we wouldn't have." Rose said perplexed.

"Hmm, I dunno about anyone else but I'm really freakin' out now." Jack stated.

"Yeah so am I." Agreed Candice.

"What if they're working for the kidnappers?" Ricky considered.

"I really don't think so." Rose said, detesting the thought.

"Says the girl who lives with the people doing this."

"Hey, don't even go there." Said Jack in a tone so serious he was a little scary. "I said before that we're nothing like them so leave her alone."

"Geez alright, calm down." Ricky said with his hands up, trying not to piss him off any more.

"There's no need to get angry." Wyatt said frowning at Jack.

"Fine." Jack scoffed, crossing his arms.

"Anyway." Rose continued. "I hope she isn't."

"Do you think we should try and knock those men out with something when they come back?" Candice suggested to the group.

"But with what?" Ryan asked.

They looked around the room to see if there was something they could use as a weapon.

"How about that bucket?" Ricky suggested pointing behind him at the blue bucket against the wall.

"Ahm that's probably not the best idea." Wyatt said cringing.

"Oh, I see." Ricky replied, catching on to Wyatt's disdain.

"We can't even use the crayons." Stated Ryan. "If they were pencils, we could stab them."

"I can't believe this is happening." Candice said teary. Ricky crawled from his position in the circle to squeeze in between her and Wyatt to put a comforting arm around her.

Wyatt had to shuffle along up beside Jack who looked at him with a grin. He looked away without returning the favour.

"What if we take the table apart somehow?" Suggested Rose as she looked past her brother at the small table sitting beneath the crayons and paper.

"How would we do that?" Jack said back.

Candice wiped the tiny tears from her eyes. "Oh c'mon

muscles show us what you've got." She teased. Ricky looked at her in astonishment.

"Aw ha-ha." Jack said to her mockingly.

"Yeah, we could take the table apart and break the light so it's dark." Ryan said hopeful they were onto something.

"No, we'd have to take the light out. The last thing we want is broken glass on the ground when we're trying to bash them and leave." Rose said sounding tactful.

"You're right." Ryan agreed respectfully.

They sat quietly before Jack suddenly got up, making his way over to the table now looking at it closely.

"What's he doing?" Candice asked Rose.

"Probably seeing if he can actually break it."

"I think I can." He said from the corner. "Everyone move back and look away in case something comes loose and flies into ya' faces." They did as he asked, letting him get to work on dismantling the old table. It was thin so it seemed an easy task. There were sounds of cracks, snaps and the occasional grunting of curse words from him.

Rose stood up, asking him for the chair. He slid it over to her and went on with his mission. She centred it the under the light, having to push two of its legs against the mattress to try and get it in the right spot. She put a foot on the seat of the chair and heaved herself up to place the other foot beside its partner. She could reach the bulb easy, but it was the fact she had no way of turning it off to touch it was the problem here, the switch was outside the door.

"I can't touch it." She said annoyed as she got back down.

"Okay... Is it an Edison screw or bayonet?" Ricky enquired.

She looked back up squinting. "I think it's one of the push ones."

"Well you could fold that paper and use it to shield your hand if you do it really fast." He suggested.

"I don't know... What if it burns?" She said worried at the thought of burning her hand.

"I'll do it." He said bravely.

"No I can do it." She said quickly.

"Don't argue with me lady." He said as he walked over to Jack. "Dude, can you help me gather the paper for a sec?"

Rose looked at Candice who shrugged her shoulders, she spoke in that universal tone that unites all females; "*Men.*"

"Oh so I'm a man now am I?" Ricky asked from across the room.

"Not yet, you haven't proved it." She teased, trying not to sound too suggestive.

"If he sets something on fire..." Started Wyatt who was trying his hardest to put aside their sexual banter.

"He won't, if he doesn't leave it on the actual light for too long." Ryan assured him.

Rose sat down in Ricky's spot beside Candice and watched as the two boys went about their missions. She didn't have the heart to tell them all that when the time came they were going to be fighting not only for freedom, but for their very lives. She wondered if Jack had thought about this too, surely he would have noticed the lack of masking on Al and Daz's faces.

Beside her Candice retrieved a stick of bubble gum from the pocket of her jacket, put one in her mouth and chewed nervously. She offered some to Rose who declined, so did Ryan and Wyatt when she offered.

"Ricky? Do you guys want some of this?" She asked politely.

"Nah I'm okay gorgeous." He replied before asking Jack. "You want some gum dude?"

Jack looked up and saw Candice offering her hand out from across the room. "Yes please." He eagerly walked over to her. "I need somethin' like that right now."

She assumed he meant because of nerves and worry but Rose knew he would be hanging out for a relaxing session on his own with a stick of weed right about now.

"Thank you." He took the gum from Candice before unwrapping it, placing it joyfully inside his mouth where it was chewed with steady gusto. He walked back and spoke to the room. "I think I've done as much as I can. There's the four legs and a few big splintery things."

After gathering it all up in his arms he walked over to the others and placed the bundle on the ground. Each of them picked up a piece of wood and sat with their weapon, watching to see what Ricky would do.

He got up to stand on the chair, reaching up with the makeshift paper barrier. They all watched riveted, hoping he wouldn't stuff up.

"Ah, so it is bayonet. Good." He said before placing his hand over the globe, gently pushing on it, turning to free the little light giver. His palm could feel the heat but there was no chance of burns. Before they knew it the light left them with no fuss, they were in absolute pitch blackness.

"Whoa, I don't like this." Ricky said into nothing, trying to safely get back to the ground. He decided that crawling to the others rather than walking would be safer. He threw the paper away to the side of him and left the bulb on the chair against the seat back. With his hands feeling around in front of him, he listened for the direction the others were in by their breathing and scuffling. He could feel the rug and then a piece of the table that Jack provided, beyond that, a foot. "Whose shoe did I just touch?"

"It was me." Rose said. He knew it wasn't Candice's voice and there was one other girl here. A hand gently touched the top of his head.

"I'm here you douche." The sweetly familiar voice of Candice advised.

He squeezed himself between her and Rose who slid over to make room.

Wyatt was seated on the end squished up beside Ryan, the darkness had them all on edge. He jumped at the feel of a body squishing itself to the other side of him. "Who's that?"

"Jack." He replied hoping he won't be told to move away.

"Oh okay. I'm kinda scared of the dark." Wyatt simply said in a small attempt at trying to explain his jumpiness.

"Me too." He whispered closely. "It makes me need to *tinkle*."

Wyatt could smell the fruitiness from the bubble gum on his breath. "That's still not funny." He said with a tiny giggle.

"I never thought it was funny." Jack stated quietly, leaning himself closer so he could speak directly into his ear. "*I thought it was cute.*"

"Fair enough." He replied. This was all too much, way too confusing at a time like this.

Jack felt for Wyatt's arm, pulling itself away slightly. He didn't try harder, it was really feeling like a lost cause. In a sigh of dissatisfaction he looked ahead into the nothing of solitary. But, it wasn't lonely for long. He felt the most careful and gentle little touch he'd ever felt.

Wyatt's hand had unexpectedly come under and around Jack's arm, felt for his hand, now securely holding it in place. They were sitting with arms entwined and hands softly holding, he could feel the bracelet they'd given him still around his wrist. Jack felt as though he might combust in admiration.

"Everyone got their wood?" Ricky asked obnoxiously, breaking the uncomfortable silence.

"You just couldn't help yourself, could you?" Candice said

disapprovingly.

"Get your mind out the gutter Fineman." He scoffed back to her.

There the six waited together for something to happen, waiting to hear the dreadful footfall of the captors before they entered, and the group were to attack.

Rose felt tired tears fall down her cheeks quietly in the blackness of the room, with the person she loved most in the world and four random people beside her, under the house she'd lived in for most of her life. She closed her eyes to picture the tree standing outside, magnificent and grounding.

~ 3 ~

Standing together in the dark of night, the faces of Violet and her companion in the dog, were lit peacefully by the street lights of Augustus Street.

A drunken man left the warmth of the pub across the road, looked at them briefly before staggering to his motel room some fifty metres from the pub doors. He lingered for a while trying to work the lock, before he entered and closed the door to the world.

Violet stood by staring the house they graced with their presence. She often wanted to visit this sidewalk, not to do anything, just watch. The dog sometimes came with her when he didn't feel he needed to be anywhere else. He didn't mind joining her, there was something about the house that was apparently important to a part of Violet.

"Good boy, Buddy." Her hand on his solid head, comforting. He himself had a special place that he liked to go when he wasn't obeying, it wasn't a house though. It's a most peculiar spot, the place where townspeople leave their crazy rubbish and unwanted goods. It is in fact the tip, a junkyard only just outside town.

There was the sudden, hooting call of an owl and the whistle of cool wind.

Together they listened, just as they do most things together.

They wandered away, leaving the sidewalk to its empty fate of the night, nothing more there for any alcoholics to see.

~ 4 ~

Standing out of view in the hall, Ethan looked at the glaring cold screen of Thelma Kersh's phone. He didn't want to go too far so that he could put it back fast without anyone catching on. It didn't even have a lock password on it which made him think that there probably isn't anything she wanted to hide in it. After cringing at the sight of the device wallpaper (a distasteful selfie of herself and the Raisin) he scanned through the message conversations. From what he could see there was nothing too shifty, nothing about kids being kidnapped. He tried looking thoroughly but in his defence, it was a hard task to try and sift through conversations on a snatched phone with the notoriously cruel owner in the house.

He quickly opened the tab for web searches to see what her recent browsing histories were. There was a noise to his right coming from the doorway to the dining room and kitchen, nothing was there. He could hear the sound of gleeful cackles coming from the kitchen though.

Continuing on with his mission, he looked back at the screen to see the search history had been cleared.

Damn it... Don't tell me it was all for nothing!...

He exited the programs and shut the screen off before heading into the lounge, placing it in the exact spot he'd gotten it from on the arm of a recliner.

Without knowing what to do next he joined the oldies in the

kitchen where Raisin sat cross legged on a bench stool, holding another glass of wine.

Still untrusting he asked them what they had planned for the rest of the night.

"Oh, we'll probably just diddle daddle like the crazy ladies we are! Isn't that right Thel?" Raisin answered clearly under the influence of her drinks.

Raising her own glass up to her friend's, Kersh replied. "That's exactly right!"

The sound of a loud, tinny phone rang from the lounge across the hall, Thelma rudely stopped what she was doing and left the room to retrieve it.

Ethan's heart skipped a little beat with the relief of not holding it when it began to ring, who knows what would have happened then.

Everyone was quiet, the parents hadn't hung around with Raisin alone much. Thelma usually had her around when the parents were out somewhere else. Those times were worse than this because Raisin's cradle snatching advances were worse towards Ethan, and to make it even worse, Thelma let her. She came back into the room declaring in a horrid I'm-so-good voice; "I have to go, Georg you'll have to drive yourself home."

"Oh what?! Why what's the buzz?" Raisin asked upset.

"Nothing you have to worry about." Thelma snapped. She then continued on down the hall and made her way to the guest bedroom turned her bedroom.

"Well it was a pleasure spending the evening with you Georgina." Said Mrs Jonson, probably not really meaning it.

"Same to you! Bye everyone, I'll be back... Soon." She waddled towards the front door before calling back to Ethan.

"Hey Ethan! Would you like to come with me? I could show you my other car... It's *real* nice!"

He was about to decline the disturbing offer when he realised, he might be able to use it to his advantage.

Maybe I could get her to follow the old cow... Unless I'm being paranoid... Something wasn't right with that phone call... Why didn't she say what's up?...

He turned to his parents to ask for their approval.

"Sure son, but if she drives like a maniac call the police." His father said.

His mum seemed disjointed but let her husband lead the approval. She kissed him on the forehead for a goodbye.

He nodded loyally to his parents and headed for the door, grabbing his jacket off one of the coat hooks on his way past.

"You're gonna *love* my place, trust me." She said like a pro sleaze.

Inside Raisin's small, compact car Ethan found himself wishing he'd never agreed to do this. In the space of mere seconds, he made the decision to get out of the car without saying anything. Her slimy movements, the smell of wine and cigarettes, just too much for him take. Thoughts of the car crashing with a thundering wave crept through his mind. Or worse, she could try to molest him or something.

"Oh c'mon, don't be shy! You'll be missing out!" She called from the window in an attempt to entice.

"Nah I'll live." He replied without the slightest bit of regret.

Without anything but a scoff she started up her car and left the roadside, leaving the street with a noisy automobile grumble.

With a small shake of the head and a look to the left he realised that his aunts car's still here, he could sneak into the carport and hide somewhere in it.

Silently, he snuck through the side door of the garage and felt around in the dark for the car's handle.

Thank god it's not an alarmed car he thought pulling on the handle. It made that deep, clunking sound and opened.

What are the chances?!...

He carefully climbed in with all the reluctance being pushed aside by adrenaline and concern. It smelt in here like cigarettes and something like dead fish. Now that he was on the back seat, he closed the door with firm carefulness.

Kersh came into the carport with no sign of daintiness. The only light emitted from the doorway to the house that she'd just come through. Her dark silhouette was that of a monstrous burden in the eyes of the Jonson boys.

She strutted around to the driver's side of the car and got in, sitting behind the wheel now, never even noticing Ethan's feet disappearing into the boot of the car through the seat hatch.

As he lay curled up in the tomb of the Kersh vehicle, he thought about why he was actually putting himself through this. He could be acting on some strange boldness he developed from something his aunt said in conversation, risking a lot here. What would everyone think when they found out what he'd done?

Ryan this better be worth it...

~ 5 ~

Still huddled together and not really knowing if they would survive the night, Ryan broke the cold silence with a whisper to Wyatt, who still held onto Jack.

"I'm really sorry about the things I said when we had that fight, I really am."

"Ryan it's okay, I'm sorry too."

"No, I shouldn't have been such a giant arse. If I wasn't then maybe this wouldn't have happened. I'm... I'm seriously really sorry."

In the cover of dark, Wyatt took in Ryan's guilty apology.

Jack had basically ended up hugging the arm Wyatt had offered earlier and for a while now had deep, steady breathing. Considering the new person by his side at this moment he found he didn't mind the goings on. Of course, he was furious at the situation and the feeling of impending doom involving his big sister, two best friends and the Angel twins. But that was just it, if he had never had that fight with Ryan he might not have been taken and wouldn't be here now with the twins, possibly giving them a chance to have a better life, to get away from kidnappers storing people under their house.

"Ryan, really it's fine. Nothing is your fault."
Jack's innocent heaving continued against him in the dark.

"How long do you think we've been here for?" Candice asked deliriously.

"It feels like forever." Ricky answered with tired sighs.

Rose grunted as she thought to herself. "I haven't heard a single thing. My mum would most likely be home by now..." She waited to hear Jack console her from wherever he was sitting in the group's line against the hard wall.

"Jack, *Jack*!" She whispered loudly.

"I think he's asleep." Wyatt informed.

"Can you wake him up, it's not really the best time to take a nap." Rose said sounding furious.

Wyatt pushed his warm body in an effort to wake him, he only squirmed with a small, annoyed groan. "You gotta wake up buddy." He said to Jack's ear as he tried to wriggle the dead weight of him.

Jack woke from his little slumber with the confused wiping of his eyes. For a moment he'd forgotten where he was and what was happening. "Shit, sorry." He said to Wyatt beside him. "Guess I was tired."

"It's okay." He kindly replied.

"You done napping now?" Rose said irritated in the dark.

"Yeah, sorry Rose." He still sounded sleepy.

"I wish *I* was comfortable enough to sleep. Actually, I wish it was all a dream." Candice exclaimed holding Ricky tighter.

"Me too." Ricky agreed.

"Me three." Ryan joined.

They sat quietly once more, the only thing to look at was the very thin line of dim light coming from under the door. The only thing to hear were themselves as they sighed and shifted limbs every now and then to prevent the uncomfortable feeling of pins and needles.

"They're prolly tryin' to figure out what to do with our bodies when they kill us." Jack said out of nowhere, casually not holding back such as Rose had for ages.

Wyatt sighed a sullen sigh as if he thought the same thing.

"You really think they'll kill us?" Ricky asked, wishing it wasn't said.

"Well they usually wear something over their faces when they're doin' shifty shit so nobody sees what they look like."

"Yeah, the one that was bringing me food had a bandanna over most of his face." Wyatt confirmed.

Jack continued "But I guess 'cause they were surprised to see us on the road they didn't bother with it."

"It's a mad world..." Ricky said lost in thought.

"Okay... So, we're really going to try and *kill them* when they come back?" Ryan asked uncomfortable at the thought.

"Before they kill *us*." Ricky continued.

"I guess we'll have to." Wyatt said. Hearing *him* of all people say that surprised Ricky, Ryan and Candice, who all stayed quiet.

"I haven't heard mum Jack, what do you think happened up there?" Rose asked her brother.

He let a deep breath leave him to answer. "I honestly don't

162 ~ ASHLEA RAYWOOD

know sis."

The twin's mother had actually been held up by the fact she crashed her car, just like the 'stupid man' that fathered her children. She was alive but the person that hit her wasn't so lucky. Georgina the raisin was in fact mangled in the wreck of the cars.

She'd been driving in the opposite direction along the wide road that eventually leads to where the teens are being kept. She had decided to go for a spin around town before going home, thinking of the way that boy had declined her, when in the corner of her wine-blurred eye she saw her mobile phone slide off the dashboard onto the passenger seat floor. Without giving the road a second thought, she reached for it, leaning her foot firmer on the accelerator, feeling around with her hand for the important device it seemed she needed so badly at that moment. The car went without guidance straight into the oncoming car, the sound was horrific to say the absolute least. They danced around each other, tires screeching on the tar, Georgina's small vehicle rolled over several times before coming to a loud heaping stop into a thick eucalyptus tree on somebody's nature strip.

The car that Wyatt had been transported in when he was taken, kept going down the road until it rolled once and slid down into a ditch a little way up, where the road turned to a Y intersection.

Residents of the nearby houses rushed out in their warm night clothes to see the wreck. Before too long the disturbing scene was coated in the flashing red and blue lights of the emergency services.

Thelma had to take a detour, a crash or something blocked

up ahead. Now she's pissed off, not giving a flying rat's arse that people had possibly died, only angry at having to take a detour.

She eventually arrived at her destination, the car came to a stop. From inside the boot, that was all Ethan had gathered. He felt relieved because the whole drive had him feeling motion sick and the smells didn't help.

He could hear her the open door and felt the car's suspension bounce up as she got out. The door slammed shut, she never bothered to lock it. Her hurried footsteps crunched gravel as she stomped away from the car.

He listened out carefully just in case it wasn't safe to show himself. All he could really hear, it sounded like wind blowing and the distant waves of water crashing, like at the beach. He slowly pushed open the seat hatch and angled his body so that he could peer out. It was pretty dark, but he could see better than in the boot. He climbed out and pushed it shut again. After looking around outside, he decided it was time to finally get out of the stupid car.

Once out, he looked around again and hid behind a bush in the front yard of the driveway she'd parked in. He concentrated on the house, seeing if he could spot something through a window; that's when he felt a small, firm hand on his shoulder. He whirled around ready to attack, but laid his eyes on a girl of maybe ten years old. Behind her, a great looking dog.

"Have you come to help?" She asked in a calm voice.

He didn't know what to say. "Help with what?" He asked, trying not to be too loud.

"To get my friends out." She stated. The dog whined behind her.

"I don't know what you're talking about." He began to feel so wary.

"Bad things have happened, and I want to fix it. We can tell you're not bad, and it'd be swell if you were here to help." In the moonlight he could see that she was smiling now.

He stared back with the unknowing of what she meant, the cold air was freezing his fingers and toes.

"Ryan is in there, in danger." She said gravely. "Come with me and we can save him, save them." She began to walk towards the backyard of the house with the dog beside her, Ethan thought quickly for a moment and instinctively ran after them. If she was telling the truth, he was wasting time about whether or not to follow her.

"How do you know my brother?" He whispered shakily.

"He is one of them."

"Uh... Who is *them*?"

"He's one of the people they wanted." She spoke calmly still, releasing the driveway gate and letting it come to a rest on the rear of a van parked in the yard. Her hands didn't seem to touch the steel, yet it did exactly as she wanted. The small clinking sound made him shudder.

"Shouldn't we close the gate?" He asked worried.

"No." She simply kept on walking without looking back.

~ 8 ~

Now, a stumbling crash outside the door, it sounded like it was coming from the end of the long hall.

"What the hell was that?!" Ricky exclaimed.

They each stood up all at the same time, ready to be attacked but not ready for what actually happened. It sounded like a bad struggle out there, sounding to Ryan like the violent sport of wrestling that was sometimes watched on the television by his older brother. Misunderstood grunting of words, bodies stumbling and feet scuffling filled their ears.

In the dark they couldn't see but they each had the same

expression of perplexed wonder on their faces.

"You guys ready?" Rose asked the group gravely.

"Yeah I'm ready." Ricky said seriously.

"I think so." Candice replied in worry.

"I am." Ryan declared coarsely.

"Yeah, I am too." Wyatt said bravely.

"I'm not." Jack confessed truthfully, his hands shaking.

Wyatt placed a comforting hand on his scared friend's back. "Hey, we'll be fine."

Jack smiled, trying to settle his nerves with a deep breath.

Before they knew it the door's lock broke as it swung open with huge force, hitting the wall behind it with a smash, the room opened itself up to the light brightness of the hall.

They all went to attack with eyes still adjusting to the new light, every nerve and fibre ready to fight for their lives, hearts raging together when Rose yelled. "STOP! Stop!" Almost tripping on each other they all realised that it was Al and another young guy fighting.

Ryan instantly recognised his brother, Ethan was here and fighting with one of the captors. Almost immediately he jumped on Al, who had stood up temporarily leaving Ethan on the ground. Ryan had his arms around Al's neck and was yelling for help while he was being shaken off. Ethan got to his feet like a true athlete and punched the man in the lower stomach, he crumbled as Ryan got his own feet back on the floor.

Ricky appeared like a prayer's answer, hitting the man over the head with a piece of the trusty table, a loud smack as it collided. Al completed his fall to the ground with a dizzy swirl, finally hitting the surface of the rug with a grunt. The baddy now lay there silent and still.

"Whoa." Said Jack, who had instinctively stood in front of Wyatt and the girls while the situation escalated.

"You're not wrong." Ricky said panting.

Ethan yanked his phone from his pocket. "Of course, there's no reception."

"Ethan what are you doing here?" Ryan asked amazed.

"This weird girl got me to come in and get you guys." He said looking around at them all.

"Violet?" Rose enquired with interested.

"I have no idea. Hey Ryan, it's all worse than what you could imagine. Aunt Thelma is-"

"Completely innocent." A shrewd voice interrupted from the end of the hall.

The scared teens all looked to see who had joined them now.

"Shit." Ricky said astounded. "It's Ronald McDonald in the flesh!"

The dark light she was surrounded by had really given her a frightening appearance. She looked just like an escaped mental patient. Her maroon perm uneven and messy, her makeup smudged, giving her a worse look than Ronald McDonald could ever have. She even only had one shoe on.

"What are you doing here?!" Ryan said fearlessly.

"Shut up you little shit!" She snapped angrily.

"She's behind it bro. She took you guys." Ethan explained, not taking his eyes off the monster.

"I should have known." He said shaking his head.

"You two know her?" Rose began. "She's one of their drinking buddies."

"The kidnapper's friend." Jack clarified to them.

"Just stop talking!" She yelled in high pitch fury. "Daryl! Get down here now!! And bring the others!"

The group moved in close and held onto some part of one another, as if to boost their courage.

"Where's the girl?" Rose whispered.

"She was up there with a dog, last time I saw them they were a distraction to give me a chance to come get you guys." Ethan answered sounding upset.

They could see Thelma at the bottom of the steep little stairs, she kept looking up at the trapdoor and back, making sure they weren't trying to escape. Daz began to creep down the stairs with two other men, they were tall, looming behind him.
Thelma mumbled something to them before they began walking towards the group.

"Shut the door!" Rose yelled as she ran over to slam it, they saw the three thugs running up the hall. Behind her Ryan and Ethan ran to hold their weight against it, joined by Ricky, Wyatt and Jack who all had to step over Al's lump of a body on the ground.
Candice stood back panicking, watching the light around the door swell up and down as the wood pushed against the others trying to keep it shut.

"They're too strong!" Wyatt yelled.

"I don't know what else to do!" Rose yelled back.

"I don't know about you guys.... But I really don't want to get to know 'em." Ricky said with his hands against the door.

Ethan spoke up. "You all stand.... Back slowly and go back there... then I'll release the door and we'll... Get 'em."

"You sure?!" Ryan asked concerned.

"There's not much else we can do." He replied in a grunt.

"Let's do it!" Ricky exclaimed.
As they left the door one by one to join Candice standing on the mattress, the door threw more light as it became easier for the angry mad men trying to enter.

"Okay, ready?!" Ethan yelled.
They replied with a synchronised 'Yes.'

What happened next couldn't have lasted more than a few,

horrendous minutes.

Ethan ran over to his comrades, the door swinging viciously open behind him. Without hesitation the low lives advanced the group, who retaliated after the terrified screams of Candice.

Ryan got pushed by someone in the struggle and fell to the floor near Al, not moving.

One of the men grabbed a firm hold of Ricky, soon having Ethan grab him from behind kicking while Ricky struggled and scratched at the grotesque arms that had him. He could see the other man holding Candice with an arm around her neck to strangle her, she as wriggled around failing to get free.

The others were occupied on the other side of the room by Daz, who tried to stab them with that same hunting knife. Ricky shook his glasses from his face, trying to bite the man, who swore viciously as he tried to kick Ethan.

"CANDICE!" Ricky called struggling, trying to get someone to do something.

Rose looked, she'd noticed Candice but wasn't sure how to get over to the man when this crazy son of a bitch was lunging at them with his big knife.

Jack stood beside her and Wyatt who held each other. He looked past Daz and saw in the bad lighting that two great big ugly hands were now around Candice's neck, slowly squeezing like the owner was enjoying the feel of her young life leaving her.

He looked over at Wyatt, hysterical at the sight of his big sister dying, not being able to do anything. In a fleeting moment, with his breathing slowing down, Jack watched the tears forming in Wyatt's shiny, innocent eyes as he and Rose held each other. His heart broke with such an agonising shatter that he began to form his own drops of swirling tears.

With all his hidden bravery coming to stand by his side, he stood up tall and powerful.

Watery eyes confronted the person he hated and feared most in the world.

"Hey, arsehole! Why don't you come here and give me a *kiss*?!"

All attention turned to him, with a piece of the very table that Al provided to the kiddy room, he swung with great force and had it land at the back of Daz's hard neck. He fell to one knee yelling in pain and anger. "You STUPID little faggot!" He tried to swipe him with a knife but Jack was too fast and bounced back, probably feeling like a ninja.   With his fury so concentrated on Jack, Rose was able to take the chance and let go of Wyatt. She went up to Daz, who stood once more, looming over Jack. She pulled her leg back and thrusted it so hard between the chunky legs of the evil man that her shin hurt afterwards. With his body in crippling agony, Daz lay on the ground trying to swipe around at the twins with only his knife to defend him.

"Do it Jack!" Rose yelled exasperated.

Jack slammed the wooden splinter onto the side of Daz's head without the slightest shred of remorse. It was in that moment that all the rage of his repressed soul had come out to drive his adrenaline.

His drinking mum, his dead dad.

His sister being a part of constant, horrible things.

Bullied for his suppressed sexuality.

The sight of that wonderful boy distressed.

It all flooded through him and out into the blood splatter across that ugly paisley rug.

He might have hit again if it weren't for the look of the blood everywhere, if he kept going he would most likely vomit his insides out.

While the twins were giving Daz what he surely deserved,

Wyatt had run to help his sister the moment Rose let go of him.

The man was kneeling on the side of the mattress with Candice's struggling slowly ceasing, her legs beneath her backside. Wyatt saw nothing but the desire to stop those hands. He came up behind the man, scratching at his eyes, he didn't even care about the feel of wetness, whether it be tears from irritated eyes or the blood from furious scratches. The thug let go of Candice and began to attack the boy behind him. That's when Ryan got to his feet, stumbling with his whirling, dazed mind to help his friend. He had one of the table legs in his hand and used it to smash the red face of the crazy killer. It seemed his nose was split, blood gushed out in horrible clumps. Ryan gave him another merciless whack to the head, this time the man fell to the ground without another move. Ryan looked down at what he'd done, dropping the wood in his internal horror.

Wyatt sat with Candice trying to get her up while Ryan ran over to help Ethan get the man off Ricky.

"Let go!" He yelled as he clung to one of the trapping arms. The three of them struggled until Rose came over with one of the splintered table pieces, jamming it into the side of the creep with squishy force before pulling it back out. She will probably never forget the feel of that splintered thing entering the flesh of the man.

Blood flowed out as he let go of Ricky to hold the hole that now gaped on him, staggering backwards against the wall, slowly sliding down, staring with widened eyes at the fifteen year old girl that had just stabbed him to death.

Ethan looked out the doorway to see an empty hall. "Stay here." He said to Ryan before he left them. Ryan watched him go up the hall and cautiously leave through the trapdoor. He turned around to see a heart-breaking thing.

Sitting on a mattress surrounded by the bloody bodies of

people they'd probably just killed, was Rose who had Jack's arm, he had his other one around Wyatt who had both hands holding Candice's limp arm, then there's Ricky who held her head in a panicking and devastated embrace, sobbing hysterically.

It stunned Ryan, after everything he'd been through in his whole little life, this was the worst part to witness.

"What do we do? I don't know what to *do*!" Ricky screamed barely, sounding like he was speaking English. His face was drenched with the saltiness of flowing sadness.

Ethan came back in behind Ryan who understandably jumped from fright at having someone behind him. "She's not out there, and neither is that girl or dog." He reported.

"We've got to call an ambulance." Wyatt said crying.

Ethan stared, almost as stunned as Ryan was before.

"We'll go upstairs and call them, uh, Rose what's the address?" Ryan said trying to sound composed.

She looked up at them, looking like the very act was strenuous on her neck. "It's... 42 High North Road." She spoke with the saddened memory that this was her home.

The two brothers turned and went upstairs with hurried footsteps.

Candice's dry and exhausted brain could only comprehend the touch of Ricky's hands lovingly holding the head it lived in.

His teardrops fell onto her lifeless face with heavy wetness.

There was no reaction from her whatsoever.

TWO

Finding The Sunrise

~ Eight ~

WASTED AND WOUNDED

~ 1 ~

Alone.

Completely alone is how Ricky Benson felt. He knew for sure that he wasn't physically alone, he had friends and family that loved him to the moon and back; but now without Candice everything was useless, pointless. He had only been close to her for a couple of days, but it had felt longer than that, kind of like they'd been together for all those years that he wished she was his. Then she *was* his and he was hers, they still belonged to each other, he thought maybe forever.

He didn't know what being in love was, he knew how it felt to love his parents, he knew what it felt like to love his friends, he also knew what it felt like to love his favourite food or songs. But he just felt like he was *in love* with Candice, and he wanted to tell her. He wanted to tell her that he longed for her like an instrument of music longs to be played, and that he needed her like trees need the sun and rain.

If he had to describe exactly how he knew he was in love to his friends, he supposed he wouldn't exactly know how to describe it other than that.

He lay on his bed, no vinyl turned to play its hearty sound, there was nothing but the sounds of life going by outside his window, and his mum clanking things in the kitchen.

It was a beautifully sunny day, so beautiful that it hurt him on the inside.

His glasses sat on the turntable, only a little scratched up from being thrown to the ground only a few nights before.

A soft knock sounded on his door. He didn't want to have company but decided he might as well go ahead. Who knows, maybe he'll end up wanting it.

"Come in." He called out.

The door carefully opened with a small creak that didn't faze him because he was so used to it. In came Jack with a warm cup of hot chocolate.

After the events of Tuesday night, the twins were left with nowhere to go and their mum in hospital. Feeling a mix of pity and gratitude for them, Sally and Noah Benson kindly offered to take them in until things could settle down for them.

"I thought you might want this, it's about the only thing I can make in the kitchen. Other than maybe cereal but I could probably set that on fire." Jack said standing by the bed. "Ya mum said you like 'em."

Ricky sat up and took the mug of warmth. "Thanks mate."

"Never seen a record player before yours." Jack said trying to get a positive reaction from him who just sat there, expressionlessly holding the mug.

Jack sat down beside him. "You okay?"

"Seriously, do I look okay?" He answered hastily.

Jack looked down at the floor.

"Of course I'm a lot more okay than Candice." Ricky said lowly.

"I'll be back." Jack said leaving for the door.

But is it love or just an obsession? Maybe he was so used to the idea of her that he only believed it was love but didn't actually feel it. Aren't you supposed to 'just know'?
There's just so many questions with no way to get a sure answer. His thoughts plagued him relentlessly.

Jack entered the lounge room after searching around for the phone book which he now scanned through, holding the landline phone in his hand. It was odd using a landline, it wasn't something you'd find in his other house.
Rose continued to nap on the couch while Mrs Benson cooked up a storm in the kitchen.

~ 2 ~

Wyatt lay on Candice's bedroom floor, his mind playing on repeat what had happened that night. The whole thing was like a nightmare, absolutely horrendous and almost like it had never happened because of how unbelievable it all was. The television and radio reporters kept the ordeal alive for everyone with their frequent news stories and updates. Kidnappings of this manner are fortunately not something you hear of on Australian soil, especially that of small Tasmanian towns. So a much more adaptable youth might turn the tables on their experience and be glad to be safe, taking a proud change in being a celebrity of sorts for as long as the novelty lasted.
Wyatt is no such youth though.

He tried to stare at his sister's belongings to drive away the bad thoughts, it was worse when he closed his eyes. His mind flared alive with things he didn't want to see and things he didn't want to know. After being taken to the hospital that night, he'd been poked and prodded by nurses and asked questions that strained his very ability to comprehend anything he was experiencing. His mother gripped to him against the professionals advice.

Where is she now? When he wanted someone the most.

His father appeared at the door, stating there's a phone call for him.

Wyatt sat up. "Is it a nice one?"

Since the group was found his dad has barely let him out of his sight, even allowing his disturbed boy sleep in the bed with him. If it wasn't a phone call Donald Fineman didn't trust, he wouldn't have said anything to his son, he would have called the police out of paranoia. "Yeah son, it's a nice one." He said with strange softness.

Wyatt stood up and left the room, almost reluctantly. He made his way downstairs to the very phone his mother spoke to Daz on that horrid day. He held it up to his ear and said hello.

"This is Wyatt, yeah?" The voice asked.

"Jack?"

"Sure is dude."

Wyatt sighed, scratching his head. "It feels like I haven't seen you guys since... forever."

"Yeah well I reckon we gotta change that."

"What do you mean?" He would really love to see an angel right about now.

"Ricky is kinda, well... depressed, and there's only one thing I can think of to change that, maybe, depending on what happens..."

"Uh... What are you planning?"

"He seriously needs a visit to you-know-where."

Wyatt closed his eyes then opened them just as fast. There are too many monsters lurking under the darkness of his lids. "Jack, my mother hates him now more than ever."

"Well I don't mean to be rude, but she has to wake up and grow up."

"Well... I could go through my dad. He isn't so... He's different to my mum."

"Atta boy! You can do this man, I'll be grateful forever."

Wyatt felt himself blushing and tried to push the fact aside. "You know I'm doing it for Ricky."

Jack stayed quiet for moment before answering. *"Yeah, I know."*

"Anyway, tell everyone I said hello for me."

"I will. And don't you forget to talk to ya dad." Jack hung up, leaving him with the dial tone.

He hung the phone back up on its seat and stood in the hall thinking in the quiet.

What to say?...

He eventually made his way into the lounge room where his dad had seated himself in one of the recliners with his feet up.

"Have a nice talk?" He asked his son.

"Yeah, it was okay." He sat down on the other recliner.

"That's good." He sounded awkward.

"Hey dad... I have a request."

"What kind of request son?" He asked worried.

"Well, it's Ricky. He deserves to see where Candice is." He felt the lump of sadness in his throat.

Donald looked at his son with regretful eyes. "Wyatt, you know how it is. Your mother wants nothing to-"

"I DON'T CARE!" He stood up from his chair. "I don't *care* what mum wants! Right now, she should be happy we're even alive! Ricky was.... *Is* her boyfriend! Or whatever, I don't even know! Sorry for yelling at you daddy but right now I don't give a *shit* what mum likes and doesn't likes. She has to wake up... And GROW up!" He stood panting in front of his stunned father.

"Okay Wyatt. I see." He said merely looking at him. "You know what? You're exactly right son, I agree with you." He stood up and firmly hugged his not so little boy. "I'll see what I can do. Might be able to arrange a visit for this afternoon, how's that?"

"Yes please, thank you." Wyatt replied, returning his politeness.

His dad left him standing there in the lounge, the wooden clock ticked it's never ending rhythm. He decided he'd better ring back to tell Jack what happened.

Back in the hall with the phone he dialled the Benson's home number and waited.

"Hello?"

"Hi Sally, it's Wyatt."

"Oh hello darling, how are you?"

"I'm okay, could be better."

"I'm thinking of you okay, and you're welcome here any time."

"I haven't forgotten, thank you very much."

"Want me to get Ricky?"

"Uhm, not this time. I'm actually after Jack."

"Ohh, well I'll just get him, silly little bugger could be anywhere." She laughed.

Wyatt heard her call Jack's name, he felt excited at the thought of him walking to the phone.

"Yello?" His humble voice sounded.

"Jack, it's Wyatt."

"Pfft I know, Sally just told me."

"Oh, well I spoke to my dad. I think he's going to make it happen and have a visit later today."

"Aw you little beauty! I knew it'd be easy."

"Yeah well I'm unsure of things sometimes."

"I'm sure that I can't wait to give you a hug for doing this."

Hearing that made him feel sick in the stomach, not the bad sick but the strangely nice one. He stood holding the phone not saying anything.

"You okay?" Jack ended up saying.

"Yeah, I'm fine. I have to go-"

"Tinkle?"

A brief smile found itself across Wyatt's face. "Maybe."

Now Jack was quiet for a few seconds. *"Well, enjoy yourself."*

"I will do. Goodbye Jack."

"See-ya, quiet little Wyatt."

More dial tone beeps.

He hung the phone on its spot again.

What is it with him?... He wondered as he left for his own bedroom. He had to find something to wear for later. He amazed himself that he even cared about his clothes right now, it's just who he is though. Besides it would be totally distasteful to turn up underdressed at such an occasion as this.

Since being free and alive, so far one of the best things has been showers. Hot, cleaning showers. After those days underground a simple shower was absolute bliss. He'd been incessantly washing his hands too. Finding it hard to let go of that feeling, the man's face shredding under his nails. It haunted him almost hourly.

On his way up the stairs he realised that he'll have to call back to give the details of when they'll be leaving.

He grinned the rest of the way to his room.

~ 3 ~

If you asked Ryan Jonson how he felt on this sunny Friday morning, he might of told you kindly to piss off.

He was mentally troubled with himself from the moment he brutally took the life of that man in that nasty little room. It wasn't like he thought the psychopath didn't deserve it but even that worried him. Not only was the sight and experience of the events on Tuesday night horrific but the killing of those people scared him, and it hadn't hit him properly until Wednesday night when he was by himself for the first time.

With the Aunty he hates now on the run from the law

-probably shacked up in a bogan house somewhere or a motel he thought- he did feel a lot more free, like there were no barriers of cruelness keeping him from staying downstairs. He and Ethan were sort of getting along better ever since. Ethan even hugged Ryan and said the 'L' word to him when they were at the hospital. Ryan returned the favour and hugged his brother tight, he had no idea what could have come of himself and his friends if Ethan hadn't of showed up that night, it was like a real life miracle. Except for what happened to Candice, which had everybody uptight and upset.

Especially Ethan, although he hadn't let on until now.

Ryan lay on his bed staring up at the ceiling of his bedroom. So many days and nights he wished he could walk away and never see it again, he lay there now, grateful at the sight of the off white paint that covered it. There was a soft knock, similar to what Ricky recently had on his own door.

"Yeah?!" He said aloud and uninterested.

"It's just me." His brother said from the other side of the door.

"Just come in!" Ryan called.

Ethan walked in to sit on the bed awkward and sullen. "Watcha doin' in here?" He asked quietly.

Ryan watched as he approached before resuming his staring competition with the roof. "Not a lot." He answered.

"Oh okay."

They were quiet for a long minute while Ethan looked around the room. "Can I ask you something?"

Only briefly looking at him he replied "Ah yeah, sure."

"Okay, um.... Do you think that I could have saved that Candice girl if I had paid attention and realised what was happening?"

Ryan instantly sat up. "No, it's not your fault okay. Don't even go there."

"It's just that I was the only one able to get to her for ages."

He looked away making it so his face was out of sight. Ryan assumed he was going to cry and he really didn't want that, nobody wants to see their tough, big brother cry.

"Trust me it's nobody's fault but that Thelma freak's."
Ethan turned back around nodding, looking at the carpet of Ryan's room.

"At least you weren't passed out on the floor. I can still feel the spot on my head." Ryan said rubbing the side of his head with a painful face.

"Yeah, I just can't believe what happened. It's all so..." He threw his arms up in the air and gave up trying to think of a suitable description.

"Besides, we can't change what happened now and we're not professional fighters, it's not our fault." Ryan said trying to sound wise.

"That's what mum's been saying."
"Yeah I've been telling myself that since she said it."
They were finishing up their small, boyish heart to heart when they heard the voice of their mother calling them both from downstairs. Together they went to investigate the calling of their names.
They were in fact being summoned to be told about a phone call from 'the Jack boy'.

~ 4 ~

Now that he'd managed to let Ricky be able to see Candice, Jack excitedly made his way to Ricky's bedroom ready to tell him the news.

Jack seemed overall more joyous than the others. It could merely be because he and Rose were finally away from Daz, now around people that were just so damn nice, something totally refreshing and totally new to the twins. Their mother's in the hospital recovering but as soon as she was able there was no doubt she'd go to prison for accessory to kidnappings, possible child abuse, attempted murder and to polish it all off, possession of stolen goods and narcotics. Jack and Rose were definitely upset about it but they discussed with each other that at least she might be able to get back on the straight and narrow path of life if she's in there. Jack just had to remind Rose that it is prison and their mother they were discussing, after that they hardly mentioned it again.

What they were more worried about, is what to say to the Benson's. They'd been so kind towards them, now they didn't like the thought of leaving. Even if the house is small with five people in it.

"Ricky?" He said through the bedroom door.
He heard a simple 'yeah' answer him, so in he went with a pep in his step, still careful to respect Ricky's space. He saw him laying on the bed with his body facing the wall, totally non respondent to anything that was happening in the world around him, other than Jack's recurring presence. "If it's more drinks, I'm gonna have to say no this time. Soz man." He didn't even lift his head from the pillow.

It upset even Jack to see this guy like this, it was a mood that obviously didn't suit him. "No drinks, just an invitation to join me on a trip today. It won't do you good to say no."

Ricky sat up to politely face him. "I'm really not up for it mate."

With a manly hand on his hip and the other one numbering the things on his list, he recited in a rather adult tone. "Okay Ricky, I have just used your phone, pulled strings that I shouldn't have been able to pull, I've-"

"Jack?" Ricky interrupted hazy and distant.
He looked back at him, worried at what he was going to say.

Maybe he was going to say 'piss off ya queer', maybe he was going to say he means it when he says he's not going, or maybe it'll be telling him to take himself and his sister somewhere else away from his house...

"Have you ever been in love?" Ricky asked, totally unexpected.

Jack thought for a moment, he had never been as far as he knew. He's fifteen, although he does have a bad love and lust relationship with marijuana and lollies. Maybe Chelsea, but most likely not. "Is this about Candice?" He asked as he sat down beside him.

"Well yeah. You didn't answer my question though." He said stoically.

Jack scratched his head and finally answered "No."

Ricky nodded and looked to the ground in front of the neglected turntable stand.

Jack wondered if he was at all thinking about anything else since he banished himself in here. He wanted to ask if he thinks about those thugs and how violent it was... All that blood everywhere. "Well if you love her, you better come with me today. And if you don't, that'll just make you a prick wanker."

Ricky looked at him with wide glassy eyes, the watery coat of premature tears made the green seem to go on endlessly into the back of his head. "What do you mean?"

"I mean I got Wyatt to convince his dad to convince his mum to let you go."

Without another word said between either of them, Ricky grabbed hold of Jack in a brotherly, hugging grip. "Thank you, thank you man. What the *hell*, I don't even know what to say!"

The stunned Jack hugged him back, worried that it was too much of a 'boy on boy' moment. Jack didn't care about touching him, he was glad Ricky was so grateful... but it's *other people* that have made him worry about going near other males. "Nah mate it's all good. That's what buddies are for."

Ricky stared at him for a small moment, making his friend a little uneasy. "You and Rose seem really familiar, you know."

"We actually thought the same thing about you and Ryan. Wyatt told me that you guys went to Pier Ripple, so I thought maybe we saw each other a couple of times or something."

"Yeah, maybe." He answered.

~ 5 ~

Trying to look their most presentable while they were standing in a row outside the Benson home, Ricky and the twins watched as the big, fancy seven seater car Donald Fineman had bought a year ago turned into the street, pulling up out front. The three of them approached the car working out the spots they'd be sitting in.

Wyatt remained sensibly in the front passenger seat and Ryan in one of the extra seats at the back on the driver's side. Ricky got in first, followed by Rose who sat in the middle with Jack on the other side of her.

"Mr Fineman, I just want to thank you for taking us. I um... Really appreciate it." Ricky said nervously.

"No, no it's okay." He turned the ignition. "Let's go shall we boys? And girl." He said trying to sound joyful.

After the first greeting and expressions of 'it feels like forever since I saw you', most of the drive everyone stayed quiet, looking at the scenery outside the windows. A lot of long distance country driving around here is quite satisfying to bored passengers and excited tourists alike.

After about half of the forty five minute drive there, the tension inside the encaging box of the car was beginning to be too much for Jack. Every time he looked around at everyone, they were looking out a window or something, even Rose was fixated on the windscreen.

He looked ahead through the gap of the front seat and the side of the car to look at the little mirror outside. He could see Wyatt looking off into nowhere like the others, except he was mouthing the words to something, but there wasn't anything playing on the stereo (which made the trip worse by the way). Jack continued to watch as the sun flashed its warm yellow over Wyatt's serene face, the shadows of trees passed over him when they blocked the sun's effect.

He was feeling more and more fascinated with him each time they interacted. To put it simply, would be to describe it as Jack has always tried to hide his queer side, with Wyatt he didn't care if he knew, in fact he might even be comfortable. Which is why he had been 'accidentally' letting that side of himself creep out lately. Same goes for all these friends really. Maybe Noah and Sally too. He still won't let it on though.

He'd already admitted to himself that he has an obvious thing for Wyatt, but there's bad factors like the circumstances of how they met, the fact that everyone is traumatised by what happened and the worst part; he didn't know what was happening in Wyatt's head. So he tried to bury it down and stomp the very feeling into nothing beneath layers and layers of all other emotions and thoughts. But damnit, that one memory in the dark of the dodgy room, it wasn't much but it was the sweetest way of being touched that he knew. And he wanted it to happen again.

He nudged Rose in the arm to get her attention, which he got. She looked at him and asked 'what' with her furrowed brows. He reached his hand out past her and over to the surface of Wyatt's unsuspecting, perfect-looking hair to gently pull on a strand, pulling his hand back fast. Wyatt's own hand quickly felt the top of his head and flattened the hair back down with poise, going on as normal, waiting for the destination. Jack repeated what he'd done before, not without Rose trying to get him to stop it but failing. This time he pulled harder, Wyatt turned around to see what the story was and only saw Rose sitting there looking at him, Ricky and Jack were looking out their windows.

"Is someone touching my hair?" He asked innocently.

Rose shook her head and Ricky turned to look, as did Jack.

"What are you on about?" Ricky asked confused.

"Someone is touching my hair, I swear." He answered full of mistrust.

"Must be a ghost." Jack suggested, grinning.

Wyatt playfully squinted his eyes at the sight. "It was *you* wasn't it?"

"No... But I can if you want." He replied still smiling.
Ricky and Rose looked over at Jack and then back at Wyatt, totally intrigued.

"I don't like my hair being played with and pulled." He declared sternly.

Jack sat back in the seat and replied comfortably. "I can respect that."

Wyatt stared back and said nothing, looked at his dad beside him, then sat in his seat properly once more. The silence joined them again, the wind rushed outside as they bobbed up and down with the bouncy movements of the car.

Ryan sat in the back behind Ricky with his mouth slightly ajar in reaction to the small conversation of hair pulling.

After more lengthy minutes of silent window watching, the scenery slowly turned from grassy green to concrete grey, they had finally reached the city.

"I haven't been here for ages." Jack said looking around.

"Yeah I know, it's nice to see it again." Rose said. "We've been stuck in that town for so long I almost forgot that other places existed."

"I feel like that too." Ryan concurred, feeling glad to be gone from there.

They were passing many old style houses and tall buildings, several small businesses were crammed in between the historical structures looking like gems stuck between rocks.

"Okay kids, when we get there I expect everyone to be on their absolute best behaviour." Mr Fineman said as he drove through a sea of vehicles, a lot of these streets are one way, sometimes making it a confusing pain in the arse.

"Yes dad, of course." Wyatt said politely.

"We will be Mr Fineman." Ricky confirmed obediently.

The others nodded in agreement.

They wound up at the bottom of a steep hill. The car smoothly took the weight of its passengers up the tar hill and successfully made it to the top without a fuss, then it was a right and a little way up the road they could see the hospital.

The vastness of the hospital's car park made it so they so they had to go on a tiny hike to get to the front of the huge building. After they entered the doors, they walked sensibly behind Mr Fineman, looking around fascinated as they passed random art on the hall walls. Ryan thought they were beautifully abstract, he also wondered what it took to get your painting on a hospital wall.

They followed Donald into an elevator and watched as he pressed one of the buttons to go up. They had the carriage to themselves much to their relief. Although it was rather spacious, being cramped with strangers in a hospital is a jarring ordeal.

Jack pretended to nearly fall over when the elevator moved, making the others giggle a little. Mr Fineman turned to see everybody standing still and quiet.

It came to a stop, they exited between the thick, silver

doors. Up they walked through a corridor, turning into a wider and busier one. Nurses and patients walked around looking like they'd been here forever, knowing every pattern on the floor and grain in the walls.

Mr Fineman walked up to a reception type desk and explained he was here to visit his daughter with some friends of hers. This made each teen feel nice and fuzzy on the inside, looking around at each other. *They are friends.*

The lady gave him the okay to go ahead and see her. They followed him down another little hall, stopping outside room number 208.

"Alright, here we are. Ready?" He asked looking at the group. They all nodded enthusiastically.

Ricky was nearly overcome with the suspense of the door opening, he wondered what she looked like, he wouldn't care how she actually looked he just wanted her to be okay.

Mr Fineman casually knocked and opened the door. They walked in to find Mrs Fineman sitting by the bed, taking in a long look at everyone before getting up and leaving. Candice remained on the bed with her legs crossed under the blankets, a gleeful grin on her tired face. A few girly magazines scattered on the bed in front of her.

First she got a hug from her dad, who kissed her on the forehead with a 'Hello sweetheart'.

Wyatt went over for a big hug, he was the only one of the group that had seen her since that dark and dreary night under the house. She hugged back with a pat on the back. "We brought the others with us this time." He said happily.

"I was strangled, not stabbed in the eyes you dork." She joked with a slight hoarseness clinging to every word. Wyatt giggled despite hating the subject, standing back to let the others get to her. Rose went over with Ryan behind her. Jack was stood shy in the doorway.

"I'm so glad you're okay Candice. They're gone and can't hurt anyone ever again." Rose said triumphantly. Candice reached over and hugged her as a response.

"Oh man, it's so good to see you looking okay!" Ryan exclaimed from behind Rose.

Candice let go of Rose and told Ryan to come over for his turn. He went and hugged her immediately with no sign of awkwardness. He now stood back out of the way so that Ricky could finally get to her.

Ricky looked at her as she held her arms out, inviting him with all the grace and beauty that he'd been thinking about for days. He rushed over and tried to gently hug her, he was worried she'd crush under the slightest touch. Candice on the other hand didn't hold back, she squeezed his ribs with firm affection, even kissing his cheek three times.

Ricky began to tear up, he tried to hold them back but they flowed out without the slightest care of his worries about crying in front of everyone.

"What's the matter?" She asked still holding him.

"I... Don't really know." He answered shyly.

She giggled internally, making them both jiggle for a couple of seconds. "How do you not know?? You're so weird sometimes, you know that?" She said remembering back to when he had said that to her during the night they first bonded.

He stood back a little so that he could look at her, she smiled with pride at reciting the line.

"Stop crying you doofus, you'll give me the impression that you're upset to see me." She joked awkwardly, still with that dialled down hoarseness in her voice.

"Really? Don't even *joke* about it Fineman." He said with mock authority, his eyes still drenched.

The others stood back against the wall watching. Wyatt with mixed feelings. Even though he'd known that they'd gotten close, it was strange for him to actually see them being affectionate and saying lovey dovey things to each other. He thought to himself that he'd better hurry up and get used to it.

Ryan and Rose tried to look elsewhere out of respect for their privacy.

Jack and Mr Fineman both looking on with smiles at the wholesome sight.

Ricky sat down in front of her on the bed dodging the magazines. "Hey um... Candice?" His voice sounding nervous.

"Yeah?" She turned to face him again, he looked at her with a serious expression.

"With what happened and stuff, I mean I know I shouldn't even be asking but I've barely slept and I can't help but think of stuff, I guess sometimes I just think too much and probably-"

"Holy shit! Just spit it out you dork." She jeered encouragingly.

"But are we like, you know, *together*?" He said the last word with a breath of relief following its wake.

She looked down at the floor, raising his doubts for moment. "Do you *want* to be together?" She asked comfortably.

He briefly looked at her dad and back to her again.

You only live once...

"That turntable in my room, I have never worked so hard for anything in my entire life."

"Yeah I remember your little story." She assured.

"Well, I'm saying with absolute honesty that I would throw it into a pit of lava if it meant that I could say we're together."

She really didn't know what to respond. What *do* you say when someone says something like that? "You really are amazing, I actually don't know what to say." She finally croaked out. Maybe honesty was the way to go.

"Well thanks, but you're the amazing one." He claimed like a modern Romeo.

She decided it was time to take some initiative with this brilliant person before her. "Richard 'total nerd' Benson, will you be my boyfriend?"

He grinned. "Actually I've been talking to this girl online from the Philippines..."

She laughed, reaching out to give him a playfully gentle punch in the shoulder.

"Yes Candie, I will be your boyfriend." He said in a pleasantly calm voice.

As they warmly embraced each other, Rose started clapping excitedly at their pairing, starting a rampage of colliding hands from around the room. Even Wyatt joined in a little.

Candice looked over at Jack. "You think I have girl germs or something?"

Jack laughed. "Well yeah but I was just givin' you some space."

"Space? Get over here you hero, you." She demanded nicely.

Jack walked over wondering what she could mean by 'hero'. It made no sense, maybe she was talking shit because of delirium or something. As he bent down to give her a hug, she quickly whispered in his ear. "*My brother told me everything you did that night, he thinks you're wonderful.*" It sounded like there was a lot of effort in the simple act of her whispering, but just as always, she got her point across.

Jack stood back and thanked her with a small smirk.

"No, *thank you*." She said with a sly look.

"Now what do we do?" Wyatt asked innocently.

"Sing Kumbaya." Ryan said mocking Ricky.

"Ha ha Ryan." Ricky answered.

"I'll leave you guys to it for a while okay. No mischief, I mean it. And Candice, take it easy with the talking." Mr Fineman said as he went out to find his wife.

"Hey Ryan, where's your brother?" Candice asked after her dad left them to their peace.

"He didn't feel up to coming, I tried to get him to but... yeah." He said upset by it.

"I really wanted to ask him what happened to the dog." Candice said looking down at her hands playing with the blanket.

"Yeah, I wanna know what happened in there as well." Rose said thinking about Violet's weird behaviour.

Ryan began to speak again. "He told me that she said she was there to help us, and he would be helpful or something like that. He also said that she knew my name, and called all of us her friends." Originally reluctant to share what his brother had said, now that they're all together, he felt it was okay.

"Her friends?" Ricky asked confused.

"What about the part of her knowing my name?" Ryan said uncomfortably.
They all thought in silence, waiting for something to tick over in their minds, for something to make sense. Which nothing did.

"Wait so, should we just try and talk to her about it?" Jack asked. "She's always given me the creeps to be honest."

"Me too." Wyatt agreed. "Ever since Ricky and I saw her and the dog in the street."

"But Ethan said she was trying to help him." Rose reminded them.

"Yeah so where were they when we got out?" Jack said trying to raise the discussion further into sense.

"Well how do we get a hold of her?" Ricky said looking at Rose.

"I don't know." She replied shaking her head slowly. "She was just always showing up, at the right time I guess."

"Hold on a second." Ryan began. "She's mentioned that she knew bad things have happened and knowing us- "

"She was working for the bad guys." Wyatt said interrupting Ryan's realisation.

"That would explain why she showed up and why she was stalking Wyatt." Ricky said stretching his limbs uncomfortably.

"So... you guys are sayin' that she's some girl with a circus dog, working for Ryan's crazy aunt?" Jack said untrusting the thought.

"Yeah a dog that led a stranger from one house to another across town." Ricky added.

"So she might really have been on their side." Rose said looking to the floor.

"That is insane." Wyatt said expectedly.

"You said it yourself Wyatt." Candice stated.

"Well she did help Ethan get us out, whatever she did in the house paid off." Ryan said hopeful.

"I don't have the brain power for this." Ricky said laying back over the bed.

"Well if anyone sees her, make sure you ask what her problem is and what the hell is going on. And how the dog is." Candice said tired, indulging in a great yawn.
Everyone nodded silently.

"And make sure you tell us what she said and stuff." She continued.

"I'd just like to know where she vanished to." Jack said standing up straighter.

"Me too." Rose agreed.

They now stayed in the little room together discussing the hospital food, and the bad midday television movies they have on all the time that Ricky described as 'Home and Away on steroids'.

After her gracious guests had reluctantly left her alone in her bleak room and her parents traded guardianship duties, Candice lifted the thin blankets off her legs to escape the confines of her temporary accommodation. The whole stay so far, she'd managed to push her curiosities aside and not wander the building to see what happens around her while she sits bored and uncomfortable in bed.

She crept over to the door as though she were being watched, carefully opening it to peer her head out. The attention of her dad seemed temporarily appointed to a phone call he'd accepted when he was still sitting on the chair by the room's single window. He now stood about eight metres away looking out another window past the nurse's station.

Probably going to be talking business for ages... She thought feeling satisfied at maybe having time to herself.

Her body followed the lead of her head as she stepped out into the hall to power walk in the opposite direction of her dad. As her feet hit the plastic feel of the floor she felt glad of the socks she had on, the thought of gross old fluids or anything touching her skin is a vulgar image.

A huge map of the hospital thankfully sat on the wall at the intersection for the stairs and elevators. Her eyes took in the titles and directions as well as her brain could understand over the bird's eye view of the building.

So much stuff... Rooms, nurse station, x-ray... Yada yada blah... Maternity... Where Wy was born, maybe Ricky too...
Her mouth formed a soft smirk of fondness. She shook her head and jiggled her limbs to subtly regain her concentration.

Okay, downstairs... Emergency, nope... Gift shop... Cafeteria, yas queen!... Recreation area, oh my God yes, fresh air...
Deciding that downstairs seemed more the place to explore

she turned for the elevators, where she pressed the button with her sleeve for protection.

What am I thinking?... I can clean my hands easier than my clothes, duh...

She slid her hand out from the sleeve and promptly pressed the button with her finger. Leaving her no time to feel eager for it to happen, the doors opened to expose the carriage inside where a sophisticated looking business lady stood alone. Briefly looking up at her, the stranger's sad, soaking eyes gripped her in a vulnerable gaze before lowering her head, stepping forward to leave the elevator quickly. She disappeared around the left corner into the hall.

Feeling a little discontented by the woman, she stepped into the elevator and pressed the button for the floor she wanted. The door closed and the carriage made its unearthly movements, leaving her with lonely thoughts of what could have possibly made that lady so sad.

It wasn't her concern she tried to tell herself, as she watched the doors open to the world of 'Ground Floor'. Out she stepped trying to ignore the fact she was about to be facing several strangers without wearing a bra.

Oy vey... If I can face Ricky and the others without one on... First world problems, get over it you strangle victim...

Shaking her head in spite of herself, she continued on to the left down the now carpeted hall. Where she was heading directly, she had no clue. Rather she continued to put one foot in front of the other in obedience of her curious wandering.

Several nurses and people with big trolleys of all kinds passed her in the wide halls. The further along she walked, the more curious she got. None of the workers stopped to enquire about her presence, which she was glad about. They'd either smile as they went past or tried not to look at her at all. After observing a small sign on the wall for the recreation area outside, she headed down a quiet hall brightly soaked in natural daylight thanks to the large windows down one side of it. An enormously bountiful tree stood tall and powerful outside. She couldn't resist the temptation of staring at it for a moment in the glory of its eternal standing show. The likes of Miss Rose Brandis would have told her she should have seen it when the sun was directly above the tree, shining through the leaves giving them a truly heavenly effect.

Her eyes looked ahead at the sound of a dainty cough, a young lady waddled along who Candice assumed to be pregnant considering the roundness on the front of her thin frame.

A tall, handsome man in smart enough clothes walked along maybe a metre behind her. The pair of blacked framed glasses tucked onto the front of his collar and his sleek curls of brown hair strangely highlighted with black piqued her curiosity.

The pregnant girl walked by sharing a speechless smile with her.

With his hands in the pockets of his pants, the young man approached her in passing with a big smile in her direction. She crossed her insecure arms over her chest and tried to return it but felt as though her small smirk could never match up to the grin he had.

"Hi." She said trying to be polite as she started to walk on. The girl turned back to look at her and briefly smiled with what seemed to be a look of confusion as she turned back to walk faster around the corner Candice had just come from. She looked warily back to the guy, who still smiled.

"*Ask him why Ashton isn't first.*" She heard him whisper quickly on the way past without even stopping. At least she's sure it was him.

She turned to look at him once he was walking away behind

her. "Excuse me, what was that?" She asked aloud, unable to help the urge to ask.

He didn't turn back, he kept his pace as he disappeared in the same direction as the girl and her unborn baby.

What the hell is... Who the hell is Ashton?...

She gathered all her golden hair in her hands and coerced it to rest over her shoulder in disturbance of the weird incident.

Deciding that the surroundings had closed in on her confidence, she hurried all the way back to her dad. There he was, still in the same spot, finishing up on the phone.

"Hey dad..." She began a little nervously at the ridiculous thing she was about to ask. "Do you know anything about Ashton being first? Or him not being first for something?"

"Candice, no I don't." He put a hand on her shoulder. "Are you okay?" He asked looking at her in concern.

"I'm fine. Just something I heard... On TV." She answered worried he thought she was crazy like her mum.

~ Nine ~

VANILLA AND SPICE

~ 1 ~

By the time they got back to Gerryville from visiting Candice, it was decided that they'd all stay at the Benson's for dinner, minus Mrs Fineman. She'd put her paranoid trust into the Benson's so Wyatt could be with his friends for a while. A miracle in itself.

The whole drive back, their raised spirits had to keep a lid on the giddiness. Ricky orchestrated the dinner plans by messaging Ethan to ask his parent's permission for Ryan to stay there.

Now at the old round dinner table, Ricky seated himself between his dad and Wyatt, who had Jack to his left and Sally sat between him and her husband.

Because of the small table, the lounge coffee table was pulled into the cramped dining area. Ryan and Rose politely volunteered to sit at the small table, so they were now seated at either end of it, crossed legged on bean bags.

Sally felt absolutely thrilled to have the 'kids' over. Seeing her only son still alive and happy again is something she was celebrating with tonight's dinner. She also loved the other boys. With what Wyatt had gone through she was only too ready to accept feeding him a great meal. She'd made a generous amount of creamy potato bake accompanied by a never ending supply of black currant cordial.

"So how's Candice guys, was she happy to see you all?" Sally asked as a great hostess.

"Yes, she loved it." Wyatt answered. "She's actually looking a lot better."

"Oh that's great, isn't it?!" She said looking over at Ricky, who nodded happily.

"It is great, she was a lot chipper than I thought she'd be." He admitted.

"Did she tell ya's the food is shit?" Noah asked before taking a bite of the precious potato.

A giggle ensued from all around when Wyatt. "She actually did. Even told us the broccoli tastes like flatulence."

"Again with the big words Wylie. Next time just say fart." Ricky said grinning to which Wyatt grinned back with a small shake of the head.

"Yeah, she's a real sweetheart. She kinda reminds me of your mum back in the day." Noah informed Ricky.

"Oh really?" He answered intrigued.

"Yep, so if you guys are anything like we were I'd watch it if I were you." His dad said freely in front of everyone, with a wink at him.

"Dad! Can you not!" Ricky said now with cheeks red as a party balloon.

"Oh stop it you!" Sally said to her husband, taking a sip of cordial.

"Yeah Uncle Noah." Ryan began from the floor. "You guys should have seen them the other day-"

"Shut up Ryan." Ricky interrupted quickly.

"Ohhh what happened?!" Jack asked amused.

"Please, I'm trying to eat!" Wyatt exclaimed looking at his plate.

"Hey, it's not my fault they can't be trusted alone." Jack said to Wyatt with a smile.

"That's my sister you're talking about." Wyatt replied with a plain frown.

"Yeah stop it before I come over there and make you. I'm a pugilist." Ricky said from across the table.

"What's a pugilist?" Jack asked interested.

"Wyatt, please explain to this person what a pugilist is." Ricky asked of him, making out Jack is of little intelligence.

"It's someone who fights with their fists, like a boxer." Wyatt said happy to be informing people with information.

"Ohhh I see. Mate, you can try but... You felt the muscles..." Jack said nodding his head with pride. "There's no way you could take me on, sorry to say."

Ricky went to get up and playfully attack Jack, but his mother advised him to finish his dinner before doing anything else, especially attacking guests. "Fine. But you won't be so lucky next time, Hercules." He sat back down looking at him through squinted eyes.

Jack began to laugh so hard that for a second he thought he might pee himself right then and there on the kitchen chair.

"What's so funny?" Wyatt asked his table neighbour. The hysterics had slightly rubbed off on him.

Jack had to try hard not to laugh just to be able to speak. "It's just that... At school, there's this mean guy who gives me a hard time... His name is Harley, and he calls himself Hercules!"
Now everyone began to laugh, including Mr and Mrs Benson who thought it was the most ridiculous thing they'd ever heard.

It was almost as though they had never gone through the violent ordeals of Tuesday night. Friendly warmth around the

202 ~ ASHLEA RAYWOOD

tables tonight, no sign of the black cloud swollen with depression ready to rain down and drown these people. The visit with Candice had done them all the world of good.

"I forgot about that!" Rose said in joyful hysterics.

"What a loser!" Ricky jeered.

"Rose punched him the face the other day! Right in the big nose he's got." Jack said proud to be able to say it.

"Oh good on ya darlin'!" Noah said impressed.

"That's pretty wicked." Ryan said to her from across the little coffee table.

"Thanks everyone." Rose said embarrassed, not knowing what to say. Being praised for violence isn't exactly at the top of her most wanted list.

"Honestly, who calls themselves something like that?" Wyatt said totally puzzled at the concept.

"Do any of you guys have nicknames?" Jack asked curious.

"Yeah." Ricky said seriously. "They call me, *Channing Tatum*."

"Pfffffft!! Good luck with that name mate." Jack replied.

"They call Ryan... 'Gosling'. I am *not* lying." Ricky said trying to be completely serious.

"Oh they do not." Ryan said shaking his head.

"Cause he's Goz gift to women, am I right?" Jack asked jokingly to which everyone laughed.

"Oh my god, that's hilarious!" Rose said completely amused by the nickname statements.

"What about you guys?" Sally asked gesturing to the twins. "Ever get any Titanic jokes?"

"Oh, only literally all the time." Jack answered with Rose nodding her agreement. He turned to Wyatt and spoke in a low tone ideally to be just between them. "What about you, what's yours? *Tinkle-bell* The Fairy?"

This was followed by one loud, synchronised and humour

injected 'Ohhhhhhhhhhhh!'

Wyatt, who was trying to finish his dinner, turned to look at Jack. "That is *still* not funny."

"Like I said already, I never thought it was funny... *Tinkle-bell.*" Jack answered confidently as he merrily resumed his dinner eating.

Ryan and Ricky looked at each other with silent conversation. They had caught on earlier today that something was weird with these two.

Wyatt looked down at his plate again, those brown angel eyes of Jack's were burnt into the underneath of his eyelids, searing the darkness with beautiful memory. At least it wasn't images of blood and gore with his sister being strangled. "Don't call me that." He said quietly while everyone else was occupied by Rose explaining the moment she punched the son of a Greek god in the face.

Jack placed a hand on Wyatt's shoulder. "Don't worry dude. I'm just muckin' around."
Wyatt only nodded his head and smirked nervously.

Satisfied that her food had filled everyone's bellies with hot comfort, Sally retired to her bedroom. Noah had stayed out in the lounge room with the television, a cold Carlton Draught in his hand.
The teenagers had all gone to Ricky's bedroom to hang out before Wyatt had to go home.

"Does your mum use coconut oil?" Rose asked sitting on the floor near the turntable.

"You mean like, in an oil burner?" Ricky asked as he cleaned his glasses with his shirt with Ryan and Wyatt beside him on the bed.

"She means for cooking." Wyatt said laughing.

"Good job." Ryan said in spite of Ricky's obliviousness about his mum's use of coconut oil.

"Shut your face, Ryan. Um, yeah, she does." He said to Rose as he held the glasses up to the light.

"Your parents are so awesome." Jack said, sitting against the closed door, a fruit pastille whirling around in his mouth.

"Yeah they are I guess." Ricky said putting his glasses on.

"Too bad they had such a douche bag of a kid." Jack said trying to get a reaction.

"Jack!" Rose remarked worried.

"Alright Wylie, hold my glasses." Ricky stood up handing the glasses to Wyatt. "You were warned Hercules." He went across the room and tackled Jack mercilessly. The laughing and grunting while their bodies flew around on the carpet had everyone in stitches.

"You morons!" Rose yelled laughing.

Ricky was on top before Jack ended up tickling him on the sides under the ribcage, many years of practice with a sister came into play. Ricky laughed in the way you do when you're tickled, he tried to fend off Jack's hands but failed immensely. "Someone help!" He yelled to the others.

"I'm not helping you!" Ryan said back.

Rose shook her head simultaneously with Wyatt.

"Who knew Channing Tatum was so ticklish!" Jack teased as he kept going.

"Why don't you go help him?" Ryan said to Wyatt. "I'll give you five bucks."

"No way, I'm not risking a broken bone just because Ricky can't handle some fingers."

"Ten bucks?" Ryan offered.

"Fifteen! I'll give you fifteen!" Ricky tried to say from underneath Jack.

"Oh alright, fine." Wyatt got up off the bed. He went over,

quickly grabbing Jack from behind. With his arms gripping him around the middle, Wyatt pulled him off Ricky back towards the door. It'd be a lie to say Jack wasn't totally thrilled with it.

Ricky stumbled to his feet to help get the wriggly Jack to the ground.

Rose looked over to Ryan. "Can you believe this?"

Ryan smiled and replied honestly. "Yes, yes I can."

She looked back to see that Ricky and Wyatt were both holding him down, they had an arm each.

While his legs were trying to get them off Jack spoke up. "It's two against one. Your name should be *Cheating* Tatum."

Wyatt giggled while Ricky felt like a loser. Jack looked up at Wyatt and smiled at the sight of his giggles.

"Yeah well what fighter tickles his god damn opponent?" Ricky said trying to defend himself.

"Just let me go, I promise I won't get you." Jack said to Ricky.

"I'm not scared." Ricky said as he cautiously released his grip on Jack. Wyatt followed Ricky's lead intending to sit back on the bed, instead Jack pulled him back down, they almost fell into Rose on their way back down to the floor. Jack got himself over the top of the struggling Wyatt with his knees on either side of his torso, then began to tickle him just as he had with Ricky.

Wyatt laughed so hard it felt like he was going to asphyxiate. After a good minute of trying to break free, he finally managed to get him back by reaching at the sensitivity under Jack's arm, leaving him a brief moment of chance to sit up and turn the tables. He pushed him backwards, lingering over the top of him with both his hands on his wrists.   He looked down into those gentle eyes and melted, he was beginning to feel addicted to them, the smile that appeared with their glisten made him feel this strange affection all the more strongly. He didn't quite have this feeling when he looked at his other friends.

He could feel the soft flow of blood beneath his palms, he couldn't tell if it was his own or Jack's.

Wyatt smiled back to kind face.

A knock at the door followed by Noah's voice broke the concentration they had. "Ya mum's here to pick ya up, Wyatt mate."

"Thank you Noah." Wyatt called. He looked back down at Jack, who raised his brows.

He got off him, standing up to face the others, who'd pretended not to notice anything. "Okay, where's my fifteen?"

"Do I look like I'm made of money?" Ricky said. "Nah just joking, I'll give it to you next time I see you."

"You better." Wyatt said as he picked his jacket up off the bed and put it on, then stroke his hair out to the side. He wouldn't actually follow up with it, he knew very well his family's wealthier than the Bensons. He wasn't going to take any off Ricky whether it's a two dollar coin or a hundred dollar note. "Well, bye everyone." He said with reluctance. He wanted to stay with them, not go back to the loneliness of his bedroom. It wasn't nice knowing that Candice wasn't in hers up the hall.

"Bye!" Ricky and Ryan said at the same time.

"It was good to see you man." Ricky said genuinely.

"You too!" He said back happily.

"Bye Wyatt." Rose said holding her arms out. He bent down to hug her. "Hopefully we'll see you real soon." She said as he stood back up.

"Yeah hopefully." He agreed.

"Well we could always chill out at your joint." Jack said from the floor against the bed frame, he placed another fruit pastille in his mouth.

"Yeah! What he said." Ricky said in agreement.

"I dunno... It can be pretty boring there." Wyatt replied,

slightly shaking his head.

"Oh I find that hard to believe." Jack said offering him a sugary lolly. Wyatt politely declined the offer.

"I gotta go guys. See you when I see you." He left them and headed for the lounge where his mum was with Noah. He thanked him for dinner and left the house with his very quiet mother.

Rose soon left and went to bed on the lounge futon when Noah went to join his wife in slumber.

Ryan was going to sleep near Ricky's bed in several blankets but first he had to go to get ready, leaving Jack and Ricky in the bedroom.

"Well, I better hit the hay too then." Jack said as he got up and walked over to the door.

"Hey Jack."

He turned around to look at Ricky once more. He expected another question like earlier today. He didn't know how to handle those sorts of questions.

"Wyatt's more of an ice cream guy." Ricky said with a kind smile.

Jack wasn't at all sure what to make of this, his shyness tried to creep in again. He did feel good with Ricky though, so let his comfortable side glow. "Is he just?" He said interested.

"Yeah, he hardly ever eats lollies or fizzy drinks because of you know, *cavities*." He said the last word in an annoyed mocking voice.

Jack laughed in fondness of it all.

Ricky continued. "But he loves ice cream, especially vanilla or strawberry."

Ryan came back in, promptly laying down on his place by the bed.

"Well, thanks for the info there. Catch ya's tomorrow." Jack said trying to seem as casual as humanly possible as he went for the door.

"No worries man, goodnight." Ricky said getting up to walk over to his volcano to get changed into his pyjamas.

"Night Jack." Ryan said as he lay there, his eyes closed and fingers entwined under his head.

Jack left, closing the door behind him, heading for the lounge room where he too changed his clothes and joined his sister on the fold out couch.

As he lay there in the dark beside Rose's heavy breathing, he thought of nearly nothing other than Wyatt and his cute affiliation with ice cream.
He felt a little exposed at Ricky telling him that small detail, but it wasn't just what he said, it was *how*. It was like Ricky was helping him get close to Wyatt... That couldn't be, surely.
In all his life he had never felt this way with anyone, he was beginning to think that he won't die alone after all. Except still, what if Wyatt didn't like him like that?
Only time will tell he told himself.
Time, and ice cream.

~ 2 ~

The next day proved just as beautiful as the last one, sun rays shone down from the morning sky, the serene feel of the big star's warmth on your skin is enough to revitalise your very being.

Candice stepped out of the car, looked up and smelled the clean air. She's finally home.
Against her mother's request she'd decided she was well and ready to come back. Seeing the others yesterday fuelled her decision into prompt action.
She couldn't wait to see her room, what she always thought of

as 'her place'. The hospital bed was okay but compared to hers it was gross, the whole room was cramped and suffocating, and she couldn't help but feel like everything she touched in there was riddled with disease germs, thinking that her hand would rot away slowly upon contact.

But now her dad had driven her back. As she approached the front door, she thought of the last time she was here, when she saw that dog on the grass. Wyatt opened the front door with a smile.

"Welcome back." He greeted with gladness.

"You won't be so happy after a couple of days, I bet." She said as she passed him and entered the house, being sure to take her shoes off.

He followed her all the way to her bedroom, he never admitted to her that he had spent most of his time in there while she was gone.

"Has anyone seen that girl yet?" She asked him after she lay blissfully down on her squishy mattress with her familiar blankets.

"Not that I'm aware of. I had dinner with everyone at Ricky's house last night." He was now sitting at the desk chair.

"Oh cool, you mean *everyone* was there?" She asked.

"Yeah, it was pretty awesome."

"Aw I wish I was there!" She said in honesty.

"We'll have to have another dinner with everyone. Maybe here... Jack suggested visiting sometime anyway." He said without much thought.

"Hmm so Jack wants to visit?" She asked still laying on her back.

"Yeah I was thinking it'd be fun."

"Well let's get them here tonight then. Maybe he could stay over." She said now leaning on her elbow to look at her brother.

"Candice, there is no way mum would allow it. Especially if Ricky-"

"Oh my god, who cares? Honestly, I'm done." She snapped, instantly annoyed.

"Well... So am I but still." He turned to play absentmindedly with the stuff on her desk. "I'm not sure about Jack anyway."

"What's that supposed to mean? He's amazing!" She said raising her voice slightly, now that she *could* raise her voice.

"I know but..." He stopped and didn't continue.

Candice hoped he'd confide in her, she'd her suspicions of him in the past. "But what?"

"Oh I don't even know, never mind." He said as he waved his hand.

"Tell meeeee!" She nagged.

"It's nothing I'm fine."

"Okay, well just remember you can tell me anything. *Anything.*"

Wyatt nodded and tried to change the subject to the weather.

"I'm going to invite everyone around." Candice said picking up her mobile off the bedside table where she'd left it. A ton of notifications waited for her, most of which were from Bethany. She went straight to the 'Little Richard' conversation and typed out a message:

'U should totally come round and make me one of those milos' She hit send with a smile on her face.

The message found its way to Ricky's phone fairly fast. He didn't see it straight away, he and Jack were playing the PlayStation on the lounge room TV to pass time.
Ryan had gone home by now and Rose was with Sally down the street doing whatever females do when they go out.

"Whoa got a message." He paused the game to swap the controller for his phone. He instantly grinned. "No one told me she was coming back today!" He simply left the room. Jack was left on his own and not knowing what's happening. Before he knew it, he was being told to get ready to visit the Fineman's.

"Well, what do I wear?" He said worried about his appearance.

"Uh, my guess is clothes." Ricky said leaving the room again.

Jack rolled his eyes following him to the bedroom. "Yeah, but from what I've gathered they're like, friggin' royalty."

"Nah man you'll be fine. I've been around them for years." Ricky said putting socks on.

"Yeah and look how much mummy dearest likes you."

"I'm telling you it'll be fine, they're not that scary anyway. Except now that I think of it... The last time I was there she screamed at me."

"What?!"

"Just kidding." Ricky lied.

"I just won't go." Jack stated leaving the room.

Ricky shook his head, following. "You were all for it last night!"

"That was last night."

"Look it'll be fun. If she has a problem with you, she'll have me, Candice and Wyatt to answer to." Ricky assured him confidently, causing him to stop and look at him. "Otherwise, you could just sit 'ere alone, and be a loser."

Jack swayed from side to side in the lounge entryway before he finally just went with it. "Okay, I'll go. Just lead the way."

After a hurried twenty minute walk through the town's streets they arrived at the Fineman's house. Its poised position and clean look in this prissy avenue made Jack feel uneasy.

As they reached the front door Ricky explained the shoe situation.

"Wow, that's not fancy at all." Jack replied sarcastically.

Ricky knocked on the thick wooden door waiting for an answer.

"You sure I look okay?" Jack asked quietly.

"Dude, stop asking. Seriously, you look fine." He assured him.

Without much of a wait Wyatt opened the door to greet them. "Hey guys." He said moving aside to let them in.

They walked in leaving their shoes behind. Jack's first impression of the inside reminded him of those ridiculously mansion-like houses that ordinary people always seem to have on American movies. "Wow, you never told me you live in a castle." He said to Wyatt.

Wyatt scoffed. "It's not at all a castle. If it was, I'd insist we have a moat."

"That'd be so cool." He said still looking around.

"Get a moat anyway." Ricky said before leaving their company to go straight upstairs to see Candice. He opened her door to see her laying on the bed where Wyatt had left her.

"I don't see any Milo." She said with cheekiness about her.

He went over grinning as he joined her, laying between her and the wall once more. "I'll get it, I just had to see you first."

"Now aren't you turning out to be a romantic little guy." She said mockingly.

"Shut up Fineman." He said before kissing her mouth, something he'd been wanting to do for days. She kissed him back just as eager.

"So... Where's your parents?" Jack asked Wyatt downstairs.

"My mum is visiting her friend's mum in the nursing home or something, and my dad's in the study."

"Oh okay. I'm gonna be honest with you, I'm kinda scared of your mum already."

"Don't be, she won't do anything."

"I'll take your word for it." Jack looked around some more, peering up the stairs. "So where is it?"

"Where's what?"

"Your bedroom, silly." Jack answered in boyish giggles.

"Oh. Upstairs." He began to ascend the stairs, leading him to his bedroom. Jack walked the whole way with a pep in his step. The scary mum wasn't here and now he gets to see what the bedroom is like, you can tell so much about a person from the look of their room.

"Here it is." Wyatt said opening the door to let him in.

Jack walked in with curiosity seeping through his every motion. It was very neat, just as he had expected. One of the first things he noticed was the big box of comics, he walked over and had a look. "You like comics then?"

"Yeah, I read them when I'm bored."

"What's your favourite ones?"

"Superman, it's awesome."

"Man, that is *so* adorable." Jack said looking through the books.

Wyatt turned to see if anyone was in the hall and looked back. "Why do you always say stuff like that?"

"Like what?" Jack replied still fascinated with the comics. Some of them looked fairly old and some looked really new. There are so many different versions to see.

"Like, say I'm cute and whatever."

"Pfft, because you are. Simple." Jack said still not looking at him.

"The only other person that says stuff like that, is my mother."

Jack finally looked up at him. "Ha, maybe me and her will get along after all."

"Have you guys seen Violet yet?" He said obviously trying to quickly change the subject.

Jack sighed as he said "No, haven't heard from her still.

Haven't seen the dog either."

Wyatt went over and sat on his bed with his legs crossed. Jack continued to snoop out the room, he was taken aback by the actual size of it, in his opinion it was like a small lounge. "You guys must be totally loaded."

"You're making me feel guilty or something." Wyatt stated uncomfortably.

"Oh, sorry." He said as he completed his circle around the room, now coming to sit down next to him awkwardly.

"So what do you feel like doing?" Wyatt asked trying to be a good host.

"Hmm... Anything. I'm up for whatever."

Wyatt looked around unable to think of something. It was especially weird because Ricky was in Candice's room and not here. This was something he wasn't sure he'd get used to. "Ahm, I have no idea what to suggest." He said with a small laugh.

"Oh well done." Jack said sarcastically.

"Hey I tried to tell you you'll be bored."

"I'm not bored." Jack said looking at him. The close range was making Wyatt nervous, he didn't want those strong feelings to come back, even if they were really, really nice to feel.

"You hungry?" Jack asked after he didn't answer him.

"I guess I am a little bit."

"You guys got ice cream?"

"Yeah, I'm pretty sure we do. We could go get some?"

"Yes please, lead the way sir." Jack said with a salute.

Wyatt laughed again and led him down to the kitchen. After opening the wide freezer door, he just had to ask the important question. "Now, do you want this one which is like chocolate with caramel and stuff swirled through it or plain vanilla?"

The chocolate was screamed at Jack from across the kitchen but he had to choose vanilla to try and rack up brownie points with Wyatt. "I'll go vanilla."

"Me too! I can't believe that." Wyatt said excited as he walked over to the bench with the tub. "Everyone has to have some crazy flavour, but vanilla is great. Besides, you can do more with it when you're adding toppings and stuff. You can't do with other flavours what you can do with this."

Jack was blown away at how much he opened up, Ricky was right. He only said he'd have the vanilla. "Yeah, I totally agree. Vanilla all the way."

"And strawberry, that's just awesome."

"Oh I know." Jack said trying to sound just as enthusiastic.

"Sometimes if I'm feeling wild, I'll mix strawberry and vanilla together." He said in a near whisper as he scooped it into bowls. Jack noticed the freezer must really do its job because Wyatt was really trying hard to dig into the ice cream. He was loving every second of the sight.

"Feeling wild? *Fucking hell*." Jack said unable to help himself.

"What?" Wyatt asked stopping what he was doing.

"It's just, you're so... You."

"Oh, is that a good thing or a bad thing?" He replied resuming his task, now putting the lid back on the tub and walking over to the freezer.

"It's a bloody awesome thing. You're so... Argh, I wish I was like you."

Wyatt started to blush again as he handed one of the bowls over. Jack took it with a hungry stomach yelling at him.

"I wish I was more like you." Wyatt said shyly.

"Me? No, you don't." Jack said shaking his head.

"Yeah, you do your own thing and live free."

"I wouldn't exactly say *free*." He answered with a mouth full of coldness. "I wish when I was feeling wild it meant mixing two ice creams together."

"Exactly, I'm so boring. Sometimes I feel like I'm just annoying Ryan and Ricky. Then I got everyone involved in what happened."

Jack got intensely serious. "Hey, there is no way that was your fault. Don't be so fucking stupid."

"But if I hadn't of walked off like a wuss then I wouldn't have been taken."

"I hardly know what you're talking about but I'm here to tell you that it could've happened anyway, those guys were evil, take it from me. It's *their fault,* not yours or anyone else's."

Wyatt began to tear up, it was obvious he was trying not to. "It's just that... I don't know. Maybe if I was different then-"

"I'm telling you for right now, it's not your fault." Jack interrupted. "It's over now and you don't have to worry."
Wyatt didn't reply verbally but started to actually cry.
Jack really didn't know what to do.
What was the protocol here?

He figured he'd do what him and Rose do when one of them have a depressing moment. He got off the bench stool and walked around into the kitchen to hug him. To his deep surprise, just before he had a chance, Wyatt reached out and hugged him first. He clung to him like a koala joey clings to the front of its mother.

Jack just held him with complete concern, Wyatt was starting to let out some serious emotions. The crying was muffled against Jack's shoulder, but it was still hysterical enough to completely slash at his heart strings. He was starting to feel useless, and it was torture to him, he didn't want him to be this way at all.

"It's okay man, I promise."
Still more crying and no words.
He must be letting all the bottled up stuff out...
One of Jack's hands began to gently stroke Wyatt's perfectly

placed hair. He instinctively did this; it was something his own mum used to do when they were much younger. It always comforted him.

It seemed to be working, he began to calm down. Though his breathing still disrupted with jerky movements.

"Everything's okay." Jack said in a low and peaceful way. "We're all here now, free to go wild and eat as much ice cream as we want."

He felt some giggles, at first he thought he was crying again.

"You okay, Tinkle-bell, you?"

"Don't call me that. And stop touching my hair." Wyatt said as the first thing since he started to cry.

"Make me." Jack said softly, still boldly stroking the hair.

There was a small pause before Wyatt unexpectedly said "No, I don't think I will."

To describe that there's a pride of lions doing the peppermint twist in a pool of Coca-Cola and Mentos inside Jack's stomach would be a massive understatement to how his excitement felt.

The arms around Wyatt tightened, the hand still on his head. Much like how Candice felt when hugged by Ricky, he hadn't felt this secure for a long time. It was warm and soft here with him, his firm body like graceful security. If this person right here wasn't a real life guardian angel, then they truly must not exist. Even the scent of distant smoke on his clothes gave Wyatt comfortable feelings; underneath it the unmistakable Lynx Africa, though impressively Jack seemed to wear it modestly, unlike so many others at school, always blasting the stuff everywhere obnoxiously. The subtle way he wore it complemented the scent, rather than have him detest it.

"It's going to melt." He announced, purposely bringing himself back to the scene from the guy's armpit smells.

"Huh?" Jack said with his eyes closed.

"The ice cream, it's melting."

"Oh, right." Jack let go as Wyatt stood back and walked over to his bowl. Most of it was melted down, he didn't like eating melted ice cream.

"Nope, I can't eat this now." He said wiping his eyes with his hand.

"If you won't, I won't." Jack said confidently, hiding the fact he'd prefer to just have both bowls to himself rather than throw the food out.

"Hey Jack!" Greeted an excited voice from behind them. It was Candice with Ricky.

"G'day you! You're lookin' a million dollars there!" Jack answered enthusiastically, hoping they hadn't seen them hugging like that. He didn't dare to begin thinking about if the dad had walked in, even if it was just an attempt at comforting a friend. Candice laughed and shrugged as she sat on one of the bench stools and waited for her drink. Ricky took to the kettle and began to make them. "You guys want one?" He asked the boys.

"Yeah sure." Wyatt answered without even needing to be told what he was making.

"What is it?" Jack asked.

"A macho Milo my good man." Ricky replied in a weird voice, similar to that of what you'd think a clown in a sombrero may sound like.

"Well how can I say no." He replied funnily.

"Wyatt, you been crying?" Candice asked worried. She could see how red and sad his eyes had been.

"Just for a second, it was nothing." He said not wanting it to be spoken about, crying's for wimps.
She looked at Jack who only smiled and shrugged while Wyatt cleaned the bowls they had used.

~ 3 ~

Rose settled herself by the small park in the Main Street, the sun inviting and calm. Little kids screeched the joys of childhood play as they climbed the colourful manmade structures standing firm in the ground of wood chips. She soaked it all in with nostalgic senses, it's times like these she always hoped the parents didn't think she was planning something bad. She wasn't of course, she only admired their free will and careless natures. Though only fifteen she felt like those days were completely over for her, and she wanted them back.

The way she sees it, you have the rest of your entire life to be a 'real adult' and act grown up, but you're only *that* young for a decade of quick years before society ages you fast.

Mrs Benson had reluctantly left her here at the seats while she went into the bank to clear up something up. Sally was worried about leaving her alone, but Rose persisted in telling her it will be fine. They could see each other from across the road through the wide windows of the bank's small building front, which was a little load of worry off Sally's shoulders.

"Rose."

She swung around fast to see who'd said her name, suppose she was still jumpy after stabbing a man to death with a piece of table. Standing behind the bench seat was Violet, finally showing herself. "Where have you been?" Rose stood up to face her properly.

"I've just been away, here and there and everywhere." Violet said in her airy, lightheaded way.

"What happened to you on Tuesday night? How did you know Ethan and Ryan?" She thought she should try to get as much information from her wandering friend as possible before they didn't see her for ages again.

"You ask so many questions now, like Wyatt was."

"That's because we need to know what's going on Violet, you're creeping us out... Creeping *me* out." She wasn't even sure what the Wyatt comment meant.

"If you all wanted to know, what was happening... Maybe the right questions should be asked."

"I've been trying." Rose said growing impatient.

"Ever notice how we both share our names with a flower?" Violet looked to the children.

Rose couldn't be sure where this was going but decided to go along with it anyway, maybe it would lead to some good information and explanation. "No, I didn't notice. That's funny."

"I think that might be why we're such good friends." She still watched the kids play chasies as she spoke, her dark brown eyes deep as they darted around.

"Such good friends, you sure?" Now Rose was totally unsure of where it was going. This wasn't normal, whatever it was. Violet just isn't normal.

"Of the group." She said focusing her attention on Rose's face again.

"You mean my friends."

"My friends."

"So you mean me and-"

"Ryan, Ricky, Candice, Wyatt, Jack and you, Rose." She said each name with a small nod of the head. "You should keep an eye on Ryan. He bumped his head real bad."

Rose stood looking at Violet's near blank expression. She looked as though she had just successfully recited a poem in front of everyone at the whole school assembly. "So why are we your friends now?"

"I think I was supposed to do something, do as I was told, but I didn't."

"What stuff, bad stuff? Who told you to?"

"Buddy helped me too of course."

"Violet, you're not answering me. We can't be friends if you don't answer me. Friends answer each other."

"He knows things too, but I can't find him."

Rose felt totally perplexed now, she was talking absolute nonsense but... If it's nonsense, why did she make it feel like sense? "Is Buddy the dog?"

"Yes!" She seemed happy to say it.

"So... Did you know my mum's boyfriend?"

"I don't want to talk about him."

"Is the Kersh lady your mother or something?" She felt so stupid asking the question but in a conversation like this there was nothing to lose. Except maybe your sanity.

"Never." Violet was nearly frowning now, looking towards the ground. "She's the biggest bully."

"Why don't you come with me? We can work together to put her in prison."

"It's impossible." She replied with a tear.

"Why don't you tell me where you live then? We can go talk to your parents."

"Because..." Violet began to drift away, Rose could see it in her expression.

"Because *why* Violet. Why?"

"Because of the water."

"What?... What water?!" Rose began to panic from the sheer unusualness of what was happening.

A car honking from the road caused Rose to turn around and look in surprise. She saw that Mrs Benson was waiting to cross the road, looking over intently at her.

"Violet please." She turned back to see that once again the place where Violet stood is now bare, nothing but concrete and colourful, hollow leaves. She looked around but couldn't spot her anywhere.

With spooked chills, she immediately pulled out her phone and began to tap the screen, typing a message out to her brother. They all needed to talk as soon as possible. That was far too weird to ignore. The fact Violet can leave your side in the space of five seconds really didn't sit, it made the whole thing even scarier.

Jack had messaged back saying they were at the Fineman's house.

"Okay, we should be right to go back now." Mrs Benson said, finally reaching the spot where Rose had been waiting.

"Mrs Benson, would it be too much trouble to drop me off at where Wyatt lives?"

"Oh no of course not." She said like it was a silly thing to say. "Does this have anything to do with that person you were talking to just now?"

"It actually does." Rose said with her head to the side.

"You know what darl, I'm not even going to ask." She said smiling and began to walk towards the car.

~ 4 ~

As Rose recounted what had happened with Violet in the Main Street, all she had in return were the confused faces of Ricky, Candice, Jack and Wyatt. They were sitting in a circle on the thick floor mat in Wyatt's carpeted bedroom.

"So the dog's name is Buddy. Did she say where he is or if he's okay?" Candice asked eagerly.

"No but I think he's okay. She wasn't talking like anything bad happened to him." Rose told her.

"But stuff like this just *can't happen* guys. There is no such thing as girls that can disappear at the drop of a hat." Wyatt said in disbelief of Violet's riddles.

"I hope there is." Jack said. "Then I could ask her to top off my weed supply for free."

Ricky and Rose laughed, Candice only smirked but Wyatt wasn't at all impressed. His mother had drilled into his brain that any kind of recreational drug is the devil's work.

"You shouldn't do that." He spoke like an angry parent.

"Yes sir!" Jack said amused at Wyatt's sudden authoritative backbone. "Truth be told I haven't used any for ages."

"Guys, be serious. We're talking about our possible future of being a ghost's bitches." Ricky interrupted.

"She's not a ghost." Wyatt said flatly.

"You wanna know something that makes no sense to me Wyatt?" Jack said to him with a serious face.

"What's that?" He asked in reply, genuinely curious to know what this was.

"If you can't believe in ghosts and shit, how can you believe in God?" He asked with the eagerness to know clear in his eyes.

The others stayed silent and waited to see what would happen next, surely Wyatt was going to have a massive tantrum and give Jack the silent treatment for the rest of their lives.

He simply looked to the floor in thought, then slowly shook his head. "I *don't*... I don't think I do." He said in such a low tone it was almost inaudible.

Nobody answered, it was so silent you could probably hear the beating of their hearts.

"What I do believe in though, is *us*." Wyatt continued. "I mean with Ryan too. The five of you are more of a miracle to me than any... Bearded guy walking on water."

Jack thought that if it were a free world he'd lean over right now and mercilessly smooch the absolute hell out of him. Nicely of course.

"Wow Wy, that's a pretty amazing thing to say." Candice said with overflowing affection for her little brother.

"Yeah, where did that come from?" Ricky said completely moved by Wyatt's comment on their friendship.

"Well, I guess I'm just trying to say that my 'beliefs' have taken a different turn lately. If what this Violet girl is saying is true, then I believe in what we do as a group. I won't believe in supernatural stuff, but I believe in the ability of evil people and the science of the planet. This girl was probably forced to do bad things and regrets it now, and I feel like she really did help us escape that night."

"That's a really cool view you have there Wyatt." Rose said impressed.

"You've gotten real deep in your old age Ol Wylie." Ricky said imitating an old man's voice.

"I'm being serious." Wyatt said, irritated.

"We know you're serious." Candice assured him.

"I'm thinking we should talk about this when we have Ryan here." Ricky said wisely.
They all agreed it'd be better to discuss the happenings of Violet when all of them were here.

While they were all occupied by Ricky's mad and amazing (so described by him) Batman skills on Wyatt's PlayStation, Jack was feeling comfortable and decided it was time to try and improvise an invitation.

Sitting behind the other three he whispered to Wyatt. "You know I wish I had somewhere to stay for a night. Just so I had a little break from Rose and everything."

"I thought you two were inseparable?" Wyatt replied in surprise.

"Yeah but even we need our breaks, ya know?"

Wyatt began to catch on. He's not the most social person, but he's not dumb either. "Do you guys have any other friends you could stay with maybe?"

"No. Well Rose does but I don't. I was pretty much a complete loner before you guys. I doubt Ryan's place will take me..."

Wyatt had a little sigh to himself. He wasn't sure if his mum would let him stay over. Then again, why wouldn't she? She knew nothing about him, and he presented himself well, she couldn't call him riff raff, surely. Most importantly, Jack isn't a girl. "Well I'll ask my dad if it's alright if you can stay here, how's that?"

Jack tried to act surprised and appreciative. "Oh? That'd be awesome! Thanks dude."

Wyatt decided then and there that acting was definitely not one of Jack's greatest skills.

~ 5 ~

Jack sat at the neat Fineman dinner table with the four residents of the house. It was laid out like the perfect families had there's on TV. He decided that tonight he would just relax and pretend he's just as privileged as the people he was visiting.

"So Jack, let us get to know you." Mr Fineman said cutting his chicken fillet.

"What would you like to know Mr Fineman?" Jack answered. He was trying so hard to sound naturally posh.

"What's your middle name? That's a nice start." Mrs Fineman said. It seemed she was giving her children a looser rein for once. Ever since she got home, she'd been really nice to Jack and let him stay over without much convincing.

"My middle name is actually William."

"Oh that's nice. Much better than Jack." She said sincerely as she took a sip of water.

"What's yours?" He asked Wyatt to his right, dismissing her weird judgment.

"Mine's Clark. It was my grandfather's name." He answered proudly.

"Ohh, I get it, just like Superman's name." He said nudging Wyatt's shoulder with his elbow.
He nodded back grinning.

"Mine's Emmeline if anyone cares." Candice informed feeling a little left out. She felt rather glad the boys had bonded so much today though.

"That's so random." Jack replied to her.

"So have you and your sister always been in Tasmania?" Donald asked.

"Yes we have, unfortunately." Jack replied.

"Unfortunately?" He answered as if he were insulted.

"Well I just want to get out and see the world, you know what I mean?'

"You have the rest of your life for that, don't worry." Donald said in a fatherly manner.

"It's just that Rose and I sort of feel, well I do anyway, like this place is tiny. The whole state is like a shrinking... Sponge or something." Jack said as he stabbed his broccoli with the fork. He had extra vegetables because of his hate of meat on his plate.

"It's a lovely place to be." Patty Fineman said to the guest. "We have clean air, abundant nature growth. The church systems are prolific as well."

Wyatt began to think of what his mother had said about the clean air and wild nature. Not even in such a beautiful place as this can you escape the torture and mayhem of human destruction.

"I suppose you're right Patty." Jack said with smile. It was of course sarcastic, only Wyatt and Candice would pick up on that small detail. Jack doesn't even know what prolific means. "Your broccoli tastes divine, not a hint of flatulence at all." He said with humoured politeness.

Candice and Wyatt giggled profusely as their mother remained quiet with confusion.

With dinner over, Donald relaxed in the family's lounge with his wife, who resumed her attempts at clothes making. Tonight would be the first time since the day the Devils called her on the phone. They'd in the lounge until around 9:15pm, then they'd hide themselves away in the comforts of their huge bed until the morning.

Candice headed to her bedroom to sleep the night away. Her trip back home had turned into a long day and she was rather exhausted. Tomorrow she'd have to ring Bethany to let her know what's happened. The poor girl has been worried as all shit because of Candice's silence.

She's probably more upset that she hasn't been able to tell me her news or whatever...

She would, however, be a sad and concerned friend after hearing the details of what she's been through with her brother.

"Night Candice!" Jack said enthusiastically as he waved to her in the hall.

"You make sure you behave yourself." She said with a pointing finger and a stern face as fake as a soap opera, making Jack laugh sheepishly.

"Goodnight Candice." Wyatt waved, happy to be saying it.

"Night guys." She turned and disappeared into her bedroom.

Inside Wyatt's room, Jack waited for him to come back with the bedding he was going to use while he stayed for the night. He sat on the carpet looking at one of the comics. He'd never really thought much in the way of comics. He liked the superhero action movies, really who doesn't? But he wasn't too inclined to read the material in which they originated.

Wyatt came back into the room using the pile of blankets he

held as a means to push the door open. Jack started laughing at the sight.

"You look like a one of those pack horse thingies!" He said as he got up to take them off him.

"Glad you didn't say donkey. I just thought I'd get some extras because it's getting cold. And it's always colder on the floor." He explained as he handed them over.

"Oh man you're so nice." Jack said gratefully.

"It's just how I was raised I guess." Wyatt replied. He was always too modest.

"So where do I set this up anyway?" Jack asked still holding the bundle.

"Anywhere, doesn't worry me." He looked around the floor. "How about just here?"
He pointed to the area of space beside the bed.

"Perrrfect." Jack said as he walked over and began to set up his spot.

Wyatt watched for a moment as his friend spread himself out across the floor in an attempt to lay out the big blankets. Seeing him do something so innocent, so normal, just the thing he needed to see at the moment. He hadn't at all felt right since coming home. His parents and police officers were talking about counselling. He couldn't go to counselling, that's for crazy people... isn't it?

He looked away from Jack's blanket laying skills to get his pyjamas out of the closet. He left the closet door open and walked around to the other side pulling the door to the bedroom back so that now he was behind both in a makeshift changing room. He always loved the feel of clean pyjamas slipping onto his body at the end of the day. It was like his day clothes were suffocating him through the sunlit hours without him realising, and then when he let the pyjamas sit on him he could feel the difference, like a small soft freedom. He often wondered if any-one else thought of their night clothes to this extent.

With the wonderful feeling of pyjamas on, he casually came out of his hiding place to put his used clothes in the dirty laundry basket. On his short walk over to it he became aware that Jack was stifling giggles, he looked over to see that he was indeed sitting there on his roughly finished floor-bed with his hand covering a gleeful grin.

"What's so funny this time?" Wyatt asked uptight.

"Your pyjamas." Jack answered trying to stop his light gig-gling. He was looking at him standing there in a white bed shirt and loose, cotton Superman pants. The red 'S' crest flowing around him from the waist down, dancing around as he moved.

Wyatt looked down at his clothes. He was irritated now. "Why is that funny? Really Jack."

"No, no. I was laughin' because I love it." He replied with casual ease, a hint of shaky nerves too.

"Oh, well that's okay then. I think." Wyatt said as he walked around the room to switch the bedside lamp on and switch off the main light that glared from the roof.

"Hey um, you got anything I can borrow or something?" Jack asked shyly, getting to his feet. It seemed that within himself he was all confident for this situation, but now that he was actually with Wyatt here in a comfortable place, he felt he was too ner-vous to stay the night. Chelsea never made him this nervous.

"Hmm..." Wyatt said looking over to his wardrobe in the warm lamp light. "Well how big are you?"

Jack's mind instantly greeted the dirty gutter, he couldn't help it. "Ahm... Probably not much bigger than you." He replied with upmost sensibility as he falsely scratched the back of his head.

Wyatt walked over and revealed the insides of his dark ward-robe again. After going through some draws, he walked back over with a folded set of his own clothes. "Here you go. I hope they fit well but if not, you should be warm enough in all that." He said looking at the blankets on the floor.

"Should be fine, thanks." He took them, beginning to change right then and there.

Wyatt walked past him for his comic box. He grabbed the new one off the top and proceeded to walk back and climb onto his bed where he sat, still purposely not looking at him.

"Yeah it's good enough!" Jack said, giving him reason to look up.

"Oh yeah, that's fine." He said in all seriousness. They're a little tighter than what they should have been because they were older clothes, but it looked comfortable... *Really* comfortable.

He didn't bother to look away as Jack kneeled on the floor to get in his own little bed. There was something intriguing about the way his dark hair was starting to fall down over his forehead as he was busy doing something casual.

Just seeing his shape here with him made him feel something, complete in a sense. He imagined what he'd look like with wide, graceful, feathered wings. His guardian angel was here during the night, and it felt so...

Stop, just stop. He's a friend like Ryan and Ricky, that's all...

"I can't believe your middle name is Clark, that's just so weird." Jack said from the floor. He was now laying on his back with his hands under his head.

"It's a pretty great coincidence. Here, I almost forgot." Next thing Jack knew there was a pillow hanging down the side of the bed frame. "You definitely won't be comfortable without that."

"Right you are." Jack said as he took it gladly. "You know it's a good thing your last name is Fineman, because you are a *fine man*."

Wyatt laughed as he opened his book. "I hardly am but okay."

"Whatever you say, Mr Wild Strawberry and Vanilla."

"You always seem to find something to call me."

Jack just laughed as he pulled out his phone to check Facebook. It'd been a while since he did. Things like that didn't seem to matter lately, it was like child's play now.

They stayed like that for a while, Wyatt reading about Superman's unreal adventures and Jack scrolling on his phone through people's exposed personal lives.

The only sound between them was occasional sighs and the soft scraping of book pages turning over.

~ 6 ~

Rose and Ricky sat together on the lounge room couch while Noah Benson drifted off on the armchair. They were sitting with the blaring television presenting them with one of those late night true crime documentary shows. They were talking about the rise and fall of some leper looking killer.

They were hardly paying attention, Candice had occupied them for a while by messaging Ricky. After she'd gone to bed, she decided she was upset with being alone. Ricky suggested going into Wyatt's room to stay in there with them overnight so she had company. She replied by saying she'd prefer to give them some quality guy to guy bonding time.

"I think she fell asleep." Ricky said yawning.

"Oh good, I was worried for a second there. There's nothing worse than not being able to sleep in the dark and on your own." She replied.

"Tell me about it." Ricky said. He had a question he'd been wanting to ask. He figured now was as good time as any. It was just that he didn't really want to ask in worry of being rude or something. "Hey Rose, is um…. Is Jack *gay*?"

She went blank for a moment then smiled a little. "He is,

why's that?"

"Thought so. I was just wondering." Finally, it's done, awkward time over.

Rose casually spoke. "I hope we get together with Ryan tomorrow. I really want to know what's happening here." She began to nearly whisper as if she didn't want Ricky's dad hearing. "I'm not sure about anyone else but if I'm going to be randomly spoken to about these things, I'd prefer to know what she's even talking about. It's really scaring me."

Her serious statement was answered by his guilty admission. "Shit... I haven't really been thinking about it."

~ 7 ~

With a tired sigh Wyatt placed the comic book on the edge of his bedside table. He glanced down to see what Jack was doing, which was still laying there on the floor looking at his phone screen.

"You need the light?" Wyatt asked trying to deny the fact that he himself didn't want to be in the dark.

"Oh nah, it's all good." Jack replied relaxed.

Wyatt flicked off the lamp beside his pillow, leaving them in total darkness except for the blue glow of Jack's mobile phone. From the bed it looked like there was a little glowing alien sitting down there.

"So what happened with Superman tonight?" Jack asked trying to make conversation.

"Uh... Just some robberies and stuff. Things like that." Wyatt said. He honestly felt a little embarrassed of his Man of Steel hobby.

"Sounds nuts."

"I guess so."

Now it went completely dark. It seemed Jack had finished with his social media update. Wyatt tensed up in uncomfortable fear of the blackness.

"Your speech thing earlier about God n' shit was the best thing I've ever heard. And I've seen videos of Lady Gaga in concert." Jack stated randomly to the dark.

"You think I give a better speech than her?" Wyatt said with an airy laugh.

"Well actually, I imagine you'd probably give a better everything than anyone."
It seemed that laying in the dark brought out both of their willingness and confidence with each other.

Wyatt smiled, that was a nice thing to say to someone. "Thank you... I think."

"I'm surprised you even know who that is."

"Yeah well. Suppose there's a lot of things I'd surprise people with."

"Ooh, like what?" Jack asked excitedly curious. *Please say you're gay, please say you're gay...*

"Oh I don't know... I'm fond of musicals."

Close enough... "You serious?"

"As a preacher." Wyatt laughed.

"What else?"

"Uhh... I once tried to do an autopsy on a slater."

"What?! One of those little bugs that curl up when you poke 'em?"

"That's the one."

"You're a bloody weirdo!" Jack laughed, shaking his head.

"It was a while ago, and I promise it was purely for science!" He explained, now laughing.

"That's what they all say! What's something else?"

"I've said too much already. What's something weird that you've done?"

"More like name something weird I *haven't* done... There was this one phase I went through of showing up at a playground the same time and day for weeks."

"What's so weird about that?"

"I was trying to see if anyone would notice so they'd come and ask me if I was okay." He said sounding low.

"Did they?"

"No."

"If I would have noticed, I would have said something. Definitely."

"You reckon?"

"Actually, I don't really talk to strangers. But the thought would occur to me."

Jack laughed a near silent laugh. "I'm really glad we met."

"Me too." He began to think back to the moment Jack first stood in front of him in that terrible little room. The darkness in his bedroom was really unnerving him now. "Jack, can I ask you something?"

"Yes of course you can." He replied eagerly.

"Will you think I'm a loser if I need a light on?"

"Oh my god, no way I would. Don't be silly. Want me to turn it on?"

The genuine niceness in his voice gave Wyatt a feeling of overwhelming emotion erupting inside. "Yes please. There's a night light just on the other side of this table."

There was the sound of Jack scuffling around and trying to feel for the light, then the sound of a switch flicking, they now had soft light over the room.

"Thank you." Wyatt said gratefully.

"Not a problem Tinkle-bell." Jack said getting back under his blankets.

"Hopefully I won't need it soon, I hate that I need it."

"You know what I hate?" Jack asked knowing that Wyatt was currently self-hating.

"The state?" He answered with a scoff.

"I don't *hate* the state but yeah. Anyway, I hate pimples, they're so gross."

Wyatt laughed a little. "I really wasn't expecting you to say that. I don't really get pimples."

"I noticed. You're so lucky."

"Well maybe when I'm your age they'll get me like there's no tomorrow."

"*My age?* You basically *are* my age!" Jack said laughing in slight confusion.

"I guess. I'm actually currently thirteen but I'm turning fourteen soon."

"Somehow that makes me feel prehistoric."
Wyatt cracked up laughing trying not to be too loud in case he woke up his family.

"Now *I* can ask, what's so funny?" Jack said.

"You, you're always funny." Wyatt said calming down.

"I'm glad I can make you laugh." Jack said sincerely.

"Me too. You know what? I think this night over was the best thing to happen."

"Really?" He asked surprised.

"Yeah. Ricky is going to always be with Candice now instead of hanging out with me, but you're here now. It's like you and Rose came along with perfect timing."

"Are you forgetting how we met? I wouldn't exactly call it perfect."

"I don't think I could ever forget. But even then, it was perfect, you guys still saved me." Wyatt said looking at the darkened ceiling.

"Oh don't say that. Saving people is for Superman."

"You kind of are like Superman, in a way."

Now Jack started laughing, he thought of himself flying through the air in a skin tight body suit. "How? Like what the hell makes you say that?!"

"I don't know, never mind. I must be tired." He said blushing out of sight.

"Nuh-uh Tinkle-bell, spit it out mister." Jack insisted.

"Well... I don't know. You both help people and you even kind of look like him. Especially in the eyes. Even if his are famously blue and yours aren't."

"Oh holy shit... I think I just received the compliment of the century!!"

Wyatt could only answer after he finished giggling. "You're welcome."

"Keep up compliments like that with me and they'll be calling you a poof pretty soon."

"What's a poof?" He asked honestly not knowing what he meant.

"You know, gay." Jack said nervously.

"Oh..." He began to panic a little, it was strange conversation. "Why would they? You can say nice things to someone without being gay."

"I guess you can." Jack said without the slightest bit of enthusiasm. "So, you're not then?"

"No, you?" Wyatt said rather quickly.

Jack paused and didn't answer right away. His heart was beating strong against his decision to say "Nope."

"I'd better try and get some sleep now, I don't want to sleep in." Wyatt said, much to Jack's irritation to his already irritated mood.

"Fair enough. Night."

"Goodnight Jack." Wyatt rolled over and fell asleep fairly fast.

Jack lay awake on his own for another hour before he finally began drifting away.

~ 8 ~

Rose woke up to the sound of her phone ringing. She knew it was her brother because the ringtone is the song that plays on the credits of 'Twins.' Hers on his is the same, because nothing beats the reminder of Danny DeVito and Arnold Schwarzenegger twinning it in all their opposite glory.

They'd set each other with the distinctive song so that when it rang, they'd instantly know it was only the other, not their mum or worse.

She picked it up pressing the answer button and held it to the side of her sleepy face. "Hello." She said unenthusiastically.

"Rose, what are you doin'?"

"Well I was sleeping and now I'm talking to you." She spoke low in case people in the house were still asleep.

"Sorry."

"What's wrong Jack? Just spit it out already."

"I'm alone and I'm too... like scared to do anything."

"Where's Wyatt? Where are you?"

"He's asleep and I'm hiding in the bathroom. I didn't know where to go to make a phone call."

"Oh shit, what's happened? You didn't upset anyone did you?"

"No, only myself."

"Okay, well whatever's happened doesn't matter, get off the phone and wake up Wyatt. Ricky told me he's an early riser anyway, tell him you want to come back."

"Okay Rosie, love you."

"Love you too. See ya soon alright."

As soon as they hung up she flopped back under the covers for a quick five minutes before getting up out of the warm to clear up the futon.

After the talk with Ricky last night about Violet, she was feeling a little like maybe only her and Candice were taking it seriously.

Must be because girls mature faster than boys she thought on her way to the toilet.

~ **9** ~

Wyatt awoke to the strangest morning call he'd ever experienced. In the throes of dream sleep, a pleasant voice began to drift in and flow through his unawakened mind. It wasn't until he opened his eyes that he really heard it for what it was.

Jack was shaking him gently and saying "Wakey wakey, shake it baby."

What in the world is happening? He thought with hazy words. "Jack, I'm awake." He said starting to sit up.

"Well it's honestly about time."

"Why, what time is it?" He asked rubbing his eyes with his hands.

Jack rolled up the blankets on the floor as he said "Like, eleven thirty. I gotta get back to the Benson's."

"Eleven thirty?! I must have missed mass."

"Yeah well, you don't like God anymore anyway so who cares, right?"

"I guess you're right." Wyatt said looking at him, something was different here.

"So I gotta get back, should I just walk you reckon?"

"Yeah well if my parents aren't here then you'll have to. I can walk you, I don't mind."

"Oh nah that's not a problem. I'm used to it."

"To walking alone?"

"Being alone."

"You've got Rose, and us." Wyatt said smiling.

Jack looked at him briefly, nodding his head with a shrug before gathering his clothes from the floor and placing them on the back of the desk chair. He then began to casually take off the clothes he had on, seeming to have not a single self-esteem issue within him.

Wyatt soon covered his eyes with his hand when he noticed. His uptight modesty must have been badly offended at that glance of Jack's perfectly sculptured shoulders and the blue boxers sitting comfortably around his waist. "That was really random." He said uncomfortably, still covering his eyes.

Jack pulled his pants up over the shorts and looked at him sitting there all innocent, like always. "You don't have to look away you know. We're all straight here remember. Besides, I'm covered." He said as casually as he could manage.

Wyatt trustingly took his hand away from his face to see Jack looking at him with a lot of skin and not a thread of shirt. "You said you were covered." He said flatly.

"Seriously dude, it's my top half. You can't be *that* awkward around other guys."

Wyatt wanted to speak his honest thoughts and tell him that it's only him he's weird around. His mum and religious life had always taught him that lying was bad, but these feelings he felt towards another boy felt like they shouldn't be spoken.

He got off the bed and spoke in a tone his friends would associate with him trying to prove himself. "I'm *not* awkward around other guys." He too took his shirt off as he walked to his wardrobe.

Though angry, Jack couldn't help a tiny smirk sneak its way in. "Good for you mate."

"Yeah, it *is* good for me." He said angrily while he slipped on one of his trusty polo shirts. He then went ahead to pull his Superman pants off to reveal his own undergarments, pulling on some track pants; because it's Sunday after mass don't you know.

Jack stood there kind of shocked but tried not to show it, still shirtless and watching. At least now he didn't have to wonder if it was boxers or briefs. "I'd watch it if I were you, don't want them homos getting the wrong idea." He put his shirt and jumper on, picked his phone up off the floor and headed for the door.

"Where are you going?" Wyatt snapped like they hadn't spoken about it a few minutes ago.

"Back to Ricky's. I might even pick a girl up to boink on the way!" Jack called from the hall, realising Candice had just come out of her room. "Oh, thanks for having me, Candice." He turned around to see Wyatt in his doorway and turned back to Candice. "Cya round." He kissed her on the cheek before going downstairs to leave.

Candice simply stood there stunned and confused before slowly walking over to Wyatt's room. "What the hell was that?"

"Nothing." He said flatly walking into his room, she followed him. If there was one thing she was going to do today it was find out what had happened just now.

He sat on his bed and was soon accompanied by her in doing the same. "That wasn't nothing little brother. I'm old, you can tell me."

Wyatt sat with all the signs of internal turmoil on his face before replying. "He woke me up and decided to be grouchy. That's honestly what happened."

"Oh pfft, come off it. There's more to it than that. Why was he saying that stuff about picking up a girl going home?"

"It's complicated."

"That's what everyone says about their lovers tiff." She said in a near inaudible voice.

"What?" Wyatt asked brazenly.

"Nothing. Look, does this have anything to do with... Maybe one of you saying something about each other?"

Wyatt thought for a moment. "Nothing weird happened between us Candice!" He said with a raised voice as he stood up to walk away. "We're just friends. We're guys!"
He left the room, she didn't know if she'd ever seen him have a tantrum quite like that before.

"You're the one getting emotional over it." She stated to the empty room.

<h2 style="text-align:center">~ 10 ~</h2>

"Like seriously Rose, he's so gay. I fuckin' swear!" Jack exclaimed, pacing angrily in front of his sister at the dingy little playground near the Benson's street. Rose sat on the wooden plank bordering the playground, watching him walk back and forth for ages, shoes crunching on the wood chips as he ranted about the incident with Wyatt.

"He was complementing me like, the whole time, and I swear to God he likes it when I touch him. But seriously, I swear he likes me. I am *not* bullshitting."

"Jack I think he's just shy and confused." Rose said kindly.

"Aren't we all?!"

"Well, you told him you weren't gay." She said raising her shoulders.

"Nuh-uh. This morning everything was so damn obvious. There was so much queer in that room that there was probably glitter flying out the windows."

"Do you have to word it like that?" She laughed.

"Seriously Rosie, he's.... Ahhh he's so frustrating!" He whined as he kneeled on the wood chips, face in hands.

A little kid on his tricycle pedalled himself past on the footpath by the playground, judging them curiously.

"Maybe you should just give it a break for a while, it's only been like... A week since he was kidnapped, remember." She tried to explain so he'd understand.

"But that's another thing, I think he feels better when I'm around. Like safer." He said looking up to her.

"Hang out with him for now and be his friend until he gets over whatever is getting to him. Just be there for him at the moment. He's been through a lot recently."

He nodded his head understanding that she's right, she usually is about everything. "I know.... I just want... you have no idea." He said sounding exhausted.

She stood up with her arms offered, he accepted her sympathetic hug. "I know." She said with motherly softness, patting his back as she held him.

"What's up with you guys?" Ricky asked walking up to them, mobile phone in one hand. They separated, Rose stood behind Jack.

"Nothing." The twins said with perfect timing together.

Ricky nodded and looked to Jack. "So, how was *the visit*?" He asked in a low and suggestive voice.

Rose stood out of Jack's view with a panicked face, waving her hands from side to side trying to signal him to stop.

"It was okay... pretty average." Jack said flatly.

Ricky replied with uncertainty after seeing her strange dance. "Oh okay... Well that's good."

"How's Ryan? Rose told me you were gonna ring his house." Jack asked trying not to think about Wyatt.

"Well, he can't hang out at the moment because his mum and dad are taking him and Ethan to some counsellor or somethin' like that." Ricky explained.

"Oh, so his parents are being nice to him now?" Rose said annoyed at the thought it takes Ryan to almost die to make his parents show they love him.

"Apparently, I just hope it lasts." Ricky resonated.

"They can't be any worse than ours." Jack stated in a positive gesture. "Besides, they have to get used to that aunt bein' behind all the crap."

Ricky and Rose nodded in agreement at what he said. Though left unspoken, the whole group hated the idea of her being out there somewhere. She could be plotting to murder them all when they aren't expecting it.

Something went off in a distant place inside Rose's mind. The one that bossed Daz happened to be Ryan's aunt... *Peculiar.*

"Anyway, I'm going round to Candice and Wyatt's house, you guys wanna come with?" Ricky asked unknowing of that morning's event.

"Nah I'm not. I might just hang out at your place." Jack said. Ricky felt a little concerned at Jack's overall mood. "My parents have gone out. They're trusting us to behave n' stuff but, feel free to chill in my room." He turned to Rose. "You?" His happy face of expectance is hard to say no to, especially in this sunny setting.

"I reckon I will." She said with a smile.

After parting ways in the park, Jack went straight back to Ricky's house, went inside after retrieving the hidden key from inside an old boot sitting casually on the concrete veranda. Walking to the kitchen to put the key on the bench, he contemplated his next move. He wasn't sure what to do with himself right now, and wasn't sure what to do with this boy that had his head spinning 'round like a faulty carnival ride.

Thinking he's smart, figuring he'd feed two birds with one

scone, he found the only stash left from his past with the effervescent past with Mary Jane. The cops never went through his schoolbag. Without the slightest feeling of regret, he took it to Ricky's room, let a 90's rock medley CD play its angst driven sound on the floor by the wardrobe, sat under the window he just opened, and rolled a joint to smoke himself more stoned than the Moai statues of Easter Island.

Like to see him sleep tonight without me... See how he likes that... Then he'll wake up to himself... Fuckin little faggot...

~ 11 ~

"Oh what the hell is going on with those two? They're so weird." Ricky said to the girls while they sat in Candice's room. Candice had just told them what she had witnessed this morning. Rose had told the other two what Jack said happened.

"You should have seen Jack when he came back. He was so highly strung about it." Rose informed.

"Wyatt's never been one to get close to people in *that* way. I think he's just confused." Candice said breaking off a piece of chocolate from the block.

"That's pretty much what I said to him. I told him to just be his friend and stuff for now. Between us three, he really likes him. If I wasn't sure, I wouldn't say anything." Rose said confidently.

"I'm still trying to sort of get used to it, but I'm totally fine with it." Ricky confided. "The other night I told him what Wyatt's naughty weakness is." He said after swallowing his own bite of chocolate.

"Vanilla ice cream?" Candice asked with a smirk. Ricky nodded with a grin.

"Jack is convinced Wyatt likes him, in *that* way." Rose said.

"Well as one of his closest guy friends, I can honestly say I've barely ever seen him without clothes so... Jack got him wound up enough to strip in front of him." Ricky said, hardly believing the words he'd just let out.

"I'll be totally honest and say I've thought it for a while, years. I think he does like him. It's just that with our mum and everything..." Candice stopped her sentence due to not knowing how to word her point.

"He's reluctant to admit it to himself?" Rose suggested like she's an expert on the subject. Candice nodded at her. Rose continued by saying "Yeah, Jack's known he's gay for years, I don't even remember when he started saying stuff about it. But with our life he's tried to hide it from the world. Until now I guess."

"Oh it's so sad!" Candice said seriously in a whiny tone. "They'd be so cute together."

Ricky scratched the back of his head, imagining the scenario.

"Not to mention it's something nice to concentrate on after what happened. Wy hasn't told any of us what it was like for him." Candice continued.

"Maybe he could go see who Ryan and Ethan are seeing. A counsellor person." Ricky suggested.

"Yeah and they might even help him with the gay thing." Rose agreed.

They sat there thinking about it with slowly nodding heads.

"Do you have to go to school tomorrow?" Ricky asked Candice.

"No, you?"

"No but I'm wondering if I should. The longer I stay away the harder it'll be to get me to go back." He said laughing with Rose joining.

"I know what you mean." She said with a semi roll of the eyes.

~ 12 ~

Wyatt lay on his bed. He could hear them laughing in

Candice's room.

They're probably laughing about me...

All day now he'd been in a stormy mood. Eccentrically storming on his own by choice. Never before had he felt this way, this fearful, this confused, this massive deepness inside him.

Ricky had knocked on his door a couple of times earlier when he got here, he said he had Rose with him, but he didn't want to answer the door. There was no point.

He put his pillow over his head, watching the dark memories from the times he got all these bruises and scratches all over him. The time he stayed under the Brandis' house and of the time his friends and sister were being attacked by evil men, the blood everywhere, the cries of struggle and fear. The death.

Jack's eyes, his face, his smell, touch... Everything...

He could feel something churning within his chest. It's uncomfortable and black with fear of newness. He lay on the sheets, his head buried deep until he couldn't take it anymore, having to try and release some of this mass within his being. He screamed into his pillow as hard as he could, tears of frustration flowed from his eyes, soaking into his bedding. If anyone heard him, he didn't care, he kept going until it felt like his lungs were going to come out his mouth. His throat ended up sore, his face red and his hair ruffled. Did he care? No.

He stayed there for the rest of the day, not eating and not communicating.

~ Ten ~

TWEED HATS AND SWEET
THINGS

~ 1 ~

A clock ticked away on the wall, a television showing one of the morning shows, the other patients sniffling and reading magazines. A little girl and a toddler boy playing with toys from the kid's area, their parents trying to keep them quiet.

Ryan sat between Ethan and his mother waiting for this droning day to finally be over. Now Monday, the day him and Ethan were to be meeting with a counsellor. Neither of them were interested in the situation, it wasn't that they didn't appreciate the help and concern. They just don't like doctors of any sort or practice, especially Ryan.

"Hey I'm sure I'll be fine, I don't need to go I'm telling you." He said in a polite tone.

"No Ryan, you've got to do this. They can help you with things that are troubling you." She said like it was the most important thing in the world. "And quite frankly, it's just the right thing to do."

She'd been really good ever since the kidnapping incident. Ryan supposed she felt like shit on a stick because Thelma

247

Kersh was living under her roof while she organised all these terrible things. Even their dad was better, and that was saying something because he's as grumpy as the dwarf.

"Let's just do it. I mean we'll just go this once after we act like we're fine." Ethan noticed his mum look at him. "Which we *are* fine, we're fantastic." He said with a fake grin.

"I just don't want to go." Ryan nagged.

"Too late, you're already here. It'll be fine, okay." She said right before a voice calmly called out Ryan's name. His stomach tightened with reluctance to do as he was being told. He stood up and began to walk in the direction of the person that called him, he didn't even look back at his family.

A woman in one of those tight grey skirt suits stood there smiling at him as he walked towards her. She must be in her early thirties he figured. Round framed glasses sitting on her face, dirty blonde curls fell down around her head. Her teeth bright white as she smiled.

"Ryan?"

He kept walking and nodded.

"Hello Ryan, my name is Dr Kraus." She said offering her hand out to him. He took it and let her shake it, not bothering to even try to fake a smile.

He followed her down a hall to a room quite quaint and friendly, although it had no positive effect on Ryan's enthusiasm to be there.

"Just take a seat." She said as she sat herself down on a big chair in the middle of the room. He sat across from her in another, actually quite comfortable chair. Squishy enough to not make you feel like you're trying to murder your backside by sitting there for ages.

"You can call me Amanda, out there I'm always 'Dr Kraus.'" She said with a laugh.

"That's funny." He replied still barely cracking a smirk.

She crossed her legs. "Okay Ryan, this is a free environment. You can say as much as you want, or as little as you want, but no matter what, you will not be judged."

"Okay." He nodded indifferently.

"Tell me about yourself. What are some of your hobbies?"

He shook his head slowly. "I don't know.... Drawing, hanging out with my friends..."

"Oooh what sort of drawings?"

"Like, grey lead. Mainly portraits and stuff."

"Wow, well done. I can't draw, couldn't to save my life!" She said with no reaction from him. "So, what are your friend's names?" She asked.

"There's Ricky and Wyatt... I guess now Rose, Jack... And Candice." He said as he disliked how she was writing things down.

"That's a lot. Do you know them all from school?"

"I met Ricky and Wyatt at school years ago. Candice is Wyatt's older sister, and I met the twins, Jack and Rose... Just the other day really." He really didn't want to say how he met them.

"Interesting!"

"Yeah sure." He said uninterested in her interest.

"What do you guys get up to?"

"Nothing out of the ordinary. Just video games, music, we walk all the time. Just hang out." He answered shrugging his shoulders.

"You guys must be the most well behaved teenagers of the decade, honestly."

Finally, Ryan smiled with even another shrug of the shoulders.

"I mean it too!" She said laughing. She got serious when she asked the dreaded and inevitable. "Now, is there anything troubling you? It could be anything, anything at all."

He couldn't decide whether or not to actually confide in this stranger and tell her all the things that were on his mind. How do you even do that anyway? When you've been stewing in your own thoughts for so long things only make sense in your head and not when you try to tell someone. But, he could say things to her he didn't want to burden his friends with, or things he didn't want to say to them in general. He supposed the meeting of the twins was a good place to begin the tales of his troubles.

"You know how I said I met Jack and Rose the other day?"

She seemed genuinely interested to know what he was going to say. "Yep, the twins."

"Well, I actually met them properly when they were helping my other friend Wyatt escape from the kidnappers that were keeping him under the house they lived in. He was kidnapped by the person that was living with my family that's supposed to be my Aunty."

She stared back at him with calm surprise. "Hmm. Would you like to tell me more about it?"

Ryan began to tell her the whole story from his point of view from beginning to end. He paid no attention to how long it took for him to tell it, but one thing was for sure; he left that daunting building glad that he'd done it and glad that he'd met Dr Amanda Kraus.

~ 2 ~

Candice was beginning to think that by the time she's old and wrinkly her greatest skill would be knocking on doors.

"Wy come on." She said as she knocked on his door some more.

No answer.

"That's it, I'm coming in."

She opened it to see he was just laying in bed. She hadn't seen him since Sunday morning, it was now Monday afternoon. Her parents told her to just give him some space but if they knew that all he was doing was laying in bed up here they'd surely not say that.

"Wyatt?" She said softly as she approached the bedside.

He's breathing thank God...

She could see the blanket moving up and down slowly. She leaned over him to see if she could see his face. His eyes were closed, he looked as peaceful as the ocean down by Plastic Park on a quiet morning.

Oh man, what am I gonna do?...

She reached a hand out and shook him gently, saying his name. He squirmed, opening his sleepy eyes to look at her. "Candice, what are you doing?" He said in a not so pleasant way.

"You have to come and have something to eat."

"No, I'm fine." He said and rolled back over.

"Please Wyatt?"

"I just said no." He asserted as he covered his head with the duvet.

"How come you're sleeping all day? It's not like you at all."

"Because I can." He said sounding muffled under the covers.

She looked around and noticed that literally nothing in the room had moved since she was in here yesterday morning. The clothes, bedding, books and all were exactly the same.

"You have to-"

"Oh my god Candice just leave me alone!" He said with a raised voice, still under his bedding.

She didn't reply, only staring in amazement that he'd just spoken to her like that.

Little dorky, perfect haired, sensible Wyatt was laying in bed all day, yelling at her to go away. She didn't know what to do other than obey him. She turned around and left the room with a soft slam of the door behind her.

She quickly walked to her own room to think over what she was going to do. She had to help him, no doubt about that.

But how?...

She figured she should give it a few days before bringing the others into it. That would give him a chance to get up on his own or for her to convince him to come out. Having more people around might make him feel like he's trapped or something. She felt herself beginning to feel more scared for him now than when he went missing.

Now look what you've done, you good for nothing dirtbag...

He was finally sleeping, and she woke him up, but he still felt the guilt of talking like that to her. He didn't want to feel guilty, he didn't want to feel anything. All the feelings he possibly had within himself felt like they were turning into one big, razor edged feeling, sitting in the dark hole where his heart tried hard to beat.

It all felt raw, his insides felt red and raw.

Why? Because of everything. That was it, everything.

He kept his eyes closed as they began to threaten tears. He'd love to try and sleep while it was still daylight. He of course never slept last night, the dark got to him so much he couldn't get up to put a light on, even to just reach out to the lamp beside the bed.

If Jack knew this, he'd feel like the shittiest shit on the planet.

~ 3 ~

"Hey mum, we should get some of these." Ricky said holding a bag of clothesline pegs.

"What the heck for?" Sally answered.

"For when dad's eaten too many beans at dinner." He said

completely casually. Rose and Jack both laughed so hard there were people going past looking at them strangely.

"Oh my... I have to admit though that was pretty good." She said to Ricky with a smile.

The four of them were doing a small shop at the supermarket for something to do so they weren't sitting around bored at home, plus they needed a few bits and pieces before it was actually shopping day.

"Oh, shit Ricky, you're like... A comedian man. Seriously." Jack said relaxed.

"So I've been told." He replied with a laugh.

"Okay guys what else do we actually need?" Sally asked in seriousness.

"Mum, I don't bloody know. We gotta start writing lists." Ricky said looking around.

"What about washing powder?" Rose asked.

"Oh yes, that was one of the things!" Sally exclaimed. "See this is why I always wanted a daughter."

"I'm standing right here you do realise." Ricky said pretending to be offended.

At the checkout, they looked at the many bunches of flowers near the front of the service desk. At the sight of them, Rose was reminded of Violet and her strangeness.

Where is she?...

It made no sense to her that if the group is so important, why doesn't she stay in touch and let them know what she's actually talking about? It was also seeming that the more she didn't see Violet, the more she was not actually thinking about it, like it was being buried fast under other thoughts and memories. She was beginning to care less and less about her and the dog.

"Hey Rose, would you like some of those?" Mrs Benson asked still at the register.

Rose realised she was talking about the flowers. She didn't even know what they were called or anything. Purple, orange, white, pink and so on. It smelt absolutely gorgeous too. "Oh no, it's fine Mrs Benson." She said smiling.

Jack walked up behind her, insisting they get some. "How 'bout these?" He held up a bouquet of several white ones. They kind of looked like little lilies.

"They're so pretty, let's do it." Sally said taking them from Jack, who seemed pleased with himself.

Rose knew straight away that he'd started up his friendship with Mary Jane again yesterday. He was hazy and carefree when her and Ricky got home from seeing Candice, acting as though he didn't care about a thing they said about Wyatt.

He's back to the version of himself that he was before they tried to help the kid under their house, except he was happier now than back then. That certainly didn't mean it was the version Rose was happy to see again. The Bensons let on in little ways that they knew, but seemed to let him have space to do the right thing on his own terms.

"We don't need flowers." Ricky said shaking his head as they left the shop.

"You be quiet mister." His mother told him.

"Mum, you do realise Wyatt's mum is a florist. We could get some for free."

"Yeah right, she hates you for fiddlin' with her daughter." Jack said amused at what he'd stated, a small coughing fit to finish.

Rose hit him hard in the arm and Ricky gave him a totally unimpressed grimace. Sally stopped walking for a moment. "Hang on, what exactly happened?"

"Nothing mum, don't worry about it. Jack's just being a douche bag."

"Richard if something serious happened I'd prefer to hear from you than somebody else." She said unlocking the back of the station wagon.

Ricky couldn't decide whether it was a blessing that Mrs Fineman hadn't rang his parents up and explained that he tried to defile their daughter or if it was actually rather strange and off putting that she *didn't* do that.

"Not now mum." He said putting shopping bags into the back of the car. Jack and Rose lingered quietly.

~ 4 ~

For days Wyatt didn't comprehend anyone's attempts to reach the personality he used to have. His mother prayed for him every night, which was driving her husband mad. Candice tried to talk to him every day, she even offered to have him sleep in with her in case he was scared of sleeping alone. He accused her of calling him a useless wimp. Which she'd never say... seriously.

He'd occasionally leave the room to go to the toilet or go downstairs to get a slice of bread and go back up again. He looked like a hobo compared to his usual appearance. He'd probably only changed his clothes once since Sunday.

Sitting on his bed unenthusiastically looking at a slice of bread, he pondered the fact that he'd made the effort to go all the way downstairs just to get this squared piece of baked yeast. He didn't even want to eat but his very inner self understood he had to eat something in order to carry on.

Carry on with what? Is there really any point?...
Suppose these questions to himself went to a further place beyond his current understanding.

He doesn't *want* the bread, he *needs* it. He doesn't want to need it but here it is in his hand, right here and ready for the taking.

The slice of bread is here for him, and whether he wants to eat it or not, there's a part of him that needs to eat it.

Now Wednesday, Ryan dropped by hardly knowing what was going on. Lately he'd been away from the others while he was sorting things out with his family and the counsellor. He was let into the house to be told by Candice what was up with Wyatt at the moment. She didn't say the true extent but said he probably wasn't in the mood for visitors at the moment.

He walked on up to his bedroom and knocked on the door to have no answer like everyone else. He walked in to see him under the covers. It's extremely weird for Ryan to witness, it was so unusual that he considered he might have finally cracked and it's a hallucination.

"Wyatt buddy?" He said trying for a reaction.

Wyatt sat up and looked at him. Ryan tried not to react, but he looked so different.

"Watcha doing here Ryan?" He asked sleepily.

"I just came for a visit. I haven't seen you for like, ages really."

"Oh, yeah. Well not much is happening here."

Ryan looked around the room. "Yeah, I can see that. Are you okay?"

"Please just don't ask me." He said looking up at him with the most exhausted and pleading face he'd ever seen in real life. This image of his poor friend will probably inspire some art later.

"I met my counsellor on Monday, she was really nice." He said as he sat on the edge of the bed. "I was really not wanting to go but it turns out she's pretty awesome and has some solutions to stuff, she even had some of her own stories to tell."

"Not my kind of thing Ryan, but its good it's worked out for you."

"There was this one story she was telling me about her grandad from when she was little. He wore this tweed hat that frayed in some spots, but he refused to get another one 'cause he knew and loved the one he had."

"Look Ryan, I'm not really in the mood." He said wiping his eyes with his hands.

"Okay well let me know when you want to hang out."

He lay back down and rolled over as if Ryan wasn't there. Not knowing what to do with himself he left the room to ask Candice what was really going on. They stood in the hall as she told him the gist of the situation.

"So, he's really got a thing for Jack?" He asked thinking it over.

"I'm pretty sure, yeah." For a second, she thought Ryan was disagreeing with Wyatt liking boys, but he came through like a true friend.

"Well get Jack round here if that's what his problem is."

"I guess I could. It's just that it might be more than that with the whole kidnapping thing."

"Candice, let's just try and get Jack 'round here." Ryan said sternly. "What have we got to lose if we try? If we don't try something, we'll lose Wyatt."

She pulled the phone out from her jacket pocket and dialled Ricky's number.

~ 5 ~

Ricky was in his bedroom with Jack when his phone rang. He always got so excited when he saw it was Candice. Whenever she rang him, GIRLFRIEND sat boldly across the screen.mHe put the phone to his ear and spoke into it with that ridiculous posh accent. "Hello, my fair lady."

Jack watched as he spoke to into the phone, he ended up getting all serious and saying things like 'why didn't you say anything?' and 'what if I can't?' and blah like that.

Just couples stuff Jack figured.

He lay back across the bed looking at the ceiling, everything's so crazy when you look at it from different angles. So many angles and so many things to look at. On different angles. He scratched his head trying to see if that obscures this angle's view in any way. It hardly did.

"Okay, see you soon." Ricky put the phone down, looking at Jack laying there staring intently at the roof.

"How's ya ladeh?" Jack asked still observing his angle.

"She's not that great actually."

Jack sat up now with concern. "Is she okay?"

"She would be, but her brother has been hiding himself away in his room for several days." Ricky said intensely serious.

"Oh... Ahm, that's not good." Jack mumbled. He honestly didn't know how he should react.

"You and I are going over there right now, come on." Ricky ordered as he stood to get a jacket on.

"No, I'm not going." Jack said worried.

"Yes, you are, you've got no choice mate. We're all friends, and when one of us is in trouble, we interfere."

"I can't go like this." He said lowly.

"Yes, you can. By the way you gotta stop using my room for your smoking, my parents will think I join." He said with a slight laugh at the thought.

"Oh man, why me?"

"Because. Now let's go." He left the room, Jack followed behind like a mischievous puppy in trouble.

The boys left Rose and Sally in the kitchen making the dinner together and headed for the Fineman house once again.

"Hey why doesn't Rose go instead?" Jack asked when they were up the street.

"Because she's busy." Ricky said trying to think of an excuse.

"But Ricky she's just-"

Ricky turned to speak sternly. "Jack just man up and come with me. Nobody cares what happened, he's our friend. Don't act like you don't care."

Jack looked back in verbal defeat. Ricky took it as his cue to turn and keep walking. He was followed quietly.

The walk there was pretty lacking in conversation. They didn't really speak until they found Ryan and Candice at the front door where they were given the lowdown on the situation. Jack began to feel uncomfortable when they explained it's been since that morning they had the disagreement thing. He was confused at how much everyone knew about it.

"It's like after that happened, he just snapped." Candice said. "I've been trying to help him, so have my parents but nothing's working. I read once, you can't help someone unless they want to be helped."

Ryan turned to Jack, his bedazzling eyes level and unreadable. "We think he might talk to you. Reckon you can help him out?"

"Not if I caused it somehow, I don't wanna make him worse or some shit." He answered seriously.

"Nah, I think you'll be okay." Ricky said kindly, putting a friendly hand on Jack's shoulder.

"Pleeease Jack?" Candice pleaded.

"How the hell can I say no? Honestly." He said of their faith in him. He began to walk up the stairs. The others stayed to give Jack space to do his thing, whatever that may be.

He walked up to the door and knocked on it like so many before him. There was no answer. Opening it slowly, it squeaked a little as it went. He stepped across the threshold into the land of Wyatt's depression. He shut the door behind him and had a look.

Wyatt lay asleep on the bed, but only Jack would notice that he's actually wrapped in the blankets he himself had used when he stayed that night.

He walked over to try and push him awake, which didn't work. His body only flopped back when Jack took his hand away.

"Oi, wake up ya little weirdo." He said softly. Still Wyatt only breathed the shallow breaths of sleep. His hair clearly ruffled, darkened skin around his eyes, he'd definitely not been sleeping well at all.

Jack looked around the room a second time, deciding to pick up the clothes and things laying around so that when he did wake up, he wouldn't have to tidy. When he'd done a number on the room he stood back and admired his great work.

Perfect, even if I do say so myself...

He looked at Wyatt who rolled onto his back with his face facing the wall so it was out of view. He walked over and casually climbed up to get over the top of him, now on the other side between him and the wall. With his elbow holding him up, he began poking Wyatt in the face in an attempt to wake him.

Oh my Christ, how does someone not wake up to that?!...

He frowned at his still sleeping friend, deciding it was time to harass the hair. He got a few strands between two fingers and pulled. Wyatt almost instantly woke up, but he looked at Jack for maybe three seconds before closing his eyes again and rolled over.

Jack was absolutely amazed. *This guy is nuts!...*

"Hey." He said quietly. "You might wanna wake up for your guest."

Wyatt looked back, promptly sitting up when he woke properly, realising there's actually a person there with him. Jack simply grinned back.

"What are you doing?!" Wyatt asked totally surprised.

"Apparently, you've had it rough the past few days. Your sister and that wanted me to come and see what's up."

Wyatt simply sat in near disbelief as he held his blanket up over his clothed self like a naked girl.

"What's up, Tinkle-bell?" Jack asked in a caring way.

"I um..." Was all he seemed to be able to conjure.

Jack sat up, holding his arms out. Wyatt looked back for a moment as if untrusting of a peasant offering a handshake. Before another second past he leaned over and accepted his warm offer. He was so happy to be here with him again, it was like his sadness was being chased away by Jack's angel light.

"Jack, I'm sorry for whatever happened."

"Yeah, me too, whatever it was."

Wyatt began to sook again when they let go of each other.

"Hey I wouldn't be too sad about it. Worked out fine for me."

Wyatt looked at him with a confused face and sad, red eyes.

"Well, I got to see you take your pjs off." He said nodding his head with a grin.

"Oh my goodness." He replied with a shy laugh.

"It can't just be our argument that's eatin' ya."

"I'm scared of the dark." He blurted out.

"What about ya little light over there?" He asked pointing towards the nightlight switch.

"I don't want to need something so babyish."

"Oh, you little douche, it's not babyish! I can't believe you were in here for days for that. You should have rang me or somethin' so I could help out."

"It's not just that, it's everything. When I close my eyes, all this bad stuff is there. I can't stand it."

"Look, it's okay to wanna face these things on your own, but sometimes you just gotta let people in and help you. Don't push your family away man, they're worried as. So are all your friends."

"You make sense. But there's also something else that's troubling me a little. It's weird."

"That's okay, just explain the best you can." Jack said positively.

"All the bad stuff goes away... When you're around." Wyatt couldn't look at him as he confessed.

Jack's big heart melted at the sound and sight of him saying this, he almost didn't react. "That's okay, I really don't mind being here for you."

He looked back at Jack with big watery eyes, they'd probably never looked so troubled.

"Why does that trouble you though?" Jack asked suspiciously.

"Oh I don't know, don't worry." He answered quickly.

"Want me to stay tonight?" He offered, asking in his own way of shyness.

Wyatt smiled, his nodding head was to Jack the cutest thing he'd seen since the baby bunnies at the petting zoo that one time. He wanted so badly to lean over and kiss him, instead he reached out to put his hand on his shoulder, but before he could Wyatt placed both of his own gentle hands around Jack's and just held it. They looked back up at each other, Jack using his free hand to slip itself around Wyatt's neck to hold the back of his head, pulling him close against his shoulder for a strongly affectionate hug.

"You're amazing Jack." Wyatt whispered with his eyes closed against Angel's shoulder. He didn't even care that he smelled of the Devil's weed.

"You're such a sweet thing, you know that?" Jack felt totally at peace with the world. "What's wrong with me though? I'm so..." He stopped mid sentence, unable to explain what he's thinking.

"There's nothin' wrong with you Wyatt. For real." Jack replied pulling away to look at him. "Really there isn't, you're just havin' a rough time." He used his thumbs to gently wipe the tears from his cheeks.

"But-"

"Nope, there's no 'but' about it. The only thing that might be wrong with you right now is you haven't showered for days. Ya smelly dude."

Wyatt began laughing with genuine amusement. His smile clearly there but his eyes remain tired and lost.

"Why don't you go and have one, you'll feel better."

"I will, seems appropriate. Will you wait?"

"Yeah of course. If I'm not here I'll be downstairs with the others or something."

"The others are here?!" He answered worried.

"Yeah, Ricky and Ryan. I'm tellin' ya, everybody wanted me to come and set you straight. Pun intended."

Dismissing the joke, Wyatt shook his head as he got off the bed to get a change of clothes from his wardrobe. He noticed that it's all tidy since he last looked. "Did you do anything in here?"

Jack looked at him with a big grin. "Maybe."

Wyatt let out a big sigh. "You really didn't have to. You're too nice."

Jack also got off the bed, walking over to put an arm around him. "It's nothing. Just go have your shower." Wyatt smiled, leaving the room. Soon the muffled sound of rushing, clean water could be heard.

Jack wandered on back downstairs where he found the others in the lounge room, sitting and waiting. They all sat up straight with interest the moment they saw him.

"What's going on?" Candice asked eager to know the answer.

"He's having a shower at the moment." Jack replied as he sat down on one of the foot stools.

"So, he's okay then?"

"Yeah, I think so, he's just sad. Struggling with stuff, ya know?" Jack said looking to the floor.

The three of them nodded in thought. Candice asked another question that made them all look at Jack with concern. "Has he been... like, hurting himself at all?"

"You mean physically? Not that I saw." Jack said trying to think back, he didn't see anything on his arms or anything, so he hasn't been slicing himself open there.

"I don't think he would anyway, it's Wyatt we're talking about." Ricky stated refusing to think of him that way.

"Yeah, but after what's happened to him, I don't think he's one hundred percent the same person." Ryan said dauntingly.

"Um, Candice... Do you reckon your parents would be okay with me staying the night?" Jack asked, almost sounding too shy to say it.

"I'm sure it'd be fine, don't worry." She said with a small smile as she tied her hair up in a messy bun on the back of her head.

"Do you think I can too?" Ricky asked, sounding polite and innocent.

"Ahm... Probably." Candice pictured her mother's reaction to the proposition of having him stay the night. It's okay for Jack because he's a guy like Wyatt, and at least then he's not isolating himself. But Ricky's already on thin ice when it came to Candice, ever since that bloody belt incident.

"Surely she's over all that stuff by now, we almost died!" Ryan judged in a frown.

"Yeah but..." Candice began. "You know how she is. She's-"

"Freakin' scary." Jack said seriously.

"She likes *you!*" Ricky said annoyed. "What's your secret?"

"I'm not chasing after her only daughter." He said with cheekiness about him, making Ricky laugh and Candice giggle.

"Oh, I know what to do. I'll invite Bethany over, so it looks like one big sleepover." Candice said thinking she found a solution.

"Candice, that defeats the purpose a little doesn't it?" Ricky said imagining Bethany taking over so much that he can't even speak to Candice. "What if we try to get Rose here. Hey Ryan, you wanna stay?"

"I don't think I've gotta be anywhere tomorrow, so I guess, yeah." He wondered what he's supposed to do while everyone else is occupied with each other. At least if the Rose girl is here, he'll have someone to talk to.

They heard the bathroom door open then someone walking through the hall. Jack turned to the others with a nod and left for upstairs.

In Wyatt's room, Jack was telling him that Ricky might be staying the night too. He wasn't really wanting to talk to anybody just yet so the thought of Ricky being here overnight was getting to him already.

"What's wrong with Ricky?" Jack asked folding the bedding from Wyatt's bed. He was tidying up some more except Wyatt was helping this time.

"Nothing, I just feel stupid after how I've been acting." His hair remained a little wet and the strands splayed out in all directions. It's a look Jack was quite enjoying.

"You'll get over it. Besides I think he'll be hangin' out with Candice, unless we actually go talk to him. They're all for giving you some space." With one arm holding blankets and sheets, he ruffled Wyatt's hair with his fingers. "Don't worry Tinkle-bell."

After receiving a big smile in return, he walked over to the laundry basket and placed the bedding in it, noticing that the colourful bracelet Rose had given him sat around the neck of a Superman ornament on a shelf above the desk. He picked it up with a smile and went over to the window. He pulled open the curtains to light the room with beautiful natural light. He then opened the window to let in some much needed fresh air, it's stuffy in here after being closed up for a while.

He turned back to Wyatt, the pedantic straightening out of a sheet over the mattress made him smirk. It seemed it just *had* to be perfect. "You know I made this thinkin' you were only a little kid." Jack said holding up the bracelet as he walked over.

"Well, I really like it." Wyatt said as he took it from him.

"Even considering how you got it?"

"Yes, the whole thing has turned out okay. I mean we're all alive, Ryan's aunt is on the run, you and Rose are better off."

"Looking on the bright side now, are we?" Jack replied in a higher, playful tone.

Wyatt shook his head with a smile, looking down at the colourful piece of jewellery only to look back at him. "Besides... It's really *cute.*"

"You are." Jack replied without even thinking.

Wyatt turned away blushing, putting the bracelet around his wrist before he continued to finish the bed making.

With that to keep a pep in his spirits, Jack noticed the bin mostly had bits of bread sitting in it atop a pile of scrunched papers and tissues. "You been keepin' ducks in here or somethin'?"

"Pardon?" He replied turning to see him referring to the waste basket. "Oh, no it's just what I've been eating."

"Well you can't have been eating much if it's all in there."

"I didn't really want to throw it away. I mean I needed to eat, but suppose I was just reluctant."

"Well stop chuckin' things you need. Today, that stops!" He pointed his finger towards him like an officer talking to a street urchin, complete with his hand on his hip.

Wyatt nodded with an accepting smile at his authoritative care.

~ 6 ~

Just before dark now, after organising who could stay and sorting out who was sleeping where, the get together on this night turned out to be the best possible thing for all six of them. They needed their bonding time.

"My mum's turned into a damn bodyguard." Ricky said to the others while they sat in the lounge room.

"Isn't that better than not caring?" Candice asked, it should be a given.

"Well yeah, but she didn't want us to come here tonight and that's for sure." He said referring to himself and the twins.

"I think she was also a little upset that she'd made dinner for five." Rose explained, sitting on the floor with her phone. She kept it close because Jack was messaging from upstairs with 'updates' on Wyatt's social confidence.

"Hey at least there's leftovers so she doesn't have to do more." Ricky said trying to justify himself.

"God, you're such a doofus." Candice bantered. Ricky's reply was a hand ruffling the hair on the top of her head, which she now had to take out and put back up.

"We should play twister or something." He suggested casually.

"Okay, why're you so obsessed with Twister?" She asked, making it sound as though he's a creep.

"Um, because it's a bloody hilarious game. Duh." He rolled his eyes as though she's an idiot.

"Man, I haven't played that for ages." Rose said amused at the memory of playing with Hannah and Jack. *I should have seen if Hannah could be here...*

Ricky laughed. "Let's do it then, I know you guys have it."

"Okay, I'll just go get it." Candice unenthusiastically. It wasn't her most favourite of games.

"This is gonna be funny." Ryan said to the other two, who laughed at each other with cheeky grins.

~ 7 ~

"You know what I hate?" Wyatt said as he moved his pawn to the square ahead.

"Please say playing chess." Jack said pretending to be bored. Wyatt was trying to teach him how to play, Jack was saying he hated it even though he'd never played properly. Only when he and Rose were little and even then they were only using the pieces as action figures.

"No. When people don't recycle their rubbish. I mean it's so easy these days and so many people don't bother."

"That... Was just so random I don't know what to do with myself."

"Well, I just get thinking sometimes."

"More like *all the time*." Jack said while he was trying to remember the pattern in which the knight moves on the board. "But yeah, I totally agree with you." His phone lit up with a message from Rose. "Haha, yes! They're playing Twister downstairs, we have to go join them. Rose *sucks* at it!"

"You can go, I'll stay here and... Do something." He replied without the slightest idea of what he'd actually do.

"Nah-uh mister, you're comin' with me." Jack demanded happily, possibly enough to make Wyatt do anything he asked of him.

"Okay but I'm not playing."

"That's okay, you'll have the best view of Rose fallin' flat on her face." He said as he got up, Wyatt stayed sitting on the floor. "Nobody thinks you're stupid so stop worrying." He said offering his hands out.

Wyatt took them, letting Jack pull him up and lead him out of the room still holding one of his hands. He didn't let go until they were at the bottom of the stairs.

They walked into the loungeroom to see they'd already started, the foot stools moved to the sides of the room so that the whole centre of the lounge was free. Ricky stood by laughing with Ryan standing on the side of the Twister mat, Candice stuck in a weird squat and Rose trying to balance on a hand and foot.

Jack walked over while Rose exclaimed "No, no no don't!" with her arm out to stop him before he promptly tickled under the arm holding her up. Wyatt sat on one of the recliners and watched as she fell to the ground, making Ryan stumble backwards and Ricky laugh hysterically.

How could I have been too nervous to see my own friends?...

They played for ages while Wyatt watched, smiling at their carefree stupidity. They balanced ridiculously over each other, stumbling to the ground in clumps of flying limbs, their laughing and shouting was amazingly not attracting the attention of an irritated Mrs Fineman.

He began to yawn in between the giggling at the sight of these amazing people. It occurred to him that even though there's evils out there ready to grab him and try to tear apart his soul without remorse, he's glad to be a part of this moment, to be a part of their lives.

Candice pushed Ricky out to the side because he kept helping Jack cheat. Turns out tickling people when they're trying to balance is more fun than the actual game.

"Oh come on, it's just a game." He said to Candice who was trapped underneath the other three.

"No, go away." She said angrily.

"What about him? He started it." He argued, humoured as he pointed at Jack.

"He's a guest so he gets away with it." She stated un-apologetically.

"What am I?" He frowned.

"Single if you don't drop it." She said with an evil smile.

He shook his head pretending to be serious and got to his feet. He looked at Wyatt and decided to go squish himself onto the chair with him. Wyatt tried to move over so he had room, not that it mattered because there wasn't any.

"So temperamental." Ricky said talking about Candice.

"She tends to be really competitive." He replied as his thoughts turned deep. "Suppose that's something you'll have to get used to."

Ricky looked at him, unable to resist placing his arm around his shoulders like he usually does. "I've really missed having you around Wylie Coyote."

"Can't say I missed you calling me that." He replied, loving to hate it.

"Don't be stupid Wylie!! You love it!" Ricky said giving him a huge hug, basically sitting on him.

"Calm down!" He said amused.

"Hey is anyone hungry? We should totally order pizza!" Ricky said to the room, still on Wyatt.

"Us and what money?" Candice asked kneeling on the floor. She had to giggle when she saw her little brother smiling under Ricky.

"Who can contribute what?" Ricky asked.

"I can pay for it guys, I don't mind." Wyatt said trying to sit up straight.

"No way, we can all pitch in." Jack said in protest as he sat up on another recliner, knowing damn well he only had three dollars... Still back at the Benson's house.

Wyatt knew that the twins especially wouldn't have much money to their names. But he had a stash in his room from his allowance, he's an excellent saver. "Honestly it's fine, don't try to argue." He said in a friendly way.

After Wyatt had asserted his paying for pizza authority, Ricky rang up the shop and ordered to get three pizzas. The phone call was interesting due to the fact they didn't decide what they wanted beforehand, so Ricky had to listen to their requests while trying to tell the shop clerk what they were saying.

Eventually they had their precious pizza in front of them. Mr Fineman insisted that he be the one to pay and answer the door. He didn't trust anyone now, even pizza boys.

"How can you have pizza without meat? Isn't that like having a milkshake without milk?" Ryan asked Jack while they sat around the coffee table like Japanese diners.

"It tastes fine, better even." Jack replied, then took a bite from his meat free piece.

"I'd think there was something wrong if it had no cheese." Ricky added.

They all nodded their agreement.

With their bellies full of warm cheesy pizza, Wyatt declared that he was too tired to stay up any longer. They all understood considering he looked like his eyes were going to drop out of his head.

"I'ma hit the hay too guys." Jack said following him out of the room. While Jack made his way upstairs, Wyatt took one last look at his friends. His affection towards them made him feel even sleepier.

After putting his freshly cleaned pyjamas on and brushing his teeth, he made it back to his bedroom to see Jack had already changed into his own pyjamas, now setting up his spot on the floor again.

"You're totally sure you want to have no lights on?" Jack asked when he finished laying the blankets out.

"Yeah, I should be okay."

Jack looked at him with squinted eyes and a playful smirk. "I don't trust you."

"Well, you can have the light on if you want." He stated confidently.

"Just don't even try to act tough with me Tinkle, I know your secrets." He said pointing at him.

"But I'm not." He said getting into his bed. "Thanks again for staying."

"No worries, spices up my boring life." He answered walking over to the light switch to turn it off. "You ready?"

"As I'll ever be."

Jack flicked the light switch, leaving them in near total darkness. The moonlight shone through the cracks of the curtains. Wyatt hated to be in it, the tiny light from the moon seemed to make it worse. Hearing Jack scuffle around made him feel better though, so that's something.

He remembered him saying he was afraid of the dark too. That night under the house while they were waiting for something to happen.

Is he really?...

Wyatt dozed off into darkened sleep before he knew he was even drifting.

~ 8 ~

Ricky switched rooms with Rose so that now he could be with

Candice in her room while poor Rose and Ryan stayed in the spare. If the prison guard personality of Mrs Fineman caught on to their shenanigans, there would definitely be hell to pay.

"I kind of feel bad for leaving the other two on their own." Ricky said to Candice in the dark.

Candice was already under the blankets. "They'll be fine. Besides, they might get to know each other better."

Ricky felt his way over the bed to lay beside the wall. "Could you imagine if Rose and Ryan got together, and Jack and Wyatt? What are the chances we'd all happen to find each other like that?"

"It'd be crazy but amazing." She said with a drowsy voice.

"I'm scared your mum is gonna see me in here." He said getting comfortable with an arm over her waist.

"Don't worry about it."

"Easy for you to say. What's the bet you'll regret saying that?"

She searched with her hand for the arm sitting over her and smiled at the feel of him being there. It still felt foreign to have him, because of the sheer fact the entire experience is new to her, but also because of who it is. Bethany didn't know they were together, what would she think? All that aside it felt right to her. Right now, she wouldn't have it any other way. "Stop panicking and just enjoy being here, will you." She ordered, thinking of his body beside her.

"Oh I am." He said as he moved closer to her, burying all his senses in everything that is Candice Fineman. Valiantly ignoring the inevitable flow of natural appreciation down below, his hand subtly stroked over her stomach as he thought of how the pizza she'd eaten was all cosy in there making her a little rounder.

Shit that's so cute...

He was beginning to think that he wouldn't ever find the right time to let her know how much he actually loves her. He felt ridiculous because they'd only been together for not even two weeks. He's wise enough to just enjoy the relationship in its early form before going into the deep feelings he had. He did however, excruciatingly hope that she felt the same way as him.

~ 9 ~

Rose wasn't used to sharing a bed with someone else, unless it's Jack she got uncomfortable. Ryan had offered to set himself up on the floor, but she was too nice to say yes. She couldn't let someone sleep on the floor just because she was uncomfortable.

They now lay there awkward in the dark, trying to sleep but not really succeeding. If one was drifting, the other would move or something, accidentally pulling them away from their sleep attempt. It'd started to rain, which usually helps with sleep.

Eventually Rose had to speak. "They totally owe us."

Ryan wasn't up for conversation but figured he might as well engage in it considering he's still not asleep. He rolled onto his back and sighed. "Yeah. If Candice's mum finds us and them, she'll freak."

"The last thing I need is to make trouble while Wyatt is recovering from himself, and Jack has found a good friend in him." Rose said also shifting onto her back.

"I can't help but think it's all so they could make out." He stated flatly.

"No, no, I highly doubt it. Jack's just as shy as Wyatt at the moment." She answered seriously.

"Ah no, I meant the other two." He said slightly put off.

"Oh yeah well they just want to spend time together I guess, even if it just means creating elaborate plans involving their trusted friends so they can make out and do it on the sly."

Giggling a little at her word use, he repeated them. "On the sly."

"They're probably getting it on as we speak." She said sounding casual and amused.

"Oh stop!" He said laughing. It was all jokes to him. He knew Ricky would tell him if they actually had been or did 'get it on'.

"My pleasure... or theirs!" She said laughing at her sleep deprived humour.

"You're actually terrible."

"My brother is worse."

"I'm still trying to get used to it, Wyatt I mean." He said somewhat seriously.

"They're just people, like us."

"Oh yeah, I know that, I'm okay with it. It's just still a little weird, because it's Wyatt. I've known him for ages, and I guess it's... I dunno."

"I know what you mean, I think."

"I kinda just hope it works out for them you know? He can be slow with change and stuff."

"Yeah, I hope it works too." She said with a yawn.

"But there is one thing with Wyatt, when he loves something, he *really* loves it."

"Ryan, you're quite the romantic, aren't you?" She said playfully.

He laughed, trying not to be too loud. "I wouldn't say that at all."

"Oh, come on, you're an artist, right?"

"Yeah, sort of."

"Artists always have a sensual side to them."

"I'll have to show you some of my stuff sometime." He said thinking about his art back in his own bedroom with the bed he'd kill to be in.

"I'd love that actually." She said delicately.

"Really?" He found her interest feeling genuine, quite up-lifting really.

"Yes of course. I have a friend that can draw, that's worth indulging in."

He could hear the smile as she spoke, evoking his own. "You talk like a poet."

"Oh wow, now you're just making stuff up."

"I don't make stuff up. Unlike my counsellor."

"You have a counsellor that makes stuff up?" She asked with another yawn.

"Yeah, she was telling me this story about how her grandad had an old hat that turned out to be worth hundreds of dollars."

"Whoa okay. Wish that'd happen to me."

He laughed again. "Yeah, me too."

"I have this friend from school and her dad collects old stuff. Sometimes he comes across expensive antique stuff." She said referring to Hannah's father.

"Wicked. Ricky would love that."

"I like that record player he has."

"So do I. And his bike."

"Oh my God I know right. That thing is huge, you should draw it." She suggested.

"Seriously? Suppose I could..."

"Do it, Mr Van Gough." She said with a small laugh.

"I might... So, how's it been staying at Ricky's anyway?"

"They've all been so damn nice. I really get along with his mum. Ricky has been so good with Jack, they're like brothers."

"That's awesome." He said smiling in the dark, glad that this deserving person gets to live his dream. "It's so cool how we're all friends and stuff."

"I know. I feel privileged."

"Only a poet would say privileged."

"Totally not true." She said pushing his arm gently.

"Whatever you say Shakespeare... -ette."

"Ette." She laughed. "Very funny."

Now they both yawned, it seemed the act of conversation was leaving them more tired.

"I think I'll try and sleep again." He stated.

"Same here, fun chatting to you Ryan." She said as she rolled to her side facing the edge of the bed.

"Yeah same here, Rose." He replied doing the same.

Now they both whisked themselves away into the floating world of their subconscious minds, free to dream of whatever they opened up to.

~ 10 ~

The sound of someone flushing the toilet startled Wyatt awake, much to his disappointment. There's no way he wanted to be awake right now, it's so dark. The rain too, it gushed onto the roof with heavy drops. How can he sleep through rain and wake up to a flushing toilet?

Doesn't matter, he's in the dark now. Dreaded thoughts of something he couldn't see doing unexpected things like viciously pulling the blankets off him were troubling to the extent of being immobilised. He can't stay like this but there's also no way he'd be able to fall asleep again.

He didn't want to move but remembered Jack is right there on the floor. He could reach down and get his attention... But what if a strong, prickly hand grabs hold of him and pulls him into the nothing of dark death?

Doesn't matter, he'll do it because it's Jack. If he could just get him awake it'll all be fine. He hesitantly rolled over to dangle his arm over the side of the bed, feeling around.

This is so flipping wimpy...

He felt something that was most likely Jack's shoulder and shook it back and forth. "Jack, you awake?"

There was a small grumble before he replied. "I am now, what's the buzz?"

"I woke up." He whimpered.

Jack sat up with half closed eyes and rubbed his forehead before standing up.

"What are you doing?" Wyatt said in a near whisper to the darkness.

"Just move over." He answered drowsy.

"But-"

"Again, 'but' nothing. Move over and let Superman do his job." He demanded in a deep, croaking drowsiness, starting to climb into the bed. Wyatt moved over towards the wall so they could fit a bit more comfortably. He's now fully under the covers thinking how it's so much warmer up here than down there on the carpet. "Now come here." He said rolling over to face Wyatt.

Wyatt hesitated at the request.

He can't be serious... But why shouldn't I?...

He moved himself closer to Jack, who promptly put his arms around him with the same forceful grace that he's already getting used to. Oh, how he does love how Jack feels.

Squished up against his chest with his arms crossed, his face somewhere around Jack's neck, he could swear he could hear his heartbeat, or was he *feeling* it? It's steady and strong, the perfect sound he needed right now.

"Better now?" Jack asked still sounding sleepy.

"So much better." He replied content. He felt movement, then the unexpected soft force of a kiss against his forehead. Jack moved back to how he was, letting out a deep breath before falling asleep. Wyatt's eyes sat open with surprise during Jack's display of affection.

Oh my goodness, that was a kiss... He just kissed me...

He closed his eyes to the room's darkness to see much the same thing beneath his eyelids. Doesn't matter, he's being held by his Angel. This was by far the strangest, yet most comfortable moment of his life so far.

He began to fall away into sleep as he listened to the beating of Jack's beautifully strong heart. The rain continued to pour outside, promising to not ease its flow as the drops hit the roof, soaking the ground and all that's out from under cover.

At least the Earth drank well tonight.

~ Eleven ~

ABILITY TO TRUST

~ 1 ~

Debra Shepherd was making a slow stride along the path headed for the Main Street. It was a nice morning, the rain from last night had the ground wet but as sure as you can be about anything, the sun will soon dry it. This iss the first proper outing she'd had since her daughter left forever.

No, not forever... She'll be back, she has to come back...

There were times she swears she saw her lost girl. There were moments she'd go to shut the curtains and see someone outside. Once she went to see if it was her Lily but when she got to the front door, there was only a dog sitting there.

Nothing but a lousy dog.

Lily wanted a dog, and a horse like most little girls. Debra too does love horses but there was no way she was going to buy her daughter one, too much work to look after them. The next thing on her list was a dog, which Debra considered but never acted upon.

Now that she's gone, she felt terribly guilty. Like she should have done everything Lily ever wanted, gotten her all the things she wished she had.

How was I supposed to know?... I told her not to leave my sight... No, don't blame her... It's not Lily's fault...
It was amazing, the number of times her mind said these things. It's like it's on repeat, just a loop of sadness, anger and guilt. It wasn't bringing her back though.

Just as she approached the crossing onto the wide road that led into the Main Street, she took a moment to take in the view of the catholic school over the black tar across from her. Lily's school. She had only been going there since the start of the year, but she loved it a lot better than the other one. She made better friends, though it didn't stop the bullies. She used to ride her bike to school, that's how the other kids found out she couldn't ride without training wheels.

She loved that purple bike...
She began to think back to the moment Lily finally learnt to ride without the training wheels, she was so happy and so proud of herself.

Now she'll never be able to show them all she could do it... No, don't say never...
She waited for a break in the cars and began to cross quickly, the last thing she wants to do is be hit by a car and be spread across the road, just in case she's still out there alive.
She made it to the other side safely, trying desperately not look at the schoolyard. Children would be arriving and going inside to start their day of being educated. Parents and their healthy children, it isn't fair.

After a long walk by the school grounds she kept going, passing the town's RSL on the other side of the big roundabout that separated the Main Street from the road she was just on-complete with an underpass full of graffiti, and another one that could eventually lead out to where the Brandis twins used to live.

After she crossed the decorative wooden bridge through a well-kept green area, she made her way to the shops where she wasn't at all impressed with how life seemed to go on here like nothing happened. Of course people have to live their lives, pay bills and feed their families but it felt wrong.

She wanted to pay her bills and feed Lily... The parents of those older kids got to have them back, so her own little one should be here. Surely it was the same people that took her, no matter what the police say.

She walked past the Golden Dragon Chinese restaurant, one of the little real estate offices, the takeaway across the road from the milk bar Ricky basically lives in and past one of the two small banks. Seeing herself in the windows upset her, she's a shell with no insides.

Debra didn't even know what she was going to do while she's here. Maybe get a few bits and pieces from the supermarket. Even the thought of that seemed purely pointless.

She turned a corner to go down and look at the sea water when she ran into Noah Benson and another man, he was familiar... The guy from the tip. That's who it was, the dump man.

"Hey there Debbie." Noah greeted respectfully. He knew her through his wife. Her and Sally were Gerry Craft Club acquaintances before the shit hit the fan for Debra.

"Hello Noah, how's Sally?" She asked hoping he doesn't say anything about her missing daughter. If nobody mentions it, she should be okay to talk.

"She's good. How're you holding up?" He held some sort of car part, probably here helping someone with their car issues, he's that kind of perfect nice guy. Many women at craft used to hassle Sally about how jealous they are.

"The best I can, I think." She said with a deep breath.

"I lost ma dog." Said the dump guy. "Actually, he wadn't

mine, but he used to 'ang out with me all the time at the tip. It's not the same without the funny doggo chasing seagulls an' goin' through the rubbish."

Debra looked at him as if he were a mental patient blabbering absolute nonsense.

"I just mean, I know what ya' goin' through." He said quietly.

"I better go, goodbye Noah. Tell Sally I said hello." She said and went on her way around them.

"Will do!" Noah yelled out after her. He turned to his tag-along mate. "Good on ya Randy, I'm pretty sure you just made that poor woman's day." He shook his head in disbelief.

"Aw don't be like that, I was just tryna help." He replied as they began walking again.

"She just lost her daughter not her junk dog." He explained sternly.

"I know I know. Lucky you got your boy back."

"Yeah there's no way I'd be able to walk around like she is if Ricky never came home. Little shit's at his girlfriend's house as we speak."

Randy chuckled. "That can't be good. Gonna have a bunch of little ones runnin' 'round."

"Oh nah, won't be like that! Pretty sure he's smarter than what I was. Then again it worked out for Sally and I."

"Don't jinx it mate."

"God forbid."

The two men had a laugh together as they walked on through the street. The sun shone bleakly through the morning clouds as they walked, not aware they were being watched by two brown eyes hiding between the bushes in front of the corner Laundromat across the street.

The eyes of a very loyal and very good boy.

~ 2 ~

"Riiickeeeya, wake up." Candice nagged to Ricky beside her. She'd just ensured her face is pretty enough and her body perfumed for being seen first thing.

He started to speak incoherently, sounding like a crazy person, but it's hilarious. "If you don't wake up right now, I'm going to take a video of your mumbling and post it on Facebook."

He opened his eyes and turned his head to see a blurry Candice meaning business. "Go ahead and post whatever you want, I won't be embarrassed." He said as he sat up.

"Why?"

"Because *you'll* be the one that has to explain to everyone what *I* am doing in *your* bed."

"Well that's true. I'll just tell them you followed me home from the pound, and being the good natured person I am I let this stray stay the night."

"Oh but poor Robbie Brannon, how would he ever recover?!" He said in a concerned tone, almost like a widowed woman. "Knowing that a younger and less popular schmuck was in his Candice's bed."

"Jesus, you are such a juvenile." She said handing him his glasses.

He took them, placing them on his face. "My name is Ricky, not Jesus."

She gave him a small punch in the shoulder and got out of bed. "How do you even know about him anyway?" She asked.

"I'm in a different grade, not universe." He watched as she put her magenta dressing gown on. He wondered if she even realises how elegant her every movement is. He felt as though he could just sit here and daydream about her and her body forever.

You dick... She's your girlfriend now, don't be a wimp...

He got off the bed and walked up behind her as she opened the curtains to the dreary sun of the morning.

"You can touch me, you know. Lord knows I tried to touch you that day." She said with cheeky reminiscing, making him feel as though she'd just read his mind.

His nervous hands gently slid around to the front of her waist with affectionate touch. She turned around, smiling at the feel of him. Her arms flung themselves around his neck when she kissed him rather passionately. It seemed the more they did it, the better they were. She giggled on the inside at the thought that they're practicing with each other. The sheer fact that neither of them cared about each other's un-brushed morning mouths should be enough indication to convey the passion between them.

He abruptly stopped. "How do you always smell like berries or something?"

"It's a little thing I like to call 'personal hygiene,' you may have heard of it." She replied, pulling him to her again. She felt his hands sneak inside her robe to glide over her ribs. Her heart began to beat faster as he had one hand on her hip and the other measuring the circumference of her left breast. "Oh god let's just do-" She began to say when there was a knock at the door.

Ricky jumped and stepped away when he heard it, as if she's now a radioactive threat. "Whoa shit!" He said in a low tone.

"Who is it?!" Candice called out doing her robe back up properly.

"It's Rose."

He put a hand to his chest, pretending to pant. "Phew, that was a close one. At least there was a knock this time. Oh, my heart."

Candice shook her head smiling as she went and opened the door.

"Ryan's still asleep and I thought I'd just come and see if

everyone else is awake." Rose said happily.

"Typical morning person you are Rose." Candice replied. "Why don't you see if the boys are awake, and we'll be out in a minute?"

Rose agreed and went on her merry way up the hall to Wyatt's room. Seeing the family photos on the wall made her feel a little sad. She often had that melancholy feeling with things like that. She knocked on the bedroom door, getting a sleepy *"Yah?"*

Totally my brother...

"You guys awake?" She called out.

Jack dangled half off the bed when he woke to Rose's knocking. He looked over at Wyatt facing the wall, squished up against it sleeping away. They appeared to have gotten too warm through the night and had moved apart. "Yeah sort of." He yelled to Rose.

"Okay well everyone else is getting up so I'll see you downstairs alright." She called from outside the door.

"Sure thing." He heard her walking away. He sat up and looked at Wyatt again, looking so peaceful laying there with his wall.

Time to disrupt the peace!...

He nudged his shoulder to start with. No reaction. Next, the gentle poking of his nose. He only shifted to hide his face. Now it's time to touch the hair.

Man, that shit is soft as heck!...

All he did was wave an arm over his head.

"Oh shit Tinkle-bell! Wake up."

This time he opened his eyes and sat up. "What's the matter?"

"The matter is that it's morning. I'm gonna have to start calling you Sleepy-bell."

Wyatt laughed and rubbed his eyes. Jack decided that if he says anything about that kiss on the forehead he'll try and pretend he doesn't know what he's talking about. He was too paranoid to go into it. Even though there was obvious attraction between them, Jack was still unsure of the boundaries here. "Rose reckons everyone is goin' downstairs."

Wyatt looked at him with a smirk.

"What..." Jack asked slightly concerned, the unexpected occurrence of the smirk intrigued him.

"Just... You look quite nice in the morning." He said sounding comfortable with his life and totally innocent.

What... The... Fuck... Did he just say that to me?...

Jack giggled nervously, and it's finally him blushing instead. "You're not lookin' so bad yourself." He replied with flirty handsomeness.

"I really appreciate you being here, you know."

"I'd be upset if you didn't."

They stared at each other smiling with happy eyes. If you were there, you'd probably crack the shits and leave the room out of impatience at the sight of them.

"Well we'd better go have breakfast." Wyatt said climbing off the bed, heading for the door.

Jack watched as he did so. "Hey Wyatt."

He stopped to turn around and look at him. "Yes?"

"Are you aware of how you sway your arse as you walk?"

He looked back with the face of surprised embarrassment. "No..." He awkwardly brushed his hair down with his fingers.

"Well you do. Or it's just my imagination." Jack said feeling pleased with himself, and a little terrified.

Wyatt smirked unsure, nodding as he opened the door to leave the room.

Jack sat alone, scratching his thigh as he began to think about his hungry stomach. Suppose the likes of Miss Mary-J lingered with him, the sassy bird. She does tend to hold on for as long as she can until the next play date.

What do posh people have for breakfast?... Seems like a good hour for a spot of tea and caviar my good Sir!...

Wyatt made his way to the bathroom, now beginning to question how he walks. He had never given care to the thought, but now...

"Morning." Ryan greeted, walking out of the bathroom.

"Morning Ryan. Sleep well?"

"I did eventually. You?"

"Um, yeah, I slept okay." The familiarity of his deep, icy blue eyes were comforting, though the way they stared made Wyatt feel obliged to tell him more, like 'yes, I'm fine now that Jack is sleeping here again, thankyou for making it happen.'

"Cool. See you downstairs?" He answered in his usual manner, his gaze subsiding, thankfully.

He nodded, and Ryan walked off in the direction of the stairs.

After finishing up in the bathroom Wyatt went back to his empty room, which is good. He wanted to change in privacy. Jack's statement seemed to have brought back his shyness and modesty.

Downstairs, they were all sitting at the dining table with an assortment of cereal boxes lined up between the small decorative flower bouquets that his mother loves so dearly. She changed them at least once a week.

When he was first taken by the kidnappers all he wanted was to get back home and see his family again. He won't forget in a hurry how much he wanted his mother, but it seems ever since his ordeal, he wasn't so much that way inclined anymore. He'll always love her, that goes without saying, but he's beginning to feel he wants to be more like himself and not turn into... That.

But what *is* himself? Who is he? These questions had haunted him for days.

He even contemplated taking down the crucifix sitting morbidly on his bedroom wall, like it's poisoning the air with some sort of airborne virus that'll turn him into a preaching, uptight, posh narcissist that can't seem to understand the concept of other people's values and how they lead their lives.

He went to the kitchen to get a bowl out of the cupboard and a spoon from the draw, went back to the table and sat next to Jack, feeling glad that she's been making herself scarce during this sleepover. Only Daddy has been lingering, just in and out of rooms occasionally.

"Hey, why don't we get a little wild and mix cornflakes and rice bubbles?" Jack suggested in his low, attractive voice.

"*Fabulous idea.*" Wyatt whispered as he began to pour the cereals into his bowl.

~ 3 ~

Over the next week, August turned quietly into September. Wyatt's sleeping improved dramatically, although he was worried how he'd go without his 'bed buddy'. Jack was allowed to stay all that time due to Candice's wise words: 'But mum, Jack being here is helping Wyatt get back to normal. If we don't let him stay, he might never get better...'
Jack actually convinced him to try out Ryan's counsellor. He was going to meet her on the day of Ryan's next meeting.

Father's Day came and went. The Jonson boys celebrated it with their dad by organising a fishing day trip to Beauty Point. They didn't catch anything but the three of them had some quality father and sons bonding, it was well overdue.

Ricky gave his dad a custom novelty mug with the words 'I may eat beans and create embarrassing scenes... But my son loves me more than just a tad, because I'm one hell of a Dad!' written over its side.

The Fineman siblings simply went out for dinner that night with their parents while Jack hung out back at the Benson's. A lot of questions about the twin's dad arose at this time. They could only say that he died in a car crash when they were really little. They barely remembered him but knew he was a good person. There's a shoe box in the twin's old bedroom that's full with photos of him. A lot of them showcased a happy man with his young family, unknowing of the death he'd unfortunately endure much too early.

Aside from the remembrance of their dead father and jailed mother, it seemed things were looking up for the twins. They were allowed to pick up some things from their old home, including the photo box which they showed the rest of the fascinated group.

Rose met up with Hannah to have what turned out to be a really nice day together. She couldn't believe what had happened at their house and it was the ultimate test of friendship, Hannah continued to be the same old friend Rose loved so much. Many other people would avoid them like the plague after learning what they used to live with operating out of their house.

Jack and Wyatt were getting to know each other well. With Wyatt becoming more and more comfortable around him, Jack was beginning to feel like he now had his first boyfriend, but he wanted to wait before broaching the subject with him. There's no need to rush something so delicate that's great just as it is... For now.

Ricky was trying to get ready to go back to school, so was Candice. Ryan, however, wasn't ready to face the other people with allegations against the child abductor he was living with for several months. Dr Kraus told him that in time people will find something better to occupy their gossiping mouths. It still unnerved him.

None of them had seen or heard from either Violet or the dog. Rose gave up bothering to worry about it. Why bother when Violet never answered properly or told them what the story is with her and the things she says about them?
Besides, they had their lives to get on with.

Nobody knew where the Kersh evil was lurking. Everybody is hoping she died a slow and painful death after what she'd done.

The group was healing physically and mentally, slowly they were each letting go of that nightmarish chapter of their lives. Ricky was secretly trying to avoid touching Candice's neck, he didn't want to hurt her just in case. He was also worried about freaking her out like if she felt somebody touch her neck she'd turn into a scared nutcase. It was out of love and care of course, even though she personally did not care in the slightest. She'd much prefer to forget that was even a thing that happened.

~ 4 ~

The day of Wyatt's meeting with the counsellor was now upon him. Ryan went with him, as well as mummy dearest. He was reluctant to go in just as Ryan was, but when he followed her into the room he felt comfortable, this wasn't scary at all. Completely not what he was expecting, which left him to wonder what it was exactly that he was expecting.

She introduced herself and asked him a few quick questions, so far nice and easy.
Then she asked him if anything is troubling him, she also ensured that he doesn't have to tell her anything but he is completely welcome to, it was confidential.

"So my mum won't be able to ask you things about what I've said?" He asked sitting in the same chair Ryan had.

"Nope, I won't tell anyone. Except if you or somebody else is in danger." She said with a humble face. Wyatt nodded and thought off into space.

His mum had managed to tell her about the kidnapping and the bout of depression he had, but she wouldn't let him know unless it was necessary. She was expecting to hear about how upset he is about the whole experience. "Wyatt?" She said. He was still in a deep thought, her voice brought him back to grounded reality.

"Sorry, I was just thinking." He focused on her face once more.

"What about? If you don't mind me asking."

Ryan was right, she is really nice... "No, I don't mind. This is what I'm here for isn't it?"

"I suppose so, yes." She said with a laugh.

"Well, I'm um..." He said beginning to get nervous, his breathing short.

"It's okay matey, nothing you say will affect this environment." She said encouraging him.

"It's just hard because I haven't really spoken to anybody about it." He cringed in discomfort.

She nodded in understanding.

Next thing he knew he just blurted it out like he couldn't hold it anymore. "I... I'm pretty sure that I like a boy. As in *like like...* A boy."

"That's okay! Tell me all about it!" She said excitedly without the slightest bit of judgement about her. It gave Wyatt a new lease on life, being able to talk to someone with such a carefree aura. He was able to tell her about Jack without feeling like he's a freak or a weirdo, or even destined for hell. He explained how they met and that having him around lately has driven the bad stuff away. He's still haunted by the memory and supposed he'll never forget, but Jack is teaching him that it's okay to live with that in the past, enjoy the present and be excited for the future.

"That is so, so wonderful. I'm really happy for you Wyatt." She said with a big smile.

"He wanted to come today, but I told him it'd be fine."

"Oh that's nice of him."

"It's just that I feel weird when I think about my family and friends finding out." He said fiddling his fingers.

"Well, tell them when you're comfortable. People can be difficult with change, but they can be very supportive. It doesn't matter whether you like boys or girls or if you're pink with purple polka dots!"

He laughed . "Try telling that to my mother!"

"You see Wyatt, Jack is good for you. He sounds like a brilliant friend and wonderful support. Don't throw him away in fear of judgement by people who should love you for you, like he does." She leaned forward with her elbows resting on her knees, both sophisticated hands around her pen. "You have the right to feel any emotions you want, especially if it's beneficial to your happiness as a person. Never be ashamed of what you feel."

"You're very wise Dr Kraus." He said seriously.

"Please, call me Amanda." She instructed kindly.

"I also worry that he doesn't really like me like that. I guess that's stupid because of what he says and does but I really have no idea what I'm doing." He said with a nervous sigh.

"Wyatt, you'll be okay." She said warmly.

He went home that night with a weight lifted from his shoulders and an obvious happy air about him. Ryan was pleased that his friend felt better after seeing Amanda. It made him feel like he'd accomplished something by seeing her other than the positive progress of his own personal wellbeing.

"So, we're dying to know! How'd it go?" Candice asked with Jack when Wyatt got home. It was nearly dinner time by the time they got back from the city. Ryan got dropped off at his house, Mrs Fineman had waited in the driveway until he went inside. For her, she maybe couldn't care less if Ryan made it home or not after what his Aunty had done to her son, but she had a reputation to uphold.

"It was actually really good, she's really nice." Wyatt informed them.

"Oh man that's awesome." Jack said happily.

"Yeah! You already seem better to me." Candice said as she tapped his arm.

"Don't be silly Candice." He answered.

She didn't react to his reply, only started to type a message on her phone with a deadly serious face.

"What are you doing?" He asked her.

"I'm updating Ricky. He told me to tell him how you went. I'm going to say 'Admits lady was nice, denies any progress'. There, sent!"

"Candice stop it, you're making me sound like a freak." He said trying to get the phone off her. They squabbled a little while Jack laughed on at their silliness.

After failing due to his sister's macho phone saving, Wyatt began to go upstairs to his room where he'd chill for a while before dinner. "You coming?" He asked Jack when he got halfway up the staircase.

"Actually, me and your big sister have a game of chess we gotta finish."

"Chess?" He asked surprised.

"Yeah, turns out I like it." He said with a wink.

"Well enjoy your game guys." He said smiling as he left.

Candice smiled sheepishly when Jack looked at her.

"What?" He asked warily.

"Nothing. Just that I see young love blossoming on the savannah." She said like she's giving a speech on romantics.

Jack blushed a little. "You be quiet, you got no idea what you're talkin' about."

"Mmhmm sure." She said walking towards the lounge with him following her to try and end their chess game.

~ 5 ~

"You ready for school?" Rose asked Ryan as they approached his front door. It's a cloudy Tuesday that had an obvious chill upon the air, pleasant but dreary. An atmosphere this town had always expertly generated.
It's also really the first day Ryan had been out walking since the kidnapping. All the parents disliked the idea of anybody being out now, but they slowly loosened the reins. He'd met up with her halfway to bring her back.

"Ugh, no. I can't be bothered with everyone crapping on about that monster."

"Yeah I know what you mean." She said tucking her chocolate copper hair behind her ear. In Ryan's honest opinion she looked lovely today, she always does but today she seemed extra girly. She's wearing a flowing floral dress, the hem past her knees with little buttons going down the front, her hair out by the sides of her head with little clips holding it back off her face. He thought Ricky might describe her as a 1970s-esque beauty, had he not been possessively claimed by Candice.

"From what I hear I could hire you as a bodyguard." He tried to joke as he opened the door.

"What do you mean?" She asked with a confused laugh.

"You beating up that bully at your school."

"Ohh." She waved her hand like shooing a fly away. "That was nothing, I just punched him in the nose."

"That's pretty badass if you ask me." He said as they walked into the house.

Her first opinion on the interior of the Jonson house is 'gold'. She'd developed this weird imaging in her head of all the houses as if they were colours. Hannah's house would be white and brown, the Benson house is some sort of red and purple, the Fineman's is greyish green and brown. Lastly the Jonson house, deep yellow and gold.

She followed him through the hallway as he told her what door led to where.
When he pointed to the lounge she had a quick peek, flabbergasted at the size of the television. It's like a car's windscreen. "That's huge."

"Oh, yeah." He laughed indifferently. "My dad and brother love their sports so I guess a big TV is a must have." He shrugged with little interest.

"It's a mammoth compared to what I'm used to."
They went upstairs to Ryan's room where she looked around fascinated at all the random artwork covering some of his olive green walls. "Cute bear." She stated wholesomely, pointing to a fluffy stuffed bear on one of the shelves above his draws.

"Oh, um yeah. Thanks." He answered embarrassed, handing her his drawing folder. He watched as she looked through them, seeming to be rather impressed with what she saw with every page turn.

"Ryan these are gorgeous. You should do this for a living." She didn't look up from the art.

"Thanks, I just do it for fun really." He said casually.

An amused smile spread across her face. "Even this one?" She held up the folder to show a loose piece that's in fact the naked girl. He'd put it in there ages ago after deciding that it didn't matter if anybody saw it, it's just a drawing. But now that somebody's looking at it, especially a girl, he felt like snatching it off her and running downstairs to burn it in the fire place.

"That's just, yeah I was seeing if-" He stuttered, trying to quickly think of something that made sense.

"It's fine." She put the folder back to browsing position in her arms. "I really like it, it's beautiful."

"Seriously?"

She looked at him as if he's a fool. "Of course." She reassured.

"It's different to what I usually do so I wasn't really sure it's actually any good."

"Well I think so." She said looking at what seemed to be a depressing sketch of a boy sitting naked and shamed with fairy wings. The face was obscured by heaving shadowing. "That's different." She said showing him. "I love it actually, I really do. Where do you even get the ideas for this stuff?"

"Funny you ask actually." He scratched the back of his head. "I got the inspiration for that one, from Wyatt."

"Seriously?!" She said surprised, looking at it again. "I get it... Now I like it even more."

Ryan smiled with happy pride.

"You've got such a mature view of the world." She said sounding impressed at her findings of him.

"Just don't tell him, will you?"

"That you drew him naked and full of despair as a fairy? Of course not." She said with a laugh. "Except if I ever find a freaky one of me in there, I'll be forced to punch you in the nose."

Ryan laughed as he tried not to picture what she looked like under her dress. He didn't go around purposely wondering what people looked like naked but with his artist mind, her comment suggested to do just that. "Don't worry, you won't."

"This one's cool too, like that's obviously you and the others on that track?" She said holding the book up to show him his drawing of himself, Wyatt and Ricky standing on the track talking.

"Yeah, I just wanted to have a memory of more than the bad stuff that happened that day." He explained, shrugging off his feelings again.

"Well it's one of my favourites." She said with a smile, looking back down at it, resting on her arm again. "I love how you even have that art bag." She said pointing to the very bag on his bedroom floor, sitting against his desk. "And how Ricky has his arm over Wyatt."

Her grin finally made him smile, a real proper, genuine smile. "I guess it's a pretty alright one." He said feeling good about himself.

"And the trees, ugh I just love it. You should do it in colour." She closed the book, wanting to see more of what he'd done. "Do you have any others?"

"Yeah, I'll just grab the box. It's got A3 to A5s. I only have those in there because they're my best A4s." He said referring to the folder.

She sat in the middle of his bedroom floor for ages sifting through his drawings. Some of these ones were coloured, it was greatly entertaining her. They were all so fascinating. He had to answer her questions of inspiration for nearly every one.
A couple were of a parrot that seemed to never have the same colour, it mainly just had the colour of mystic, starry rainbows. He ended up explaining that it was a bird he had that recently got given to someone else because of Thelma Kersh convincing his mother to do it. Rose was so enraged at hearing the story she told him to say no more and changed the subject to a rough drawing of an old shed in a paddock.

While Ryan had gotten up from his chair to go through his draws to look for the old pencils he'd used for a particular piece, Rose soon found herself looking at a bunch of odd drawings that made her stomach drop and eyes widen with surprise. She flipped the pages over to reveal the dates he drew them. She was about to raise her concern about what she was looking at when she jumped from the suddenness of somebody else's presence in the room.

"Hey Ryan." Ethan said standing in the doorway.

Rose turned around startled. "You're Ethan right?" She hurriedly placed all the art back into the box.

Ethan walked into the room. "Yeah, I was your rescue party that night."

"Thank you for what you did. I'm Rose." She said offering her hand.

"I remember." He said in such a friendly way that it made Ryan feel uncomfortable.

"What's up?" He asked him, diverting his brother's attention.

"I was just wondering if you know what's up with the Wi-Fi password."

"I'm actually not sure. I think dad did something again."

Ethan shrugged, turning back to Rose. "You staying for dinner?"

She looked over at Ryan. "No, don't think so. I'm just checking out Ryan's awesome art."

"Oh, well if you ever wanna have dinner here, just ask." He smirked the smirk, the one Ryan associates with Ethan and his 'babes'.

"Thanks." She said seeming unaffected by his charm.

Ethan turned to leave, stopping to ask if they'd seen the girl that helped him that night during the great escape.

Ryan began to reply "Oh yeah, she's-"

"Really evasive. We haven't really seen her at all." Rose quickly interrupted.

Apparently not picking up on that weirdness, Ethan left them to their privacy. Probably back to his own room where he'd play

300 ~ ASHLEA RAYWOOD

video games or plan nights out with his mates, Ryan assumed. "So why did you just shut my brother out about Violet?" He asked her confused about what just happened.

"I just think we should keep it to the six of us for now. Until we really know what's up, if we ever find out. I don't want to worry any more people with it, you know?" She said trying to make sense. She'd only just decided this view on the situation.

"Am I missing something?" He asked suspiciously, it seemed she wasn't as poised as she thought she was. His furrowed brows atop those prominent eyes made her nervous.

"Nope." She looked to her phone. "I guess I better get back to the Benson's." She said getting up from the floor.

"If you wait a little longer my mum could take you back." He said with concern. There was no way he'd let his friend walk nearly all the way back across town close to the end of the day, especially alone.

"It's still daylight I'll be fine."

"None of us should be walking around on our own. What if your mum's boyfriend's buddies grab you?"

"They were all arrested for some sort of crime each. I'll just get Ricky to get his mum to pick me up, if she can that is."

"Rose-"

"But she probably will."

He looked at her, still with a face full of suspicion and concern.

Without too long of a wait she went home with Sally and Ricky, who went along for the ride.

As Ryan went to the lounge room to hang out on his own with the TV- now that he can do this sort of thing with that trash bag gone- he thought that if he's to draw Rose, he'd have to include flowers. Maybe in her hair or something... Maybe even the only thing covering her modesty.

Man, stop wanting to draw people you know naked!... It's creepy...

Truth is, he found it easy to draw people without clothes. Not to mention it somehow adds depth to his pictures. He often thought that he must be the only guy his age that thinks of naked girls as art.

With the television windscreen turned on he thankfully lost that train of thought, concentrating on the evening game shows.

~ 6 ~

Jack entertained the likes of Patricia Fineman by trying to play the family's old heirloom piano. He'd managed a version of Twinkle Little Star with a little of her guidance, there was only so much he could remember from when he was younger. He'd dabbled in it a little at school in music class, that and a few other instruments, most notably the drums. Though he loved it, he never pursued it after his home life began to really spiral downwards. This was the first time in ages he'd touched any black and white keys, and this was a beautiful old style piano.

Wyatt sat on the stairs listening to the commotion coming from the lounge as his mother bonded with Jack over the big musical instrument.

It was getting late, and Candice was on her way upstairs when she asked him what he was doing.

"Not much. Just listening." He said quietly.

"To that?" She said referring to the laughing and mottled piano playing. "Sounds like he couldn't play to save his life."

"It's not *that* bad." He said with a small laugh.

"You should go show him how to *really* play." She suggested playfully.

"I might."

"But when mum's gone."

"Yeah, she might try to take over and point out all my mistakes." He said sounding irritated.

"Exactly. Plus, I think it'd be better that way." She patted him on the shoulder, continuing her ascent up the stairs.

He remained seated on the stairs for a little longer with his chin resting on his hands. He closed his eyes and sighed before getting up to walk on into the lounge.

Jack was sitting on the piano stool, his mum standing beside him pointing and teaching. "Oh hello honey." She greeted when she saw him behind them. "Look, Jack's almost got the hang of it already."

"Like I said Mrs Fineman, I had a good go at it in primary school." He said with a charming smile.

How is he so naturally... Beautiful?...

"Well, you know Wyatt has been having lessons for the last six years. He's quite the little Mozart, aren't you darling?" She exclaimed with bountiful pride.

"No mum, I wouldn't go that far." He said modestly.

"You didn't tell me that! Why don't you show me?" Jack moved over on the stool so that he could sit beside him.

"Not right now, maybe another time. I haven't played for a while." He said with the thought of his mother looming over his shoulder as he tried to play.

"Well boys, it's getting late so if you play make sure it's not well into the night. Goodnight." She kissed her son on the cheek on her way out, much to his dislike of her doing it in front of Jack.

"Goodnight." The boys said in unison as she left the room. Jack turned back to the piano and began to try the nursery rhyme once more. It was better than before, you could tell he was remembering which keys to press now. Wyatt stood there and watched as he concentrated so wholeheartedly to play the twinkle.

Jack started to think it was a lost cause when he felt him sit down beside him on the seat.

"At least you can tell what it's supposed to be." Wyatt said to him encouragingly.

Jack looked at him. "I suck, just admit it. What can you do?"

"I'm not the next George Gershwin or anything." Wyatt answered anxiously. "I can do a few bits and pieces, like nursery rhymes and from movies... Church stuff and other classics. Christmas carols."

"Aww yes! Please do some wicked piano playin' for me." Jack begged innocently.

Wyatt felt reluctant. "I don't know what you know though."

Jack didn't care what it was really, he just wanted to see him play an instrument. "C'mon, you can think of something. Please?"

He sat quietly to think it over, concluding with something that should make him laugh. "Okay, I think I have the perfect one for you."

"Go ahead." Jack said excitedly.

He watched as Wyatt's shaky hands approached the ivory keys, waiting patiently for him to begin. At first it was a little broken, but soon turned into a lullaby-esque version of the Titanic love theme. Jack moved closer to him when he realised what he was playing. He sat quietly beside him in the warm lamp light, watching the graceful movements of those hands dancing over the black and white dance floor, his face so pure and at peace, his lashes fluttering at the movements of his eyes gliding over the elegant sound his hands were creating. He was one with the old piano, and in Jack's opinion, at his most handsome.

If Jack had ever thought anything was astonishing and beyond words, this moment blew it right out of the park. He put an arm around him without thinking too much about it. Wyatt smiled and continued with the flow of musical beauty.

304 ~ ASHLEA RAYWOOD

At every tone of the keys, Jack could hear the song's words in his head. He hadn't heard it for years. "You're amazing." He said to the side of his face, he looked up and smiled again. Jack couldn't resist, if there were ever a time to try, it might as well be right now at this raw and tender moment. He leaned over and ever so gently kissed him on the lips.

Wyatt stopped playing, the sudden silence jarring. He looked back at him with nervous shock and adoration. In the quiet, Jack looked away, thinking he'd messed up big time. He found that horrid regret chased away by the feel of Wyatt returning the favour with a light kiss on the cheek, right before he looked him in the eyes, smiling his approval of their intimacy.

Jack couldn't be sure if there really was, but he felt there were tears forming on his eyes. It was in the face of each other they could see the open doors of their souls, offering the young promise of unconditional affection and security for one another.

They said nothing, Wyatt only looked back down to play again. This time it's a fuller version, more confident than but just as beautiful as the first attempt. Jack grinned with delight at the sound of hearing it again, watching contently by his shoulder.

The rest of the family were serenaded in their beds upstairs with Wyatt's muffled piano playing, falling asleep at the peaceful elegance.

Candice had a smile on her face as she fell asleep listening to her brother's comfortable presence in the otherwise silent home.

~ 7 ~

Ricky found himself dreading the next Monday, that was when he was to go back to school. Mainly because Ryan wasn't going back with him. There's no way he wanted to go back after all this time after all that happened, on his own. He'd have to face everyone like nothing ever swirled in, disrupting the casual motions of being a teenage boy in a small town. At least he had Candice, he could see her during lunch and recess.

He'd been thinking over the whole situation. If Wyatt had never gone missing, Candice wouldn't have gotten close to him as soon as she had, not that he wishes it all upon his friend. He could wait another year to be with her if it meant Wyatt never got kidnapped.

The new day's relatively decent, and he really wanted to go somewhere with The Ferrari. Actually, he wanted to go to Ryan's but apparently that's suddenly too far away, according to his mother.

"What if you ask if both of us can meet up with him and the others somewhere? She let me walk with Ryan yesterday." Rose suggested. They sat side by side on the back doorstep, Ricky was complaining about being caged like a trick monkey when it's off duty.

"I would but I kinda don't wanna see Candice right now." He said uncomfortably.

Rose instantly got confused. "But... She's your girlfriend. You guys okay?" She asked genuinely fascinated.

"Yeah..." He leaned closer to whisper. "Can I tell you something private?"

Oh crap, why is it always me? "Sure. Unless you plan to murder someone."

"No." He chuckled to shrug off the murder plot accusation. "I was actually going to talk to Ryan about it, but I can't get round there, and I don't wanna talk on the phone. This is probably better anyway, 'cause you're a girl."

Rose badly wanted to bring out the sarcasm coping mechanism but decided not to because he's getting ready to confide in her. "Okay, you can say. I'm not gonna think you're weird or anything."

He nodded slowly, looking at the hardly used backyard. He turned back to her, letting his held breath go. "Okay, so I really do love being with Candice right, but since we did get together it's like all she wants to do is sort of, you know... Get in my pants."

"Guess she's bolder than some..." She mumbled to herself.

"What?" Ricky asked, not hearing her properly.

"...and that's a bad thing? Aren't males all about the pants getting into?" She asked amused.

"Well I'm not, okay. Jack isn't like that is he?" He said slightly defensive of his gender.

"Ha, please. You wouldn't think it but Jack's basically a lollipop-sucking, obnoxiously dancing stripper covered in glitter with a halo of innocence." She explained with a small laugh, though sounding serious.

"Um, that's an image I didn't need." He said making her laugh a bit harder. "Now I'm praying for Wyatt." He pretended to be serious as he put his hands together to pray, looking up to the sky.

"I know, that's what I thought!"

Ricky laughed a little too, stopping when he realised they were off the subject he wanted to ask about. "Anyway, what do I do about Candice?"

Rose stopped her giggling to get her serious and ready for business face on. "So have you guys actually..." She carefully slammed her hands together, looking like some weird Kate Bush wannabe. It took him a moment of watching to realise what she meant.

"Oh! Ah no, we haven't." He answered shyly.

"That's okay, that's good actually. Way to go." She said encouragingly. "So, I assume the problem is that you don't quite want to yet?"

"Oh my God yes." He turned back to her, relieved at the understanding. "I just don't know what to say to her because she's always trying to do *that*, I mean I don't mind touching and stuff but I don't want to do *that*."

After ceasing a cringe she tried to hide at the 'touching' comment, she said "Well I'm sorry but you're going to have to just say it to her. Be honest Ricky, she'll like you even more for it anyway."

"Do I bring it up randomly, over the phone or in person? Or when she's doing it again?"

"In person when you feel the time is right." She answered hoping it was the right thing to say.

"Thanks Rose. I have a feeling this talk went better than if I had it with Ryan."

"That's okay, and good luck." She said with a kind smile. He held his arms out offering a friendly hug that she accepted. After the brief show of appreciation, Ricky asked when the stripper was coming back here to stay.

"I don't even know." She said looking at the long grass in the yard, The Ferrari standing still by the shed in the small breeze. She wondered if she'd ever be as close as she was with her brother ever again. Earlier this year when he broke up with Chelsea, she was happy about it not only because she hated her selfishly fashioned guts, but also because it meant they could go back to being just the two of them again, which is exactly what happened. Until Rose decided she'd help the kid under her house, to which she has no regret, but she missed her twin. He's always been her companion, freakishly loyal to each other no matter what.

"How is Ryan anyway?" Ricky asked her.

"He seems fine. I met his brother properly."

"Did he hit on you?"

"No... He was just nice." Rose said looking at him like he's a fool.

"Never mind."

"So many of Ryan's drawings feature vines wrapping around stuff. It's weird but I like it." She said wondering if he could elaborate on the subject.

"I just think he likes to draw them or something. I stopped questioning his abilities years ago man. He's just epic."

"I'm thinking it's more than just enjoying drawing that sort of thing."

"Okay you've lost my understanding and piqued my interest." He said turning to her.

"Well, when I was going through them, I noticed you can tell the difference between the ones he made up vs the ones he would've had a model or picture for, stuff he's had in front of him."

"Don't tell me you're trying to say some of the weird art he's done, is real."

She nodded slowly, doubting herself after hearing someone else say it.

"Nah, surely not. I mean he's always been creative and deep, I wouldn't worry about it."

"No, Ricky some of it revolves around Violet."

He looked at her almost disbelieving. "Must have been after the kidnapping then."

"The dates are from *before* the kidnapping. One of the portraits has a totally obvious likeness to her."

"Rose, I really don't want to open that can of worms again. I would much prefer to go on with life as normal as I possibly can without having to worry about Violet and her creepy agendas."

"Look I feel the same way, truth be told I've hardly thought about her recently but after seeing Ryan's pictures it's all come back. I can't help but feel that it's rather strange how her and that dog were popping up everywhere for each of us, and then when we're all together she just disappears into nowhere."

"She's just strange though."

"Like where is her house, her family, her parents?"

"What are you saying? Besides I should be asking *you* that because you were her friend before we even knew you guys."

"I think I'm seriously believing she isn't purely human, and the things she was saying might really be true."

"Rose, dear Rose." He said putting a hand on her shoulder. "This isn't the movies, okay. We're not living inside a Stephen King novel. Although I get we're basically a Losers Club, but just stop worrying yourself about bloody Violet and be glad that we all know each other now... and we're all good. Not to mention Ryan wouldn't hide anything from us, especially big, crazy stuff like that."

She looked down to the backyard grass in defeat of trying to convince him. She wasn't even sure of what she was trying to say herself. She placed her face in her hands and breathed deeply for a moment.

I think I'm going mad...

"Rose, you don't think Candice only wants me because of *you know what*, do you?" He asked her trustingly.

She looked at him with honest friendliness. "You're a really great person Ricky... and *I* know that *you* know you're incredibly witty and intelligent. So, I'm gonna to say this as your good friend, okay."

"Okay." He answered with a grin, waiting to hear more of her great complementary wisdom.

She looked right into his welcoming green eyes and spoke flatly. "Don't be so fucking stupid."

~ 8 ~

It wasn't until Wednesday's afternoon that Wyatt knocked on Candice's door. He had something to confide with her. He found he couldn't quite keep this to himself and just *had* to get it out. His heart and mind told him that he could trust her with the touchy subject, whether it's plain instinct or sibling trust. Amanda Kraus had advised him to involve his loved ones with his life, suppose this could be a positive step in that direction.

He walked in, closing the door behind him. Candice sat up on the side of the bed putting her magazine down. She noticed he looked a little timid. "What's up?" She asked concerned.

"Can I tell you something?" He asked quietly.

"I told you, you can tell me anything." She said patting the bed beside her.

"Okay, but you can't laugh, and you *definitely cannot* tell mum, or dad." He asserted gravely as he sat down.

"Hmm. Now I'm kinda freaking out." She nodded her head slowly.

"Seriously. Do you promise?"

"Yes, just spit it out." She laughed, holding a pen she kept clicking. Somehow it distracted him from what he was thinking.

"Okay, you know how you told me to play the piano last night?"
She nodded.

"Well I was trying to play the score, and ahm..." He hesitated before he finally blurted out the exciting statement. "Jack kissed me."

Candice stopped her pen clicking much like Wyatt stopping his piano playing the night before. She looked at him expectantly. "Where?"

"In the lounge."

"No you dweeb. Where'd he actually kiss you?"

He looked uncomfortable when he answered "On the lips."

Candice was getting the impression he wasn't impressed with what happened. "Where is he now?"

"He went to have a shower. Since it happened everything has been super casual."

"Well what did you do when he did it?" She asked fascinated.

"This is the part I'm weird about... I didn't actually mind him doing it." He said with a light smile, shaking his head.

Candice couldn't hide the smile on her own face as he said this. Her shy and poised little brother is growing up. "Aww my god! That's awesome!" She squeezed him in a hug.

"You're going... to kill me." He said restricted of breathing ability.

She let go and asked more questions. "So, did you do it back? What're you going to do now?"

"I did it back on the cheek. I'm clueless about kissing and stuff. Then I played through the song again and went to bed. And I don't know what to do now."

So that's what that pause in the music was... She thought amusing herself. "Don't worry about that, you'll learn how to kiss and stuff eventually. So're you guys like... A couple now?"

"I don't know, I'm kinda scared. I don't know *how* to have a partner, and he's a boy. Could you imagine mum?!"

"Oh you know what she can just get over it. Besides she loves him, unlike Ricky. And she's known *him* for years."

"Yeah I know." He turned his attention to the window, his expression deep with thought. "I think I do want to... Be his boyfriend." He said freely.

"Well it sounds to me like he wants you to be as well. And why not? He's friendly, caring and not bad looking." She nudged him in the arm with her elbow.

"I know right, tell me about it!" He replied enthusiastically.

A sudden soft knocking on the door interrupted them. They both silently identified the sound as Jack's knocking.

"Come in if you're single! And ready to mingle!" She called, resulting in a playful push from Wyatt.

Jack came in with his own style of innocence as he sat down casually on the desk chair. "I'm always ready to mingle." He replied in a boyish giggle. His hair had grown out to be rather shaggy over the last couple of weeks. It now sat dark and damp on the top of his head. He resembled something like a member of an early 2000s rock band.

"So, what're you guys doin'?" He asked, picking up a bottle of perfume from the desk to inspect it absentmindedly. Laid back comfortably, he didn't realise the sheer coolness he exhibited.

The siblings looked at each other, giggling helplessly.

"You two are weird." Jack said shaking his head with a confused grin, swaying himself slowly side to side on the swivel office chair.

"Oh, *we're* the weird ones?" Wyatt said laughing. "Anyway, I have to go shower too." He got up and left for the door.

Jack smirked with ease. "Have fun."

"Will do." Wyatt smiled back as he left through the doorway.

Not having a single clue that she's about to embark on a similar conversation that Ricky had just had with Rose earlier, Candice asked Jack if she could ask him something kind of... Private.

Oh man, Rose is better at this stuff... "Yeah! Sure. Fire away."

"Well, how can you tell if your kissing sucks?" She asked a little shy, sitting cross legged on her bed.

Guess she thinks she can 'girl talk' with me 'cause I'm a poof... "My guess is don't pretend you're a vacuum cleaner." He said jokingly.

"I'm being serious!" She said laughing.

He put down the perfume bottle and paused to think for a moment before answering. Unable to understand why she was even asking him the question, he decided to ask her one back. "Hey why? You and Ricky are always goin' at it like cannibals, he doesn't seem too upset with what you're doin'.'"

"We so don't!" She defended amused. Jack simply mouthed the words 'Yeah you do' nodding his head like a professional shit stirrer.

"Anyway I was just wondering because he always manages to stop like he's disturbed or something. I don't want him to be disturbed when he kisses me..." She continued like Bethany's ranting.

"Wait wait." Jack said, pausing again. "Is he stopping the kissing, or it going further than that?"

"Ohh..." Candice said as she went into deep thought, memory and a little realisation. "I'm not entirely sure actually."

"Well I wouldn't worry about it, seriously." He sat back comfortably again.

"Easy for you to say!" She said still worried.

"Well I'd offer to be your crash test dummy but, ya know." He said smiling devilishly, raising his brows.

"Yeah... It might mean we'd both be cheating?" She said as sly as any fox.

"What do you mean?" He instantly sat up straight.

"My brother may have told me a little something about you from last night."

Jack immediately left the chair and hurried over to the bed to sit beside her. "What did he say?" He asked riveted.

"Wow, you're really dying to know what he thought aren't you?"

He gave her an unimpressed look of impatience.

"He likes you, and your kisses." She said unable to keep the grin off her face.

"You seriously not messing with me right now?" He asked with about as much hope as a young aspiring actress trying to make ends meet.

"I'm seriously serious." She confirmed.

He placed his hands over his mouth, resting his elbows on his knees as he relished in the fact Wyatt had actually said this to someone. "This is too good to be true."

"Don't tell him I told you. He never told me not to but, yeah."

"Nah I won't." He gave her a hug and thanked her for the honesty.

"It's fine. But if you hurt my brother, I'll totally flipping end you." She said playfully serious.

"Note taken. You don't have to worry though, I'm basically an angel." He circled his head with a finger, signifying an invisible halo.

Candice shook her head in amusement at his absolutely ridiculous statement.

~ 9 ~

With it seeming to be confirmed that he's in with Wyatt, that night Jack decided it's time for some fun and fresh air to lighten up the hopefully new relationship between them. He wanted to do something good and nice for him, something more than any old kiss at a piano.

How would he do this exactly?

By bending the rules with his mischievous charm of course.

He'll wait a while to plan out exactly what and when he'll take such action. This whole thing was very new and exciting but also very scary to say the least, so it felt important that he do everything as perfect as he could possibly manage.

But when does that ever really happen for any of us? Having

something planned out to go exactly how you imagined it to perfectly go. Granted there are the few exceptions, you can't be too negative on life because no matter how bad you feel or believe it gets for you, you can never deny that it does in fact have its beautiful and purely magical moments.

Rose even found a small, wondrous beauty when she'd helped Mrs Benson with dinner one night. She was cutting the vegetables to be put in an Italian inspired stew when she had to stop and admire the purple cabbage half. It had the look of an eighties psychedelic tie-dye, the swirling white and burgundy had her attention for a solid minute before she continued the chopping. In that small moment she fully trusted in her planet's beauty and all it has to offer her. Whether this perspective will stay with her, she didn't know, nor did she care to think about it. She always enjoyed to just live in the moment, like when she watches the little kids play in the park.

Really, if you can't trust your planet and its nature, what *can* you trust?

The humans? No way.

She trusts in fate and the higher powers that glue the little bits and pieces of your life together. She believed herself and the other five were all together for a reason, she just wasn't exactly sure what that is.

If they weren't together for a reason, then what could she believe in?

Religion? No God damning way.

Besides, she supposed her brother and these friends *are* her religion now anyway.

~ Twelve ~

PIERS FOR FEARS

~ 1 ~

Now as he sat at the dinner table unsuspecting of Rose's accusations about his involvement with random vines and Violet, Ryan contemplated whether to tell Amanda about how him and his friends killed bad men and left them bloody and broken. He'd come to terms with the fact that it had all happened but there was still that irritating, sunken feeling of knowing that it had happened. They killed people and that was weird to him.

Life and death is something that had always fascinated him. That became evident early on, with him drawing graphic pictures of lonely car crashes at the ripe old age of four. He knew his mother nearly killed him but had decided not to. He'd thought deeply about it many times and now contemplated how the mothers of those men wouldn't have known the lives they grew inside them would grow up to torture and try to kill other ladies' babies.

It amazed him that his grandparents harboured a sadistic freak alongside his own mother and real Aunt all those years ago; and that she was nearly the end of his young life that'd already been threatened before he was even born. Not just his but also his dear friends, it just wasn't acceptable.

For weeks these thoughts began to twist his way of viewing the situation, therefore he began to work out that it's actually Thelma Kersh who killed those men. It was with the teen's hands they died but it was in fact, because of *her* that it happened.

Everything led back to that greedy son of a bitch, and he wanted nothing more than to have her pay for what she'd done. Imagining vines wrapping tightly around her neck simply wouldn't suffice.

For the time being though, he's so very glad that she'd disappeared. It didn't matter that she wasn't found yet.

"Hey mum, can I go to Ricky's tomorrow?" He asked polite and hopeful.

She let out a deep breath. "I suppose you can. I'll drop you off at around eleven?"

"Yeah alright." He said gleefully.

"Righto, go and ring them up to make sure." She demanded aloofly.

He promptly ran over to the phone and dialled the Benson's number.

Waiting... waiting...

"*Hello?*"

"Hey, is that you Rose?"

"*Uh, yeah. Ryan?*"

"Sure is."

"*You sound different on the phone.*"

"Everybody does, I guess. Can you please do me a favour and ask if it's alright if I come 'round tomorrow at eleven?"

"*Yeah hang on.*"

He waited as he heard muffles of sound.

"*Yeah they said it's fine.*"

"Okay awesome. See you tomorrow."

"Yeah I guess you will, Ryan."

"Okay, well bye Rose."

"Bye... Hey Ryan!"

"Yeah?" He said relieved he heard her before he hung up.

"Are you okay?"

This struck him as odd, but there's a part of him that found it sweet of her to ask. "Yeah, I'm okay. Why's that?"

"Just making sure, that's all."

"Are you okay?"

"Yeah I'm fine."

"Okay, good."

"Look if there's anything you're going through or anything has happened, you can tell us okay. You can tell me."

"I know. Same here."

"Yep. We'll have a good night, Ryan."

"You too, bye Rose."

Then she hung up on him. As he placed the phone handle back on its seat, Ethan walked by. "You okay bro?" He asked after noticing the perplexed expression on Ryan's face.

"Yeah. Girls are so weird." He said turning to look at him.

Ethan chuckled freely, placing a firm hand on his shoulder. "Oh man, you have *so much* to learn."

Ryan half smiled at his brother's remark.

What's to learn?... "How? We're just different genders, not species."

"That's what you think now." Ethan said before ascending the stairs, leaving Ryan to his apparently juvenile views of men and women.

~ 2 ~

"Oh my god, Ryan isn't hiding anything!" Ricky said growing frustrated at Rose.

After getting off the phone to him, she'd been asking if they should mention to Ryan what she'd been thinking about Violet after seeing the drawings.

"I'm not trying to upset anybody or anything but-"

"Well to be honest, you're upsetting me!" He said washing the dishes as she dried them. He didn't like to be stern with Rose, or anyone for that matter, but right now she's well and truly pushing it. He has a soft spot for all his friends but it's an especially soft spot when it comes to Ryan.

She breathed deep and quietly as she wiped the suds and droplets off a bowl. "I don't think he's evil or anything, he just might need a bit of a push to tell us what he knows."

"No!" He threw the dish scrubber into the sink, his shirt got a little darker where it splashed him. "He'd tell me! He tells me everything alright! You're just obsessed with Violet! Or you're just obsessed Ryan!"

Rose flinched, standing back as his yelling progressed, his arms jumping around intimidatingly.

"Like I'm sorry that you and Jack have nowhere to live, but it doesn't mean you can just keep reminding everyone of some... *weirdo*, then start accusing one of my best friends of hiding paranormal links to said weirdo! Just drop it!"

Sally came hurried in with perplexed worry. "Hey, what's up in here?"

"Bloody nothing." He answered sternly before leaving the kitchen, going to his bedroom.

Sally looked at Rose who only stood there, totally still and looking like she was about to burst with emotion. "You okay honey?"

Her sad eyes looked to her. "There's madness in the air Mrs Benson." She noticed the confused face looking back. "I think I just annoyed him a little, that's all."

"Alrighty. Well boys around his age tend to be all over the place. If he's not ready now, maybe in the future?" It was obvious she didn't really know how to handle the situation she thought she'd just stepped into.

"No no, nothing like that." Rose said with a deflated half laugh.

"Ah okay. Honestly if there's anything I can help you with, just ask me sweetie pie."
Sally held a comforting hand to Rose's face. Her cheek rested against her motherly offer, eager to accept the comfort.

"What's going to happen to my brother and me? All we have is you guys. If the social services get us, we'll be separated and no doubt end up with horrible people."

"No darling, you'll be okay, just-"

"I'm fed up with horrible people, I can't stand it anymore. I just want..."

"Look Rose-"

"I just want a normal life."

Sally held her head gently so that she's looking directly into her face. "Noah and I won't let anything happen to you, or your brother."

Rose looked back and nodded as if she's to obey an order. "I'm sorry for getting all weird just now."

"No, don't apologise. You two have led crazy lives, let's not try and pretend you haven't. You guys have been fantastic, and to say the very least you're family to us now no matter what. You're the daughter I never had."

"I love being here, Mrs Benson." She replied, gripping her in a parentless embrace.

"You get some rest alright. Tomorrow's a new day baby." She petted her on the back.

After Rose left the kitchen, Sally made her way to Ricky's

room where she opened the door without bothering to stop for a quick knock.

"Geez mum, trying out boot camp tactics?" Ricky said laying on his bed, glad that he wasn't doing anything personal.

"I know I raised a good boy, so tomorrow you apologise to Rose." She demanded.

"I was planning to, but don't you even want to know my side of the story?"

"Richard, I don't even know hers. I'm not going to pry into your social life because God knows I hated it when my parents did that to me, but her and Jack have been through a lot more than we could ever imagine."

"Yeah I know-"

"Regardless of what happened to little Wyatt, right now it's this family's responsibility to make these two feel safe."

"Even though Jack's barely ever here now."

"Ricky I'm being serious."

"I know mum. I snapped once and I hardly ever do. I'll apologise."

"Good boy." She walked over to give him a kiss. "Goodnight honey."

Just before she left the doorway, Ricky took a chance on his trusted mum to ask about his budding social life. "How did you know dad was you know, 'the one' or whatever?"

A peculiar smile crept its way across her face, the kind Ricky had associated from a young age with something good has or is about to happen. Possibly another amazingly fun family adventure in the car over the weekend or maybe something so simple as she'd just been given a small bunch of flowers from his dad. She walked over to sit down beside him on the bed. "I knew he was the one when he handed my pencil back at the end of the day, sharpened and all."

Ricky sat back with humoured confusion plain on his face. "Okay mum. I was honestly expecting something a little more inspirational than that."

She chuckled at his reaction as if to laugh at his amateur take on the world. "Point is, for us it just worked out that way. Everybody's experience is different, so I won't tell you what they say in the movies."

"Oh you mean: 'It was love at first sight, I just knew he was the one.' That bull?"

"Yes that's the one." She said laughing. "I think that kind of warps people's views on things, and they end up being disappointed or miss the really important moments, miss their chances because they were unknowingly misled."

"That's a real eye opener. Being an old lady really does make you wise."

"Hey, keep up all that old lady talk, and you won't be eating dinner ever again."

"Just joking." He joked.

"Well it's getting late, and I have to work tomorrow so I'll probably see you in the afternoon again." She got up for the door.

"Goodnight mum. Thank you." He said in a wholesome, serious way.

"Anytime baby." She replied, and left down the hall.

~ 3 ~

The sun of the new day arose with the promise of honest shine and warmth, turning the blandest of people into poets in their own right. The town streets swung into motion as it does every day. Jack's outside the Fineman house mowing the front lawn. He'd been trying to do as much housework and odd jobs as he possibly could to try and keep up the winning title of polite and handy houseguest rather than freeloading stray boy.

Wyatt secretly watched on from his bedroom window while Jack pushed the loud machine from one end of the lawn the other. He observed that he's wearing a grey singlet, slowly darkening with the sweat of his labouring. His already lightly tanned arms bulged with promising muscles while the sun shone down on him. Wyatt found great satisfaction in knowing that they're the same arms that love to be around him, those are the hands that comfortably hold him, touch him.

The wonderful hair that he keeps flicking off his face, maybe now Wyatt himself is free to touch it whenever he wanted. He remembered back to when Jack commented on the way he walks.

If only he could see his own gait, like a dressage stallion... Breezy and strong... Literally looks like one of those guys in Candice's magazines... No... He's better... More real looking than them... Handsomer... Soft... So very soft but so... Firm... If mum knew I was thinking this stuff...

Who cares right? She can't touch his thoughts, they're in his head. He still felt guilt as a naughty little boy for letting himself go there regardless of her interference or lack thereof on the subject.

Jack stopped the mowing, and with it came the absence of that irritatingly loud noise. He leaned over the handle for a quick breather before heaving it into the side garage.

He is so, so perfect... But for what exactly?...

Wyatt quickly left the window when he saw him head inside and promptly continued his mission of eradicating anything in his bedroom that made him feel like a toddler or a mummy's boy. He basically wanted to stop feeling like 'Little Wyatt'.

He'd gotten a medium sized cardboard box from the garage, now putting things in there that he found to be for little kids or losers. Any sort of toy that wasn't some form of collector's item went into the box, any dorky clothes, books that're below his vocabulary level, even innocent things like colouring books went in.

Jack wandered into the room with a fresh t-shirt on and a glass of water that's clearly very cold due to the condensation on the outside of it. Tiny droplets tried to spread through the firm grip of his fingers with clear subtleness.

Warm hands... Jack's wet hands...

"Watcha doin' Tinkle-bell?" Jack asked him, curious and happy.

"Just getting rid of stuff I don't need." He replied from the floor beside the box.

Jack took a deep sip of water before placing it on the desk. He loomed over the box and reached in to pull out a pair of shorts, the kind with suspenders clipped on. "What are *these*?" He asked in a low, excitedly amused voice.

"Just something my mum used to always buy me." He tried to grab them back and failed.

"You can't get rid of these. You should totally put 'em on." He suggested with a grin.

"Jack, no way." He said flatly.

"Fine, *I* will." He took his pants off and threw them onto the bed with little care. Watching him step into these shorts made Wyatt giggle, he knew they'd be a little too small because they'd been in the back of his draws for a long time now. After successfully slipping into them and looping the straps over his shoulders, he resembled something similar to a 1940's sailor child. If his t-shirt was striped blue and white, he'd be right on.

"So, how is it?" He asked turning around like a little girl trying a pretty dress on for the first time.

"It's um... very becoming of you." Wyatt answered trying to hold back big laughter.

"I'll take that as a compliment. How's my butt look?"

Is he being serious? He looks serious... "Looks like your butt."

Jack sighed, pretending to be unimpressed at the lack of satisfactory compliments to his new attire. Truth is, the shorts mounted his butt in such a concrete way that he was sculptured into model proportions. The stallion wore the perfect saddle.

"Nope. Nuh-uh and no way are you getting rid of these." Jack said picking up the Superman pyjama pants out of the box.

"They're mine to get rid of."

"No, they're the best."

"Well they can be the best on someone else." He stood up to try and take them off him.

"You miss the point more than Candice."

"What?"

"They won't be the best unless they're on you."

Wyatt grinned. "You really don't want them gone, do you?"

"These pants are like, you. They're who you are Tinkle-bell."

"Okay... You think these pants are who I am?" He said failing to understand where he's coming from, especially given he'd decided they're of the dorkiness worthy to be passed on to the op-shop.

"Yeah, they're fuckin' legendary like you." Jack said softly.

"Oh. So are you." He replied looking into the beautifully fashioned doors of his soul.

Jack reached out and placed his hand on Wyatt's upper arm, his heart ran surprisingly steady despite being under Jack's gentle touch again.

"*I'll keep them.*" He said in a near whisper.

Jack smirked, stepping closer to speak just as quietly. "*That's my boy.*" He leaned in for what could only be a kiss, to which Wyatt panicked and turned away. He didn't dare look at Jack after that, thinking he couldn't handle whatever emotion was written across his face. He kneeled down and continued to put clothing into the box instead.

Why did you do that, wimp? Oh my goodness, no...

"Did I do something wrong?" He heard from behind him.

He turned at breakneck speed. "No, not at all."

"Except maybe wear shorts too small for me." He said folding the pyjama pants.

"Maybe." Wyatt laughed. Ideally, he would have liked to have told him 'No actually. They're perfect, because *you're* in them.'

"Why you doin' the big clean out anyway?" Jack asked curiously.

"I guess I'm just trying to start anew." Wyatt said thankful he'd completely changed the subject.

"You talk like such a fancy lad." He said sitting beside him cross-legged on the floor.

"We do have relatives in England."

"Of course you do." He said shaking his head with a smile. Wyatt shrugged his shoulders folding a shirt for the box.

Jack looked around the room in deep thought. "You know, if you want to really start up new, you could do it by doin' somethin' totally crazy that you wouldn't usually do."

"Such as?" He asked stopping his box operations to look and listen.

"Well, just hear me out. I'm not sayin' we *should* or whatever, but we *could* smoke the last of my weed."

"We could, but we really and seriously should not."

"Okay okay. Maybe you could shoplift somethin'?"

"Jack! I don't want to be arrested or yelled at by my parents."

"But that's half the fun Tinkle! Or maybe a quarter of the fun."

"My 'rebelling' at the moment is choosing to do this instead of the work for school."

"Yeah, you're a real rebel. Remind me not to let you influence me."

"I should be saying that to you."

"Hey let's burn your schoolwork in the backyard and say it vanished!"

"What'll that achieve? They'd give me more and I'd just have to do it all over again."

"Egg a house?"

"Jack."

"Flaming dog shit on the doorstep of someone you don't like?"

"Ew, no."

"Itching powder in Candice's underwear draw?"

"What? No."

"Okay I got it. Jump off the pier in your clothes."

"I'm not the best swimmer. Especially if I was wearing clothes not suited for swimming."

"Well you could wear nothing, even better."

"No way!"

"Why not?"

"Because everyone will see me naked."

"Yeah and they'd be like 'Oh I wish I was as daring as that strapping young rebel over there! Oh, that wonderful naked body-"

"Stop, just stop!" He said unable to hide his laughter.

"Come on it'll be fun. You won't drown or anything cause I'll be there."

He sat on the idea and pondered it for a moment. "Okay I'll do it."

"Yes!" Jack jumped up with such enthusiasm it made Wyatt somewhat amazed at how four bland and ordinary words could make him so damn excited.

"Just so you know, I'm wearing this." He strutted out of the room with both thumbs gripped to either suspender.

"Wait, you mean go now?!" He called out after him.

He walked back into the room. "Yes, I mean now. There's no time to waste."

"But I've got stuff to do, and I'm not dressed to go out!"

Jack let out a deep breath, looking at him with his head tilted. "Will you just relax? The whole point is to just go and do it, and yes, I mean without tellin' anyone."

Without offering his hand to let Wyatt decide to take it himself, he bent down to grab him by both wrists, encouragingly pulling him to his feet. If he had the guts to admit it, now would have been a good time for Jack to try a kiss. For reasons unknown to him, being handled like that made him want it.

"What if my mum comes home and we're gone?"

"Then we tell her all about it when she comes to... Spank your backside..."

Wyatt noticed the subtle smile on his face as he turned to reach for the glass of water. His eyes mischievous over the rim of glass as he gulped down the water.

"What are you thinking right now?" Wyatt heard himself say.

Jack reacted with a half grin accompanied by a small laugh. "Nothin' you need to know." He placed the glass back down on the desk, then put the same hand on Wyatt's neck. The suddenness of the cool combined with wet skin made him jump. "We got shit to do boy! Let's go!" He exclaimed, then left the room. "*Gross, my hand's fuckin' wet.*" He said absentmindedly down the hall.

Wyatt didn't hesitate to follow him this time, even if it was just because every part of his being now screamed '*Do it again, touch me again Jack. I won't be shy.*'

Halfway down the staircase their mission was interrupted by Candice's curiosity. "Where're you two off to in such a hurry?"

"One time only, ya brother is going to jump off the pier!" Jack said enthusiastically.

"No way!" She said shaking her head in disbelief, to which they both nodded back at her.

"Well I'm going then!"

"Okay but you have to come now, we're not waiting." Jack said and began to walk on.

Wyatt followed, and Candice hurried after. She didn't even turn back for her phone.

~ 4 ~

You can tell me anything...

Why would she say that, and did she really mean it?

Of course she did, Rose wouldn't say something and not mean it. Especially something of that sort.

But why say it?...

Ryan was almost at the Benson's by the time Wyatt was leaving his house to head for the pier. His mum was dropping him off just as she said she would. She pulled up at the side of the road to let him out.

"Get in contact when you're ready to come home and we'll work something out." She told him.

"Yeah alright, thanks." Once he was out of the car she drove off and out of sight. He began walking up to the front door.

Don't over think everything... She was just being nice, maybe she likes me...

With that thought he stopped walking, nervously anticipating whether he could face her. What if she did like him in that way? What's a guy to do?

Don't over think...

He put one foot in front of the other and began walking on.

Inside the house Rose was on guard at the front window, watching and waiting. She'd been thinking it over and wasn't sure if she should try and make herself scarce while Ryan visited. Last night's moment of enduring Ricky's anger really ruffled her feathers. For the most part these feathers were as tough as nails, but this time round they were weak as pelican piss.

Ricky came up behind her just as she noticed the car pull up. "Hey I'm super sorry for being such a grouch last night. I'm not angry at you, I just have a lot on my plate lately." He spoke with sincerity clear on his face.

"That's okay. I *have* been talking like a loon. Maybe I'm just trying to make sense of things, I dunno." She replied. His choice to come up to her felt like a load off but she also felt guilty about it, like she should be apologising instead.

"Ah look we're all loonies." He said offering himself up for a hug. Accepting the offer, she realised that lately hugs are one of her favourite things to engage in. This guy does give awesome ones, and the Anarchy of his scent attracted her unapologetically. She was about to tell him Ryan should be here any second when a knock at the front door happened.

"That's probably Ryan now." He said letting go of her.

"Want me to leave you to it?" She asked still feeling the shame of voicing her theories.

He paused to look at her. "I don't want you to do anything but relax." Off he went to answer the door.

It's true, she thought. There's no need to worry. Ryan knows nothing, so it'll be easy to pretend nothing happened. She could hear them coming back towards the loungeroom and quickly darted back to the window where she gustily spread open the curtains.

Relax...

She turned around just in time to see them enter the room, instantly recognising a change in Ryan, but what was it exactly? He simply walked in, yet something was definitely different.

He didn't smile at me...

She smiled casually at him, and he looked away without returning the favour in which he normally always naturally does. To make it worse, he never even said hello.

As the three of them were seated on the homey lounge furniture, the visit progressed into a stressful paranoia trip for Rose. He's completely fine with Ricky but when Rose comments on something or says anything in general, Ryan's face expresses serious uncertainty and he'd verbally ignore her completely. The most unnerving part about the whole experience was how she noticed he'd look at her when he thought she wasn't paying attention.

It was so clear he knew something. There was no time for relaxation with this unfolding the way it is. The questions of what does he know and how, ate at her from the inside out. Her tough feathers were probably starting to resemble moth eaten rags.

Ricky wasn't picking up on this weirdness, or if he is, he's a bloody good actor by the way he's been his completely casual self, blabbering on and on.

~ 5 ~

"So do tell me Jack. How'd you end up in those?" Candice asked walking behind the two boys. The sun powerfully shone down on them as they quickly walked towards the front of town. The occasional cloud covered the magnificent star, sending small shivers through their bodies when the light feigned.

"My shorts? They're the best!"

"I can't believe you're wearing them in public... Wait, yes I can."

"Don't diss the spender-shorts, sister." He said gravely serious.

"You look like an old man turned stripper or something."

"Ooh, I like the sound of stripper!"

Wyatt walked on in quiet fretting. It's a ludicrous idea and he didn't want to do this, not completely. He barely participated in school events at the pool. But maybe that's why it's right. "Are you even allowed to jump off the pier anyway?" He asked them in a sort of ploy to begin talking them into thinking it's a bad idea.

"Ah, no." Jack said with a nod of his head.

"Then we can't do it!"

"Wyatt, that's why we're doing it remember. Because it's crazy."

"If mum asks, I was trying to stop you." Candice said joking, but also not joking.

"Besides, we could be doing a million other things *way* worse than this."

Wyatt stayed quiet, only nodding his head at their statements.

It's true though, could be worse...

Before too long they reached the quaint street that led out to the boat docks and fishing platforms. To their advantage and Wyatt's relief there weren't too many people around and maybe a total of three down by the actual pier. Most of the action was happening up the other end of the street where it had one the few op shops, the masseuse and hypnotist, the Maritime Display House, and soon it joined onto the Main Street.

"Here we are!" Jack said excitedly.

It was so obvious Wyatt was reluctant to jump. But truly on the inside he was kinda pumped to do it.

"Come on let's get over there!" Jack encouraged, beginning to walk towards the pier.

Candice took Wyatt's arm, saying nothing in silent encouragement, guiding him over behind Jack. Sea gulls soared about over their heads as they got closer to the jetty.

Wyatt stepped over the threshold, tar turned to thick, aged wood. To him, the only thing that isn't unsettling about the place is the clean, fresh sea breeze. But even to an extent that seemed big, like forces of nature daring him to do it, to be unlike him or for that matter, try to *find* himself. He continued to walk along. Suppose he's walking the plank, the plank of uncertainty and bravery to be tested. The swaying wobbliness of the jetty is like him, how he is on the inside. Unsure of direction and never able to settle, even on calm evenings or peaceful mornings.

Jack began to run, the thud of his feet vibrated throughout the whole jetty. With arms stretched out and face to the wind, he reached the end of the jetty and jumped. A well-formed dive bombing if ever there was. Enough to leave onlookers with their own blood pumping ready for exhilarating action.

"Holy shit!" Candice said surprised. "Off you go then!" She ushered Wyatt forwards as an attempt to get him to follow in his footsteps.

"Ohh my fuck! Temperature change!" Jack said in a hilariously high pitch, wading in the splashes of ocean. Candice laughed at his statement.

Now feeling as though he may be able to do it just as Jack had, Wyatt stepped onwards to the edge, heart beating fast and breathing growing ever faster. Maybe as a mistake, he looked down over the edge of the old jetty into the water, hesitating any further proceedings into the ocean. It's a faceless mass of mossy blue tones, hissing with white foam from Jack's recent haste of a descent into its body.

"Come on Tinkle, you can do it!" He called out still treading water.

He looked deeper into the abyssal water, and it looked at him. It reached out in its own way now working with the wind, taunting and daring him once more.

Do it, I dare you to defy yourself. Defy yourself Wyatt or stay lost. Stay un-dared and stay uncared.

His distorted reflection only aided in favour of the decision to take the leap. Without thinking, he got onto all fours to crawl over to the corner of the jetty. As one foot descended over the edge and came to rest on one of the thick ladder rungs, Candice asked what he was doing.

"You're supposed to be *jumping* in!"

The water lapped at his body with eager saltiness. When he'd reached two rungs down the ladder, he stopped to carefully turn around to face it again. Much closer now and just as frightening as before. He closed his eyes, trying to push out the thought of sharks and stingrays. With one deep breath and his eyes closed tight, he lifted his leg as if to casually walk ahead, taking the plunge to let himself be engulfed by the wet and suffocating hug of the sea, clothes and all.

It's a warm cold that engulfed his body. Call him crazy but that's what it felt like, the water hugging his very being, swallowing him whole. He didn't open his eyes as he let near lifeless limbs relax, feeling the silk of dangerous absence around him. This is it, this is him.

It's mindless wandering down here while the cool opened him up and exposed the being of his mind. He's suspended in body, just as he is in mind. He didn't even try to swim, he didn't want to try. Two lungs inside began to panic but his brain's far away and not listening to them, instead it conversed with the ocean, listening to the message it had for him.

Let go, be free.

The very finger tips that had reached for mother's jewellery as an infant now drifted down, down into nothing. Was it worth reaching for anything?

They could let go now, it would be okay.

But through it all and with or without a God, heaven has angels. These forsaken hands gripped onto his beautiful guardian with a strange but comforting thankfulness whether his brain told them to or not.

Taking his first breath of air at the unsettled surface since the descent, he opened his eyes to let the sun in, too strong at first so squinting's the only option as he reached out and held onto the jetty.

"That was so cool dude. You're like, James fuckin' Bond or something!"

He turned to look at Jack, who seemed to be totally thrilled with his present life. Looking at him now with his shiny, sun kissed hair and a grin that could stop traffic or even an asteroid flying, Wyatt realised something... It definitely wasn't his mind that held Jack with his hands. It was his heart.

"Next time though, make sure you resurface. I could do without the heart attack."

"Yeah me too!" Candice said from above, leaning over the jetty.

"Sorry guys." Wyatt replied with little idea of a good answer.

"We should start heading back. I'm kinda getting paranoid now." Candice said, she wandered away a little back up the jetty.

It was Jack who spoke next, after he made his way through the water to grip the slimy jetty just as Wyatt had. "So, you feelin' like a rebel now?"

"Am I supposed to?"

"Well a little rebellion is always a turn on." He said in a low voice as though to ensure nobody would hear him.

Wyatt answered with a simple "Hm?"

Jack looked back at him with affectionate confusion on his face. "You know, it's hot and fuckin' sexy."

"Oh." Wyatt said with a smiling frown as he flicked water

at him.

"Hey!"

Suddenly there was an uproar of water slinging. The salt found its way through their smiles, Wyatt hated that but loved everything else. An unexpected graze of some sort on his upper thigh caused his fright of the water to heighten, but he figured it was Jack after he'd moved closer not long before he felt it.

"Hang on a sec..." He said ceasing the water antics. "Did you just touch my leg?"

"No..." Jack replied seeming seriously freaked out.

Almost instantly they both tried to scramble up and out of the water. Wyatt had visions of a giant shark with big black eyes and serrated off white teeth breaching the surface to chomp him into pieces like in Jaws. He had nightmares for weeks after Ricky showed him that wretched movie.

After almost falling backwards back into the depths with the beast of the big blue, he'd made it onto the warm surface of the wood, lucky not to get irritable splinters under his fingernails by the way he reached and scraped for dry land. Their bodies flopped over the jetty surface with a heavy, drenched relief. Candice quickly came running back concerned at the sudden burst of urgent escape.

Jack started laughing hysterically as Wyatt still tried to get over his panic. "Okay how the heck is that funny? We could have possibly died!"

Jack got a grip on himself and croaked out the answer. "It was me."

Wyatt lay back panting on the thick wooden planks. A soft grin appeared in the light of the sun over his face.

"I'm not even gonna ask." Candice said shaking her head.

~ 6 ~

Cheese flavoured rice crackers were Rose's excuse to get out of the lounge room to try Jack again. She'd already used the toilet excuse once and now she couldn't get hold of him again, not even Candice.

She retrieved the crackers from the cupboard and emptied them onto a serving tray to take up more time. If she can't get a hold of her own brother when she needs him then what the hell could she do?

Thinking he was possibly in some sort trouble, she picked up the tray of distraction biscuits, making her way back to the lounge where the boys remained seated on the floor in front of the couch playing some random, boring video game.

I could leave and they probably wouldn't notice anyway...

She went over, leaving the tray on the coffee table in front of them before trying to walk off without their prying input.

"Thanks Rose, where you goin'?" Asked Ricky, barely letting his eyes leave the screen.

"Um... Just going out for some air."

"Aren't you feeling well or something?"

"I'm just gonna go and... Talk to Candice... about girl stuff."

"Say no more." He replied, dropping the concern.

While she was quickly heading for the back door, Ryan's character was too easily beaten by Ricky's. "God's sake." He muttered faintly.

Ricky swapped his controller for the tray of crackers. "She didn't have to go all out and put 'em on a plate. Makes me feel like a bossy old prick or some shit."

"She's the one that offered to get them."

"Yeah but I just mean, never mind. What's up with you today? You're being weird."

"I am not." He defended flatly.

"Ah, yes you are. The whole time you've barely said a word to Rose, and you've been looking at her weird, like she's gonna savage you. Not to mention I just kicked ya butt when I was hardly trying."

"It's just that... nothing. It's stupid."

Ricky gasped excitedly as the penny dropped in his head. "Oh my God, dude, you have a thing for her, don't you?"

"No!" He said too eagerly, leaving Ricky with a perplexed expression. "Not that she's not really pretty or whatever, and kind. But I think *she* has a thing for *me*."

"Okay, cool." Ricky replied nodding his head slowly, knowing Rose's recent opinion of him. "What makes you say that?"

"Just things she's been saying lately, I guess. I told you it was stupid."

"Nah it's not stupid. I mean, who knows. I've been into Candice for *freakin' years* and she was always kinda mean to me. Next thing I know she's tryna to rip into my pants. Oh my God Ryan, it's the Uptown Girl complex!"

"What're you talking about?" He asked in a small laugh.

"You know, the song. Billy Joel. I am literally living Uptown Girl." He replied with a shake of his head, biting down on another rice biscuit.

"Girls are crazy."

"Tell me about it. But then again look at Jack and Wyatt, relationship complications one oh one, huh. Cracker?" He offered the tray to him.

He took one. "It's kind of insane that he likes the son of his kidnapper's girlfriend. Like when does that ever happen?"

"I know, the past few weeks have felt like we're living in a movie."

"Hey, what about you and Candice. Have you two you know, done it?"

"Dude! No, we haven't." He answered nervously.

"I thought you'd tell me if you did." He said as he casually nibbled his cracker.

"Yeah for sure, it's like the biggest thing ever. Pun not planned but now intended." Ricky informed proudly.

Meanwhile, Rose tried to be quiet holding the big side gate open as she slipped through, swinging it back again to latch it. Tip toeing her way out of the driveway she risked going out onto the footpath out in front of the house, keeping her eyes and attention on the lounge room window.

Shit, should have closed the curtains, nah they won't see me any-
She walked right into a dampened body, the shock of it scared the life out her. "Oh, sorry!" She looked at her collision victim, not expecting to see what she did. "Jack?"

"I'd say the one and only but it's a popular name." He replied, hardly seeming surprised himself.

"What're you guys doing here? And why're you two wet?" She asked referring to him and Wyatt.

"They decided to be spontaneous and jump off the pier." Candice explained, proud to have been there.

"What?!!"

"Let's just go in and tell everyone the story shall we?" Jack said. "What're you even doin' out here?" He continued as they walked towards the house.

"Oh nothing, don't worry." She answered quickly.

Jack opened the front door and walked in with the others. Entering the lounge, they were greeted with the absolutely dumfounded looks on Ryan and Ricky's faces as they stood by watching them walk in like it's all totally normal.

Candice ran over and threw her arms around Ricky, something he still wasn't exactly used to happening. "So when Rose said she was going to talk to you she meant outside, not on the phone. What the hell?"

"What do you mean?" She asked unknowing.

"They just turned up actually, I didn't know they were coming." Rose said from the doorway.

"Wicked. Are you guys wet?" He asked pointing at Jack and Wyatt.

"That's personal Ricky!" Jack exclaimed humorously.

"Just a bit damp now, we jumped off the pier!" Wyatt answered excited, thoroughly proud.

"You bloody *what?!* And didn't invite me?"

"Had to do it fast or he wouldn't do it." Jack explained.

"It was pretty cool." Wyatt continued. "Even the part where we got chased off by some angry council men."

"Oh no." Ryan laughed at the image of it.

"Yeah we're badass, aren't we?" Jack said looking fondly at Wyatt.

"I guess so. I think the worst is yet to come though, that's if my parents found out."

"We'll just come up with some weird excuse." Candice assured.

"What's with the new thirst for danger?" Rose asked, delighted at the happiness about him.

"Guess I just felt like it." He answered honestly.

"I'm gonna go get some dry clothes 'n shit." Jack left for the bathroom.

"Ricky, could I please borrow some clothes for a while?" Wyatt asked politely.

"Yeah go for it, just use whatever."

He smiled in appreciation and left for Ricky's room.

Now those two weren't there, the other four moved in close together to quietly discuss what had just happened.

"What the hell is going on?" Ricky asked still processing it.

"Jack's influencing Wyatt, that's what." Ryan stated casually.

"And what's that supposed to mean exactly?" Rose asked getting on the defence.

"I just mean that he wouldn't have done anything like that on his own. He's not like that."

"So you think Jack's a bad influence on him?" She crossed her arms, challenging him.

"No, well yeah kind of. I mean Wyatt's been different since he's been around."

"Oh, I get it. Look Wyatt was gay *way* before we ever came along." Her smug face of defensiveness had him unnerved.

"That's not what I'm saying." He tried to keep a neutral tone to convey his peace.

"If you have a problem with them whatever, but don't try and pull that 'bad influence' crap on my brother." She frowned relentlessly, her brown eyes firm in judgement.

"I'm not being mean. Why are you attacking me?" He asked growing impatient of this.

Ricky and Candice looked on in still silence, their eyes moving back and forth at the whispering argument.

"I'm not attacking you. You'd know if I was, trust me."

"I wasn't trying to say anything bad, I was just pointing out that it's Jack's fault Wyatt is doing weird things." The foot in his mouth apparently won't budge.

"Oh my god, instead of calling it 'weird things' maybe you should stop judging and be happy for your friends being happy."

"I am! But that doesn't change what's going on! There's a difference between being happy, and being dangerous and getting in trouble."

"Whatever, I'm not arguing." She stood firm, turning away to look anywhere but at him.

"Before you guys, he was almost completely different to now." He said calmly.

"Oh I see. You were all better off before us. Well, I'm sorry for the inconvenience Ryan. Have fun up there on your high horse with your bags of cash and homophobic opinions." She stormed off down the hall somewhere.

"That's not what I was saying." He stated sounding totally defeated.

"Am I missing something?" Candice asked him. "Last I knew you two were getting on great."

"Don't know, I thought we were too."

Ricky hated this conflicting situation between his friends. "I don't know if it's related, but just before she said something about girl stuff, so..."

"You trying to suggest it's her time of the month?" Candice asked, a smirk to accompany her crossed arms.

"Just saying." He shrugged.

"You are such a typical guy." She said amused. "My personal opinion is that she's just defending Jack. They're really close, and she understands things that maybe you just don't I guess."

"Yeah, I'll just agree with you. I haven't done anything to her that I know of."

"My God it feels good to be out of those wet shorts. I was chaffing!" Jack announced, bursting into the room.

"Why the hell were you even wearing them?" Ricky asked genuinely curious.

"Found them in Wyatt's room and thought it'd be fun."

"I haven't seen him wear those for ages." Ricky answered remembering them fondly.

"Where's Rose?" Jack asked.

"Dunno." They all said shaking their heads.

Wyatt came in with a plastic bag that had the folded wet

clothes heavily inside. "Thanks for the clothes Ricky."

"No worries, man!"

"A flanny looks good on you!" Jack stated kindly.

"It's just clothes." Wyatt answered feeling anxious.

"He's totally right. Maybe I should get mum to get you some for your birthday." Candice said trying to smooth it over.

"You reckon?"

"Yeah, then we can twin it!" Ricky said. "Hey your birthdays only two weeks from now."

"Yeah I know. Don't remind me."

Birthday! That's the perfect time for 'operation romance'... Jack thought.

"Don't be such a sour puss Wylie." Ricky said walking over, putting an arm around him. "Birthdays are the most important things in the year. Other than Christmas, obviously."

"And Easter." Wyatt added as though it's rude to dismiss it.

"Oh, duh self. And Easter." Ricky chuckled in humour of his quaint friend.

"I just don't want a big deal made out of my birthday this year."

"Shit man! You could have told me that *before* I payed for the strippers." Ricky exclaimed disappointed. Sometimes it was hard to believe he was joking by the way he said things so convincingly, no matter how absurd the statement was.

"You're such an idiot." Candice laughed.

"People love me for it." He replied in a shrug.

"I'm thinking of going back to school when you guys do, so that we're doing it together." Wyatt stated confidently.

"That'd be awesome!" Ricky said picking up his vibrating phone.

"Yeah, we'd be like the three musketeers against everyone else." Ryan said with a smile, receiving one from Wyatt in return.

"You know what? I will too." Candice stated just as confident. "I've only been putting it off out of laziness anyway."

Ricky answered his phone to see why his mum was ringing. It's slightly unusual for this time of day. "Hello?... Yeah, they're here, why?... Ohh, I see... mmhmm..."

The others watched on in pure suspicion and curiosity. Wyatt looked at Candice with silent sibling communication. She looked back with semi wide eyes telling him 'Yeah, she knows.'

"Yeah mum we're all good... Nah there's no need for her to be worried but I get it, yeah... Well, you get back to scanning cereal and I'll take care of this... Yep, you too mum, bye." After hanging up he slid the phone into his pocket and looked up to the fascinated group. "Finemans, you're in deep shit. Your mum knows you were at the pier, and she's been harassing my mum while she's trying to work." He said trying to sound as light-hearted as possible when he said it.

"Oh for Christ..." Candice said placing her head in her hand.

Wyatt stood by, breathing deep. Was it worth the discipline they were about to receive? Probably not. But he was glad he'd done it.

"Maybe I should just stay here." Jack said imagining Mrs Fineman with sharp teeth, a forked tongue and a bible ready to be thrown at his forehead.

"Nuh-uh. You're coming with us." Candice said sternly.

~ 7 ~

Nothing had prepared Jack for the authoritative anger and looming presence of a distressed Mrs Fineman. Not even the other two telling him how it would be and most likely go down. Naturally, none of them sat in the front seat of the car, instead squished up together in the back.

Jack expected an absolutely puke inducing scare trip caused by her furious yelling and arms waving around, unsure if he should brace for a slap across the face or not.

But instead, as the threesome sat in a row at the dining table, she stood quietly in the kitchen with her arms crossed. Her lips pressed together, her breathing hard, the crossed arms slowly moving up and down against her chest. They'd all been like this for at least ten minutes. Somehow, he felt this is scarier than what he'd expected.

Wyatt shifted uncomfortably in the chair. "Mum, we're fine so we can move on now." He said in an innocent tone.

His mother looked at them with a straight face clear with anger. "Candice. How could you do this? Every single time I'm starting to believe you're on the right track and that I've done my job as a mother, you turn around and throw it in my face."

"What?!" Candice said downheartedly distressed.

"And today with your little brother?" She slowly walked over to them. "He was kidnapped! Have you forgotten that?"

"No as if I'd-"

"Don't talk back to me in that tone." She said flatly. "The last thing he needs is *your* crazy influence trying to get him killed."

Jack opened his mouth to speak but was promptly stopped by Candice's firm shove of her foot against his shin.

"I'm sorry, that's all I can say." Candice obeyed in defeat.

"You should be apologising to your brother!"

Wyatt stood up fast. "Oh my Goodness, it was me! Candice just followed! Why can't you get anything through your head?!"

She stood back totally baffled.

"Don't worry about telling me off, I'm going to my room, WITH Jack." He grabbed him by the wrist. Like Ricky all those weeks ago, Jack felt scared to pass her on his way out.   She watched as they left the room with her hand placed carefully over her mouth. Candice followed in their wake, almost just as speechless as her mother but definitely not as surprised.

For the days that followed not a single word more was said about the issue. The teens weren't even sure if Mr Fineman knew of the pier jump. Jack had wondered how the mother had found out, Candice assured him that their mother has prissy spies about the town all too ready to inform her of anything out of the ordinary.

Constricting parenting at its best.

~ Thirteen ~

THE SUM OF IT

~ 1 ~

Finally it's time. Time for school and time to face relent-less prying eyes owned by curious peers. Ricky, Ryan and the Fineman siblings walked up to the building clad in the school's primary colours of sky blue and deep, dark red. Wyatt of course is the only one of the four with the shirt tucked in sensibly. Even Candice had her shirt sitting over the top of the plaid winter skirt. For her, the worst part of this whole great return to Lady Sacred is facing the nosey ways of Bethany and the unwanted likes of Robert Brannon. Already they'd noticed the fascinated faces of other students walking past them as they stood by outside.

"Well. Standing here isn't going to make this any easier." Wyatt said stepping forward and turning to face the other three. "I suggest we go in and get settled."

"Easy for you to say." Ricky said looking at the group of girls that dominate his grade walk past. "You'll have Ryan around for most of the day. Candice and I are on our own."

"Actually unlike you I have friends." She said meaning it as a friendly 'forget your worries' burn.

"Oh thanks for that, Queen Bee." Ricky answered mockingly.

"There's lunch and recess." Ryan reminded positively.

"Till then boys..." Ricky said placing a hand on a shoulder each of Wyatt and Ryan. "Try not to forget me in there. And don't do anything too fun without me."

"It's just school Ricky, it'll be like old times." Ryan said encouragingly, also trying to convince himself. "Except people know things now."

"But do they?" Ricky asked as he mischievously turned to look at Candice.

"What? Why are you looking at me like that?" She asked laughing with playful concern.

"Do people know about the little thing we got here with you and me yet?" He asked waving a finger in the air between her and himself.

For a moment her face wavered with the seriousness of self-doubt. "Don't wanna go telling the world now do we? Can't have 'em spreading rumours." She said in a joking tone trying to reclaim the proverbial grounds.

"Guess that's a no." Ricky said turning away. "This is why *I* hate Mondays. Bloody school."

"Ricky I'm just messing with you. It's just that I haven't had a reason to tell everyone else. No, I mean-"

"Nah, it's okay. I get it. Tis all good." He answered confidently. Sarcastically, on the inside he only felt a wee bit guttered at the relationship sidestep.

Candice looked at him helplessly, unable to know how to handle what she'd just accidently done. Ryan and Wyatt remained silent, trying to look away from the verbally awkward incident.

"Ahhhhhh! C!" Said an excited high-pitched female voice. They all turned to see what was happening. Candice wouldn't have needed to turn around to know exactly who it was. Ricky not so subtly rolled his eyes.

"Beth, hi!" Candice said with convincing enthusiasm.

"You didn't tell me you were coming back!" Bethany said hugging Candice.

"She leaves out a lot these days." Ricky said in his usual bubbly manner. Bethany only looked at him as though he's a squirming slug dying of bait poisoning before turning her attention back to her friend.

"Just thought I'd surprise everyone." Candice said freeing herself of Bethany's grip.

"You definitely have! Emma and Courtney are gonna flip!" She noticed Wyatt standing near. "Hey baby Fineman." She greeted happily.

"Hello Bethany." He answered politely.

She linked her arm around one of Candice's and guided her towards the school boundaries. Candice glanced back at the boys with a sorry face before disappearing into the seemingly innocent building.

"What, so I have to go around all day pretending I don't know her?" Ricky asked annoyed.

"Typical." Ryan stated. They looked at him surprised. "Well, now she's got all those popular 'normal' people back it'll just go back to how it was. Sorry Ricky but looks like you're headed for dorky-friend-of-the-younger-brother territory again."

Ricky sighed and looked to Wyatt. "You don't think, do you?"

Wyatt shrugged with a hopeless expression. "It's harsh, but maybe he's right. It is Candice we're talking about."
Ryan nodded at Wyatt's support of his opinion.

"Let's just do this then." Ricky said waving his arm as he began to walk ahead.

"I wonder if there's any new food at the canteen." Wyatt said as a distraction attempt while they walked through the glass maroon trimmed doors and that old familiar scent of education and alienation hit them hard.

~ 2 ~

This will be a good day for Rose. Now that the four friends were going back to school, Jack had gone back to the Benson house to spend the day with her. It only made sense, he wasn't about to spend his days lonely in the Fineman house with the occasional company of the dreaded mother. She'd dropped him off this morning at the end of the street after leaving Candice and Wyatt at the school. Jack tried to make small talk while he was alone with her, but she seemed a little uninterested in his bringing up of random, unimportant subjects. Ever since that pier jumping day last week, she'd been colder towards him. Not mean or rude, but colder.

"So how's it all been since you convinced goody two shoes to jump off the edge of town?" Rose asked him as they sat on the couch.

Jack laughed at the memory. Despite the crashing anger of Mrs Fineman, he loved what'd happened. "I never told you that we got yelled at afterwards."

Rose placed her hand over her mouth. "Seriously?"

"Yeah I kinda felt like I was in that nasty pig's blood, psychic chic movie."

"Just as long as she didn't start cursing about dirty pillows."

"I wish she did. That woulda been so fuckin' funny."

"And out of context. How come you didn't tell me already?"

"I dunno. Guess I just didn't have a chance or whatever." He casually answered.

"Anything else you've failed to tell your one and only sister?"

"Well there is one thing..." He formed a small smile. "I kissed him, I kissed Wyatt."

Rose looked back at him with widened eyes. "When? How'd it all go? Clearly very good by the way you're glowing right now."

"One night he was showing me his mad piano playin', and I just couldn't help it. I just... laid one on him."

"What did he do?"

"Reacted all cute n' stuff. Gave me one back on the cheek."

"Wow. So, you guys are really hapnin' over there huh?"

"There's definitely somethin' happening and that's for sure."

"I can't believe you're only telling me this now! How did you not blurt it out over the phone at least? Which hasn't been as often I might add."

"Oh I dunno Rosie. I'm tellin' you now, aren't I?" He laughed.

She faked a smile and looked away. At this moment the cluttered mantelpiece seemed like a decent attention getaway.

"So, what do you wanna do today? Man, we haven't been just you and me for ages!" Jack said excited.

"Well I've developed this habit of watching the morning shows and news." Rose said aiming the remote at the television, turning it on.

Jack looked at her with indifference. "Haven't you turned into a bundle of fun." He said sarcastically.

"You'd be surprise at the amount of stuff happening in the world Jack." She said reading the headline on the screen. "See." She gestured to it. "Some cop shot himself in the foot."

He looked at the television to see she wasn't kidding. "What a ham. Get it?" He laughed.

"That's pretty funny." She laughed back at him, pondering how much she's happy that he's here. "I've really missed you, you know."

"Aw Rosie, come 'ere will ya." He leaned over so they could throw arms around each other. She embraced him with warm affection. "Your bro ain't going nowhere."

"I know." She said with an air of melancholy.

"You alright?" He asked with belated concern.

"I'm fine Jack. Just happy you and Wyatt are moving forward. That's seriously so amazing."

"Uh, don't I know it!" He grinned. "I got him to wear the bracelet today for when he's at school with all those prancy toffee noses."

"I'm sure he's doing great."

~ 3 ~

Sitting at his desk, Wyatt's fingers played with the entwining plastic feel of the colourful little trinket around his wrist. Everything here seemed the same as it always had been. Mr Mirtskin is his same old moustached self. Wyatt could tell that the buttoned up middle aged teacher was trying his best not to pay him any special attention. Probably as a means not to make him uncomfortable in front of all the classmates because of the horrid ordeal. While the man droned on in his deep, almost muffled voice about the day's schedule into the first lesson of the day, Wyatt couldn't help thinking that Jack would probably take a leaf out of Ricky's book and say this teacher's a real work of prissy art.

Fellow classmates have been throwing him insensitive glances all morning. It took him great effort to try and keep concentrated interest on Mirtskin's teachings when wondering if their glances would last all day. He's budding a terrible worry.

All these desks... The make of them nothing like that stupid set up in the hellish room beneath the old Brandis house. Yet there's a sickening feeling within him that's the remembrance of that crucially perilous time. Ryan's presence here only comforted him a small amount.

Mum did say to tell the office if I had to go home... Goodness stop being a baby... Ryan must feel exposed knowing that everybody must know that it's his fault it all happened to me... Hold on, did I just really think that...

He turned to look at Ryan two desks over to the left, he looked tired already, slouching over his desk.

Is it Ryan's fault?...

He rubbed his temples with his hands, sighing as he did so. He's beginning to want these educational hours to speed by as quickly as possible, even though he started the day and went into this with a positive attitude.

By the time recess came around he was so excited to see Ricky again he could have hugged him right there in the school's hall if it weren't for all the other people around.

"Wylie!" Ricky called excitedly through the red and blue traffic flow of students. Wyatt thought it was kind of hilarious how Ricky didn't hold back and just simply drew attention to them. With an apple in hand he approached them with reunited relief. "Felt like recess was never gonna arrive." He said looking around the hall.

"I know right." Wyatt replied. "You're looking for Candice, aren't you?"

Ricky shrugged. "Maybe just a little."

"She's over there." Ryan said with a nod in the direction Ricky had just come from.

Ricky turned around to see her walking along in the old group of popular arseholes. This was a sight he would have been happy to never see again. It had nothing to do with her gorgeous golden hair tied back sensibly in a pony tail, the beautiful way her features are contoured on her face, the uniform skirt swaying from side to side with every motion of her hips, her arms graciously holding her books... It's how all this and more is once again being wasted on those wretched people. Her group migrated through the hall, being loud with conversation and laughter. Walking past the boys, Candice did nothing but glance back, waving briefly before returning her attention to the friends.

Laugh and smile all you want Candie, but I know exactly what it looks like when it's real...

Wyatt could tell there was real underlying hurt in Ricky's face. After all he's been through, he may have picked up a keen eye for sore souls and a soft spot for such tenderness in others. "Ricky." He said placing a hand on his shoulder. "Don't let it get you down. I think it will be okay."

Ricky looked at him and smiled at the comfort he was trying exchange. "Thanks buddy."

"Wyatt Fineman." Said an authoritative voice from behind them.

When Wyatt turned around to address the addresser, he found it's the principal of their bumbling religious school. "Hello Mr Seymour. How are you?" He asked with upmost sensibility.

"I'm very well, thank you. I've come to invite you to my office." He informed demandingly.

"Now, Mr Seymour?"

"No not now. I'll have some spare time later. Come by at the sounding of the lunch bell."

"Okay, I'll be there sir." He answered with a sensible smile.

The tall, brown tweed suit wearing principal smiled, nodding his head once in reply. He then looked at Ryan. "Mr Jonson, settling well?"

"Yes Mr Seymour." Ryan said trying to sound enthusiastic.

"Good good." The eyes behind golden thin-rimmed glasses now turned to Ricky. "Mr Benson."

"Mr Seymour." Ricky answered not holding back his disinterest.

"Keeping your teachers on their toes, are you?"

"As always sir." He laughed.

"I'm sure. Enjoy your break boys. I'll be seeing you later Mr Fineman." He gestured his hand at Wyatt, who nodded. He turned around and walked off in the direction of the offices.

"Does anyone else feel like they're talking to a military sergeant when they're talking to that pompous bum?" Ricky asked turning to lead the way outside.

"I just want to know why he wants to see me." Wyatt said concerned.

"He most likely wants to make sure you're okay and whatever." Ryan suggested.

"Yeah so nothing comes back to bite him on the arse if something goes wrong." Ricky said untrustingly.

"What could go wrong?" Wyatt asked anxiously.

"I don't get to eat this apple." Ricky said taking a bite of his royal gala.

~ 4 ~

Drone, drone, drone. Just on and on and on it goes with no break.

Can't they talk about anything worth wasting breath on?...
Candice's patience was being tested as her girly group spoke of all that she'd missed while she's been home-bound. She felt particularly horrible for having shunned Ricky by accident. It by all means wasn't intentional and all morning since it happened, she'd been trying to figure out whether or not she was really in the wrong, or if it just turns out he's easily emotionally offended.

Currently the best part about this recess is the sun on her skin. Sitting at one of the outside lunch tables, the sun's warmth seemed to calm her nerves a little and clear some of those worry webs in her mind.

"Candice? You listening?" Bethany asked. Her voice seemed to come from nowhere.

"What?" She began to unwrap a muesli bar.

"I said I guess you're wondering where Robbie is?"

Candice shrugged and swallowed her first bite. "Not really."

"He's holidaying in Bali with his family. Just imagine all that sun he's getting, sitting half naked beside a pool." Bethany totally isn't acknowledging Candice's disinterest.

"Yeah, being fed grapes by a pool boy just as hot and even bigger from all the hard work." Emma added to the ridiculousness of the subject. Bethany and Courtney laughed whereas Candice only smirked, shaking her head.

Emma and Courtney aren't as promiscuous as Bethany but they're just as attractive and ambitious when it comes to anything and everything to do with the girly throes of womanhood, and above all: the attention of males.

"He's not coming back until the 29th or something. He put a post up on Facebook and stuff." Bethany said absentmindedly playing with the screen of her phone.

"That's the day before my brother's birthday." Candice said now sounding engaged in the conversation.

"How is the little munchkin?" Bethany asked with a pouty face. It didn't take a genius to know she's asking because of the kidnapping.

"He's surprisingly okay." Candice began to let her mind float away again. It wasn't until this very moment in all its casualness that she realised how tremendously strong her little brother is. What happened to him could have sent most kids and adults into a depression of fear, distrust and a side of life loathing. Yet here he is a month later, at school, trying to move on. Being strangled by that hulky madman had taken its toll on her but within herself she felt pretty fine. Except for this Ricky business of course.

Maybe I should just act like nothing happened when I see him after school...

She started to zone back into her friends verbal shenanigans.

"I reckon when he's a bit older he'd be fine as heck." Emma said freely.

"Yeah, I've thought that for a while. I'd totally go for it." Courtney added.

"You guys!" Bethany said playfully waving an arm towards them.

"Not gonna make a difference when we're twenty and he's eighteen." Courtney laughed.

Emma nodded. "Oooh, boy toy!"

"He's definitely got the makings of a hottie in that innocent, inexperienced kind of way." Courtney continued.

"I see it." Bethany said looking towards a brickwork wall of the school's building.

Candice followed their trio of perverted gazes to see the only males over there were Wyatt, Ricky and Ryan. "Who're you guys talking about?" She asked confused.

"Your brother! Wow you're just not listening today." Bethany exclaimed amused.

"What?! Eww!" She sat up straight with a cringe on her face.

"Can't deny it Candice." Emma added with a matter of fact tone.

"Uh, yes I can. Gross. Talk like that anymore and you'll never see me again."

The girls laughed, clearly not taking her as seriously as she's being.

"Although can't say the same for Candice's pet monkey over there." Bethany stated.

They all turned their attention to Ricky.

"I wouldn't say no to him." Emma said, to which the others looked at her with confused wide eyes, Candice included. "If I was drunk and almost passed out at a party!" Emma continued. Now they all laughed at her stupid joke, Candice not included.

"He's not that bad." She said defending her unannounced boyfriend

"Oh C, you're getting too soft in your old age." Bethany said putting her arm over her.

No, you're just getting bitchier...

"Look at him though." Courtney said degradingly. While Wyatt and Ryan sat on the ground against the brickwork, Ricky walked around in front of them, repetitively tossing something into the air to catch it again, only failing catches scarcely.

"Seriously, that four eyes fag. What a loser." Bethany said with closed smile at his quirkiness, as if to love hating him.

"I know right." Emma agreed.

Candice didn't answer their tremendously misguided opinions, but left her eyes to watch Ricky being his great self over there, not hurting anyone. It's feeling as though their words could possibly break her heart should they continue with it. What if she were to tell them right now that the 'loser' is her first and current boyfriend, and that she'd probably sell both her thumbs to a cannibalistic hobo if it meant she could be hanging out with him right now and not them.

She noticed the plump body of Mrs Willis walking past the corner of the building when Ricky threw the item onto the roof with impeccably bad timing. "Oh my God." She giggled under her breath.

~ **5** ~

"Whoo!" Ricky shouted proudly with his arms over his head.

"Richard Benson! What did you just throw onto our roof?!" Mrs Willis screeched, nearly emitting smoke from her nostrils. The greying orange of her hair didn't help the look.

"Was just an apple core Mrs Willis." He answered with both hands in his trouser pockets.

"And why exactly would you do that?" The woman asked now crossing her arms.

"Just giving the possums a snack." He grinned. Ryan and Wyatt let out some laughter before receiving daggers from the critical eyes of her.

"Well if I catch you doing such things again, you *will* be punished!" She announced loudly.

"Got it ma'am. Don't feed the furry neighbours." He said with a nod.

"Pull your sleeves down and tuck in your shirt. You look like a hooligan." She snapped before continuing on her walk.

"What... ever." Ricky said slowly as he tucked into his pants the exposed parts of his shirt that aren't covered by his jumper. "Ryan yours isn't tucked in. She didn't grouch at you."

"Ricky she hates your guts, always has." He answered simply.

"Why do people keep doing that to me?" Ricky mumbled.

"They're intimidated by you probably." Wyatt stated in encouragement. "Besides, all the right people think you're the best."

"Yeah what he said. Who knows, maybe she'll pull a Candice and suddenly like you one day." Ryan said briefly holding his arms out to the side as he said it.

"Holy hot cakes! Ryan don't even put that out into the universe!" Ricky said sitting himself beside him. "Zif I want *her* ripping through my belt." He whispered so only Ryan could hear.

They laughed sheepishly, raising Wyatt's curiosity.

"Not even going to ask guys." He began to stare at his wrist. The bracelet is a bold statement as it clashed and bashed against uniform rules, but the risk was worth it. Not once has anyone said anything.

At least there's that upside to being kidnapped...

~ 6 ~

"Ha! No way, she won't go for it." Rose shouted watching the television upside down. Her two small hair buns only just weren't grazing the carpet of the lounge room.

"Nah bet ya she will." Jack said, also upside down. On the cushions they both lay on their backs with their legs draped over the back of the couch. Having the house to just the two of them was enough to get them comfortably acting as though they owned the place. Now at midday, they'd been watching TV since Rose turned it on that morning and were now munching on gelatine free mixed lollies.

"No way!"

"Told you she would." Jack said placing a ball of sweetness into his mouth.

Rose sighed dissatisfied. "Ricky's right to call these movies 'Home and Away on steroids.'"

Jack laughed. "God he's funny sometimes."

"Tell me about it." She answered with another small sigh.

Jack watched the TV screen as Rose aimed the remote and flicked through channels. "So, I have some inside word on Wyatt's b'day." He said intriguingly.

"Oh yeah?"

"You know how I said that Candice said that Ricky said that Ryan said something the other day about his brother having a party 'cause their parents are outta town?"

"I think so." She paused her channel surf to concentrate on what he's going to say.

"The guy suggested turning it into a party for Wyatt, and if that happens he invited us all. I think Candice is gonna work on the mum."

"Oh that should be fun!" She said excitedly before her thoughts reminded her of the last time she saw Ryan. "I should really apologise to Ryan. I may have been a little harsh last time I saw him."

"Whatevs. Whatever happened, somethin' tells me the tiff won't last long." He said casually, rummaging the packet for a certain lolly.

Rose looked at him expectantly just before the sound of the midday news grabbed their attention with a few collective, alarming words.

"A woman wanted by police for kidnapping has been found dead on the side of the road. Trudy Hammond has the full story..."
The twins silently looked at each other, simultaneously sitting upright to watch it with full attention.

They showed a young female reporter on location. *"The deceased body of forty seven year old alleged kidnapper Thelma Kersh was found this morning on Bridport road. Officials identified her by driver's license at the scene after they arrived. A local elderly couple had discovered the ruined remains of her vehicle by pure chance."*

It flicked to an elderly man. *"My wife and I were on our way through as we've done many times before, I just pulled up for a pit stop and found the car wreck in the bush there. I was very surprised."*

"We're told that considering the condition of the body, she crashed several weeks ago, possibly around the time she began to run from authorities due to orchestrating the kidnapping of her fourteen year old nephew's friend in quiet Gerryville. The police haven't ruled out foul play but at this stage it appears to be a classic fatal car crash.

There will be a coroner's report and I guess we'll know more after crash experts have scoured the vehicle and scene. Carmen, back to you."

"What the hell?" Rose whispered.

"Just like that." Jack said just as quietly.

They're absolutely stunned. 'The big scary' had been dead for weeks. Not only was it incredibly surprising and totally relieving, she'd crashed and died in a most peculiar area.

~ 7 ~

The sound of the lunch bell should have felt like a relief for Wyatt, but instead he had to think about making his way to the principal's office. Ryan assured him that he and Ricky would be waiting for him at one of the tables outside.

Now as he walked up to the office door, he contemplated whether or not to actually do it. As if he'd get in trouble for not going.

No, I have to do it...

They'd probably call his name out over the speakers and no doubt tell his mother. This is the first time today that he'd been without one of his friends and he's not better for it.

Knocking on the dark wooden door, and taking a deep breath for the shambles of nerves had him feeling brave.

"Come in!" The principal called from inside. Wyatt opened the door and walked in with his most sensible mannerisms. "You can shut the door behind you." Said the old man seated behind his semi cluttered desk. Wyatt closed the door quietly and stepped towards the desk. "Please, have a seat Mr Fineman." He said taking his reading glasses off his face, placing them on the papers in front of him.

Placing himself on one of the guest chairs, Wyatt couldn't resist to enquire. "Sir, why did you want to see me? Not that it isn't a pleasure of course."

Mr Seymour chuckled a little before answering. "You're always so polite, no matter what. There aren't too many students about that are quite like you Wyatt."

That didn't answer his question and it made him confused. Mr Seymour is known for his hard head and quick discipline. He'd always been kinder towards Wyatt but today he was being a different kind of soft. It seemed authentic though. "How so sir? I'm just being myself."

"Yes, of course you are." He said as though it'd been a lie. "I've always taken a certain liking to you. Not because of your parents, impeccable grades or necessarily how polite you are to my teachers. But it's the how you understand it's the way you act and the things you do that get you to where you need to go."

"Sir, I'm sorry but I'm not following."

"Hush Mr Fineman. Your respect, politeness and non-violent ways will certainly get you places. But I'm afraid not acting as your true self because of others, will warp your very being and turn you into something that you are not." The seriousness of his face and the direct gaze of his eyes got Wyatt having to take this seriously. It's incredibly unlikely for Mr Seymour to talk about things that don't matter.

"Mr Seymour, if I may ask. Why are you telling me this?"

"I'm telling you this because, in your life you will encounter many things that'll have you question everything you know and believe. It's these moments that could help you define who it is you are, and without an open mind it could possibly very well drive you mad. What I'm trying to say is, by all means be a polite person. But *do not* go through life trying to only please others. You have your entire life in front of you, with great opportunities ahead. To make the most it, be you. Be Wyatt, not what people want you to be."

Wyatt couldn't believe his ears. He almost didn't turn up

to this meeting and yet it's nothing like he thought it'd be. "I appreciate it sir, thank you."

"Don't thank me, just tell me you understand."

"I do." He said with a smiling nod.

"And always stand up for yourself."

Wyatt nodded again.

"Your sister may be older than you but it's your duty as a brother to always take care of her. I once had two sisters rather than one, and I'd do anything to spend another day with the both of them together."

"Oh... Mr Seymour, I'm sorry."

"Don't be sorry. Just-"

"I understand fully sir." He said warmly.

"Now I know I'm not supposed to play favourites but you're in fact my favourite student. Just don't ever tell your friend Richard that he comes in second. "

"Oh wow." Wyatt laughed. "He thinks all teachers and parents hate him!"

"Small minds can't handle something great. He's a court jester but he's hardly disrespectful." He offered a glass bowl of sherbet bombs, to which Wyatt refused.

"Take a couple for your friends. And here's a chocolate bar." He said getting one from his desk drawer. "Actually, take two."

"Thanks Mr Seymour, they'll be thankful for it." Wyatt said stuffing a handful of sherbet bombs in one pocket and the chocolate bars in the other.

"Now if anyone gives you trouble or you're not coping very well, come and see me or tell the office ladies you need to speak to me, and we'll see what we can work out. Coming back must be very daunting."

"Thank you. But I think I'll be okay." He answered with a smile.

"Just remember my words today, Wyatt. Now go and enjoy your lunch."

Wyatt nodded happily and made his exit of the principal's office. It was rather quiet in the halls now the students were outside.

Can't believe Mr Seymour is so wise... He's like Dr Kraus but not... He'd decided to make his way to his schoolbag, leaving the treats in his lunch box. Now time for a 'tinkle break' before returning for it and going outside to the others.

After making his way to the restroom and doing his business, he stood at the sink to wash his hands thoroughly. A quick check of the hair and he was about to be on his way outside. Too bad he was stopped by the unwanted face of Hunter Mason entering the room.

If there's a Lady Sacred equivalent of Pier Ripple's Harley Harris, Hunter Mason is it. Except what made him worse than Harley is that Hunter doesn't need other bullies around to torment others. He's perfectly fine doing it all on his own.

"Well, looky here! Fucking Fineman returns to the hellbin, and I find him alone in the shit room." His intimidating voice echoed as still stood in front of the way out.

"Um... Good to see you too Hunter." He tried to head for the door. "I just have to-"

"Oh no you don't." The gruff boy said, grabbing him by the arms. "I gotta check for any cash. See if I take your money, no more people will want to steal you."

"I don't have any on me, I swear." Wyatt plead.

"Rich people always lie. Everybody knows that." He rolled his eyes.

Wyatt tried to wriggle free. "I'll tell the principal." He said trying to sound tougher than he felt. The bully ignored, tightening his grip as the hand holding his right arm came across the bracelet. He pulled Wyatt's sleeve back to see it. "What's this?"

"Nothing. Can I go now?"

"You know who wears shit like that and says it's nothing?"

"No?" Wyatt said looking at him as though he's delusional.

"Closeted faggots." He said with an unsettling, evil smirk.

"No... You have it totally wrong." Wyatt tried to say before he was being pushed into one of the toilet cubicles. Hunter forced him against the wall. "I don't have it wrong at all. Everything makes sense now. But you wanna know something?"

"What?" Wyatt said trying to think of how he could get to the door.

"That sorta crap will send you straight to hell."

He looked to the aggressor with angry eyes. "Looks like we're both going for different reasons."

"You stupid-" Hunter grunted and held him harder against the wall with his forearm over Wyatt's chest.
Wyatt closed his eyes in anticipation of what was to come.

"Talk like that to me again I swear, I'll mess you up so bad your own mother won't recognise you."

The sound of somebody walking into the restroom momentarily interrupted the interception. Hunter quickly closed the cubicle door with his foot. Wyatt didn't even open his eyes until he heard their voices. Hunter placed a finger over his own mouth to signal Wyatt's silence.

"Yeah but if we got to their table before them, then she would of had no choice but to say something while they'd be bitchin about us in their spot."

"Ricky just go and talk to her in front of them, then she can't deny anything."

"And I'll be a fool if she denies shit."

Wyatt didn't heed Hunter's warning and yelled out for help. "Ricky, Ryan!"

It only took a matter of seconds for the boys to swing open the cubicle door to assist him. "Get off him ya dickhead!" Ricky yelled, pushing Hunter into the wall opposite. Ryan squeezed himself in, promptly punching the bully, once in the shoulder and again on the chin.

"What the hell?! You his body guards?" Hunter grunted, holding his face in pain.

"Get outta here ya waste of space." Ricky answered with his arm around Wyatt.

"I get it. You guys are bed buddies aren't ya?"

"Well I'm sure he's a better boink than what ya mum was last night." Ricky said with quick wit.

"This is bullshit." Hunter scoffed, making his way out of the cubicle andout of the restroom.

"Guys, thanks so much. He was just threatening me, I don't know if I was going to get hurt or not." Wyatt said making his way out of the small space. The other two followed.

"No problem." Ryan said looking at his hand, the knuckles feeling the impact.

"Why was he being so mean to you? He's not usually so handsy." Ricky asked.

"Yeah we thought you were still with Seymour."

"I don't know." Wyatt said doubtfully as he tidied his hair in the mirror. "Let's just get outside and have some lunch shall we."

"You sure you're okay?" Ricky asked worried.

"Ricky, I'm fine." Wyatt assured him.

~ 8 ~

Candice had been told by her mother to make sure Wyatt waits by the offices to be picked up at the end of the day. She'd been held up with Bethany back at the classrooms and quickly made her way through the halls to find him waiting with Ryan in the little arm chairs near the front office.

"Sorry I'm late."

"Doesn't matter at all." Wyatt said waving a hand.

"Where's Ricky?" She said sitting down in the chair beside her brother, plonking her schoolbag on the ground.

"He already left." Wyatt replied.

"Here's my mum now." Ryan said getting to his feet. "See ya's tomorrow."

"Bye Ryan." The siblings said together.

Candice sat back in the chair, sighing deeply with her hands over her face. Wyatt looked at her and remembered what Mr Seymour had said to him. "Candice."

"Yeah?" She said without showing her face.

He leaned on the arm rest to get closer to her. "When I first realised you and Ricky were... Whatever you are, I really didn't like the idea of it at all. I was angry, I was jealous and just... I didn't like it."

Candice took her hands from her face to look at him with a concerned expression. "What are you saying?"

"But now we're at this point, I've seen you guys together and other factors have made me realise that you both *should* be together. I don't think you should let bad people keep you apart."

"You mean other factors, as in Jack?" She said giggling.

He smirked a nose crinkle, unknowingly batting his eyelashes. "Ricky's not avoiding you by the way. His mum just got here super early."

"How'd you know I was thinking that?"

"Just brother's intuition." He shrugged.

"I like this newfound intuition."

"Yeah well. Suppose I've always had it. Just now I'm starting to realise."

"People do tend to get wiser with age. Unlike me. I think I really messed up Wy. With Ricky I mean."

"Nope, you didn't. Don't tell him I told you, but he's been talking about you all day."

"Really?" She smiled as she sat up straight.

He smirked at how excited she got. "Talking about how he's going to fix it."

"So funny. I've been thinking the same thing all day."

"Difference is Candice, he was talking to his friends about it."

"I don't need you to tell me I'm an idiot." She said looking to the floor.

"You're not an idiot. A pushover maybe but not an idiot." He opened his schoolbag and rummaged through for a moment to find one of the chocolate bars. "Here. Have this."

"Whoa so random." She said taking it from him.

"A wise old sister of mine once told me that chocolate doesn't fix your problems but it does make them easier to bear."

"Oh be quiet you!" She laughed as she put the bar into her own schoolbag. "So do you think I should send him a message, will he ignore me?"

"I don't know. He's *your* boyfriend."

"Ugh, maybe I should just- Oh here's mum." She said when she saw the car drive past outside.

The both of them gathered their bags and headed outside to greet the refreshing afternoon air. As they walked along the sidewalk, watching their mother park the car at the side of the road further along, they realised with surprise that the passenger side door opened. Out came Jack, enthusiastically jogging towards them. Wyatt grinned the biggest grin he felt he'd ever meant as he sped up his walking to reach him.

Candice shook her head with a genuine smile. *Poor sucker endured another car ride with her just to see us earlier... Well, Wyatt anyway...*

Mrs Fineman stood by the car watching. Jack reached Wyatt with suspenseful longing. His arms wrapped around him as though he hadn't seen him for months.

"Careful." Wyatt said unexpectedly. Jack didn't need to be a mind reader to know he meant 'Careful, people might see us together.' Such a small moment can hurt but Jack didn't let it get the better of him. He let go of him.

"Just excited to see ya."

"Calm down. It was only six hours." Wyatt said laughing.

"Don't tell me you didn't miss me." Jack said confidently placing his hands on his hips.

"Of course." He replied looking towards his mother.

Jack turned his attention to Candice and hugged her before she had time to acknowledge that it was going to happen. "Whoa soldier, I'm sure she didn't think anything of it!"

He stood back from her. "Gotta have me some of the more lady like Fineman too." He said suggestively.

"Ha, yeah. Because she's *so* lady like and all." Wyatt scoffed and began to walk on.

"Hey!" Candice said defensively. "I *am* lady like."

While the siblings walked ahead of him bickering with each other, Jack felt that he just had to say something about Kersh. He couldn't tell them right at this moment and no doubt their mum knows by now, so she'll probably be the one to tell them. It's unlikely she wouldn't, she does appear to love jumping on the grief wagon given the chance. He followed them into the car quietly.

~ 9 ~

"So she's actually dead? Just like that, gonza?" Ricky asked at the dinner table in near disbelief at what Rose had told him.

She'd just explained to all three Bensons what her and Jack saw on the television earlier that day. She managed to wait until dinner time to tell them because that's when they'd all be home and together.

"Noah and Sally, I'm surprised you didn't hear anything all day." She said hardly touching the meatless spaghetti bolognese she helped prepare.

"I thought some of the ladies were acting a little sheepish at work. Maybe that's why." Sally said with deep thought. "Hun, why didn't you hear it on the radio?"

Noah shook his head as he swallowed some food. "Didn't have it on today luv. It's been playin up."

"Who cares, she's dead. Good riddance." Ricky said speaking his thoughts, twirling his fork in the spaghetti.

"Ricky come on." His mother said unimpressed.

"Mum, she was an arse. Plain and simple. Personally, I hope there's a hell and she went to it. Otherwise, I wish she was still alive and being tortured in prison."

Rose looked down at her plate.

"Ricky!" Sally lifted her hand to speak. Noah placed his hand over hers and gently shook his head.

"Way I see it..." Ricky said swallowing a bite. "Death is a release, not a punishment."

Rose's thoughts turned to her mother as her dinner's sauce suddenly resembled what came out of the man she stabbed to death with the shard of a table. What had even come of her mum? Last they heard was her giving consent of the Bensons caring for her and Jack. *Not that he's ever even here now...*

"How was your first day back at school with a girlfriend?" Sally asked purposely changing the subject to something unrelated.

Ricky placed his fork down. "Oh mum, you always know the perfect questions to ask." He said sarcastically. "She's not my girlfriend. Well, she is but she isn't." He picked his fork up and used his other hand to rest his face on.

"What're ya on about?" His dad asked as though he'd just admitted to a crime.

"She kinda ignored me and stuff around her friends." He said sullenly.

"Oh what?" Sally said sadly.

Rose stayed quiet and listened.

"Man up kiddo. She's just being a girl." Noah slyly looked at Rose and Sally across the round table.

"She must be adjusting. Give it time." Sally said. "I understand it must still be a big deal for her, big change."

"Well I'm just going to ignore her back. It seemed to work last time." Ricky said referring to the months before they became close.

"Richard don't ignore your girlfriend." His mum said quickly like he's a fool.

"Like your dad said, be a man." Rose said jokingly.

"You know if you didn't help make gourmet food, I'd kick you out!" Ricky laughed.

"Nah you'd miss me too much."

"Got that right." He leaned over to grab her cheek like an old grandma does to a baby.   Rose smiled at him sideways.

Noah and Sally exchanged a quick but meaningful glance at each other when Ricky returned his hand to himself.

~ 10 ~

After his parents had failed to tell him about the discovery of Kersh and Ethan was the one to tell him, Ryan had been laying on his bed for hours thinking with the ceiling once again. Not thinking too deeply, but of how after all this time she'd really been dead. There were no plans of a violent retaliation, nothing of the sort.

Stupid woman... Can't hurt anyone from beyond the grave, can you?...

After all that worrying about it there was no need. This could possibly be the final thing to propel their lives back to normalcy, but an even better version of it.

He couldn't understand why she was driving out that way, but in the end it doesn't matter. Dead as a door nail she is, and it's the best news.

He got off the bed, went over to sit at his desk and turned the lamp on. He'd been brainstorming every now and then of how to mend things with Rose, and finally decided on drawing a portrait of her dad with her and Jack as babies. Ricky had nicked a photo from their things and brought it along to school today. They planned to return it as soon as he's finished with it. With the photo propped up on the desk in front of him, he prepared all the materials he needed to do it. For a moment he did nothing but stare at the photo. He couldn't believe those little babies were the wonderful twins. Their dad looked so kind, and it was so obvious they're related to the man.

Now just about to connect 2H graphite to paper, the lamp flickered three times before going out completely. There's still some faint sunlight keeping the room from pitch black. Though peculiarly, the atmosphere of the room is off, like something's different. He turned in his chair to look around the room, everything's the same, but he just had this feeling... What is it?

Like something's here. Something watching him. Something with him.

He got up to turn the light on, looking around at the room again. Shaking off the uncomfortable apprehension, he sat back down at the desk. Picking up his pencil, he concentrated on starting the first sketchy line of the picture when the light flicked once very briefly on the ceiling.

I'm not interested in this...

For the rest of the night he peacefully continued his drawing without interruption.

~ 11 ~

"Here's some chocolate." Wyatt said offering Jack the bar Mr Seymour had given him. He sat with him and Candice on his bedroom floor. They'd wandered up here when Mrs Fineman had blatantly told them about the news after dinner. They briefly spoke of it before Wyatt suddenly reached inside his schoolbag for the treat.

"Wicked!" Jack said totally thrilled.

"I got a Mars bar, how come he got the Snickers?" Candice said starting to wonder where he got them from.

"Oh damn, they're epic." Jack said hardly really caring.

"Oh well next time I'll do it differently. I didn't really think about it." Wyatt said honestly.

"Hey no, it's fine by me. *I love nuts.*" He said in a deep voice, holding the bar up, raising his eyebrows.

"Oh I'm out of here." Candice said throwing her arms up. Before leaving she turned back to speak. "Wyatt you sure you're okay?"

"I wish everyone would stop asking me that, I'm fine." He said kindly. "Just because she's dead doesn't mean it makes anything different. Just means she can't hurt anyone else."

Candice looked back at him hoping he meant what he was saying. She'd like to remind him that he doesn't know what it was like to worry about him when he wouldn't leave his bedroom for days. On her way back downstairs, she tried to gather up sentences in her head of what she'd say to her mum when she'd surely deny a party at the Jonson's in under two weeks.

Only pure luck can help her on this one.

Finding her sitting in the study busy sewing away, she approached confidently.

"Hello mum."

Turning her head to look at her she answered almost too friendly. "Hello darling, what's happening this evening?"

"You seem really relaxed tonight."

"Maybe I'm just happy God's will has taken that woman out of our lives forever." She said with a startling smile, still sewing as she said it. "You didn't answer my question Candice."

"Oh, well..." She approached the accompanying chair. "I wanted to ask something, about Wyatt's birthday."

Patricia's hands stopped threading fabrics when her face looked at her daughter. "Yes?"

"Ryan's older and *very* responsible brother Ethan has planned a nice little party on the same day as Wy's birthday. It'd mean so much to him if he sees that all his friends and family put something like that together."

"Candice, I can't believe you even bothered to ask me. The answer is no." She resumed her sewing project.

"Mum, I think it would be something really good after all the bad things that have happened lately. Think of Wyatt."

"I don't need you to tell me to think of Wyatt. I said no because I have him in mind. A gathering of unsupervised teenagers will most certainly have alcohol, drugs and obscene sexual acts. I will not have your brother apart of it."

"I never said it wouldn't be supervised."

"Well will there be parents?"

"I don't know..."

"No Candice. It's not happening."

"Mum we're old enough to be responsible by ourselves. We'd be fine-"

"How do you expect me to be fine with it after I find out you watched your little brother jump off the pier Candice?!" She snapped. "This has been the year from H E double hockey sticks, and I do not wish to make it any worse."

"Please?" Candice pleaded helplessly.

"No. Get to bed. It's a school night."

She got to her feet and left the room in defeat. This is the worst. *Everything would be so much better if we had a different mother...* Ascending the stairs for the trillionth time, she remembered the sad fact she still hasn't sent Ricky a message.

Damn it... He's going to think I hate him...

"Arrgh!" She grunted walking along the hall.

~ 12 ~

Later the same night, Donald was learning what Candice had asked her mother earlier that evening. "Patty I'm saying this as a serious father. I think we should let them." He said sitting up in his side of their dramatic king size bed.

"What?!" She looked at her husband in shock, pausing her pillow fluffing. "We couldn't, so much can go wrong."

"That's what you said about the flower shop."

His words played on her mind. "Don I'm worried about him."

"The sum of it is, I don't want to stop my children from living because of worry. Patty, if you don't give them consent, *I* will." He said fearlessly looking her right in the eyes.

"I can't, I just can't have this happen." She said getting under the covers.

"That's it then." He said getting out from under them.

"Where are you going?"

"To tell Candice they can have this party." He said with firmness, not even bothering to put his dressing gown on before leaving the room.

Candice was almost in a deep sleep when her door opened, jolting her awake.

"Candice kitten, you're allowed to have that birthday party for Wyatt."

"Oh, okay daddy."

"Yep. Goodnight then."

"Thank you heaps." She said dropping her head back to the pillow.

"Not a problem." He said closing the door once more.

~ 13 ~

For the next eleven days everything went by rather smoothly. The only rocky business was the drifting apart of Ricky and Candice. Sparing the occasional 'Hello' in passing at school they hardly had contact.

Mostly everyone concentrated on their presents for the day Wyatt was trying to pretend wasn't going to happen. Jack especially wanted his present to stand out and brighten Wyatt's world in a way totally unique and so special that it changes everything for the better. To say the least, he was feeling as though this 'present' could be one of the most important and defining moments of his own life. If not, guess he'll try again with something else. Either that or skip town.

Ryan worked hard on the family portrait for Rose. He'd taken his time with it and decided it was done after about a week but still hadn't given it to her, mainly because he didn't see her very much but there was a little hesitation with it too.

There was truly minimal talk about Kersh. Even when updates were on the news about the crash, nobody brought it up in conversation. They said everything pointed to her running off the road of her own accord, possibly due to speeding. There were no skid marks and no sign of any other vehicles at the scene.

It seemed as though each teen could get back on their individual path of the good life.

~ Fourteen ~

THOSE BIRTHDAY BLESSINGS

~ 1 ~

Jack lay beside the sleeping and unsuspecting Wyatt.
He looked over at the alarm clock reading 4:32am in bright, slender digital blocking. The red of digital numbers in the darkness always made him feel weird, like it's life's darkest form of watching you, counting down the days of your existence. That didn't matter right now, there's more important things to worry about. It's finally the early morning of Wyatt's birthday.

He rolled over closer to Wyatt who was again almost squished up against the wall. "Teeeenkle-bell." He said softly. A small push of the shoulder was enough to wake him up this time, much to Jack's thankfulness. It's usually too hard to try and wake him up.

"What's going on?" Wyatt asked sleepy, propping himself up with his elbows. The only useful light in the room is the bluish, bright light of Jack's phone.

"We're going out." Jack whispered casually.

Wyatt looked at the poorly lit face of the ridiculous guy next to him. "What?! No, we're not!"

"Yes we are, we have to." He answered pretending he wasn't expecting him to put up a fight.

"Not at this hour, that's insane! Mum would kill us!"

"Not if she doesn't know." He said grinning. Even in the dimness his face is hard to say no to.

Wyatt thought over the possibilities:
Hit by a vehicle, kidnapped again, trip or fall over something in the dark and continue down a hill or embankment only to stop on a hard object by landing on your head causing your neck to snap, witness a mugging or a drug deal, be mugged by a drug dealer or maybe the very worst of all possibilities... Being caught in the act by mother.

"No we can't Jack. Why anyway?"

"No we have to go. I wanna do something." He nagged.

"It's too dangerous out there at night."

"Not with me it isn't. We'll be fine, I've done it a million times." Jack said confidently.

"But.." He began to say before hearing that inner voice of his that lately seems to be saying 'Hey what the heck. Yolo.' He wasn't even sure that statement of Jack's is valid. He'd said before he doesn't like violence or the dark.

"Please Wyatt? Please? It's not even really night anymore." He begged him.

"Okay fine but if anything happens, I'm blaming you."

"Yes!" He said excitedly jumping out of bed to put warm clothes on. He threw some over for Wyatt who's still under the covers wishing he wasn't awake. He giggled to himself thinking about the situation that was unfolding.

"Come on." Jack encouraged suddenly beside him.

"I am, I promise." He sat up to put a jumper on. Jack must've decided he's taking too long because he grabbed the jumper to put it over Wyatt's head, acting like he's an unruly toddler.

Wyatt quickly got his arms through the sleeves to speak defensively. "You right?!"

"Okay I'll just wait over here." He said amused, going over near the wardrobe.

Now both successfully dressed and ready for the mystery outing, they'd only gotten to the front door and opened it slowly before Wyatt's nerves got the better of him. They'd just put their shoes on when he spoke up.

"Oh come on, we'll be fine." Jack whispered.

"I want to, but I just don't think we should. We'll just do whatever it is tomorrow, in the daylight." He replied trying to be as quiet as possible.

"Everything's so different at night though. Please? Do it for me?" He pleaded holding his hand out. There's a hesitation of doubtfulness before Wyatt trustingly took the offered hand. After closing the door gently behind them, Jack led him off the property and out into the early morning along the sidewalk. The air's still, clear and crisp with moisture. It's pleasant feel against his skin didn't even remind him of the time the twins and Violet attempted to free him from those putrid captors. He's far too thrilled to be out, though he wouldn't admit it to Jack until later.

It'd gotten a lot lighter since Jack first woke him up and as they walked on, he kept note of the brightening sky above. The clouds kept it from being too bright and hid the stars. He had no idea where they were going which made him more excited than he thought he'd be, the defying of curfew and the rush of wonder from leaving at such a nice time of the morning had his spirits high.

"What are we even doing?" His curiosity grew intense.

"Just going out for a while." He replied looking at his phone to check the time. They kept walking, heading for the other side of the main area of town towards the water.

It's so quiet at this time of morning, so peaceful. It's refreshing to witness the old streets devoid of busy people and rowdy teens yelling and throwing things at each other.

After passing all the dark interiors of the shops, they eventually wound up at the ocean lookout. Between the water and the car park are grassy areas lined with pine trees and park tables where families and couples ate their hot chips during daylight hours. There's a large concrete monument to the left of where they entered the area, near the boat docks. All kinds of boats sat waiting on the calm water, their bodies bobbed around slowly, seemingly graceful.

Jack walked away from that area and kept going to the right before finally stopping at a somewhat secluded spot surrounded by low bushes. The branches of a nearby pine tree spread out over the top of the little clearing. It's almost like a little clubhouse, the kind of spot you'd want to find as a kid. He sat down on the grass facing the water. "This'll do." He patted the ground beside him.

Wyatt stood there confused. He'd hardly ever been in this spot, actually he'd never been in this exact spot. And this whole thing is weird.

"Wyatt it's fine, trust me." Jack said looking up at him, relaxed.

He walked over to Jack's right and sat down beside him. Jack noticed he was kind of out of breath. "You okay there? You're actin' like we just ran a marathon." He said over exaggerating.

"Yeah I just don't do much physical activity I guess." Wyatt said brushing it off. "The grass is wet."

"Oh, that doesn't matter. We're here to look at this." Jack gestured to the open sky and ocean in front of them. The sun was beginning to show itself in all the glory it had to offer. They sat quietly as they watched the deep, heavenly colours of the night sky mix together with the sun's promise of day, bouncing off the clouds and onto the surface of the ocean in a poet's inspiration of emotional beauty.

Wyatt shook his head in awe and fascination. "This is beautiful." He said to Jack's company beside him.

"I know. And I also know you like science and stuff, so I wanted to show you something that's crazy and out of this world but naturally amazing, like you." He answered confidently, still looking at the sky.

Wyatt turned to look at him, he looked back with a comfortable smile. "Happy Birthday Wyatt."

"Jack.." Was all he could manage. He's totally speechless. He looked away from him to see the water again. It reflected the sky like an oil painting from heaven. He looked back to Jack who'd remained gazing at him.

"You can kiss me if you want." Wyatt said with his heart racing like a wild horse.

Jack grinned nervously. "No it's okay." In fear of him only saying it to be polite or something strange like that.

"I don't mind." Wyatt reassured.

"Really?"

"Really."

Jack sat up straight, nervously leaning over to him. The light on their faces warm against the dark surroundings, making it all feel just that bit more magical. Right before he's about to touch his lips with his own, Wyatt laughed. He leaned back a little, confused. "What?"

"Just that my mum is going to kill us." He said trying to stifle giggles.

"Why're you laughing though?" Jack persisted nervously.

"Because I don't really care." He replied smiling.

Jack made his move again, faster than before to try and avoid any more nervous laughing.

Wyatt felt his soft mouth gentle on his, it's strange but

totally okay. He stayed still at first before following Jack's lead by mimicking the feel of what he's doing. Before too long they'd managed a tender rhythm of physical affection that's all their own. With his eyes closed to the world, he felt Jack get closer to him. He reached out to clutch at the sides of Jack's jumper as he felt an eager hand glide through his hair, making his over-whelmed heart skip a beat.

He felt like this was suddenly life, nothing else mattered. Just this moment was all he needed to live. The world felt like theirs, all theirs with no such thing as fear and violence, no greed and no hurt. Just them and beautiful life-sized paintings of nature.
He could taste something sweet in Jack, something that he won't forget for a long time.
It lasted for not even a minute, but it felt like forever in the now relaxed mind of him.

They stopped to look at one another before Wyatt looked out at the water. Deep colours of orange, burgundy and several shades of blue were out there, the whole experience made him feel like he'd died and gone to heaven, yet at the same time he felt totally alive. The smell of pine, damp grass, crisp air and the sound of small waves crashing will probably forever remind the two boys of this first show of true passion towards each other.

Jack held one of Wyatt's hands in both of his. "Happy you came out now?" He asked most likely meaning the pun.

"Completely." He replied looking back at his angelic gaze.

"Can I kiss you again?" He asked politely.

Wyatt simply smiled and nodded. His readiness for it to happen again didn't go unnoticed by Jack, who leaned over with all the slow romantic movements he'd picked up off the television. Right before they touched, Jack began to tickle him around those irritatingly sensitive areas.

"Oh no! Stop it!" Wyatt said breathless through laughter,

now laying back on the grass rolling around trying to stop him. With Jack's hands groping at his humanly sensitivity, he saw the needled branches of the trees silhouetted against the sky soaked in the sunrise, and somehow, he felt at home. He felt *free*.

"Stop it! I don't want to hurt you!" He said worried about kicking him somewhere it'd hurt.

"Okay." Jack said, casually ceasing. He sat himself on top of him with his knees on the grass to either side of his body, kissing him in several different spots on both cheeks.

Wyatt felt delighted at the affection he's receiving. He propped himself up, next thing he knew, his head was being held gently by Jack's hands as he kissed him again. One hand slid slowly from the side of his face down to the shoulder. He felt the one and only thing his body could possibly be telling him. That forbidden tightness in the security of his pants screamed its presence at him.

Thankfully, before he had to do anything abrupt and spoil the moment, Jack stopped the kissing to get off the top of him to lie directly beside. "When do you reckon we should get back?" He asked slightly puffed.

Wyatt sat up, brushing the nature out of his hair and off his clothes. "Uhm... Maybe we should head back now." He said shifting uncomfortably.

Jack got to his feet and offered a helping hand. They stood together for one last glance at the rising sun. It's almost fully visible now and totally not worth going blind for by looking directly at it. The sea birds whirled around joyfully in the sky over the water at the new day ahead of them.

"I'm so glad we met." Jack said before he felt Wyatt take his arm and reply quietly.

"Me too. We may be a little in over our heads though."

Jack looked at him and flicked a leaf off his shoulder. "That doesn't worry me."

They said nothing for a minute before Jack continued. "You know I haven't been anywhere near a joint since I've been around you these last few weeks."

"Well done, that's awesome. You should be proud." Wyatt said impressed. He already knew because he doesn't smell like it anymore.

"I am." He answered through a grin.

~ 2 ~

It was nearly seven o'clock when they got back, but there were no signs of anybody being awake. They were relieved to get all the way inside without anyone standing there, asserting their anger and disappointment. They wandered into the kitchen intending to prepare an early breakfast, when Mrs Fineman came in with a huge smile, her arms stretched out to engulf her son, which she did against his internal resentment of it. He felt stupid being with Jack like he was and now being hugged by his mum.

"Happy Birthday my little fourteen year old!" She said releasing him from her grip.

"Thanks mum."

"Did you have a good sleep?" She asked still holding his shoulders.

"Yeah it was quite a fantastic sleep actually." He said looking at the smirking Jack.

"Well now, that sounds great." She said as she walked over to the pantry. "Why don't you go upstairs and change while I make everybody breakfast?"

Wyatt looked down at his clothes. They weren't exactly dirty but guess a mother just *always* knows.

They ran into Candice on their way back downstairs. She was

overly excited to see Wyatt and gave him a big old birthday hug. "How does it feel to be so damn old?"

"Oh please, I'm younger than you."

"Yeah but for me I can still remember all the years of little you walking around in nappies!"

"Oh so not much has changed then?" Jack laughed, getting a weak backhand on his forearm from Wyatt.

"Whose side are you on?"

"I'm sorry, no jokes or burns on your birthday."

"That's more like it."

"You two really kill me." Candice said studying their brief conversation. Their faces looked back at her confused. "You're really lucky to have each other, you have no idea."

Having things still not mended properly with Ricky is eating at her terribly, especially seeing these two as giddy as they are this morning.

Wyatt subtlety held Jack's fingertips with his own. "I have a pretty good idea actually."

"Dad. Dad's coming." Candice informed quickly.

The boys refrained from any touch as Mr Fineman came around the corner of the hallway and greeted them. Wyatt of course got a one armed hug. "What are we all doing at the top of the stairs?"

"Just planning our future career endeavours." Jack said straightening his posture.

Mr Fineman chuckled and scuffed Jack's hair like you would with a puppy. "You're a weird kid, don't ever change."

"Right back at ya Don!"

Mr Fineman glided quickly down the stairs shaking his head, still laughing.

"Seriously? What's your secret? Ricky is still basically an outsider when it comes to them." Candice said unable to understand how he does it.

"There is no secret. Your parents just love me." He said sounding totally cocky.

They began walking down the stairs with Wyatt in front.

"I mean I used to think it was funny how they didn't like him but now I'm his girlfriend it pisses me off."

"Like I said, it's probably just because they know he's into you and shit." He took on a lower tone now. "I mean if they *knew*, I have no doubt I'd be kicked to the curb."

Although Jack said it acting as though it didn't bother him, hearing him say something so simple yet so gruesome really made her want to cry.

Once downstairs, they were instructed to sit at the dining table by Mrs Fineman. There were new flowers in the display vases. Medium beauties of chrysanthemum and freesias sat nestled in baby's breath expressing themselves colourfully, noticeably cheering up the neat and sophisticated room. The soft sound of piano classics in the background complimented the atmosphere quite adequately. She could be a real piece of judgmental work sometimes, but Patricia Fineman knows how to create a certain mood for a room and that's for sure.

"Sometimes I swear it's like a forest in here." Jack said quietly.

"I hope that was meant as a compliment Jack." Patricia walked into the room with serving trays.

"Oh always Mrs Fineman." He said courteously, looking at Wyatt and Candice with wide eyes, signifying his brief fear of being in trouble.

"Holy cow." Wyatt said of what she's serving.

"Yes!" Candice said ecstatically. "I feel like it's my birthday too!"

Jack looked at the food with a small, unsure smile. Looking at the piles of thick, bread looking chunks in the shape of noughts and crosses boxes, he felt out of place having no clue what they were and what the big deal was.

"It's a special day and special days call for special breakfasts." The mother said sounding proud. "I'll just go get the toppings."

"Forget the toppings. I'll just eat 'em all plain!" Candice said like a true glutton.

Jack whispered in Wyatt's ear to inconspicuously ask what it was.

"They're Belgian waffles. Trust me you'll love it."

"Jesus, sounds so fancy." He whispered back.

"In a way yes, but hardly." He said placing a light weighted hand on Jack's forearm under the table.

"Here it is everyone, enjoy." Mrs Fineman said placing another serving tray on the table, bearing the goods of ice-cream and mixed berries.

"Ice-cream first thing in the morning, Mrs Fineman you've out done yourself today." Jack said in his own charming way.

"Oh Jack, one day you're going to woo the shoes off a very lucky girl." She said sitting down at her royal spot at the end of the table. Candice really tried but couldn't suppress the giggles as Wyatt stayed uncomfortably quiet.

"So they say." Jack replied indifferently.

His first bite of waffle was plain. He straight away understood Candice's comment on eating it without the interference of toppings. On its own it tasted like the expensive, sugary dessert pastries you'd find at an exquisite bakery or European restaurant. In his opinion it was totally awesome.

"And that's not all." Mr Fineman said as he entered the dining room, his hands behind his back as he sported a curiously enlivened smirk.

"What do you mean?" Wyatt asked with interest.

"We have spiced ginger beer!" He exclaimed in a cheery voice,

390 ~ ASHLEA RAYWOOD

showing his hands to have one holding a small wicker basket of
stubby glass bottles.

Wyatt's face formed the look of pure delight, his hands
covered the shock displayed by his open mouth. "It's not even
Christmas time!"

"Might as well be, love you son." The father said as he placed
the basket on the table. Candice immediately leaned over to
get hers.

"Oh my goodness, I'm just so excited right now." Wyatt stated
as he picked up his own bottle carefully, as if it were a block of
pure gold.

It humoured Jack to see this entire thing, so funny to see
Wyatt get excited over his food again.

*Spiced ginger beer?... What the fuck man... Must be on some sort
of fancy, rich mother fucker's planet or somethin'... Cause it ain't the
world I grew up in...*
He decided to stay quiet in his lack of knowledge in 'brand name'
soft drink flavours.

"Okay Wyatt." Mr Fineman began. "Today there's a bit of a
schedule." He said as he sat on his own seat at the table.

"A schedule?"

"Yes, after breakfast your friends are coming over, then
there's a special evening."

"What kind of evening?" He asked calmly but clearly curiously cautious.

"You'll have to wait and see." Candice said with food in her
mouth.

"Candice, manners!" Her mother scolded.

"Around five thirty you're going to Ryan's house for a party."
Mr Fineman continued.

"A party? What *kind* of party?" Wyatt asked sounding almost
untrusting.

"We're trusting Candice to take care of you but from my understanding, the older boy Ethan has organised an evening with some other children." Said Mrs Fineman.

"Do you have to say *children?*" Candice said feeling condescended by her mother once more.

"So you're letting us go to a house full of other people, for a party? How late?" Wyatt chimed in.

"You'll be staying the night I believe." His mother said looking down at her plate.

He looked to Candice and mouthed 'What the?' to which she nodded proudly with a closed mouth grin. Jack shoved him gently with his elbow, which Wyatt grinned in reaction.
This was going to be a crazy day.

~ 3 ~

By lunch time on this particularly fine day, Ryan was the first of the others to arrive for the present giving. Wyatt wasn't even aware that his friends had prepared presents. He did tell them on more than one occasion that he didn't want anything from them. It wasn't at all anything against them, just that for some reason he couldn't stand the thought of having the whole day revolve around him. In moments of being honest with himself he felt that just having his friends around at all is gift enough for him.

Now as he sat on the couch unwrapping the gold paper from around the gift Ryan had given to him, he felt overwhelmingly conflicted with gratitude and irritation. All eyes on him as he did so, the mantelpiece clock ticked on with painstaking accuracy of its time counting. For some reason he always tries not to rip the paper as if it's total taboo.

Just something else that makes me disturbingly different...
It's an intriguing flat and stiffly shape this present. Finally

pulling back the last flap of wrapping paper he could see it's two pieces of cardboard. Pulling them free of the paper to look between them he smiled at the sight of a drawing. There in a plastic pocket for protection is a cartoonish rendition of Superman standing proudly atop a building, in his hand a flag pole with of course a flag. It was obviously meant to be waving in the wind, given the way you could easily see the purple of it with a golden owl crested in the middle of it. Wyatt's grin intensified when he looked at Ryan.

"Ryan, this is amazing. Thank you so much!"

"That's okay. Just wanted to do something special."

"Cool." Candice said nodding her head as she lingered behind the couch.

"What's the flag thingy mean?" Jack asked pointing at it.

Wyatt turned to him to explain. "When we were younger, we had this army crest for our trio." He began to point at parts of the little flag. "Purple is for loyalty and trust, gold is for strength and courage, and the owl is for wisdom and knowledge."

"Yous were weird." Jack said grinning. "I was never that deep."

Wyatt turned to Ryan again. "I can't believe you brought this up again. I thought I was the only one that thinks of it now." He placed it carefully on the coffee table next to the expensive watch from his parents and stood up to hug his friend. Ryan hugged him back, it was nice to engage in such pure and kind physical acts.

"Hey uh... Anyone know when Ricky is getting here?" Candice asked the room.

"Should be soon." Ryan said sitting back down on the foot stool.

"I can't believe you still haven't spoken to him." Wyatt said shaking his head.

Before she had a chance to answer him, her mother spoke crudely. "Candice, instead of wondering about your own affairs, why don't you explain why you haven't given your brother a present on his birthday?"

"Well, I didn't really get one in time." She said shamefully, to which the mother huffed.

"What about the afternoon that Ricky was here to help you with it?" Mr Fineman asked, seated in an armchair with a glass of wine in his hand.

"Um, yeah... About that... Didn't work out in the end." Candice said sheepishly trying to not look either parent in the eyes.

"Honestly I don't mind. It's okay." Wyatt tried to reassure his mum. She smiled at him before turning to Candice with a disappointed scowl.

The doorbell dinging had Wyatt leave the uncomfortable room before anyone else could react. He hated the blatant favouritism his mother has been exhibiting lately. He felt it's disgusting and unnecessary. What if Candice came to resent him because of it? He couldn't bear to think it.

Jack promptly followed him to the front door to find Ricky and Rose waiting for entry. As soon Wyatt opened the door, a grinning and overly enthusiastic Ricky burst through the threshold to grab hold of Wyatt in a warm bear hug.

"Oh whoa!" Wyatt grunted in surprised.

"Happy birthday Wylie!" Ricky yelled still hugging him.

"Thanks Ricky."

"Carful there, a guy might get jealous." Jack giggled somewhat nervously.

Ricky let go of Wyatt and turned to Jack. "Sorry man. I know how you feel about me. You get a hug too." He mischievously hugged Jack briefly.

Jack shook his head with a smirk at Ricky's hilarious stupidity.

"There's a present from me and one from mum and dad in here." Ricky said offering Wyatt a plastic shopping bag.

"You shouldn't have!" He answered taking the bag from him.

"I only have this cake." Rose said still standing in the doorway. "Happy birthday Wyatt." She spoke with a lovely smile across her face.

"Rose, it looks fantastic." Wyatt said honestly. It's plain, just as it should be.

"Yeah Rosie. Really outdone yaself." Jack said impressed.

"But does it taste good?" Ricky said with a sceptical voice. "Open your bloody presents already!" He said to Wyatt.

Obeying him, he walked away and stood by the hall table.

"Where should I put this?" Rose said holding the cake up.

Mrs Fineman came from the lounge room and spoke with sudden guidance. "Here, come with me." She began walking in the direction of the kitchen. Rose reluctantly followed.

Wyatt reached inside the plastic bag and got his hands on a small present wrapped in pink floral paper. He looked at Ricky untrustingly. Jack laughed at the innocent sight.

"All we had at the time." Ricky shrugged. "That one's from mum and dad."

Inside the wrapping is a blank, faux brown leather notebook. "This is nice." He said genuinely meaning it.

"I think mum just thought it might help you out a bit. You know, write down your problems and stuff."

"You'll have to thank her for me." He said placing it on the hall table between the lamp and vase of flowers.

Ricky was nodding his reply when Ryan came in to join the viewing.

Next is Ricky's present. In the same floral paper it has the weight and shape of a CD case. He carefully took the flowery envelope off to eagerly find a homemade CD insert sitting in the case with badly drawn Superman crests, surrounding the words 'Music To Bother With' boldly scribbled in the middle. On the back, a handwritten list of the CD's tracks.

"This is awesome!" He said laughing happily at the thoughtful gift.

"Every song was specially chosen for the mix by myself." Ricky said with fake pride, holding a hand to his chest. "And remember, it's 'N' Roses. Not and Roses."

Wyatt walked over to hug Ricky, handing the CD to Jack. "Come on let's go in here." He gestured to the lounge room. They all began filing in when Candice was on her way out.

"Hey who the hell are The Smiths?" Jack said as Ricky and Candice smiled awkwardly at each other, passing in the archway.

"I better get the book before I forget." Wyatt said going back through into the hall.

"Look at one of the first pages!" Ricky called out.

Wyatt picked it up and flicked through curiously. Candice once again hovered around beside him, also curious. Before too much of a look he noticed something. In Ricky's handwriting, a small paragraph of peculiar words read:

There's a guy in the south known as Wyatt
Sometimes I think he might be super
Even without his friends and diet
I know he'll pull through 'cause he's a trooper
Smart and sensible is his only way
Can be annoying I have to say
But without this loyal friend
I'd surely go round the bend

"He's amazing." Candice said quietly.

"Yeah. He is." Wyatt replied with watery eyes.

~ **4** ~

It's time for any curiosities and expectations of the party to be laid to rest, hopefully satisfied. Of course Wyatt's nervous but at least it's happening, he's at least going into this with his friends and this wonderful boy now always by his side whenever he needed him. If he had of known about it days beforehand he surely wouldn't go to it. The anxiety would have built towers upon itself and forced him to opt out.

Walking up to Ryan's front door had never been this peculiar. Obnoxious music and many voices emitting from the house, accompanied by the exciting flares of party lights coming from inside. It's enticing and frightening to all inexperienced senses alike.

Ryan had made his way back home from the Fineman's house an hour beforehand.

"Wow, his brother knows how to throw a party doesn't he?" Rose said taking in the first impression of the night that followed.

"Looks like we're gonna have an epic night guys." Jack said in a manner that almost sounded like a warning. The five of them got to the front door and waited patiently after several door knocking attempts.

"Let's just bloody walk in." Ricky said from the back of the group.

"Okay." Jack casually opened the front door like he lived there.

They filed inside trying to leave all insecurities outside the house.

Ricky whispered into Candice's ear. "Would it kill 'em to play some *real* music?"

She smirked playfully at his little interaction with her over the dislike certain modern sounds.

It was immediately notable they seemed to be the youngest there, the rest of the guests are mainly older teens like Ethan. Dancing and gyrating themselves around the lounge room and up the halls, Wyatt thought they were fascinatingly ridiculous, and Candice found herself intimidated by all the seemingly grownup girls. Groups of people here and there talking, and a group of more sophisticated looking teens stood in the kitchen with all the snacks and munchies offered on the bench.

Most of these party goers they'd seen at school, even from Pier Ripple. It suddenly dawned on Jack: What if Harley's here somewhere?

Candice thought the same thing about Rob Brannon. He and his family would be back in town by now and he's definitely the kind to celebrate being back by turning up to an event like this.

"Where the hell is Ryan?" Ricky asked agitated, looking around the sea of moving heads.

"I don't know but there's Ethan." Candice replied pointing at him as he stood in the kitchen laughing with a bunch of dudes.

As they all tried to move forward through the crowd towards the kitchen, a random dancing blonde girl already totally off her face, plunked her arm over Jack's shoulder expecting him to react the same way. He politely took her by the wrist and guided her into the group of people beside him. To his relief she just went with it, laughing and all.

He turned to look at the others who were stifling giggles, even Wyatt.

In the kitchen, Ethan informed them that Ryan's probably upstairs in his bedroom to which Ricky left to retrieve him. Waiting for him to come back, the others tried to stay out of the way as much as possible. Standing in the corner of the kitchen by the pantry, Wyatt's out of place insecurities were making him really want to hold Jack's hand, who stood beside him leaning against the sink with his arms crossed. Such a subtle yet big display of companionship wasn't ready to be shown, it was still feeling weirdly wrong to him when it came to other people.

"My friend Hannah will be here soon." Rose said trying to make conversation.

"I'm kinda excited to meet her." Candice said.

"I'm sure you'll like her. Will Bethany be here?"

"She already is." Candice replied. "She's the one in pink and black with brown hair, surrounded by a bunch of guys."

"Oh, cool." Rose said not knowing how to respond to that.

Ricky's return with Ryan didn't aid any of them in knowing what to do next. Jack knew exactly how to party but was trying to be reserved for Wyatt.

Ryan took one look at their unsure faces and felt as though this was a bad idea after all. "Hey Ethan!" He shouted. "Maybe we should just go upstairs or something, it's a bit weird."

"No bloody way!" Ethan replied giving them his full attention. "I promised a hell of a party for the little guy and that's what he's going to get!"

I'm not a little guy... Wyatt thought angrily.

"HEY EVERYONE!" Ethan shouted so loud it made Rose jump. "It's this guy's birthday!" He shouted pointing at Wyatt, to which everyone clapped and cheered regardless of whether they knew who he was or what was even going on. "This shindig is for fourteen and over, know what I'm saying?!" He now turned to the wary group, telling them to relax and grab a drink from one of the eskies in the dining room before he walked off.

"Is there alcohol around? Because they're all being weird." Wyatt said referring to everyone here.

"There's gotta be. I'm assuming that's what he meant by grab a drink." Rose answered. She looked down at her phone and smiled. "Hannah's here, I'm just gonna go and meet her outside." And with that she left.

"Okay let's do it." Ricky said looking to rowdy crowd. "Let's just join them and have a drink."

"Yeah it's not like anyone's going to catch us." Candice agreed.

"Guess I'm up for it." Jack said.

"Why the hell not?" Ryan shrugged.

The four of them looked at Wyatt who was beginning to feel the same way. "Yeah, we're here so let's just go for it." He said with a shrug.

"I'll go get us some!" Jack said, leaving all too eagerly.

"Is anyone else getting pissed off with this so called music?" Ricky asked trying to sound less irritated than he is.

"It's not my thing either." Wyatt concurred.

They found themselves accompanied by Bethany who walked right up to Candice and hugged her without warning. It's obvious Candice is used to it. "What up C? Had a drink yet?"

"No not yet."

"Robbie is here and he's in a real good mood if you know what I mean. I'm sure he'd *love* to see you!"

"Nah, I'm good here."

"Why? Come on Candice it'd be perfect."

"I'm here with someone."

"Oooh who?"

"Ricky." She took his arm in hers. He smiled, flashing a waving hand at Bethany.

She laughed at the silly joke. "Candice it's not April Fools. I think Robbie is in the lounge."

"I'm serious, he's my boyfriend."

Bethany's face turned unsure and obviously wanting this to be untrue. Jack came up behind her with Rose and Hannah behind him. He had several bottles in his arms. "And who is this?" She asked impressed, turning her attention to him.

"I'm Jack. You are?"

"Well Jack, you can call me Beth, and I'll be just over there if you wanna get to know me." She said with a hand on his upper arm as she walked away.

"Anyway, here's your drinks everybody." He said handing them out. "I got only red and blues, 'cause Superman." He said smiling at Wyatt.

"What is it?" He said silently appreciating the quirkiness of Jack's colour logic.

"These are Vodka Cruisers. Basically, lolly water. So be careful, they're easy to drink."
After getting the lids off they each took a sip, satisfied with the taste.

"Tastes totally different to my dad's beer." Ricky said nodding his head.

"Guys this is Hannah." Rose announced. "Hannah this is Ricky, Candice, Ryan and Wyatt who is Candice's brother, and it's also his birthday today."

"Oh Happy Birthday!" She said enthusiastically to Wyatt.

"Thanks, nice to meet you." He answered politely.

As time progressed, Ricky was opening his fourth drink, the others were halfway through their second and Wyatt was still on his first. While Candice followed Ricky's loose antics around the house, Rose, Ryan and Hannah were talking somewhere in the lounge room, Jack and Wyatt remained in the kitchen now discussing the food.

"Okay who has mini cookies at a party? That's way weird." Jack said, looking at the bowl of cookies.

"Really? I think it's an awesome touch. They look like the ones Ryan has at school sometimes. Ethan probably saw them in the cupboard and used them."

"Guess you're right, as always."

"I might have one."

"Let me guess, plain?"

"No way! When it comes to cookies, choc chip is the only way."

"Ooh I like this rule."

"Besides, we're at a party so rainbow chips are essential." He placed one in his mouth.

Jack thought that if he kissed him right now he'd be able to taste that cookie. Despite thinking it was weird, somehow it made him want to do it even more. "You're quite the little charmer, you know that?"

"I might. But maybe I picked it up from this charming boy I know."

"Wow, vodka does strange things to you." He giggled wholeheartedly.

"So do you." Wyatt said deeply, the cheekiness in his eyes obvious.

Jack grinned, looking around a little nervously. This is by far the most sexually intriguing moment of his life, and he had no idea how to react. Is Wyatt seriously trying to flirt right now? Maybe he's just simply less uptight because of the drink.

"In a good way I'm hoping."

"Have to say I like it better than I like vanilla ice cream." He downed the last of the blue liquid. "I have to use the bathroom, I'll be back."

"I'll be waiting." He finished his own drink and went to get more, not realising that he'd been followed back into the kitchen.

"I do believe in fairies, I do I do!"

He turned to look after jolting with absolute surprise at the sudden exclamation from behind. Even through the loud tunes he knew what's happening. It was indeed Harley and one of his goons. Why he turned up here is something Jack couldn't make sense of.

"Just please leave me alone." He pleaded. The very last thing he wants is to be bullied in front of Wyatt.

"I don't believe in fairies by the way, I think you should all piss off." Harley said while his stupid friend laughed.

"Seriously what's with you? Go away." He looked at his friends, they hadn't noticed them yet.

"Don't talk to me like that ya fag." Harley said pushing Jack's shoulder with a few pudgy fingers. Jack unusually retaliated by pushing back with both hands. Harley hardly budged but became totally furious.

"You wanna die you idiot?" Said the other menace.

"Come on even I'll admit that was a sissy shove." Jack said in a feeble attempt to diffuse.

Harley got up in his face, throwing absurd insults and threats. Jack closed his eyes tight and braced himself for violent impact, even though at close range Harley had to look up at him. Instead, he heard the faint scuffling of Harley being pulled back and Wyatt's steady voice. "Stop and back off."

"Who the fuck is you to tell me what to do?" The bully asked taking a small step back.

Wyatt stepped between them and spoke again, this time in a deeper tone than before. "I said back, the hell off. You illiterate swine."

"Hey, don't worry about it." Jack said placing a hand on Wyatt's shoulder.

"They must be butt buddies!" Stated the tag along bully.

"Fuckin' gross." Harley laughed, showing yellow teeth.

"Leave him alone, or I'll finish what his sister started." Wyatt demanded, crossing his arms.

"Is that so?" Harley said taking a step forward. At this point the others came over which deterred him from coming any closer. He slowly retreated, turning to leave through the crowd followed by his friend. As they left the house Ricky asked who it was.

"That boys and girls, was Hercules." Jack said shaking his head.

"No bloody way!" Ricky said amused. "Oh, bye bye all mighty son of Zeus!" He called out.

"You guys okay?" Ryan asked Jack and Wyatt.

"Yeah we're fine." They answered in unison.

"It's like he really wants Rose to beat him up!" Hannah stated.

"Way to go little brother, you showed him who's boss!" Candice said proudly as she walked away with Ricky. Ryan wandered off with Rose and Hannah to see if Harley had actually left the property or not.

Wyatt returned to his spot at the bench island in the kitchen. Jack didn't move, only stood in significant awe at the simple presence of him in his eyes.

Amazing, he's amazing...
Of all the terrible things that have passed him by in his fifteen year span of life, this is worth it. Really worth it all. He walked over to join him. "These are ours." He passed Wyatt another full bottle. "Thanks for scaring him off back there, that was epic."

"Oh please, he was probably scared of Rose." Wyatt said laughing.

"But still."

"They're so stupid though. What's wrong with being buddies?" He said holding a hand up beside his shaking head.

"Wait, what?"

"When his friend said something."

"You mean 'butt buddies'?"

"Is that what he said?"

"Yeah he was just trying to be mean."

"I'm not offended."

"Really?"

"Yeah, no idea what he's talking about."

Jack leaned in closer as if through the loud music and chiming voices they'd be heard. "So, you have no clue what he's referring to?"

"Not a single clue."

"Maybe I'll explain one day."

"Insults are insults Jack, they're just words that don't matter." He spoke valiantly, before taking a mouthful of drink.

Off in the crowd it was becoming clear Ricky's ignorance towards the modern sound of cool kid music was feigned for the night. He was dancing around with a bunch of other people and Candice was downing more drinks to try and loosen up about the whole thing like he had.

In the muddle of bodies Rob had finally found her. "Hey Candice!" He shouted.

"Oh hi." She answered politely but uninterested.

"I've been looking for you everywhere!" He said putting a hand on her shoulder.

"That's nice." She said trying to pay him no attention.

Ricky popped himself up out of nowhere. "Hey dude, keep your hands off my girl!"

"Go and play chasies with your friends or something, douche bag."

"Um dude, seriously piss off, she's not interested." Ricky persisted in seriousness.

"He harassing you Candice?"

"No he's my fucking BOYFRIEND!" She yelled with sudden feistiness.

"Oh." Robbie said nearly inaudible, instantly walking off in defeat.

"Hear that everyone? I'm her FUCKING BOYFRIEND!" Ricky yelled totally enthralled.

"Yeah, he's my FUCKING BOYFRIEND!" Candice screamed.

Ryan had made his way back to Rose and Hannah who were by the front door. Rose declared she needed the bathroom and left Ryan and Hannah to themselves for a moment.

"Cool party." She stated.

"Yeah it's getting pretty crazy." He answered thinking of how Candice and Ricky are becoming the life and soul of it.

"And it's all for your friend Wyatt?"

"Well sort of. My brother was going to throw a party, then we decided to make it for Wyatt's birthday because he's had a tough year."

"That's nice. How old is he?"

"Fourteen."

"Is he single?"

What the hell, what the hell?... "Umm... Yes..."

"You sound unsure."

"Nah he is I think."

"Awesome, see ya soon." She headed for the kitchen.

"Hannah wait! *Shit*..." He said failing to stop her. Rose returned and asked where she was off to.

"Look I swear I didn't mean to, and I tried to stop her, but I think she's going after Wyatt."

"Oh." She said and took a mouthful of her drink.

"I really didn't mean-"

"Ryan chill out." She said to his surprise. "Hannah has had a thing for Jack since forever. She has the worst gaydar known to man."

"Oh, okay." He said, laughing a little.

Over in the kitchen Wyatt was pouring half his red drink into a cup along with half of Jack's blue. "It just looks like swamp water." He said giggling.

"Hey I like it! We're the only ones here with swamp vodka!" Jack exclaimed.

"Hello guys, whatcha up to?" Hannah asked.

"We're mixing colours, Wyatt's kind of wild." Jack said affectionately.

"Oh nice. Just came to ask Wyatt if he wanted to dance or something?"

"Thank you, but no." He declined.

"You should go for it Tinkle-bell." Jack said giggling.

"Sorry Hannah, I don't dance." Wyatt insisted.

"That's okay. Hope you're having a good time." She hid her rejection blues and left them to it.

"You are so *harsh!*" Jack exclaimed amused.

"I am not! Why?"

"She is into you man!" He said laughing.

"Well too bad for her because I myself, am into..." He mouthed 'you' pointing at Jack.

"Is that so?"

"Very so." He said with a nod.

"Wanna go find somewhere you can tell me a little louder?"

"We could but then we'd be missing this lovely party." He answered sarcastically.

"Watch me care." Just then his phone buzzed in his pocket. He checked it to see a message from Rose. "Oh hell no."

"What's wrong?" Wyatt asked.

"My ex-girlfriend is here." He said looking around at the crowd.

"You had a girlfriend?! When?" Wyatt exclaimed.

"A few months ago. I thought I told you." He said seriously

meaning it.

"Jack!" Said a thin girl with fat, false lashes and long brown braids, walking over with two other girls.

"Chelsea, hi." Jack said trying to be enthusiastic but failing.

"Nice to see you, it's been a while." She said ignoring Wyatt's existence.

"Guess it has. This is Chelsea, my ex-girlfriend and this here is Wyatt." He said feeling totally uncomfortable.

"Hi." She said to Wyatt. "What're you here for?"

"What's that supposed to mean?" He replied annoyed.

"Nothing I guess."

"Jack if you'll excuse me." Wyatt said and began to leave.

"Where are you going?!" He asked concerned.

"To find Hannah. You lot have fun now."

He watched him walk away angry, feeling guttered at the sight. "What was with that? You want me to hate you or something?"

"He seems like the little goody two shoes type of guy who followed his older brother or sister here."

"You know what stuff you Chelsea." He frowned as he leaned his hands on the bench.

"Whoa asshole." She said holding her arms up.

"Just leave me alone."

"Why are you getting so damn defensive about it? Don't tell me you two are gay for each other!"

"Just piss off, nobody wants you here."

"Oh my god, the rumours at school are true. You really are a faggot."

"You mean the rumours YOU started!"

"Maybe you shouldn't have broken up with me then!"

"I broke up with you because you were mean to my sister and kept stealing my weed!"

"And clearly because I'm not a guy."

"You're being a total bitch, you always are."

"You really drew the short straw huh?! A big faggot with an alcoholic whore for a mother! Have a nice life dickhead!" She walked off followed by her two quiet friends with as much sassiness as she knew how to express.

The people around him looked on with curious and amused eyes. Now what was he to do?

Look for Wyatt...

He soon found him in the lounge dancing around with everyone but most notably with Hannah. It was annoying him how close they are.

Could she get any closer?...

He watched on as she put her arms around him. Around *his* guy's neck.

Fuck this...

He went over and cut in between them. To his actual surprise, Wyatt didn't care that he had. Hannah seemed annoyed with it and tried to dance her way back in, but Jack got closer with his arm around him. Wyatt resonated with the situation and put his arm around Jack's waist. Hannah finally understood. She disappeared into the people and left them once more.

"I'm sorry I didn't tell you." Jack tried to say through the noise.

"Jack, I don't care it's okay." Wyatt replied. His cheeks were showing themselves to be a soft scarlet. Was he meaning he doesn't care about Chelsea or was it more than that?

"How much did you drink just now?"

"I may have drank one real fast while you were gone."

"Bein' a rebel again are we?"

"Well you know, it's apparently hot and sexy." His entire demeanour right now is so funny to witness.

Ricky's voice suddenly demanded everyone's attention. After the music was turned down he yelled again, arms outstretched to the roof. "We need KAREOKE!!"

"We don't have karaoke, but we got sing star!" Ethan shouted enthusiastically.

"Hell yeah let's do this!!" Ricky said excitedly.
Without too much of a wait they had set up the game and were ready to play. Mostly all the people were gathered in the lounge room around the television ready to watch and get involved. A drunken Ricky and a tipsy Ethan began a not too shabby but totally dodgy duo version of 'Don't Go Breakin' My Heart'. This activity went on for what felt like hours.

"I think it's time for a game of spin the bottle!" An unfamiliar voice yelled after a string of singing. All the players made their way into the lounge and formed a large circle in front of the couch. Ricky and Candice lingered around as part of the audience while many others continued to dance to the resumed music of Ricky's choice.

Wyatt remained quietly over in the kitchen, with Jack encouraging him to eat more to soak up a bit of the alcohol in his system. They didn't go unnoticed by Chelsea who insisted they join in considering they're not in relationships.

"They don't have to play if they don't want to." Hannah said, showing them her support.

"No, no it's okay. We'll play your stupid game." Wyatt said as if to challenge Chelsea.
Jack followed him to the lounge and joined the circle assuming Wyatt had no idea what the game even was.

"Okay so no relatives, and if you land on the same person more than once, you go to the laundry for some alone time in heaven." Ethan informed. "If it's two guys or two girls just do the cheeks or something cause, ew."

Ethan spun first and landed on some girl. She then spun and had to kiss Rose on the cheek, who spun the bottle and kissed Hannah's cheek who after her turn kissed Ryan. His turn saw him having to kiss Chelsea. She spun and landed on some guy who landed on another random girl who landed on Ryan to which he spun again and got Rose. Now inevitable, she'd have to kiss him or risk looking like a loser in front of all these people.

Rose wasn't actually thinking along those lines at all. If she really didn't want to, she wouldn't. She didn't care for other people's foolish opinions on foolish matters. She got up from her cross legged position on the carpet and leaned over towards Ryan, who seemed all too ready. With onlooking faces, their lips connected for a quick peck. Oddly enough they did it again before returning to their seating positions. She wiped her mouth and spun the bottle, its open tip coming to a stop in Wyatt's direction. "Not this time." She said to Wyatt's satisfaction.

"That's against the rules!" Chelsea bossed.

"Well, no because he's like my brother and relatives are out." Rose said smartly. Ethan backed her up to make Chelsea shut up.

"Your turn birthday boy!" Ethan encouraged.

Jack had stayed totally quiet since sitting down. He hated this, hated all of it. What if some slutty girl defiled Wyatt's mouth? Only Jack had ever been there, and he wanted it to stay that way.

Wyatt reached for the bottle, even with slurred thoughts he thought of how stupidly juvenile this whole game is. With a steady, perfectly pre planned flick of the wrist the bottle spun strongly and came to an abrupt stop pointing at Jack beside him.

Jack's relief had his lungs exhaling the air they'd been holding. Wyatt kissed him on the cheek.

Chelsea pretended to cough, coarsely saying 'faggots'.

"Shut the hell up Chelsea." Rose said gruffly.

"Yeah, you have a thing against guys kissing or something?"

Hannah challenged.

"No but you must be sad to see Jack getting it on with a guy. Everyone knows you wanted him while he was mine." Chelsea scolded.

"Leave her alone!" Jack said in her defence.

"Oh so you've got her on the go too then? Man, I'm glad I'm out of that toxic shit."

"If all you want to do is bully everyone why the hell are you here?!" Rose yelled.

"Don't even talk to me you frigid idiot."

"Chelsea get the hell out of the house." Rose said in a lowered tone.

"Hell no hoe, I'm staying!"

Ricky cheered as Candice left his side to attack Chelsea, now literally being chased out of the house by the girls and a few other people.

In all the commotion, Wyatt saw the bottle still sitting there, deciding to spin it again. "Would you look at that, it's landed on you again."

"So it has." Jack laughed.

"Better follow the rules and go to heaven." He clumsily got to his feet and headed for the laundry. Jack quickly followed his lead because he has no idea what the layout of the house is. Walking towards the back of the house, away from the people and away from the noise felt relieving. The open back door let fresh air hit their lungs, making them feel like they've been in a musty cave for days on end.

They wandered on into the laundry, closing the door behind them. "Where the heck's the light switch?" Jack said feeling around for it. The smell of washing powder in here is dominant over any smell of dampness laundries have, well, the ones he's used to.

"Let's not, the dark is okay." Wyatt said. It's strange to hear him say it considering all the times he'd been frightened of the very thing he just said is 'okay'.

"But you hate the dark."

"Not if you're in it Jack. It's not that dark anyway." He answered. The smell of alcohol warm on his breath. It's true. Because the back lights were on, a glare shone through the door gaps and lit it up enough to make out simple features of the face and the various laundry items. Especially once your eyes adjusted.

"You didn't have to stand up to Harley for me earlier but, thank you so much."

"Anything for you." He replied with a kind smile.

"You seemed so brave, like a macho super hero or something."

"Oh stop it." Wyatt said doing his modest blush.

"Nah I'm serious." He moved in closer to whisper. "*I wanna take care of you now.*"

Wyatt leaned against the wall, showing his pampered teeth in an unsure smile as Jack took his hand to hold it to his chest. "You do know what I mean, right?" He asked thinking the guy may not have caught his obvious drift. He moved in ever closer, placing Wyatt's hand on his hip. "Can I *please* kiss you?"

Wyatt looked up into those gorgeous eyes, once more finding it hard to resist him in the dark. "Maybe a little."

"Thank you, sir." He proceeded to kiss his mouth.

Wyatt tried to put an end to it by pulling away. "Whoa, maybe not now."

"Cause people might see us? They won't in here. I really don't care what they think anyway, let 'em stare."

"Ryan's washing will never be the same!"

Acting as though he didn't hear him Jack tried again, this time

Wyatt kissed back a little before trying to resist. "We should stop it Jack."

"*Oh stop it Jack.*" He said imitating him in a high pitched manner as he kissed the side of his face and down his neck. Wyatt repeated himself except this time he laughed as he told him off.

Jack's hands slowly and steadily found their way around to Wyatt's backside, making the normally uptight part of him gasp in an unexpected, satisfied surprise. He began to feel the shape of Jack's shoulders, his fingertips glided over the fabric happily and eagerly. Jack's hands feeling their way around his backside is something so exhilarating that he wanted more. He couldn't place what he was wanting from him but felt the desire to have every ounce of Jack's being on his own. Before he could comprehend the absence of one of Jack's hands, the skin of his stomach felt it trying to slide down his pants.

"Hang on, what are you doing?" He asked quickly panicked.

"Well you stood up for me so much tonight, I wanna to do this for you."

"Is that what boyfriends do then?"

He laughed at the purely amazing fact of that question coming from his brain and out his mouth. "Yes Wyatt, that's what *boyfriends* do."

"Okay then." He let him kiss him again.

Tonight, he tasted not of the sweetened bliss of sugar, but instead of the reckless bitterness of adult's drink. Jack's hands were back on his body and he loved it, more than he could have ever loved any ice-cream.

Finally, one hand squeezed back down into the forbidden area, now open only to one person, free to own it and do as he will. Nestled in between expensive threads, his hand found what it's after. Feeling the gentle rub, Wyatt felt drunk on vodka and high on Jack. This is his heaven, he's surrounded by those magic wings... and of course the Jonson's dirty laundry.

"You're an angel." He whispered before he realised he was going to speak.

"What?" Jack asked, frozen in surprise.

"I think you're an angel, I've thought it since I met you."

"I liked you before I ever saw your face." He replied before proceeding to pull the trousers down just enough to be able to do what he wanted.

It's actually happening, he's really going to go there... He's really going to do it...

Now with bare skin and nothing to stop him, Jack reached for him with the same firm gentleness that he always silently sought after. Not even Wyatt touched himself like this. But this isn't awkward, and it doesn't feel wrong.

It's Jack's now, and as he let him own it he held the wild silk of angelic hair in his hands. The soft feel on his palms, through his fingers, intensified everything beyond this plane of life. Wyatt was completely in Jack's hands both literally and mentally, whether anyone liked it or not.

~ 5 ~

Back in the kitchen, Ricky had been trying to convince everyone that he wasn't drunk, only making himself look even more so.

"Yeah dude, I'm drunk and even I know you're drunk!" Candice exclaimed.

"I want cheese! You want cheese Candie?" Ricky suddenly asked with enthusiasm.

"Yes I'd love some cheese dear... Richard!" She answered sounding like a posh woman with a mild speech impediment. They headed over to the fridge and literally began to raid it for cheese.

"Maybe we should just go." Rose suggested to Ryan.

"Back to Wyatt's house?! You'll be killed."

"I don't know what the hell to do then." She said worried.

"Look, I said you can all crash here and I meant it."

Rose looked at her phone, telling her it's forty past one in the morning. "Okay, we have to cut them off. No more drinking."

"Should I get Ethan to send everyone home?"

She looked around at the remainders of party guests, a lot were still here. "Yeah I think it's been a satisfactory enough night for them."

Ryan disappeared to find Ethan and put an end to the night. Rose watched on as Ricky and Candice ate several slices of cheese, sometimes failing to remove the wrappers completely, making a right foul mess on the floor. They wrapped slices around random other foods they'd discovered in the fridge. Ricky sang along to the tail end of the current song with a mouthful of cheesy cocktail onions.

Rose couldn't help but at least giggle at their drunken stupidity. She pulled her phone out, held it up to face the fridge and began to record.

"Uh oh Candice..." Ricky yelled, taking his glasses off. "Put these on will ya!"

"Hang on ya..." She took them off him and put them on. "I got 'em, they're on there!"

"Ooh you look just..." He didn't finish his sentence, only grabbed her nose as if she's a five year old.

Rose had gotten a few minutes worth of the cheese raid when she stopped recording. Jack had walked in with Wyatt following. "Where have you been? I've been stuck with this!" She held her arms out gesturing to the cheese lovers.

"We were just... Around." Jack said trying his hardest not to seem sheepish. "What the hell are they doin?"

"Ricky decided he wanted some cheese." Rose explained with fists on her hips.

"Oh my goodness, I am *so hungry*." Wyatt exclaimed, walking over to the bench for the graveyard of near empty bowls, scattered chip crumbs and other leftover foods.

"Hey Ricky!" Jack said. "What was the song on before this one?"

"I really don't think he's-" Rose began to say before being interrupted.

"All you need to know is Tears For Fears my man!"

"Is he messin' with me?"

"I really couldn't tell you. The guy's got cheese all over his face." Rose said shaking her head. "How's Wyatt? He drink much?"

"He'll be right."

The music was suddenly silenced, Ethan's weary voice filled the house telling everyone to piss off or he'll call the cops.

"But I'm really hungry."

Everyone turned their attention to Wyatt. He stood by the bench with his hand in the cookie bowl.

"Not you dude it's your birthday." Ethan assured him.

"Cool, cool beans." He said giving Ethan the thumbs up.

"Wow." Rose laughed. "He is so not himself."

"What's that supposed to mean?" Jack asked getting tense.

"I mean he's been drinking. You okay?"

"Yeah, totally fine."

She knew now. Something had happened.

Slowly but surely all the guests left the property out into the night. A few of Ethan's friends hung around to crash in his room when they went upstairs, leaving the others in the kitchen.

"I'm not feeling well." Candice confided, sitting on the

kitchen floor.

From this point on, Rose, Jack, Hannah and Ryan nursed the other three to bed. It took Wyatt a little longer to show how affected he was but when Candice started the vomiting, he couldn't help it himself and soon joined her at the toilet. Thankfully they'd made it to the upstairs bathroom before any of it. Rose was holding Candice's hair back for her while she expelled all the food she'd taken in at the fridge earlier.

Amazingly, Ricky was the ideal drunk and went soundly to sleep in Ryan's bed without a single upchuck. Rose set Candice up also in Ryan's bed but made it so she could reach for a bucket if she should need it at all through the rest of the night.

Upon Wyatt's weary request, Jack led him to Ryan's room. They stopped in the middle of the room before it seemed Wyatt couldn't walk anymore, slowly making his way down to lay on the mat.

"Just going to crash here then?" Jack laughed.

"Hope it's okay." He answered faintly. "Can I?"

It amazed Jack that even in this state he's ridiculously polite. *"Yeah totally. I'll go grab a blanket."* He whispered before leaving the room to ask Ryan where the spare linen is. Upon his return he found him in the same position as before. "Here you go." He said gently as he placed the blanket over him.

"Jack?" He mumbled from the floor.

"Yeah?"

"Don't leave again."

Jack immediately knelt down beside him. "Sure, I won't." He said with a quiet grin.

Wyatt lifted the blanket with great effort while his eyes stayed closed and his head almost motionless. Jack placed himself beneath it, now laying alongside him.

"I think I spilt... Blackcurrant juice here when I was eleven."

Wyatt said unexpectedly.

"Really?"

"Got Ryan in trouble... I should really... apologise for that again."

Jack stared back at the exhausted face of him, amazed. "I really don't think it matters anymore."

They were quiet for a few minutes and Jack was falling asleep. He would have if Wyatt didn't suddenly speak again. "Jack?"

"Yeah?" He answered sleepily.

"I can feel them again."

Here we go... The nonsense talk... "Feel what?"

"Your wings. They're... *so* soft." he replied with a deep breath following his words.

Jack didn't know how to react. What a thing for someone to say to him. "Get some sleep, Wyatt." He said softly, getting closer to put an arm around him. Curled up under this blanket on a foreign floor after Wyatt had just puked his guts out wasn't the most brilliant or romantic situations, but to Jack it's ideal. He buried his face against Wyatt's neck and chest to let himself be taken by sleep.

Rose tiptoed in to close the door and leave it slightly ajar, not without first taking a moment to admire her brother's sleeping bliss. She went back downstairs where Ryan and Hannah were in the kitchen. Ryan had just crouched down and began to clean the mess in front of the fridge. He had clumps of paper towel, using it to gather the food and waste into a pile with a plastic bag beside him, Rose thought he resembled that of a cat in its litter tray covering its shit with sand.

"Need some help in here?" She asked.

"Nah I'm just going to clean this and go to bed, I'm stuffed." He didn't even look up as he said it.

"They're all crashed in your bedroom. Jack's asleep now too."

"That's okay, we have a spare bedroom."

"Can I stay too?" Hannah said standing by the bench, stacking bowls.

Ryan stopped what he was doing.

"It's just that my house isn't close and it's really late, it's okay if you say no." She said feeling like a hindrance.

"No no, it's fine. Of course, you can." He said resuming the clean-up.

"Awesome. Thanks."

"Is there more than one bed or?" Rose asked cautiously.

"Ahm, nope. Just the one." He said briefly looking up at her. Hannah and Rose shared a look of mutual misunderstanding of the sleeping arrangements.

"Well maybe you two could take the bed and I'll take the couch?" Hannah said looking at Rose with a cheeky smile, which received a humoured frown in return.

"Maybe *you two* could take the bed and *I* take the couch." Rose said with whimsy.

Ryan stayed quiet on the floor as they bantered.

"Nah my suggestion is a much better idea." Hannah said nodding her head with arms crossed.

"Maybe you two should take the couch and I get the bed, sounds better to me." Rose said now crossing her arms.

"I don't mind the couch. Besides, wouldn't be the first time you guys shared the bed for a night."

"Hannah!" Rose said embarrassed.

Suddenly Ryan stood up tying the plastic bag, speaking over its rustling. "You two take the room and I'll sleep on the couch. Sorted."

They stood quietly for a moment before he walked over to the cupboard to get a garbage bag. While he shook the bag to get air flow through it, Rose shook her head at Hannah to signify her disapproval of her antics and mentioning the fact she'd told her about sharing the bed with him. Hannah shrugged with a quirky smile of comedic pride.

Ryan plonked the smaller bag inside the garbage bag and sat it to the corner of the kitchen to worry about it tomorrow.

"Maybe you could use your parent's room?" Rose suggested.

"Nah no way, I'd prefer the couch." He said with a small laugh.

She smiled back. "Well I just gotta go to the loo and then you can show us where the room is?"

"Yeah sure."

She left the room but apparently left the theoretical elephant behind.

"What's with you two?" Hannah boldly asked him.

He looked at her as if she'd said something totally heinous. "Nothing. What makes you say that?"

"Well you like her don't you?"

"Did she get you to ask that?"

"No. What makes you say that?"

"Oh I don't know, nothing. I'd prefer not to talk about it."

"So there's a something to be spoken about then, huh?'

"I can see why you two are friends now." He said nervously.

She laughed. "What do you mean?"

"I just mean, she talks almost in riddles sometimes. Like good with words and stuff. I mean, when you were talking smartly, I thought of saying that. Ugh, it made sense when I said it."

"Dude! Chill out would ya?"

"Sorry." He said shaking his head. "Been a long night."

"You so like her."

He looked at her, then nervously checked the surroundings to make sure nobody was there.

"Don't worry, I won't tell her."

He nodded with some kind of relief.

"But she's not stupid-"

"Oh I know."

"As in she's going to figure it out if she hasn't already."

"Doesn't matter. She doesn't like me. Sometimes I think not at all."

"Maybe. But out of everyone you kissed in the game, she went back for a quick second."

When her statement found its way to his ears it dawned on him, opening the door of realisation. How could he not of thought of that already? He smiled at Hannah who nodded her head with cement approval of his thoughts.

"Alrighty, where's this room?" Rose said entering the room causing him to jump skittishly.

After showing them where the room is and making sure they'd be comfortable like a good host, he decided not to go upstairs to his bedroom for clothes in case he woke one of the sleeping drunks. He made his way to the laundry to see if luck would work in his favour and have some clean pyjamas in there, anything. He turned the light on and looked around, even checking inside the washer and dryer only to find his hopes were tainted with rejection from the universe.

"Christ's sake."

Flicking the light off and walking away, he realised how suspiciously tidy it was in there.

He eventually snuggled under the blanket he chose to use for his time on the couch, still in the same clothes. He disliked that he'd worn them all night but there's no way he's getting up again. It took him a few times of rolling around uncomfortably before he finally lay still on his back, looking up at the darkened ceiling.

God so stupid, how did I not notice?...

He closed his eyes and tried to remember every detail of what happened during that stupid game of spin the bottle. But it wasn't stupid because he got to kiss her...

If only he could get it to happen without the dynamics of a group involved game.

Why did she kiss me twice if she doesn't like me? What the hell Rose?...

He began thinking of how her name suits her so well. The rosy colour of her lips and cheeks, especially when she smiles. Just like a rose flower, she has a natural beauty of laced layers.

Handle it wrong, and you'll be cut by the thorns...

Wondering if she was thinking of him in the other room, sleep finally enveloped his mind and let him rest after the several hectic hours they had all just endured.

~ 6 ~

As most of them lay sleeping, dipping into the obscured dreams of the night. There was a content feeling in having just been able to let loose and act as they should. Like teenagers.

Rose though, she lay beside Hannah in the spare room double bed. Her weary head had hit that pillow like it was the most perfect pairing since cake with icing.

She closed her eyes and saw the things she'd witnessed during the night. It was good, to have seen it all. She even finally got to have a go at Chelsea, the good for nothing slut. It was pretty funny seeing Candice chase her too. Seeing her and Ricky having their little scream-athon over their relationship status left her with a tiny sting she'd rather ignore, like she had been for weeks.

She rolled onto her side, careful not to wake Hannah, so she could look at the window across the room. A gap to the world outside presented itself through the middle of the curtains. What she wouldn't give to take a deep breath of that fresh air out there.

A fair amount of light, maybe the moon's full.

That explains the amount of lunatics...

She thought of the blue in the dark sky, the way it threw the stars at you in a shower of existential beauty. If she was anything other than herself, she'd want to be a star.

They offered her an image, of the shine reflecting off Ryan's mysterious wells of blue.

Groaning in frustration at herself, she promptly covered her head with the covers. Darkness again, the perfect thing to smother any pain in the arse thought your brain decides it wants you to think about.

Just go to sleep, God damn it... Anything...

Finding something else to focus on isn't easy. All her thoughts showed her everything she's confused and insecure about; from the boys, to her independent brother, their unsettled guardianship, to the weirdness of Violet.

For now, unbeknownst to them, Violet awaits them as she always does. The answers they want, sitting comfortably in the pocket of her own sketchy mind.

The only peace Rose could find is the thought of the old tree back in her old yard. *Her tree.* Sitting there proud behind the house. She made herself envision the memory of those pretty little leaves twinkling with the sunshine in the wind, showing her their freedom. And with that, a freedom for her mind to wind down and explore things beyond her humanly consciousness.

She now lay heavy in the foreign bed as she slept along with her friends and only family, waiting for what's next. For what awaits them in the days ahead, the words they'll expose each other to, the emotions they'll experience, the things they hope to see, and what they hope not to see; in the stories of their lives yet to come.

SNEAK PEEK

Book Two of

The Beautiful Is Free
series by
Ashlea Raywood

The Circle's Point

WHAT'S THE STORY, MORNING GLORY?

~1~

Another Sunday morning in Gerryville, but this one is far from typically ordinary.

Candice awoke to a sorely head and an empty stomach. Though not unpleasant, the scent of the entangling sheets proved totally unfamiliar, the surroundings even more so.

Oh right, Ryan's house... This must be his bedroom...

Ricky had gotten up twenty minutes beforehand and tiptoed out to go downstairs, shower and find the others.

Sitting up with steady caution, she held her head with a sorry hand, noticing Wyatt curled up under a blanket on the floor, with Jack half beneath it sprawled across the rug.

"*Oh wow, Wy.*" She whispered in a giggle, searching around for her phone, finding it still in the pocket of her skirt. She took a snap of the sleeping duo and made a slow move to leave the room.

Downstairs she found Ryan and Ricky sitting on the couch together, not doing anything, simply sitting and looking totally exhausted.

"Uh, guys?" She said to get their attention. They both looked at her.

"Morning, puking beauty." Ricky said barely moving a muscle as he said it.

"Oh very funny. I think there's actually vomit... In my poor hair. I need to shower like right now." She sounded as though she's about to cry.

"Just go for it." Ryan said nicely.

Nodding her head she turned to leave before stopping. "Towels?"

"Oh, somebody actually washed some. I dried them this morning. Should still be in the machine just in the laundry towards the back there."

"Okay awesome. Thanks. Hopefully they're still warm!" She left for her deeply needed shower.

The boys sat in silence for a moment before Ricky spoke up. "Who cleans towels... At an all-night party?"

Ryan laughed. "I dunno, maybe Wyatt made the mistake of walking in there and saw how messy it was."
They laughed together, letting the sound trail out into more silence.

"Ricky..." Ryan said suspiciously.

"Yeah man?"

"Jack and Wyatt... They went missing for a while last night, and the clean towels. You don't think?" He said tilting his head as his words trailed away.

"What? They snuck off and did your laundry instead of socialising with everybody else?"

"No... Yeah never mind." Ryan said brushing off the suspicion.

It took a moment for the penny to drop. "Oh, piss off, no way! Dude you're off tap!" Ricky replied in amused hysterics.

"Yeah, as if!" He said now laughing.

"Shit, nobody tell Candice!" Ricky laughed, still joking at the absurdness.

Upstairs, Jack came out from the sleepy haze of first morning awareness. Breathing deep, he sat up only to lay back down closer to Wyatt and face him. "Oi, Tinkle-bell." He whispered to his uncomprehending face. He blew steady air onto his features, Wyatt's eyes began to flicker around beneath his closed lids before lifting slowly to the light.

The sun shone beautifully through the window, making the room's atmosphere a warm yellow against Ryan's olive walls. A positive blanket over already joyous feelings.

"What's the story, morning glory?" Jack asked grinning.

Wyatt looked at him barely moving his head. "What the *heck* are you talking about?"

"Never heard of Oasis?"

"The jungle or the band?" He replied closing his eyes again.

"The band silly." Jack answered shaking his head with an eye roll.

"Yeah, Ricky likes them."

"Of course he does. How you feelin'?"

"Like death. That's if death has feelings."

"Whoa, you're deep when you're hung-over."

Wyatt slowly slid a hand down his face and opened his eyes again. "That's one word for it I guess."

"You still look *super* handsome though." Jack stated with a sliver of shyness.

"Stop it, you're making me feel self-conscious!" He covered his head with the blanket.

"Nah don't worry. There's only a little drool on Ryan's mat." He said as casually as he could manage.

"What?" Wyatt said checking the carpet.

"Matches the blackcurrant juice."

"I told you about that? Why?"

"Hey don't look at me." He said holding his hands up. "I'm just an angel, not a mind reader."

Wyatt felt totally embarrassed, it showed on his face. "Sorry about that... So stupid." He said as he sat up slowly.

"Why are you sorry? That's the best thing I've ever, ever, *ever* been told." He said with his hands fisted against his chest.

"Seriously?"

"Hell yeah! Just call me *Jackariah... The angel.*" He said with outstretched arms.

"Jackariah and Tinkle-bell... We're so weird." He laughed at the ridiculousness.

"The best weird ever." Jack said watching him stretch. "Hey, I don't wanna get even weirder but... Are we all good and everything?"

"What do you mean?" He asked rubbing his poorly forehead.

"You know, after what happened last night."

"As long as nobody tells my parents we should be fine."

"Why the hell would we say anything to them?" Jack asked with an uncomfortable expression.

"Thing is, Candice drank too so she'll take the blame if they do find out. My mum's stupid like that I suppose." He shrugged weak one as he explained.

"Ohhh... I see." Jack said with indifference and confusion.

Does he seriously not fuckin' remember?...

"Phew, I really need to shower." Wyatt said rubbing his forehead again, looking down at himself.

"Hang on, I'll get you some water first." Jack got up to leave the room before Wyatt could answer properly. He paused halfway down the stairs for a moment, running his hand through his messy hair.

What the fuck?... What the actual?... Shit motherfuckin' shitter... He continued on down to the kitchen and looked around for a glass to fill it with water from the purifier. The steady stream proved to take a considerable amount of time to pour out the spout.

Bloody rich mofos and their fancy water...

"Oh hey Jack." Ryan greeted as he walked in.

"Hey Ryan. Crazy night huh?"

"Tell me about it." He answered with wide eyes of relief that it's in the past.

Ricky came in with his overbearing presence. "Oh, good morning old Jacky old pal."

"Mornin' Ricky." He replied with a quiet chuckle.

"So, you stay up long last night?" He Ricky asked, followed by the immediate giggles of Ryan.

Jack looked back at them, failing to understand what was so funny. "Yeah, I guess. You went to sleep before me, so..."

"How's b'day boy?"

"He's good. Could be worse." He answered, looking down at the water.

"Hmm. Sure, he's probably shitting himself about his mum right now."

"Nah he's actually pretty cool with it." Finally, a decent amount of water in the glass. He went to leave the room.

"If anyone's going to have a shower, there's fresh towels in the dryer." Ryan said informatively.

"Oh cool they're dry, thanks." Jack said and left up the hall.

The boys stood in silence before looking at each other with unbelieving expressions, Ricky shook his head for a no of denial.

"Nah." Ryan whispered.

"You guys got milo?" Ricky said changing the subject.

~2~

Wyatt lay on the carpet again while he waited for Jack to return. Closing his eyes, he tried to remember all the details of what happened in the laundry last night.

'I liked you before I ever saw your face...' He thought with a soft sigh.

He'd never connected with another person this way before, Jack had him feeling like the luckiest guy in the world. The luckiest *and* the happiest.

He felt strange for not feeling bad about it all. Surely it shouldn't have happened?

But it had, and he'd like it to happen again. He wanted it to happen as soon as he saw Jack this morning.

He found himself wondering what would happen if he were to try and do the same thing for Jack. Would he let him? Maybe even resist a little and then let him do it, only to return the favour once more...

He sat up startled as Jack came walking through the bedroom's threshold with the water. "Here you go, drink it up." He stood in front of him holding the glass out.

Wyatt smiled, taking the glass from his sacred hand, unable to think of anything other than observing Jack's 'you know what' is right there.

Right. There.

Maybe more forbidden sexual initiative should be called upon, more blissful feelings of physical togetherness...

"You okay? You're super quiet." Jack said noticing something was off.

"Yeah, never better!" He took a sip, trying not to look at him. "I'm going to go have this shower, I'm feeling pretty unwell." He now got to his feet.

"You sure we're all good?" Jack asked quickly before Wyatt left the room.

He looked back and smiled before leaving the doorway.

He so remembers...

"*Balls on a grater, shit!*" Jack grunted to the empty room. How was he supposed to fix this? He can't take back what happened. Doesn't want to anyway, he loved every second of their moment together. Why didn't Wyatt? He seemed fine with it when it was happening. Maybe he regrets all this.

But it was going so well...

He sat down on Ryan's bed with his face in his hands, trying to hold back the urge to cry as it cut at his resistance for it to happen. With watery eyes, he looked up to see the sky through the window. It's looking so simple and blue, he felt as though it mocked his very life. Such a mockery, always some sort of cruel joke played on his feelings.

Downstairs, Wyatt was greeted with the friendly faces of friends looking just as tired as he feels. Rose came up to him and placed a hand on his shoulder. Hannah had already been picked up by her father much earlier. "How you feeling birthday boy?"

"I feel a little weird, but it's not as bad as what I thought it would be." He answered truthfully.

"You're lucky. Candice is still spinning."

"Spinning?"

"*Yeah I feel like I was in a merry-go-round all night!*" Candice shouted from elsewhere.

"Maybe I *am* lucky." He said jokingly.

She enquired about where Jack was, he told her accordingly before walking into the dining room to see the others now sitting at the table. They had a pile of toast on a large plate in the middle of the table. Candice was eating a bowl of cereal with her hair up in a towel. Wyatt always thought she looked hilarious like that, ever since they were little.

The towel... Thank Mary and Jesus it's not the blue one...

"Is the downstairs shower free?" He asked the group.

"Oh well good morning to you too!" Ricky said faking offence.

"Morning all." Wyatt said with a courteous wave to the table.

"Yeah it's free. Towels are in the dryer." Ryan said, pausing his toast munching.

"Yeah I figured, thanks." He casually went on his merry way.

Ryan and Ricky shared another look between each other.

"Well while you sissies are sharing inside jokes, I'm going to go get my phone to see the Facebook damage from last night." Candice said leaving the table to do just that.

Once upstairs, Ethan passed her with a weary smile, his dirty blonde hair spiked about with dampness. "Drink much last night?"

"Too much I think!" She said with a feigned laugh.

"The best way if you ask me." He went down the stairs.

Before she could make her way to Ryan's room, she found herself looking at the cautious face of none other than her self proclaimed bestie; Bethany. She had her small handbag over one shoulder and a jacket draped over the other forearm.

"Beth? What the hell are you doing here?" She asked in high pitched surprise.

"I stayed the night in Ethan's room. You know, he's not a bad guy!"

"I know but... You spent the night with him?"

"His mates were in there. I mean I'm open minded Candice, but I'm not *that* open minded."

"Oh. So, you guys just slept. Awesome." She replied impressed.

"Yeah, for now." She said with sly intention. "What about you? You get lucky last night?"

"Oh God no, I was sick. Wasn't pretty in the slightest."

"Oh my God that was you?" Bethany laughed.

"Yeah, a real catch."

"As always. Anyway, I gotta get home and change. See you soon okay."

"Okay."

"In the meantime, you have to tell me all about your *boyfriend*. How, when? And isn't he your brother's age?"

"I'll tell you all about it at some point." This made Candice feel completely glad for Bethany's perseverance, she'd hate to lose the friend she's always had in her over being with Ricky. "We should hang out just the two of us real soon."

"I agree." She said batting her lashes as she does.

They hugged goodbye, and Bethany began walking away.

"He's only a year younger than us by the way!" Candice called after her.

Finally she had made her way to Ryan's room to find Jack sitting cross legged by the bed, his head low, she could hear sniffling. "Jack? You alright sweetie?"

He looked at her totally startled, wiping his eyes. "Uh, yeah I'm fine. How are ya?"

"Nuh-uh. Tell me what's eating you right now or I'll forever bug you about it."

"Nothing it's... It's just some guy stuff." He waved his hand forward.

"Guys have stuff? Who knew?" She walked across the room to sit beside him.

"Everyone thinks girls are the complicated ones, but us dudes are pretty messed up." He said looking to the floor.

"You upset by your ex last night? It's a little foggy but I remember she's a bitch."

"No it's not her. But she is a frickin' bitch."

"Yeah I didn't realise you were into girls, come to think of it."

"I *really* don't wanna talk about her."

"Sorry. Totally get it." She wondered what she should say next, not knowing how to cheer him up, only that she wants to. Aside from that, her natural curiosities of gossip pulled at her inhibitions. "Did something happen? Was it Wyatt? 'Cause he can be grouchy in the mornings if he's hardly slept."

"No. I mean yeah. Nah, maybe me. I dunno, don't worry."

"Dude, now you have to tell me. What did the little shit do?" She crossed her arms in preparation to hear some queen dramatics.

"I can't talk about it. Especially with you."

"What could be so bad that you can't tell me? I mean, we were all drunk last night doing God knows what all nigh-" She let the words trail out before looking at Jack, who was now looking at her concerned due to the sudden silence. "Did... Did something *happen* between you two?"

"Nope." He said looking away fast.

Candice isn't the most experienced person in all things relationships and human behaviour, but she knew the panicking lie of a male when she saw one. "Jack, if you tell me what happened maybe I can help you out." She said trying to sound as comforting and wise as she could.

He looked at her with an expression that clearly showed he's deciding whether to say it or not. "Okay... Something happened last night."

"Holy *DOODLES*! What kind of something?" She said turning her body to face him.

"Candice, calm." He held his hands up to her. "Wasn't much. Well, it was but wasn't."

"I don't follow." Her wide eyes stared, intent on hearing more.

"Okay." He leaned forward to look across the room out to the hall. Satisfied there's anyone around to hear, he leaned in closer to her. "Just a little whackin' off, is all."

Sitting back a little, she found it hard to fathom he's just admitted that. "You mean?" She gestured herself to be a male masturbating like the world's most disturbing game of charades. He nodded his head in confirmation.

"Holy crap. Where?"

"In the laundry downstairs."

"Ew, you're weird!" She said laughing. This made him smile,

making her feel a little less awkward and more like she's doing her job as a caring friend. "So what's the bad part?"

"I think he regrets doing it." He looked to the floor.

"What makes you think that?"

"Just a feeling."

"Well it's only just the next morning and he had a big night. I'm not making excuses or anything, but just give him the benefit of the doubt. He's never been one for talking about that kind of stuff at all. Our mum is super, and I mean flipping majorly weird about it."

"I guess I'll try not to worry then. You can't tell anybody about this, even him."

"I won't, promise. I just can't believe he let you go there."

"It was the best. Like I've done shit with Chelsea but with Wyatt I'm like... I dunno." His smile prevalent as he confided, the cuteness had her join in the happy display.

"So you'd never done anything with a guy before?"

"No. He's the first boy I kissed."

"Aw." She had to keep the happy squeals in.

"And last night, was different. It was kinda like... We were the same person or something." His eyes showed how deeply he's reaching into himself as they looked to her in explanation. For the most part, Jack seems so unhinged from the everyday, she's so used to seeing him be the light-hearted hero with no more than a surface level, so this deep and meaningful felt wildly wonderful to be witnessing.

"That's so nice." She answered in honesty.

"Sorry, you're probably thinkin' I'm nuts."

"No, I think it's awesome. Seriously."

"I think that's why it hits me so bad when I think he regrets it."

"You guys are so brave. I still haven't done anything like

that."

"What?! Seriously? You two are like this!" He slammed his palms together.

She laughed at his surprise. "Ricky is still weird about it. Crazy about me, but weird about getting too close. Hopefully now we're talking again things will change. It's really nuts actually, before we got together I really didn't give a flying crap about those things."

"Oooh he brings out your wild side!" Jack said mockingly.

"Shut ya face ya bloody queer!"

That made Jack laugh wholeheartedly, causing it to rub off on her. "Nobody offend the straight girl, wow!"

"I'm so lame though!" She said ceasing the laughter. "If the time came I wouldn't even know how to do what you did."

"Guess it was easy for me, I know what it's like being a guy so... yeah." He said with a little shrug.

"Can you maybe teach me?"

"Whoa, did it just get freaky in here?"

"Yeah you're right. God I'm such a loser." She said hiding her face in her arms resting on her knees.

"No you're not. Don't be so down about it. You think all the people of the world know what they're doin' the first time they're doin' that stuff? Ricky is a *bloody good* guy. I'm sure he'll take care of you when it all goes down."

"You are so right. I actually feel a bit better now." She said as she released her hair from the towel.

"Awesome. How come you haven't asked your slutty friend about it?"

"Oh she's just... I don't know why I didn't actually." She replied with deep thought, playing with the corner of the damp towel.

"Yeah well I'm glad we had this talk anyway."

"Me too." She smiled.

"Sorry you had to hear about your little brother getting' it on." He chuckled.

She laughed, looking to him. "It wasn't something I want to hear all the time, but I'm glad it was you telling me and not someone else."

Jack simply stared back at her for a moment before reaching for a solid hug between non biological family. She hugged him back just as grateful. "You got to promise you won't tell anyone you saw me havin' a sook." He said letting her go.

"Not unless you do something to piss me off." She said jokingly. He grinned back with a face of pure amusement.

~3~

All are finally reunited at the dining table together to discuss and joke around with friendly offensive banter of the night that was. Ethan proved to be the main antagonist in the shenanigans of making fun about the younger company's loose antics under the influence of alcohol, must be after all these years of being an older brother.

"Look the cheese thing is totally acceptable!" Ricky said waving a slice of toast around. Tiny crumbs flattered every move of his hand. "Who doesn't love it?"

"I'm surprised you're not eating it now." Wyatt chuckled.

"To be totally honest, the thought of it makes me ill at the moment." He replied with a deflated frown.

"What's *my* excuse though? I never think that much about cheese." Candice added.

"You were just going with it I think." Rose said reminiscing in the cheese raid.

"No, I know what it is." Wyatt began. "She just wants to copy everything her *boyfriend* does now." He teased.

"Aww that's nice. Little impressionable Candice!" Jack

tauntingly joined.

"Can you two stop ganging up on me right now?" She said and looked towards Ricky. "So what if I do anyway? His cheese fetish is worth the shame."

"That's got to be the most thoughtful thing you've ever said to me Fineman. I really should have been recording that."

"Oh shut up Benson." She said smiling.

"Ugh, you guys are so gross." Wyatt cringed with a twist of humour looking down at his crumby plate.

"Says you!" Ricky exclaimed.

"Yeah douche bag." Candice said scuffling his hair with her well trained irritating hand.

"Candice, don't!" He said batting her away.

"Yeah jeez man! Every hair on that specimen's head is precious!" Jack exclaimed, hardly caring for the quiet attention from the others.

"I've been messing this hair up for the last twelve years dude, fight me." She stood up pointing to the top of Wyatt's head at the messed, damp hair.

"I'm up for this." Jack said standing up on the opposite side of him.

"Ohhh fight, fight, fight!" Ethan began to chant, soon joined by the others.

"Thought you didn't like violence?" Wyatt said quietly, looking up at Jack.

"Not unless it's seriously serious." Jack said looking down at him smiling.

"Guys guys guys." Ricky said standing up. "We should be getting ready to get our shit together before facing the parents, not fighting over Wylie's overrated hair."

"Oh man, mum's going to know just by looking at us." Candice sullenly said as she sat back down. "Wow Wy, *we're bad.*"

"Stop it. Unless you want me to have a panic attack." Wyatt replied before taking in a large mouthful of Evelyn Jonson's calming chamomile tea.

"Hey, they should be happy you're still around to *do* stupid stuff." Ethan said casually.

Ryan kicked his brother's leg under the table, shaking his head in disapproval.

A painfully obvious silence washed over the room as faces turned awkwardly serious. Not only did the subtle mention bring back gruesome memories of blood and fear for each of them, but it brutally reminded the twins of where they really came from.

Wyatt stood as graceful as any gentleman in civility, despite his wild night and clear avoidance of talking about the kidnapping. "Ricky is right. We should get ready to go."

About The Author

Ashlea Raywood is an extravagant, forest dwelling, promotor of the peace. One with nature, she's the witchy owner of her dew-blessed cottage in the emerald bush of Australia.

Wouldn't that be ideal?
I don't have much to say for myself; I'm too busy writing about these Gerryville stooges.

~Wishing you well, stranger~